TINY

TURNER PUBLISHING COMPANY
Nashville, Tennessee
www.turnerpublishing.com

This is a work of fiction. All the characters and events portrayed in this book
are either products of the author's imagination or are used fictitiously.

Cover design: Grant Haffner
Book design: Karen Sheets de Gracia

LIBRARY OF CONGRESS CATALOGING-IN-PUBLICATION DATA
Names: Hooper, Kim author.
Title: Tiny / Kim Hooper.
Description: Nashville : Turner Publishing Company, [2019] |
Identifiers: LCCN 2018049260 (print) | LCCN 2018051270 (ebook) |
   ISBN 9781684422449 (ebook) | ISBN 9781684422425 (pbk.) |
   ISBN 9781684422432 (hardcover)
Classification: LCC PS3608.O59495 (ebook) | LCC PS3608.O59495 T56 2019 (print) |
   DDC 813/.6—dc23
LC record available at https://lccn.loc.gov/2018049260

9781684422425 Paperback
9781684422432 Hardcover
9781684422449 eBook

PRINTED IN THE UNITED STATES OF AMERICA

19 20 21 22   10 9 8 7 6 5 4 3 2 1

TINY

KIM HOOPER

TURNER
PUBLISHING COMPANY

For Mya.
All the winding roads have led to you.

ONE

NATE lies flat in bed, staring at the ceiling. When he was a kid, they had popcorn ceilings. He used to find shapes in them—Snoopy's profile, a space shuttle, that kind of thing. When he and Annie bought their house, a beach cottage built in the 1950s, the first order of business was removing the popcorn ceilings. "There could be asbestos," she said. The guy from the removal company—there are whole companies dedicated to this now—nodded in grave agreement, and they paid him to strip it away and make them feel safer.

He knows Annie is awake next to him. They're both pretending to be asleep, trying to convince each other that such a thing is possible. It doesn't seem like it will ever be possible again.

There were times—in college, between classes—when he'd lie down on a park bench like a homeless person and fall asleep. He could sleep anywhere, anytime. Annie used to make fun of him for doing push-ups in the living room while watching football games and then lying on his stomach for a quick nap. The first time she caught him, she gasped and shook him awake. "I thought you were dead," she said, slapping him on the shoulder.

The grief counselor, Pete, had told them it would take time. Nate asked, "How much time?" in hopes that there was a prescribed formula, a date he could look forward to when they would just wake up and it would be all over.

Pete chuckled in a good-natured way and said, "Unfortunately, it's different for everyone."

Annie's eyes welled up. "I don't think the next sixty or whatever years I have left on earth will be enough time." Pete put his hand over her clenched fist, like he was paper to her rock.

Annie hasn't gone two hours without crying since it happened. There's a subconscious timer in Nate's brain, counting the minutes, hoping she'll be tearless just a few moments longer than the day before. She hasn't passed the two-hour mark though. Sometimes she'll seem okay, going through the motions of existence, and then something small will happen and she'll lose it. Yesterday, she cried after finding a little pink sock behind the dryer. "It's been missing for months," she said, holding it up to him like it was the Hope Diamond.

Nate has never been a crier. He prides himself on this fact, resents the psychology community for implying he has some kind of underlying *issue*.

Pete had asked him, "Where did you learn to hold in your emotions?"

Learn? Like it was an obscure skill like building ships in bottles. Nate told him it was just who he was. "Aren't most guys like me?" he asked Pete.

Pete responded, with a friendly laugh, "You say that like it's a good thing," and Nate thought, but didn't say, *Isn't it?*

He doesn't mind being a stereotype, a cliché. It's better than losing his shit and sobbing like a little girl. Annie would cry automatic tears—the kind of tears you cry when you pluck a nose hair—if he said this out loud, if he said "little girl." She wants him to break down, to join her in misery. Pete told her, as if Nate wasn't sitting right there, "He doesn't want to open the floodgates." Nate didn't fight this conclusion, even though he doesn't think there's a flood, rivers of raging tears, waiting to break free. Maybe it's shock. Maybe he's hardened by the need to support Annie. There's an equilibrium to relationships; both people can't be completely devastated simultaneously. They just can't.

Nate gets out of bed, stretches up toward the ceiling. The clock says 3:26 a.m. Lucy, their seven-year-old black Lab mix, stirs in her dog bed on the floor. Nate got Lucy when he was twenty-eight, after breaking up with Stephanie, his girlfriend of four years, the girl he swore he was going to marry. He resigned himself to a man-and-dog kind of life. Then he met Annie. Lucy seemed to approve of her. They got married after only a year of dating. Lucy was their ring bearer.

Lucy used to sleep on the bed with them, but Annie can't bear looking at her since it happened. So Nate tries to keep her out of the way. He feeds the dog, walks her, picks up her poop. Lucy isn't the same either. There is something in her eyes— apology, maybe, guilt.

"What are you doing?" Annie says, voice soft and falsely groggy.

"Going for a run," he says.

"*Now?*" Her tone tells him this is a crazy notion.

"Figure I'll make use of the awake time. I'll take Lucy with me. She hasn't been out in a few days."

Annie rolls back over, away from him. "Fine," she says. She's used this word so many times before, as a precursor to so many arguments, when she is exactly *not* fine.

"I'll have breakfast ready for you when you wake up," he says. He's trying to make her some version of content in this new life of theirs—a Sisyphean mission so far. "What sounds good?"

"Nothing," she says.

"Pancakes?"

Pancakes had been their Saturday morning ritual, before.

She sighs something like disappointment. "Definitely not pancakes."

THE AIR OUTSIDE is crisp and cold. People say California is always seventy-something degrees, but it's not. There are thirty-eight-degree January mornings like this one. Joggers wear sporty gloves and headbands that keep their ears warm. Nate doesn't have either of these things. And his shoes are a decade old. He's only just started running again. He ran track in high school and college but couldn't manage to integrate it into his adult life. There wasn't time before work, or he didn't make time. And after work, he just wanted a beer and brainless TV. There were occasional years when he made resolutions on December 31 to start running again, but he'd maintain his resolve for only a month or so before petering out. It feels good to be back now. Or maybe good isn't the right word. Maybe *necessary* is the right word. It feels *necessary*.

He lets Lucy run next to him, off leash. He hates the leash, probably more than she does. Annie always scolds him when he doesn't use it though. She says he has to consider other people, not just himself. He has to think of the little old ladies who are petrified of dogs. He has to remember that dogs are animals and Lucy might attack an unassuming Shih Tzu. And besides, the ticket for having a dog off leash is expensive—four hundred bucks or something absurd like that. At four in the morning though, nobody is out. No cops, no little old ladies, no Shih Tzus.

On those past New Year's resolution kicks, he had a running route, a loop that went by the park and then down to the beach path. He'd run two miles along Pacific Coast Highway, ending at a traffic light that marked the start of the big hill trek back home. He could never bring himself to run the damn hill; he always walked it.

Now, though, he can't run by the park. After what happened, it's like it doesn't even exist to him as a place. So he's found another way down to the beach path. He winds through their Capistrano Beach neighborhood, a maze of streets crammed together by city planners who never expected such an influx of humans. There are no streetlights because his hippie-dippie community has an ordinance against them, the board agreeing that streetlights would make it hard to see the stars at night. Annie loves this about where they live—the people who have been there forever, who bake pies for each other and sip wine on each other's porches, talking about the good old days when they surfed in less crowded ocean waters. Nate would prefer streetlights.

He uses the flashlight on his phone to navigate. When he gets down to the beach, the air is cooler. He blows warmth onto his hands, but that helps for only a split second.

"Jesus, Lucy, it's a cold one today," he says.

This is one of the favorite parts of his run—talking to the dog. He used to talk to her a lot when she was a puppy, when he lived alone in his bachelor pad, pitying himself after the Stephanie breakup. He'd tell Lucy about his day, and she'd cock her head to one side, ears perked, like she understood, like she was genuinely interested. When Annie entered the picture, there weren't as many Lucy chats. Sometimes when Annie was in the shower and he was still in bed, taking his time to wake up, he'd nuzzle Lucy and tell her she was a good girl and ask her what she wanted for breakfast. "I can whip up some steak-and-vegetable kibble," he'd tell her. "The bag says it's meatier than ever." She'd lick his face like she was trying to get to the center of a Tootsie Pop. When Penelope started talking in sentences—around the sixteen-month mark, early according to Annie—she had full conversations with Lucy and seemed disappointed that they weren't a two-way street.

At the end of the run, instead of heading straight up the merciless hill home, he decides to take Lucy to the beach, let her run in the waves. There is something freeing about ignoring the signs that forbid such a thing. He sits on a bench and watches her, her big pink tongue flapping out of her mouth, a wide grin on her face. "It's not a grin," Annie said once. "It's just the way her face is when she's panting." She always teases him for ascribing human emotions to Lucy. But damn it if Lucy doesn't seem ecstatic right now. She comes back to him, her underbelly, paws, and the tips of her floppy ears wet. She jumps up next to him on the bench. He flinches at her cold fur on his skin. It's cold, freaking cold.

"You ready to head back, girl? Maybe I'll give you some bacon. Sound good? And don't worry about Annie. She just needs time. It wasn't your fault, what happened. It was mine. She'll forgive us though, both of us. She just needs time."

He kisses the bridge of her nose, and she licks his face in return. He crosses the street, not needing to push the button to walk for once. There are no cars. And then, overcome by a sudden burst of energy, he runs the hill home.

TWO

ANNIE has always been a fast thinker, her mind spinning, spinning, spinning. She hates work meetings, because she understands the issue at hand within five minutes while everyone else hems and haws for an hour. Sometimes she pinches her own thigh in frustration, imagining it's the earlobe of whoever's yammering on. She can't imagine going back to work now, sitting at her desk, a photo of Penelope on her third birthday in a frame next to her work phone. She just can't imagine it.

Is it because of all those years I said I didn't want kids? That's Annie's latest obsessive thought. After all, people say things happen for a reason. And the basic reason this happened was Nate's fault. But there is more to it than that. The God her Catholic parents taught her to believe in from the time she was a little girl wouldn't punish her like this if she had no responsibility in the matter. She had to be at fault somehow too. That is the only way to explain her pain and keep believing that life is fair.

In the beginning, those first two weeks after it happened, she tormented Nate with all her ponderings—*Is it because I yelled at her that morning about getting pink marker on her bedroom wall? Did God think I wasn't fit to be a parent? Is it because I told Beth that Penelope's nap time was the best part of my day?* Nate would just scoff, making her feel crazier than she already felt. "It just *happened*, Annie," he said, a bizarre mixture of anger and sadness.

Nate had never believed in God. Annie's parents warned her that it would be an issue at some point in their marriage—"bone of contention," they'd said. She waved them off, told them, "He goes to church on Christmas Eve. He humors me."

IT'S TRUE THOUGH—she'd said she didn't want kids. She'd stated it, with certainty, starting in her early twenties. Most of her friends, even her mother, dismissed her, said she would change her mind. She insisted she wouldn't. If they cared to continue the conversation, they'd ask her reasons, and she'd say, simply, that she had too much she wanted to do in her own life. The real reason was deeper than that though, just like the real reason for what happened a month ago had to be deeper than the surface details of the event.

Annie had been a happy kid, a good student. She was on the swim team at school and part of the youth organization at church. Her parents assumed they'd dodged all the major bullets: she never got involved with drugs, never missed curfew, never even had a boyfriend long enough for them to worry about a pregnancy. Then they got a call in the middle of an October night during Annie's first semester away at college—University of Notre Dame, her father's alma mater. It was the resident advisor of Annie's dorm, saying that Annie's roommate found her unresponsive on the floor next to her bed, a small pool of vomit by her mouth. The RA assumed alcohol poisoning, because that was the usual culprit, but Annie's parents couldn't believe that was it. Paramedics took Annie to the hospital. Without hesitating, Annie's parents said they'd be there the next morning.

It wasn't alcohol. The doctor pulled Annie's parents into the hallway after they'd had a chance to visit with Annie—who was groggy but okay—and said, "She had toxic levels of ibuprofen in her blood."

They looked at him quizzically. "*Advil?*" her mother said.

The doctor said he'd seen it before. "Kids, especially, don't have access to other drugs," he said. "They go online and find they can take their own lives with something already in their medicine cabinet."

They said it had to be a mistake, an accident. Annie wouldn't take her own life. She was a smart girl, they said.

"A smart girl would know that much Advil would kill her," the doctor said before leaving them to consider that.

It had started at the end of senior year, Annie told them, "it" being this nagging thought that life was just a series of obligations and expectations and pressures and challenges. Everything ahead of her—college, adulthood—seemed like drudgery. She thought, hoped, a fresh start at Notre Dame would change things. But that first week on campus, she had no desire to engage in the freshmen welcoming activities. She could barely stand to make small talk with her ever-peppy roommate. When she woke up in the mornings for class, it was like there was a twenty-pound weight on her chest. She dragged herself to classes, sometimes nodding off, exhausted by the very notion of existing. She declined invitations to parties, stopped showering every day, wore the same clothes for a solid week. Her roommate suggested she talk to a counselor, so she did. The counselor said she was depressed. She didn't disagree. She went home, looked up the word online:

depressed *adjective*
1. sad and gloomy; dejected; downcast
2. pressed down, or situated lower than the general surface

Both definitions sounded right.

The counselor was the one who gave voice to the idea percolating in her brain. She'd asked, "Do you have any thoughts of ending your life?"

Annie shook her head because she knew that was crazy, to want to end your life. She had thought about it though, passively. Like, she sort of hoped a meteor would fall from the sky and crush her as she slept. Or maybe she'd step into the street at the wrong time and get hit by a car. *It would be a grand relief*, she thought. She kept her appointments with the counselor but didn't admit that she'd started to wonder why she didn't just end her own life. If there was light at the end of the proverbial tunnel, she couldn't see it. She was sitting in the dark, knees to chest, unable to make it around the next bend. It was like the doctor said—she went online and found out, with just a few clicks, that she could take her own life with the seemingly benign medicine she used when she strained a muscle after going out too fast in swim practice.

"I just don't understand, honey," her mother said, sitting on the edge of her hospital bed, clutching Annie's hand desperately. Her eyes were wet, tears primed to roll down her cheeks.

"I don't either," Annie said.

She'd left a note, on her desk in her dorm room. All it said, by way of explanation, was, "I can't do it anymore. I'm so sorry." Both her roommate and the RA thought her suicide attempt was alcohol poisoning; they weren't looking for a note so they didn't see it. It just sat there, unread, until her parents came to pack up her things and found it. "Did you actually think that note would give us peace?" her mother said to her, her eyes pooled with tears. Annie was embarrassed—she'd not only failed at suicide, but she'd failed to leave a proper note.

Annie's father stood at the foot of the bed, arms crossed against his chest. He'd been mostly silent, stoic. Then he said,

"This is what happened to my mother." He was solemn. Annie had never seen her father solemn. He was a happy-go-lucky type.

Annie and her mother looked at him. Her father never talked about his mother. All Annie knew was that she died when he was young. Annie's mother didn't seem to know much more than that.

"What, Steve?" Annie's mother asked, probing.

"My mother, she had this . . . sadness, or whatever you want to call it," he said. He looked guilty, like all of this was his fault. "I was too young to really understand it, but that's what my father said—a sadness."

"Is that how she died? Of the sadness?" Annie asked.

Her father nodded. "My father didn't tell me about it until I was older. He said she went out to the garage to get a shovel. They'd just bought an avocado tree and were going to plant it in the backyard. When she hadn't come back after a while, he went to see what she was doing and found her sitting in the front seat of his car, the engine running, the garage door closed. She was gone."

As sad as it was, it comforted Annie that there was a reason for this. It was some kind of destiny, a familial fate.

"The doctor says they can help you, though," Annie's mother said, immediately dismissing the story, as if she was afraid Annie would envy her grandmother's success. "There are medications you can take. You have to think of it like you're sick, like you have the flu, and you just need some medication," she said. "We'll bring you home, go to church every day, get you back on track."

Annie nodded, resigned to this plan. She doubted it would work but couldn't bring herself to give up completely. She had to try—for her parents' sake.

And she did get back on track. She moved home, into her girlish bedroom with the pink-and-white quilt and sponge-painted walls. She started taking an antidepressant medication—a serotonin reuptake inhibitor, the psychiatrist said. She imagined the chemicals in her brain as little bubbles, floating around, some popping, others forming, creating a balance to keep her sane. Her mother asked if she felt different, and she said, "Yeah, I feel exactly like myself." That was the thing—the sadness wasn't who she was; it was the foreign invader, the cancer. If the medication could keep it at bay, she would take it every day, religiously, for the rest of her life.

Her mother took her to church every morning. They prayed. Eventually, they all agreed Annie could go to a local community college, take a few classes to see how she felt in the world again. She felt good. She got straight As. She started going out with friends. She was better.

She met Jeremy when she transferred to the University of San Diego to finish her bachelor's degree. They dated for a year before she told him about what had happened at Notre Dame. He didn't seem fazed by it, and she knew it was because he didn't fully understand. They moved in together after graduation. He worked at a TV station downtown, and she got a receptionist job at a law firm. It was her long-term goal to go to law school.

Contrary to popular gender stereotype, Jeremy was the one who kept bringing up marriage. Annie wasn't that interested. "We're so young," she'd said. "Too young," she'd said.

He was a good Catholic boy from the Midwest, where the majority of his friends were putting rings on their girlfriends' fingers. "I want to start a family when we're young," he said.

She hadn't thought about a family before, but when he said those words she knew immediately that she didn't want one. "I can't have children," she said. He furrowed his brows, confused. She clarified, "I mean, I *can* have them, but I don't *want* to."

When he realized she was adamant, that this was non-negotiable, they broke up. She made the final call. He still had hoped she'd change her mind. She didn't tell him about the depression—about how she feared it would come back, cripple her. She didn't tell him that she wasn't sure she was mentally capable of being responsible for another human. She didn't tell him there was a chance that human could inherit her defective genes. She couldn't live with herself—literally—if that happened.

So she got her own apartment and turned her attention to law school. She took classes at night and spent her days answering phones and scheduling appointments at the firm. Four years later, she was working at a real estate law firm in Orange County. She didn't seek out real estate law, but a former professor referred her to the firm, and that was that. She liked it more than she thought she would. It was black and white, with very little gray area. That's why she loved law—it set boundaries, corralled the messiness of life into a small area fenced by rules.

Annie met Nate in 2007 at a real estate seminar in Newport Beach. She was part of a panel discussing lease disputes, and he was sitting in the front row. They locked eyes in that way Annie thought happened only in movies. After the panel, he stood, hands in pockets, on the periphery of a small group of people asking her questions. When they were gone, he said, "Hi, I'm a local property manager, and I have one last question—will you have dinner with me tonight?" And they did. They went to a small Italian restaurant that had an open kitchen and just six four-top tables. Before they even opened a bottle of wine, Annie had a feeling he would change her, alter the path of her entire life.

She'd come to wave off marriage in much the same way she waved off kids. She didn't *need* a husband. And most of the guys she met didn't make her want one, either. This one seemed different though. She asked him if he wanted kids, figuring it best to get that out of the way.

He shrugged and said, "Sure, I guess."

"That doesn't sound very convincing," she said.

He twisted his mouth to one side, sighed, and said, "I don't know. I guess I've always assumed I'd have kids. But, quite honestly, I'm not sure I'm ready for them any time soon." He made a face that said *I'm sorry, this probably disappoints you.*

"Oh, no, me neither." That ice broken, Annie probed more and learned it was as simple as this: Nate expected that the woman in his life (whoever she might be) would want a family, and, as an accommodating partner, he would concede. Did he daydream about kids? No. Would he be happy not having kids? Yes.

They got engaged exactly a year later and got married a month after that. It was a small courthouse ceremony followed by a party with twenty friends and family members at Annie's parents' home in Trabuco Canyon. Annie didn't want any frills. She wore her mother's wedding dress—an understated gown with lace overlay—and carried a bouquet of roses from the garden. They exchanged simple gold bands, and that was that. Eternity promised.

A month after they got married, they bought their house—a thousand-square-foot cottage with three small bedrooms and two bathrooms. They replaced the carpeted floors with reclaimed wood, got the fireplace functional again, and opened up the kitchen so Annie could talk to Nate while she was cooking and he was channel-surfing on the couch. And then, when the house started to feel like home, something strange happened. Annie started envisioning the third bedroom, an office at the time, as a nursery. She started thinking about stenciling the walls—a woodsy theme, maybe. She somehow knew the occupant of the room would be a girl. During downtime at work, she browsed baby names, fell in love with "Penelope." Penny, for short.

She didn't say anything to Nate at first. She scolded herself for the fantasies, chastised herself for getting caught up in what society told her she should want. And, considering her history of depression, her genes, having a baby would be selfish—*wouldn't it?* She'd been stable, happy even, for years. But still . . . Besides, having a baby was inherently selfish, considering overpopulation and global warming and all that. Social media proved that parenthood just made people completely self-absorbed in their children, their vanity projects, every annoying Facebook post screaming, "Look how adorable our creation is!"

She asked her mother, sheepishly, "How did you know you wanted to have a baby?"

Her mother, trying to restrain excitement over her daughter's inquiry, said, "Oh, honey, I just *knew*."

"But it's so impractical. There are enough people on this planet. Kids are expensive and time-consuming and—"

"Annie, logic is no match for biology," her mother said.

During wine-fueled dinners at restaurants they could afford because of their dual-income, childless existence, Annie and Nate poked fun at their friends having kids and talked about their grand plans for life. Instead of planning birthday parties with overfrosted cakes and cartoon character themes, they could plan trips: Bali, Iceland, Italy, anywhere really. Instead of coming home from work to school assignments and kid-friendly dinners, they could get Thai takeout and watch their favorite crime dramas in peace and quiet. Instead of seeing each other as "Mama" and "Daddy," they would see themselves as just Annie and Nate, two people who adored each other enough to spend forever with just each other.

Annie didn't think Nate would be that opposed to kids, if she truly wanted them. It wasn't even *them*; she envisioned just one, two max. Nate was, after all, accommodating. He let her pick every restaurant, movie, wall color—everything. Her happiness seemed to be his, a fact she was careful not to draw too much attention to for fear of encouraging him to find his own happinesses, separate from her. And besides, she was the one who talked Nate into the no-kids lifestyle. He'd said on that first date that he'd always assumed he'd have kids. So he had to be somewhat accepting of the idea, in theory.

"You know, I don't really like traveling," she said one night as they sat on the couch, her leaning into his shoulder, credits rolling on an episode of the chef competition show they loved.

"Hmm?" he said.

"Traveling. It's not really appealing to me. I want it to be. It *should* interest me—seeing other cultures, trying new foods, exploring. It just doesn't though."

"Okay, nothing wrong with that," he said. There was never anything wrong with what Annie said, according to Nate.

Still, as if she had to prove something, she rambled on about her reasons: "I hate layovers, I'm too impatient for them. I hate long flights, period. You're just stuck there, in that cramped little seat, subjected to episodes of *Friends* and tiny packages of nuts. I hold my pee, because I don't want to get up and step over the stranger next to me and stand in that line. It's like a urinary tract infection waiting to happen with all that pee-holding. And my back. I feel like I'm elderly, and I don't want to feel like I'm elderly. And then you get there, to the destination, and you're lost most of the time, wandering around aimlessly, trying not to get mugged, all to find something a guidebook says is amazing that really isn't, because nothing can live up to those expectations, *nothing*. And you know how my stomach always gets in knots when I travel. Something to do with the time change or the food, I don't know."

He stopped her, gently, putting one hand up like a crossing guard for an elementary school.

"Honey, what's going on?" he asked. The fact that he knew her so well was simultaneously comforting and unsettling.

"If we don't travel, what will we *do*?"

"Do?"

"With our lives, our time?"

"I don't know. Just live, I guess," he said.

She was quiet again.

"Annie, you may as well just tell me what you're thinking."

She didn't turn to face him. She couldn't. She was embarrassed, really. All those people who said she would change her mind were right. She hated that they were right, that she'd become so ordinary.

"This is going to sound crazy, but I've been thinking about a baby," she said, adding a little laugh so he'd know she thought this ridiculous.

He didn't laugh in response. He said, with seriousness, "Well, we would be awesome parents."

SINCE IT TOOK years to come around to wanting kids, Annie believed, stupidly, that once the decision was made, it would happen just like that, as if God was just waiting on her to change her mind like everyone told her she would. It wasn't like that, though. Of course it wasn't. How egocentric of her! Still, even after acknowledging her own silliness, she cried— sobbed, actually—every month when she got her period, as if the blood was a result of a miscarriage. Her period always came midday, usually when she was at work. She'd sit on the toilet seat in the multistall bathroom, pull her knees up to her chest (in case anyone could recognize her shoes), and cry as quietly as she could.

It didn't help that she'd gone off her antidepressant because it could cause harm to the unborn baby, apparently. She was at the mercy of irrational emotion, crying about everything: an episode of *Dateline* about the tsunami in Thailand in 2004, rush hour traffic, her yoga teacher adjusting her in a difficult pose, a Neil Young song on the oldies station, some asshole snapping at her for inadvertently cutting the line at Walgreens, a haircut that went slightly too short so that she couldn't put her hair in a ponytail without strands falling in her face. Nate knew about her past depressive episode, but he didn't seem worried. "You're just adjusting," he told her. "Let's just get you pregnant."

But it wasn't that simple.

Every month she hoped, surprised at her own optimism or delusion or whatever it was. In that two-week window between possible conception and the date of her next period, that window when she could be newly pregnant, she analyzed every twinge in her stomach, convinced it was the beginnings of a baby. She barely slept, her heart thumping in her chest with excitement. She frequented the Due Date Calculator website, typing in the date of her last period to see when her baby would arrive. She looked up the astrological sign associated with this date, though she didn't even really believe in astrology.

She looked in the mirror, convinced she saw a small pooch forming below her belly button. Of course nobody showed that early, but she knew her body. That's what she told herself. It. Was. Changing. She knew it. She used to hate seeing those baby bump photos on Facebook, couldn't even stand that phrase "baby bump." Now she couldn't wait to take her own photos. The fence in their backyard, the one with the ivy on it, would make a nice backdrop. She would stand in front of it, in the same position, wearing the same clothes, for the most accurate representation of the progress of her very own baby bump.

She took overpriced prenatal vitamins and gave up hot baths, wine, sushi, soft cheese, and previously benign over-the-counter medications because the phobic internet said these things could irreparably damage a fetus. She even stopped using her beloved face cream because it had a supposedly disastrous ingredient in it: Retinol. She ate lots of beans and spinach after googling the best sources of folic acid. And then her period, her stupid period, would come, right on schedule, and she would feel like a complete fucking idiot. People always said to think positive, send good vibes out into the universe. A lot of good that did. It was better to expect the worst. Expecting the best just makes you look like a fool.

For a couple months, they stopped having sex completely, Annie's rationale being that if they didn't try, they couldn't fail. She didn't want to get into the temperature taking and ovulation charting, the acupuncture and weird holistic remedies. Trying that hard would just make the disappointment worse. Maybe she was right all along: she shouldn't have kids. Mother Nature knew best. She started to hate other pregnant women. She overheard one, in the break room at work, complaining about her backaches and frequent need to pee. Annie felt an urge to pull her hair, like an angst-ridden kindergartner. Who was this person she'd become? Nate, ever positive, told her to be patient. She laughed at that and said, "You're cute." Patience was never one of her strongpoints.

Eventually, they started having sex again but had an unspoken rule of never referring to it as "trying." In the not-so-far-back of her mind, Annie still tracked the days of her cycle and counted months, knowing they probably had a fertility issue on their hands if a year passed with no luck. Then, right before that one-year mark, the date she'd circled in red on her calendar came and went. She'd missed her period. And four different pregnancy tests confirmed that ever-positive Nate had been right—she'd just had to be patient.

It was a relief, those pregnancy tests, but she still worried. Every time she went to the bathroom, she expected blood in her underwear, a miscarriage. She was constantly touching her boobs to see if they were still sore. Nate caught her once and said, "You know, I can help you with that." She took comfort in the morning sickness that arrived in the sixth week and panicked when it went away, convinced there would be no heartbeat at the next ultrasound appointment. There was, though. Loud, like the steady beat of a drum underwater. She was in awe of how strong their baby seemed. The whole, mysterious process of creating that baby had seemed so fragile.

Penelope was born on November 11, 2011 (11-11-11), a date a psychic told Annie was "magical." They fell in love with her immediately. They called her the best thing that ever happened to them. They loved the smell of her skin. They stared at her when she slept, mesmerized. They couldn't even remember life before her. Every single cliché they used to roll their eyes at became truth. Every single one.

Annie had been so consumed with the seeming elusiveness of bringing a baby into the world that she hadn't considered how precarious that world could be. A fool, once again.

SHE HEARS THE front door open and shut, Lucy's nails on the tile floor in the entryway. Nate has taken up running suddenly— and cleaning, obsessively cleaning. She woke up before dawn the other morning and looked out the window to see him mopping the cement by the pool.

He's in the kitchen, making breakfast even though she told him she didn't want anything. She reaches over to the nightstand drawer, pulls it open, takes the cap off the four-year-old bottle, and pops a pill in her mouth. The label says the medication is expired, so maybe it's not even doing anything. She can't bring herself to see her doctor though, not yet. She can't bring herself to see anyone. She can't handle the pity, the unoriginal condolences. People crinkle their foreheads and say, "I'm so sorry for your loss," but what they really mean is "I'm so fucking glad I'm not you."

It's a wonder she made it through the funeral.

It's been four years since she's taken antidepressants. There were the crying fits when she first went off them, when they were trying to get pregnant, but those went away. She was fine during the pregnancy. Blissful, even. "Maybe it's the hormones," she told Nate. "Maybe," he said. She thought she'd for sure fall into a black hole after the birth. She'd heard horror stories of postpartum depression, braced herself, but she was fine then too. A little teary in those newborn days, but fine, stable. It was like the very existence of Penelope solved everything.

And now Penelope is gone.

Nate peeks in the room.

"You're awake!" he says, with too much enthusiasm. He's smiling, and she hates him for it. *How is he so* normal? Maybe she envies him. Maybe that's what's making her heart race. No, she's angry, purely angry. Somehow he can function, and he shouldn't be able to. These weeks since it happened, he looks at her like she's a mess he has to clean up.

"I'm awake," she says. She wishes she could tell him that she doesn't want to be, that she wants to sleep for a year. He wouldn't accept such a statement though. He would say something like, "Don't be silly. It's a nice day." He'd say, with the go-get-'em encouragement of a sports coach, "Let's try to get out of the house today."

"I've got coffee brewing," he says.

She doesn't respond, doesn't even sit up in bed, just stays reclined. Next step: prop herself up on her elbows. This is the new to-do list of her life. The old one included things like *make Penny breakfast, take Penny to preschool, buy craft paper.*

"Come on," he says, approaching the bed to pull her out, like she's a sullen teenager who doesn't want to go to school. And then, just when she thinks she can't hate him any more, he says, "I made pancakes."

THREE

JOSH

JOSH slumps in his chair, staring at the computer screen. He cracks his knuckles. How long has he been playing? Two hours? Twenty hours? He's lost track of time, kept the curtains pulled shut so he has no idea if it's night or day. He's in his own alternate universe, detached from reality—the type of atmosphere they strive to create in Vegas because it encourages recklessness and bad decisions.

"Are you gonna, like, do some actual work today?"

He turns lethargically to see Jess standing in the doorway, one foot turned out to the side, head cocked. It must be morning.

"I don't know, maybe," he says.

She rolls her eyes. "Dude, I'm not made of money. I'm a *bar-is-ta*," she says, as if he has never heard the word before. "I don't get it. We move in together, and you start slacking off. I didn't think you were that type of guy."

In a huff, she spins around on her heels and marches down the hallway, the old wood floors creaking beneath the force of her anger.

The thing is, he isn't that type of guy. He should go after her to tell her that, defend himself. He should tell her everything: why he's in this mood of his, why he's spent the past several weeks playing *World of Warcraft*, taking one character after another on quests in a virtual world until they reach the highest level. His latest avatar is Amphi, a female frog. Most of the time, his avatars are male and human, representing himself. He's not sure he wants to be himself anymore.

♠

"YO, YOU WANNA raid?" Brad says over the headset. Brad is his online friend, his best friend, though they've never met face-to-face. A raid is a group event with multiple players joining forces to take on a giant monster. Jess says it's "juvenile."

"I don't know," Josh says.

"We need an illusionist." Amphi is an illusionist, capable of casting spells to stun enemies so the other members of the group can attack. He likes this background role best. It reminds him of the night he met Jess at that party he didn't want to go to and she approached him, saying, "Hi, wallflower."

"I should probably do some work. Jess is gonna kill me if I don't hold up my end of the rent this month."

"Bitches be crazy."

"Yeah," Josh says, though he doesn't think Jess is crazy. He is the crazy one. Or at least he's been acting that way lately. She would understand if he told her what was going on inside his head, but he can't tell her, can't say it all out loud, can't make it real.

He logs off the game and pulls up his latest project, a website for some guy's chiropractic office. Josh is a computer programmer, self-taught. He signed up for community college last year so he could have a degree to his name. Really, though, he doesn't need any training. More often than not, he's enlightening his teachers, sharing hacks and quick work-arounds with them. He's been a computer genius since he was a kid, built his first computer twelve years ago, when he was only ten. He just never applied himself. That's what the principal said when he dropped out of high school. He got his GED, just to prove that asshole wrong, and started his own company—ComputeRx. In the beginning, he made house calls to fix people's computers. Usually, it was something quick and easy. In one case, the guy's battery had just died. Josh recharged it and left with a hundred dollar bill. He was taking advantage of people, in a way, leveraging their lack of knowledge. When that got boring, he took up website programming. He could do it at home, from his own little lair. Occasionally, he still does house calls to fix computers, if the particular case interests him or the money is especially good.

That's what he was doing a month ago—a house call. An old man called him, said he found his number in the phone book, of all places. Josh had put an ad there, specifically for this type of elderly customer. The man sounded desperate, flummoxed, said, "The machine's just a mess." Josh didn't have anything pressing to do that day. Jess was working. They'd go to dinner somewhere that night, maybe see a movie. He had the whole afternoon to kill. He didn't need the money, but there was something in the guy's voice that got to him. He reminded Josh of his grandpa, his mom's dad. Since his father was never around, his grandpa had performed the fatherly duties: took him fishing, gave him his first beer, talked to him about women. He'd died just a few months ago, after two years lost in the confusing haze of Alzheimer's.

"Do you know where Capistrano Beach is?" the man asked. "Well, actually it's Dana Point. It used to be Capistrano Beach. Those of us who live here still call it that," he rambled. It was obvious he spent most of his time alone, in silence, and enjoyed the opportunity to talk to someone. Josh didn't know the area well, had spent most of his childhood in the northern part of Orange County. He grew up in Anaheim, living with his mom until he and Jess got their one-bedroom apartment in Santa Ana.

The man gave Josh his name, Ron, and his address. "Okay, I'll find it," Josh told him, already typing the numbers into Google. "I'll be there in an hour."

After that, he can't remember much, or chooses not to. He was going the speed limit; he knows that much. He may have been going even slower than the speed limit because he wasn't familiar with the neighborhood. He saw the park on his right, caught a quick glimpse of the ocean through the pine trees. Then he turned his attention back left, scanning the numbers of the houses. That's when his memory goes black. There are no visuals to access after that point, only sounds: screeching brakes, the thud of contact, a woman screaming, his own voice—sounding so strange to him—yelling for help, sirens, a barking dog.

Jess texted him while he was at the police station, asking him where he was and if they were still going to dinner. He could have told her then. He could have said, "I was involved in an accident." It would have been simple. But he couldn't imagine discussing it, couldn't bear her questions and the answers to those questions. So he just wrote back, "Sorry, babe. I'm stuck on a job." She gave him a sad face emoji, and that was that.

They did a breath test at the station, to make sure he wasn't drunk. Of course, he wasn't. He'd had a beer, just one, the night before. Irrationally, he feared that meant he was somehow at fault. In the end, it was pretty clear it was "just an accident," a horrible, unfortunate accident. Witnesses confirmed that a little girl had run into the street, that the driver, Josh, braked appropriately, etcetera, etcetera. Still, Josh cursed his big, heavy Dodge truck, inherited from his grandfather. What if he had driven Jess's Mini Cooper instead? Would that have made a difference? Then again, why would he have driven Jess's Mini Cooper? He never did. He made fun of that car. Still, he couldn't help but consider every what-if. The officer mentioned that the little girl had died at the scene, a fact Josh would have rather not known. The parents were probably at the police station too. He didn't want to see their faces. They would hate him, even though it was "just an accident."

One of the officers drove him home. They were keeping his truck for a while, "since someone died," the officer said. "It's procedure." There was still a whole investigation to be done, as part of that procedure, before they would proclaim him completely innocent. They would examine the truck for any malfunctions or mechanical failures. They would measure skid marks. They would perform an autopsy on the girl. They would wait for the results of his drug screening. Investigators would convene to determine if charges should be filed. It was enough to make him feel like a criminal.

He walked in the front door that night and found Jess on the couch, wrapped in a blanket, a mug of tea on the table in front of her. It was eight o'clock.

"You must have made big bucks today," she said. He charged an hourly rate of seventy-five dollars. She'd been doing the math, probably hoping he'd buy them a new TV with the influx of cash.

"Yeah," he said, distractedly. He forced a smile.

She patted the couch next to her, and he sat obediently. She leaned into him like it was any other night, the two of them cuddling on the couch. She was watching one of those reality shows with a bunch of hopeful pretty girls trying to be models. She made comments throughout the episode, and he just grunted in agreement with whatever those comments were. He wasn't really listening. He googled the Dana Point police blotter on his phone and saw the incident: "Traffic accident, fatality." He'd wanted to believe it hadn't really happened.

The next morning, the story was front and center on the Dana Point news site. He was forced to learn that the little girl was only three years old and her name was Penelope Forester. He was forced to learn that her parents, Nate and Annie Forester, were "profoundly devastated." None of the reports included his name. Even the notoriously brutal media agreed that he shouldn't be vilified. So, then, why did he feel like shit?

He took to his computer because that was his safe place, his solace. He scoured for every digital footprint left by Nate and Annie Forester. Turned out Nate didn't have a public Facebook page; Annie did.

Annie hadn't posted anything about the accident. A few people who had heard posted things on her page like, "Oh my God, can't even imagine. Thinking of you," with little heart icons. The last thing Annie had posted was the morning of the accident—a picture of a pink marker scribbling on a white wall with the caption "The next Jackson Pollock or just a troublemaker?" He scrolled down her page, cautiously. Nearly every post was related to Penelope, or Penny, as Annie called her. He understood the obsession. The little girl was adorable: blonde Goldilocks hair and big blue eyes that reminded him of Cindy Lou Who in *How the Grinch Stole Christmas*. Annie had brown hair, so the blonde must have come from Nate.

There was a long post about Penelope's third birthday, just a couple months ago in November. Annie wrote it as a letter to Penelope:

My darling girl, every day I love you just a little bit more than the day before. Who knew I had this capacity? It blows my mind.

I love the little blonde hair on your legs, how it shimmers in the sun. I love how you eat raspberries by putting them on the tips of your fingers and biting them off one by one. I love how you're into telling secrets, like a proper female. You come up to me, say you have a secret, and then whisper something like, "I wanna cupcake." I love how you announce when you have a question—"Mama, I have a question!"—and seven times out of ten, it's "Can I have a cupcake?" I love how every time I ask you a "Why?" question, you just say "Because." I love that your world is so simple. I love how you try to delay nap time when you're playing with your dolls: "Just five minutes, Mama." I love how you say "Pweez" (Please) and "Shanks" (Thanks) and "Essue me" (Excuse me), though I'm not sure I can take credit for your politeness. I love how you insist I kiss your boo-boos. I love how you kissed my boo-boo when I nicked myself last week chopping veggies. I love how you have pretend conversations on your phone—again, such a female. I love how you play with the suds in the bathtub and say you're making "cake." I love how you love Lucy, how you carry her bowl to the food canister and fill it every morning. The other night, when Lucy was sleeping at the foot of our bed, you closed the door and said, "Sweet dreams, Lucy." I love how when you're cold, you say "cozy pweez," which is our cue to wrap you tighter in a blanket. I love how your left pigtail falls askew sometimes while you're at preschool—always the left one. I love how when I put you to bed and start to get up to leave, you put your little index finger in the air and say, "One more cuddle." How could I ever deny you?

After your favorite dinner tonight—chicken nuggets, of course—I've got a huge cupcake for you with extra frosting (because, let's be real, you usually eat just the frosting anyway).

It got 112 "likes" and twenty-three comments. One person said, "She is the best little girl and she has the best mama." Another said, "You two give me warm fuzzies."

"Who's that?" Jess said, peering over his shoulder. He flinched, hadn't even heard her come in the room.

"Nobody," he said, clicking off.

"I would ask if you're cheating on me, but she is ugly," Jess said.

"She's not ugly." She wasn't. She had big green eyes and the kind of silky hair you see in shampoo commercials.

"Well, she's *old*."

"She's one of my customers. Wanted me to help her manage her Facebook page." It took him by surprise that he could lie so easily.

"See, only old people can't manage their own Facebook pages."

He pulled up *World of Warcraft*, figured he'd distract himself for a few hours, or try to. Jess hovered.

"Um, where's your truck?" she asked.

"Oh," he said, searching his brain for his next fib. "I forgot to tell you. It stalled last night, on my way home from that job. I had them tow it to a service station."

She looked at him quizzically.

"Why didn't you call me?" she asked. "I could have picked you up."

"I didn't want to bug you," he said. "I knew you were probably pissed about me canceling on dinner."

Just like that, he'd avoided the subject of killing a small girl with his truck and made himself look like a thoughtful boyfriend.

"Oh, well, when do you get it back? My sunglasses are in there," she said.

Suddenly, he was sure he didn't want to be with Jess anymore. He wouldn't say anything right away, but he didn't see how they could be on the same wavelength ever again. This concern about her missing sunglasses wouldn't have bothered him the day before yesterday, but things had changed now. She was so petty to him now, so immature, almost insufferable. It wasn't her fault. He was the one who'd changed in a matter of twenty-four hours.

"Do you want me to buy you some new ones?" he asked.

"No, silly," she said. "I mean, your truck is coming back, right?"

He shrugged, "I'd assume so."

"Okay then." Her concern vanished as fast as it'd appeared. She gave him a quick kiss on the cheek, said she was going to a movie with her friend Stacy. He was relieved when he heard the front door close behind her.

Those few hours of *World of Warcraft* turned into two days straight. He got up only to pee and get food (Hot Pockets and Pop-Tarts) and drink (Mountain Dew). Jess teased him, asked him if he was becoming a hermit. During that first week after the accident, she was too busy being a *bar-is-ta* and hanging out with Stacy to notice that something was wrong. When she did notice something was wrong, she was more annoyed than worried.

They called him about his truck a few days later and said he could pick it up. It was at some police holding facility, like vehicular jail. He said he'd come get it that day, which turned out to be another lie. It wasn't that he couldn't get to the facility; he could get a ride. It was that he feared he'd get there and experience some kind of paralysis in the driver's seat. He wasn't sure how he'd ever be able to drive again.

But after a couple weeks, he did go get the truck. Jess was sick of driving him around and was starting to question why the alleged repairs were taking so long. He couldn't help but see the vehicle as a criminal. There was a noticeable dent in the front bumper. He'd hoped, stupidly, that the police would fix that, remove any evidence of the accident because Josh wasn't at fault.

His heart was pounding as he drove it, at twenty miles an hour, back home. When he parked in his spot in the apartment complex and let go of the steering wheel, his palms had left two sweat marks. He took Jess's sunglasses from the center console, wiped the visible beads of nervousness from his forehead, and went inside. When he gave them to her, she said, "Oh, I forgot about these."

The very next day, he posted an ad on Craigslist to sell the truck for dirt cheap. Within two days, it was gone. He bought a used Honda Civic to replace it. Jess said, "That's a chick car," but he didn't care. He felt more comfortable driving it, but he still didn't want to leave the house much. He drove only when he had to. He wasn't taking any house calls, or any jobs at all for that matter. That's why Jess was pissed. He was just losing himself online—in *World of Warcraft* and Annie Forester's Facebook page.

His favorite photo of Annie is one from her wedding day. She's looking off to the side, laughing. It isn't a conventionally attractive photo. Her side profile accentuates her long, pointy nose. Her mouth is wide open in a smile that creates lines around her eyes. She just looks so happy. Sometimes he talks to that photo, says, "I hope you feel this same way again, some day." Even if he wasn't at fault, he wants to apologize for being the person behind the wheel of the vehicle that killed their child. It wasn't hard to find out where they live—in Capistrano Beach (or Dana Point or whatever), just a few streets up from Ron, the old guy with the computer problems who probably wrote off Josh as a flake on that fateful day. Maybe he'll add their address to the short list of places he's willing to drive.

FOUR

NATE eats three banana nut pancakes while Annie sits listlessly across from him, elbows on the table, palms propping up her chin. He's not even hungry, but he's compelled to keep eating, to model a healthy appetite for his wife's sake. She's not even looking at him though. She's looking beyond him, at the fridge door. Some of Penelope's drawings are still magneted to it, abstract creations in crayon and marker. She'd say, "Papa, this is a cat"—though it looked nothing like a cat, only like scribbles—and he'd say, "That's a perfect cat."

Should he take them down, the drawings? There are memories of Penelope all over the house: the plastic ducky named Sammy in the bathtub, a rainbow decal sticker on the mirrored closet door in their bedroom, her worn-around-the-edges blue blanket draped over the arm of the couch. Are they supposed to leave these things where they are, as if they are treasured pieces in a museum? Or are they supposed to box them up and put them in the garage with all their old photo albums and random memorabilia? It's hard to say if these lingering things— the ducky, the sticker, the blanket—do harm or good. For now, he won't move them. He will wait for Annie to do something, say something. After all, when he closed the door to Penelope's bedroom last week, thinking the sight of their daughter's unmade bed and neglected toys wasn't helping anything, his wife yelled, "Jesus, Nate, we never close her door."

"So what's on the agenda for today?" he asks.

They used to wake up and spend every morning like this, discussing the day's events. When it was just the two of them, they talked a lot about work, a new recipe to try for dinner that night, weekend plans. When they became three, they talked all about Penelope: the components of her lunch, cute things she said, her bathroom habits, the preschool schedule. Everything else in life became so secondary. They still had their jobs and they still had weekends to plan, but it was assumed those things would just happen naturally. Penelope became the focus of their energies. And that's why it was so strange—yes, strange was the word—with her gone.

"Agenda?" Annie says, like the word disgusts her. She keeps looking down at the countertop.

"Well, I'm going to check on a few properties," Nate says. He took some time off work when Penelope died, because that's what people do. Annie's parents, Sheryl and Steve, had come to stay with them for a while, so he closed the laptop and tried to mourn properly, whatever that means. He would have preferred to work, for distraction, for normalcy.

"Okay," Annie says. Today, she seems mad at him. That's normal, according to Pete the counselor. Grief has stages, anger being one of them, blah blah blah. Pete told them to read a book called *On Grief and Grieving*. Annie read it in one sitting and then put it on Nate's nightstand. He hasn't opened it.

"You want to come with me? I'm going to the Laguna house. Tenant says there's mud sliding down the hill into the backyard from all that rain two weeks ago."

"No," Annie says, looking up now.

"C'mon. You love that house."

The owner of the place had hired him to make it a vacation rental and bring in good tenants, collect checks, organize repairs, that kind of thing. When he went to assess the home for the first time, Annie came with him to take pictures of the property. She'd stood on the back deck, looking out over the ocean, and said, "If you can find a way for us to live here, I will give you bacon every morning and a blow job every night for the rest of your life." They'd laughed.

Would they laugh again?

"I want to stay here," she says.

Since Penelope's death, Annie's left the house only once, for the funeral. And Nate's not even sure she remembers the funeral. She was in a daze, in complete disbelief and denial (that's one of the fucking stages). At the service, her eyes were big and awestruck, like she was wondering who all the people were and why her daughter's preschool photo was enlarged and mounted on a big easel next to a smaller-than-normal coffin.

"Okay," he says. "Can you promise me you'll try to go out for a walk?"

She shrugs, and he doesn't push. A shrug is better than a shake of the head.

Annie's parents are worried. Sheryl calls Nate at least once a day to ask how Annie's doing. "You weren't there when she was really depressed," Sheryl said yesterday. He hates that she is possessive of a part of Annie's history that he can never really know.

Pete the grief counselor had mentioned something called "the grief exception," saying that many psychologists don't believe in diagnosing someone with depression during the first year following a major loss because that kind of sadness is expected, not indicative of a mental health problem. Even though Nate *does* think Annie's current state might be a problem, he isn't going to tell her mother that.

"Depression is appropriate for the circumstance," he told Annie's mother, quoting Pete.

Sheryl snapped, "Depression is never appropriate for Annie."

Nate says to Annie, "Okay, then, I'm gonna jump in the shower and take off."

He rinses his plate, puts it in the dishwasher, and then gives Annie a quick kiss on the cheek, like it's any other day. He longs for a day that is like any other day.

THE HILLSIDE AT the Laguna house isn't nearly as bad as the tenant had made it seem. He was expecting mud oozing down to within a few inches of the back sliding door. But no, it's not that bad. Yes, the mud has overtaken the sandbags he'd placed a few months before, and there are some landscaping casualties, but nature hasn't done too much damage. There is no mud in the pool, which had been his main concern. The patio furniture is crowded as close to the door as it will get, as if it would have walked itself inside and locked the door behind it if it could, as if it were terrified of being out there.

The tenant is a bald guy named Ted. He's wearing a Tommy Bahama shirt, just like the other two times Nate has seen him. He has a huge belly atop skinny flamingo legs.

"I'm not trying to be difficult," he says. This is what people say when they are, in fact, trying to be difficult. "My wife bought these salmon kabobs to barbecue *two weeks ago*. We had to put them in the freezer. We can't really *use* the barbecue, that's the thing."

Nate looks at the barbecue. It looks guilty somehow, scolded. It may have tried to escape the yard, like the furniture, but it's stuck in mud.

"I'm sure you can *use* the barbecue," he says.

"Well, we can't exactly *relax* out here with all the mud." He's got his hands on his hips now. *Ted*. He's just another rich asshole. Most of them are, because this place costs eight hundred a night. *Ted*. He's staying two months.

The week after Penelope died, Ted called and texted saying he had an "emergency" at the property. Nate didn't say, "My daughter just died," because he's not the type to burden people with his personal problems. He just took note of the "emergency," realized it wasn't an emergency, and said he'd come take a look as soon as possible. Frankly, he forgot about it until the guy texted again yesterday saying he was ready to pack up and leave if it wasn't addressed. Now, seeing this guy and his irrational anger over some mud, Nate wants to say, "My daughter got hit by a car." He feels immediately ashamed for that, for thinking of using Penelope that way.

"Okay, I'll have someone out Monday to clean up," he says.

"*Monday?*" Ted says. Clearly, Monday is not soon enough. Clearly, yesterday was not soon enough. "I'm paying a pretty penny for this place, and the backyard isn't even *usable*."

"Sir, with all due respect, it's usable," Nate says. He wants to add *Maybe your wife could just replace her four-inch heels with sensible shoes*, but he knows that's probably just the anger stage of grief talking.

"Okay, then, we'll pack our bags and leave."

If he wasn't a long-term tenant, Nate would let him go. But he's promised the owner a two-month contract. He's already given him the money. If Ted and his annoying wife leave, Nate will have to refund their money out of his own pocket. And after the funeral expenses, he doesn't have much money in his own pocket.

Nate pushes up the sleeves of his shirt, a too-tight flannel that Annie got for him two Christmases ago.

"I'll do it myself," he says, "unless you require a professional."

Ted looks flabbergasted, like he's never considered manual labor.

"Uh, okay, sure," he mumbles. Just like that, Nate has proven himself to be a better man than Ted. That makes the upcoming work worth it.

He gets a shovel from the garage but can't find any gloves, so he starts digging bare-handed. Within twenty minutes, he feels the burn of blisters forming. He ignores it, imagining the earth is this man's thick-as-a-tree-trunk neck, the shovel a murder weapon. He can feel Ted watching him from behind the safety of the glass screen door. He doubts Ted has ever blistered his hands.

His phone buzzes in his pocket just as he finishes freeing the barbecue from the mud. Annie's mother, Sheryl. Before all this, Sheryl never called him. Ever. He can't remember a single phone call from her. She's always talked to Annie a few times a week, usually when Annie is in the car, on her way home from work. On more than a few occasions, Annie would come in the door, set down her purse, and say, "Sometimes, I can't stand my mother." "She's so overbearing," she'd say. "She worries about everything," she'd say. "She's so negative," she'd say.

Annie's mother is the catastrophic type, the type to wonder aloud, "What if the real estate market takes a downturn and both of you are out of work? Have you thought about that?"

The first week after the accident, when Sheryl and Steve stayed with them, Nate felt more uncomfortable in his own house than he ever had before. He thought they were coming to support him and Annie: make casseroles, send out thank-you cards, sort mail, whatever people do for those who are mourning. But no—they were there to comfort Annie, to cry with her, to hold her. Nate made the casseroles and sent out the thank-you cards and sorted the mail.

He couldn't stand it, really, watching his capable, adult wife become an invalid in their welcoming arms. They coddled her, cuddled her, seemed to relish in it. They used soft voices around her, talked to her like she was a toddler. They spoke for her; when he brought out chicken soup one night, Sheryl said, "I don't think Annie's hungry right now." Sheryl slept in bed with Annie while he took the couch. Steve didn't say much of anything to anyone, just lumbered around the house seeming (and probably feeling) useless. After a week of this awkwardness, Nate told Annie, as gently as he could, that they had to leave, that he needed some space "for my own grief," though he wasn't sure that was it. He just didn't want these people in his fucking house.

Even though they left—begrudgingly, with an insinuation that he was being somehow unfair—it's like they're still there. Sheryl calls enough to make it impossible to forget or ignore her presence in their lives. Sometimes Steve is on the line, when they want to appear as a team, hell-bent on helping their daughter through this "monstrously difficult time" (Sheryl's words). Lately, the calls are about antidepressants, how Annie needs to take them.

He told Sheryl, "I've seen her taking some of the ones she has left over, from before."

Sheryl huffed and said, "Those are *years* old, Nate," as if he's the stupidest person on the planet.

He declines the incoming call from Sheryl and goes back to work on the mud, shoveling it off the lawn and cement, down the slope. The blister in his palm opens wider, a circle of redness slowly taking over his hand. He likes the pain, in a way. Or maybe *likes* isn't the right word. He welcomes the pain. He appreciates it. It's such a cut-and-dry, simple feeling, so much unlike all the complicated ones Pete the grief counselor talks about ad nauseam.

"Do you want some water?"

Nate jumps, startled. He didn't even hear Ted open the slider, didn't sense him approaching from behind.

"Oh, sorry, didn't mean to scare you," Ted says, taking a cautious, self-conscious step back.

The morning after the funeral, Nate was standing in the kitchen making coffee because he didn't know what the hell else to do but copy previous mornings, and Steve came up behind him and clapped his hand on his back. Nate flinched, coffee spilling out of his cup. Steve apologized, in his good-natured way, and Nate told him, "It's okay, just a little jumpy." It was as if he was always bracing for that damn truck to come barreling toward him, always looking for a do-over opportunity to stop the truck with his mind, superhero style, and save his daughter.

"You're working awful hard out here," Ted says.

Awful hard? He has become suddenly Midwestern, sheepish, "oh shucks" hands stuffed in his pockets.

"Yeah, well, it's an emergency, as you said."

He doesn't look at him, just keeps working, beads of sweat taking suicidal leaps off his forehead.

"This is probably good enough," Ted says. "It looks much better."

When Nate straightens up, he realizes how much his back

aches. If it was the old days, "old days" now referring to the days that existed before the accident, he would go home and ask Annie to give him a massage. She would knead his muscles with her deceptively strong, slender fingers, grind her knuckles into the knots. One of their recorded shows would be on—*House Hunters* or *Top Chef*. She always had to be multitasking. Clearing out the recorded shows one by one was an accomplishment. "What can I say? I'm productive," she'd say.

"That's the difference between us," he'd say.

When she was done massaging him, she'd lie facedown on the bed and he'd rub her shoulders. The ambition lodged itself there, in between her shoulder blades. He'd lie flat on top of her, whisper in her ear, "You're so tense." This was their language of foreplay.

She'd whisper back, "Then relax me." They'd make love, and by the time they were done, whatever show they had been watching would be over. She'd delete it anyway, check it off her list.

"Thank you, really," Ted says, extending his hand for a peacemaking shake.

Nate shows him his palms with as much enthusiasm as Penelope had when she put her hands in the wet cement on the sidewalk outside their house. She was only two at the time, so Annie helped her, pressed each of her fingers into the ground.

Ted recoils quickly. "Oh, wow," he says. Nate has to suppress a childish laugh. It doesn't take much to unnerve this man. He's surprised Ted doesn't dial 9-1-1, claiming another "emergency."

"Do you want to come in and clean up?" Ted asks.

I'm sure your wife wouldn't approve of that, Nate wants to say. Instead, he smiles stiffly and says, "It's just a short drive home, thanks."

He lets himself out through the back gate and gets in his car. There's hand sanitizer in the cup holder. Annie always makes sure there is hand sanitizer within reach at all times. "I've become one of those germophobes I used to hate," she'd said, right after they had Penelope.

Annie didn't have any postpartum depression, but she had postpartum anxiety. That's what the doctor called it. "Totally normal for lots of moms," the doctor said with a calming smile. Annie couldn't let the baby sleep an hour without checking to make sure she hadn't suffocated. She measured out the milk she pumped every day, down to the quarter ounce, convinced it wasn't enough, convinced she would be responsible for starving their child. She had nightmares of Lucy eating the baby, of their neighbor—a round, eighty-year-old, sweet-as-pie grandmother— stealing the baby, of the baby drowning in Lucy's water dish or the puddle that perpetually formed in a depressed area of their backyard. Thankfully, the worries subsided, but the desire for hand sanitizer did not.

The alcohol stings. He winces. He's covered in a thin layer of dirt and needs a shower. Like he told Ted, it's just a short drive back home, but he doesn't want to go home. Not yet, anyway. He doesn't want to see Annie in bed or on the couch. In the old days, he would have rushed home to show her his hands and tell her about the rich asshole who did this to him. She would shake her head, laugh, say, "Some people," and pour him a glass of whiskey. Now though, he doubts she'll care about his hands. Or she'll say with annoyance, "What happened?" as if he's bringing her one more thing to worry about, one more example of how life sucks.

He decides he'll go to the gym, shower there. He hasn't been to the gym in months. He just keeps his membership as a lingering, halfhearted reminder to "get back into it."

It's busy for a Saturday night. Fairly attractive people who you would assume have plans on a weekend are running on treadmills and riding bikes. Part of the reason Nate stopped going to the gym is that Annie hated to go with him. "All that energy and nobody actually *goes* anywhere," she said about the treadmills and the bikes. "Like hamsters in wheels."

Some people watch the TVs mounted to the ceiling, staring with glazed eyes. Some bob their heads to music. Some read magazines or books, their bodies barely working in the midst of their engrossment. None of them look particularly happy. This fact is comforting in a way.

His original plan was to make a beeline for the locker room, just use the shower and leave. But now he reconsiders. The machines look more appealing than they ever did before. Between his run this morning and the shoveling, he's burned a couple days' worth of calories, but he hops on a treadmill anyway. Nobody gives him strange looks, in his dirty flannel shirt and khaki shorts. There's an old guy next to him, walking at what must be the slowest pace the treadmill will go, and he's wearing pants and a button-down white shirt. That's the thing about this place—nobody seems to give a shit.

He pushes the up arrow, increasing speed, until he's going at a fairly fast clip. It's different from running outside. Here, the belt is moving and you must keep up. There's a thrill to that, a bizarre kind of danger.

Before he knows it, four miles have passed under his feet. He slows the machine, steps off, gets reacquainted with the stillness of the ground beneath him. He walks to the showers in a kind of haze. He feels good, he thinks. Yes, *good*. He turns on the hot water, stands under it, lets it sting his hands and wash the dirt off him. He'll just stay here, in this shower, for an hour. There's a drought in California, but this is important, he thinks. And if Annie asks where he was, though she probably won't, he'll just say, "I went to work out." It will be a way of telling her, yet again, that life must go on.

ANNIE reaches to the back of the closet for a big, wide-brimmed hat. She wore it only once, years ago, when she and Nate had just started dating and they went to watch the horse races in Del Mar. She tried so hard then; she had to go to three different stores to find that hat. Last year, they took Penelope to the racetrack in response to her expressed love of "horsies." Annie wore jeans.

It's all flattened out now, the hat. The wire shaping the brim is bent and awkward. She twists it into a somewhat normal shape and puts the hat on her head. She looks at herself in the mirror, rolls her eyes. When she wore the hat at the racetrack, she wore a pretty sundress and strappy sandals with it. That's what made the outfit. Now she is wearing the same ratty gray sweatpants she's worn all week and a blue sweatshirt. The hat is out of place. She must wear it though.

As she ties her shoes, Lucy looks at her with those big, dumb dog eyes, wagging her tail. "You're not coming," Annie says. She puts on her sunglasses and goes outside, into the world. The sun seems abusively bright. *This must be what bears feel like when they come out of hibernation*, she thinks. She squints behind the sunglasses. Why is she even doing this? Because Nate told her to go for a walk? What is she, a child in need of instruction? *Yes, maybe. Probably.*

If she told Nate why she had to wear the hat and glasses, he would say she was being ridiculous. He would say it with a laugh, in hopes that she would also laugh. He wouldn't mean anything by it—the laugh, the "ridiculous." She would be hurt though. He would take her by the shoulders and say, "Geez, Annie, chill out." She baffles him.

The thing is she doesn't want people to recognize her. Neighbors, mostly. Not that she knows any of them super well. But they know her now. They have left cookies and Crock-Pots of chili and flowers and notes on the front porch. The notes say things like, "I always loved seeing Penelope. She was such a sweet girl." Who do they think they are? They didn't *know* Penelope. They don't get to be sad. They don't get to have a piece of her. Annie gets all the pieces.

She didn't like people before all this. When she first met Nate, at that real estate conference all those years ago, she'd told him, "Just so you know, this socializing thing is torture for me." She faked extroversion well, for her job, to seem "normal," but it all exhausted her—the small talk, the feigned interest in bullshit, the smiling. He said, "You have no idea how much it relieves me to hear that." They were two introverted peas in a private pod. By finding each other, they no longer had to pretend anymore. They could just enjoy each other, at home. And when there were those obligatory weddings and birthday dinners and housewarming parties, they had each other to glom on to. If one of them winked at the other from across the room, that was code for "We gotta get out of here." In the car on the way home, they said things like, "We're so lucky" and "What would I do without you?" Annie really didn't know the answer to that question. There were times when she woke up in the morning and Nate was already out of bed. She would try to imagine that as her life, waking up in bed alone, no Nate. Some days, it brought her to tears.

Part of the allure of having a baby was that they would have valid, unquestionable reasons to decline invitations: "Penelope's fussing," "Penelope has a fever," "Penelope has a school event." The options were endless.

"Kids are like built-in excuse banks," Beth used to say. Beth, Annie's best friend—or former best friend? Annie can't see how they will have the same friendship ever again, how they will ever meet up for martinis and bitch about their husbands and trash-talk women at their respective jobs who wear short skirts and flirt with whatever male is in power. Beth the architect, Annie the lawyer—two high-powered, no-bullshit, invincible women. Beth had a son, Jackson, a year before Penelope came along. Annie liked that Beth could go first, then pass on her wisdom. The "excuse bank" thing was a valid pro, Beth said. "Sometimes, I tell my boss I have to pick up Jackson from day care, but I just can't stand to sit at my desk an hour longer," Beth said. "He never argues with me. He's afraid of HR."

The two people Annie's always loved most—Nate, Beth—she can't stand anymore. How awful is that? Nate is so insistent on being positive, on seeing the glass as half full. This used to be one of his best qualities. So quickly it has become one of his worst, creating a chasm between them that she isn't sure will ever close. She imagines him on his side, calling at her: "Come on, honey, join me over here, on the bright side." Even if she wanted to go over there, how could she? She is trapped in all these clouds, this darkness. She can barely see him some days.

And Beth. Beth gets to have Jackson. And she's got the new baby girl, Emily. She has two—*two*! It seems so excessive, so greedy. They used to joke that Jackson would be Penelope's future husband. Well, not now. He will find someone else. He will have so many options for wives. The world will be his fucking oyster. And that's not fair, is it? That he gets to live and fall in love?

Nate would say it's irrational to hate Beth, but she does all the same. How can she be expected to be rational, for God's sake? The world hasn't been rational in return. Still she knows, even in the midst of her insanity, that it's not Beth's fault. It's just that Annie now has this all-consuming membership in a shitty club for mothers who have buried their children. Beth will never understand, even though they've known each other for decades, even though they grew up together, in that white-picket-fence sort of way that many people don't get these days. Beth was there when Annie sipped alcohol for the first time—wine coolers they'd stolen from Beth's mom's collection. Beth was there the morning after Annie lost her virginity. Beth was there when Annie came home from college, depressed and embarrassed. Beth was there to hear Annie gush about Nate. Beth said, "Well, I have to meet this guy." And when she did, she pulled Annie aside and said with a seriousness that wasn't usual, "He's it."

The day Penelope died, Beth was there at the house when Nate and Annie got home from the police station. Annie couldn't even remember Nate calling Beth. He must have. She was just sitting on the couch, looking strung out and devastated. When they came in the door, she stood and took a step toward them, then the same step back, unsure how to proceed. They'd exchanged so many hugs over the years, "hello" hugs and "goodbye" hugs and "you'll get through this" hugs and "I missed you" hugs. How could any hug suffice for this situation? It couldn't. She tried, hugged Annie tight and long, but comfort was an impossible thing. In those first few days, all the people close to Annie tired themselves trying to prove it possible.

Beth cooked dinner for them that night, even though nobody was hungry. It was like she just needed something to do to fulfill her role as the best friend. The pot of pasta sat on the stove for two days, until Annie's mom threw it out. At the funeral, Beth stood near Annie the whole time, like a security guard trailing the president's teenage daughter, on the watch for anyone who could do harm. They all did harm though, not meaning to, of course, but harm just the same. They all approached her with those furrowed brows, using soft, gentle voices, as if any words spoken at normal volume would trigger a mental breakdown. They all tiptoed around her, noticeably afraid of saying something wrong. Even Beth—cynical, sarcastic, "if you can't say something nice, you're my type of person" Beth—became so careful with Annie, treating her like she was made of porcelain. Just the week before the accident, Beth had playfully slapped Annie and called her a "fucking bitch" when she mentioned that she still hadn't managed to gain back the weight she lost breastfeeding Penelope. Now, suddenly, Beth was so overly considerate and painfully sympathetic. Suddenly, she was all tight smiles and sad, Lucy-like eyes. Suddenly, she was a stranger, just like everyone else.

Annie was on the internet a lot the first couple weeks, searching through blogs and message boards of people who had also lost children, trying to find people who would understand her. One of the bloggers, a woman whose newborn son died of sudden infant death syndrome, mentioned these tribal people who bash their teeth in with a rock when they're grieving so they don't have to deal with uncomfortable small talk. See, the internet understood. Until it didn't. She made the mistake of reading the comments on that blog post. One person said, "We must trust that everything happens for a reason" and another said, "What could the reason possibly be?" Someone else said, "Maybe he would have grown up to be a serial killer." With that, Annie abandoned the laptop, and some hope.

SHE WALKS DOWN the hill past the elementary school. Her face gets hot, the way it does when she's angry or ashamed. Why would Nate suggest this walk? He knew there was no way to really avoid the elementary school. They had talked so many times about how they couldn't wait for Penelope to go there. They were constantly in flux between wanting time to slow down and wanting it to speed up. There were days Annie wanted to freeze Penelope, make her a toddler forever; but then there were days she was so eager for Penelope's teenage years, when they would talk about boys.

It's Saturday, so there's no school today. Thank God for that. Annie is fairly certain she would have a mild nervous breakdown and cause a scene if she had to witness parents pulling up to the curb and saying lazy "I love you"s to their education-bound offspring while scanning their phones for more important things. *There is nothing more important*, she thinks. And, yet, how many times did she tell Penelope "Give Mommy just one minute" while she sorted through work emails?

Annie and Nate used to talk about what dumb luck they had, choosing a house close to an elementary school even though they hadn't planned on having children. "Maybe the universe knew something we didn't," Annie said one day, when she was about-to-pop pregnant and they took a walk down to the park to watch the sunset. How naïve they were, thinking the universe had some rhyme or reason to it, some grand plan in their favor.

And how naïve they were to assume their dumb luck would continue. They'd had such idyllic visions of future mornings with their school-age daughter. They would eat a leisurely breakfast as a family, not rushed by the fear of freeway traffic, not stressed by the notoriously chaotic school drop-off scenario. They would walk her there together, each holding one of her little palms in theirs. It would have been so Norman Rockwell. *Would have been.* How many times could Annie string together those three words before losing her mind completely?

She makes it to the bottom of the hill, past the school. It seems like she's traveled miles. She wonders how Nate runs as far as he does. She starts the walk back up the hill. It's an incline that has always left her winded, no matter how many times she has conquered it. She stops to catch her breath. Right before Christmas, they took Penelope to the beach. It was a weirdly warm December day, "earthquake weather," according to Nate. Penelope loved the beach, loved running in the sand with Lucy. She taunted Annie: "You better not get me, Mommy" (which Annie knew to mean, "Get me, get me!"). A chase ensued. Penelope was getting old enough to exhaust her parents in new ways. And, well, Annie was out of shape. When Penelope ran ahead, Annie said, "Sweetie, I have to catch my breath," and Penelope said, with the most quizzical, wondrous look on her face, "How do you catch breath?"

There is a "Lost Cat" sign stapled to a wood power pole. It says, "This is Ginger" above a picture of an orange tabby in the lap of a boy who looks to be ten years old or so. The white paper is yellowed with age. Somehow, this sign has survived two years on this light post. It says, "Missing since December 18, 2013" and "We'd love to have her home for Christmas." Then there's a phone number to call. There are always signs like these in the neighborhood.

The coyotes come down from the hills looking for food, and that's that. It's not their fault, the coyotes. The humans keep invading their territories, building tract homes that sell for close to a million dollars. Still, nobody can believe it. Their neighbor said once, "Who heard of coyotes this close to the beach?" Annie guessed the coyotes were thinking, "Who heard of million-dollar homes in the wilderness?"

She takes out her phone. There's a text from Nate: *Just checking in. I'll be home later than I thought. Love you.* She doesn't type anything back. What is there to say? At least one of them is reentering life, going back to work, coming home later than they thought.

It's stupid, probably, to call the number on the sign. What if they found their cat though? Wouldn't that be amazing? A reason to keep believing in something? She punches in the phone number and gets a jolt through her body when it rings.

"Hello?" a voice says. It's a small miracle that some people still answer their phones when they don't recognize the incoming number. Annie never does that.

"Hi," Annie says, immediately realizing that it's been so long since she's said that—*hi.*

There is silence.

"I just saw your sign for the missing cat," Annie says.

Again, silence.

"I was just wondering if you ever found her."

There is another beat of silence, and then: "Ginger?"

"Yeah, Ginger," Annie says, her heart pounding.

"Oh, no, sweetie," the woman says. She's older, this woman. Someone younger would have hung up already.

"Oh," Annie says. She regrets all this with an intensity that overwhelms her. She starts crying, audibly, because she seems to have lost her ability to cry discreetly.

"Sweetie, that was some time ago now. We got Phillip another cat."

Phillip must be the boy in the picture. He must be about twelve now. He probably cares more about video games than he does about cats.

"Well, that's good to know," Annie says. It's such a blatant lie. It's not good to know. It's terrible to know that people just move on, get new things to love. "I'm sorry," she adds. For their loss two years ago? For disturbing them? Both?

"It's okay, sweetie. Is there something else I can help you with?"

Elderly, she must be elderly. Nobody is this kind these days.

"No, thank you," Annie says and pushes the red button on the phone that ends the call.

She crouches down right there on the sidewalk and puts her head between her knees. That's what they say to do when you feel faint, right? The phone buzzes. Maybe the sweet woman is calling her back. No, it's her mother. Before she registers this, she's accidentally answered the call.

"You picked up," her mother says, before any "hello."

She's been calling every day. Beth too. At first, it seemed like everyone Annie had ever met was calling: old friends from high school, coworkers, acquaintances who would have been completely forgotten if not for Facebook. The calls have dwindled as the weeks pass. Beth and her mother still call daily though. She ignores Beth and answers her mother sporadically, just to assure her she's alive. After all, she has a history that would suggest she might try not to be alive in this type of situation.

"Yes, it appears I picked up."

"It's good to hear your voice."

Annie swallows, feels guilty for all the calls she's dodged. That's what she needs on top of everything else—guilt.

"How are you?"

"I'm out for a walk, actually," she says, hoping that will put her mother's mind at ease. She stands, resumes her trek back up the hill.

"That's great, honey." Her mother has always had a saccharine voice, but it seems especially saccharine today.

"Nate said I should, so I am." She sounds like a teenager all over again, compliant with orders despite the desire to rebel. This is how she was when they carried her home from college.

"I'm sure fresh air does wonders."

Wonders? She shakes her head at her mother's enthusiasm.

"Listen, honey, I really think it's time to see the doctor," her mother says, taking on her voice of authority.

Annie gets to the top of the hill, pauses to catch her breath. *How do you catch breath?* She remembers promising her mother when she went off medication, when she was pregnant with Penelope, that she would go back on the antidepressant if she needed to. "Mom," she'd said, putting a hand on her mother's shoulder lovingly, "I wouldn't put you guys through that again."

"I have some pills left, from before. I'm taking those."

"Annie, you don't even know if those still work. They're more than four years old."

Older than Penelope. A life has come and gone, and the pills remain.

"I think they work fine."

Really though, she's not sure. The label says, "Discard before February 2011." In February 2011, Penelope was three months old. What she would give to go back to then.

"If you're not *opposed* to taking them, why not get *new* ones?"

First of all, Annie doesn't want to leave the house, this walk being a huge exception that she doesn't plan on repeating.

Second, even if she was okay with going out into the world, she doesn't want to see her doctor. It's unlikely Dr. Grace has heard about what happened. It's not like they live in a tiny Midwestern town where everyone knows everyone else's business. So Dr. Grace will ask, innocently, "How is little Penelope?" She always asks that, in just that way. Annie can't imagine having to break the news. She hasn't said it out loud yet. *Penelope died.* Dr. Grace would probably cry. She's that type. Annie doesn't have capacity for other people's sadness. She can't be responsible for that.

"I don't want to see Dr. Grace," Annie says. If before she sounded like her former teenage self, now she sounds like a toddler.

Her mother does her characteristic scoff that sounds like a little laugh and says, "Well, honey, there are hundreds of doctors within a twenty mile radius, I'm sure."

Annie sighs. Her mother's not going to let this go, that much is obvious. Annie's going for a walk for Nate's sake, and now she will have to see a new fucking doctor for her mom's. It's draining, honestly, juggling the roles of dutiful wife, loving daughter, and distraught mother—or former mother?

"Fine, Mom, I'll take care of it."

And just like that, she's adult Annie again, whether she likes it or not.

SIX

JOSH follows a block behind her as she marches back up the hill. He can't believe she hasn't spotted him. She's in her own world, that's what it is, a world he and his stupid truck helped create.

He'd pulled up in front of the house an hour ago. He wasn't sure what he was doing there. What did he come to see, exactly? That they were alive and well, going on with their lives? What would be proof of that? Hearing laughter coming from inside? Smelling fresh-baked cookies? Peeking through the window and seeing them watch mindless TV or vacuum like they would on any other Saturday?

It's a modest house, a little white box from the front. Two palm trees tower over the driveway, one of their big leaves— what do you call those . . . fronds?—threatening to fall onto the Prius parked there. Maybe he should go and tell them about it, as a do-gooder. *Hey, I was just out for a walk and noticed . . .* No, that's dumb. What if they recognized him from the accident scene? What if they had gotten his name off the police report and done some online stalking, just like he had?

The neighborhood is quiet, normal seeming. There is no shrine to the little girl in the front yard, no Christian cross staked into the lawn. He shook his head at himself for expecting something that would make him feel . . . what? Better? Worse? He didn't even know. Then, just as he was about to drive away, she came out. Annie Forester, the mom of the little girl. Or that's who he assumed she was. He couldn't see her face. It was hidden beneath this big, ridiculous hat and sunglasses. There was a dog too. She shooed the dog back inside, nearly closed the front door on its snout.

She just stood there, on the welcome mat, for what felt like ten minutes. She looked up at the sky like it was the first time she'd ever seen it. She crossed her arms across her middle, the way people do when they have a stomachache, and started walking. At first he thought she was going to get the newspaper or the mail, but she walked past the driveway and past the mailbox, to the end of the street. Then she turned right and kept walking. He waited for a second to see if she would come back. When she didn't, he got out of his car to follow her.

He walked on the other side of the street, kept a safe distance. She went down the hill, past the elementary school. At the bottom of the hill, she turned around and started walking right back up. Maybe this was some kind of daily exercise ritual. She stopped suddenly in front of a wooden power pole. He thought she saw him, so he ducked behind a bush. From what he could see, she was looking at a sign of some kind, like a yard sale sign or something. She took out her phone, dialed. A few words were exchanged, and then she looked really sad, like the person on the other line had told her all over again that her daughter just died. She crouched down right there on the sidewalk with her head between her knees. Again he considered being the do-gooder. *Ma'am, I was just passing by. Are you okay?* He started to walk across the street, but then she rose from her crouched position, phone to her ear. She looked agitated with whoever was on the phone now. She resumed walking. And he resumed following.

Now he is at his car again. She has just gone back inside the house. He waits a few minutes to see if she comes out again. Nothing. The palm leaf (or frond or whatever) really does look like it's going to fall any minute. It sways precariously in the beach breeze, begging him to knock on the door and warn her. She must be home alone. If her husband was home, he would have gone for a walk with her, right? And there's just the one car in the driveway. Nobody parks their cars in the garage these days. The garage is for storing shit. He'd rather talk to Annie than to her husband, Penelope's father, Nate Forester. Even if she recognizes him, she won't beat his face in. Nate probably would. And Josh wouldn't blame him if he did. Even if it wasn't Josh's fault, you have to blame someone. You have to direct anger somewhere. It can't just hang there indefinitely, like a palm leaf (or frond or whatever) in the fucking breeze.

Sitting on the ground next to the front door is a pot with a pink ribbon around it, a gift. The contents of the pot are dead, petals shriveled and brown. He takes this as a sign to leave, abandon this ill-thought-out plan. Obviously, they are too grief-stricken to tend to basic upkeep. They don't need him complicating things. As he starts to turn around, she comes out, this time without her hat and glasses.

"Oh, Jesus, you scared me," she says. Her eyes are big and startled and a brighter green than the photos portrayed. The dog, a black Lab, starts barking behind her.

"Lucy, shut the hell up," she says, with more anger than is necessary.

"It's okay. She's just trying to protect you," Josh says with an uneasy laugh.

"No, she's barking because she's afraid," Annie says. "She's pathetic."

She closes the door behind her and looks at Josh. He awaits that moment of recognition, awaits a change in her face that says, "Oh no, it's you." There is nothing though.

Annie offers him a small, forced smile. She's pretty. He can see the sadness in her eyes, but she's still pretty. She picks up the pot next to the door, clutches it in her arms like it's a baby. Maybe she just realized it was dead. Maybe she doesn't leave the house much.

"Um, can I help you?" she says.

He's flustered now. He wants to sit with her, tell her he's sorry. Something in those eyes of hers tells him she couldn't handle it though. It's too soon.

"Oh, uh, I was just walking by your house and I noticed the leaf or frond or whatever from the tree is about to fall on your car," he says.

She doesn't seem alarmed. Maybe nothing alarms you anymore when you've witnessed your three-year-old get hit by a truck. She calmly cranes her neck so she can see the driveway, sighs.

"That stupid tree," she says. "You know, one of the reasons we bought this house was because of the palm trees. Little did we know. We have scratches on both our cars now."

"That sucks," he says. He stuffs his hands in his pockets, feeling suddenly self-conscious about the bagginess of his jeans, the sleeve of tattoos on his right arm. Most of his tattoos are computer nerd tattoos—lines of code from programs he's written, the power button symbol, that type of thing. She doesn't know that though. She's probably wondering, *Who is this kid?*

"Yeah, it does suck. I'll tell my husband though, thank you."

She opens the door again, balancing the pot on her thigh while she shoves the curious dog back inside. He should just walk away now, but he's standing there like an idiot. She gives him another uncomfortable smile along with a little wave before shutting the door.

He heads back to his car, feeling like he should do or say more. He looks up at the palm tree. Could he climb up there and get the leaf, wrench it off the tree? Maybe. He goes to the brick wall separating their yard from the neighbor's. He determines that he can push himself up on top of it, then stand and be within arm's reach of the culprit frond. He looks both ways, making sure neighbors aren't watching him. After all, it's suspicious, this kid with baggy jeans and tattoos scaling a fence and assaulting a palm tree.

Once on top of the fence, he pulls up his pants and reaches for the frond. *You have such long arms, like a spider.* Jess said that to him once. "Gangly" is what his mom calls him. His mom, who's always been short and round, told him he got his height (and lack of weight) from his dad. "I hope that's all I got from him," he'd said. He liked to assure her that he hated his father as much as she did, even though he didn't know his father at all. Hating him was as good as telling his mom he loved her.

It's more stubborn than he thought it would be, the frond. He can barely reach it, so he can't get a solid grip. He tugs on it as best he can, both arms totally outstretched. The blood drains down his arms, and they start to go numb after just a few minutes. He shakes them out, tries again. Getting a little braver, he jumps slightly off the half-foot-wide wall and knocks at the frond with his fists. After a few of these punches, it falls, away from the Prius, into the neighbor's yard. It lands with a thud. He hops off the fence into the yard and picks it up. It's heavier than you would think.

It must be trash day because the neighborhood trash cans are curbside, except for the Foresters', incidentally. He opens one and jams the frond inside, closes the lid. For a second, he feels happy. Happy in the way he used to feel before the accident, like after a good gaming session, like after figuring out a complex computer problem, like after having sex with Jess, like after one too many beers. And just as he's trying to figure out how to hang on to this bit of happiness, it's gone.

WHEN HE GETS home, Jess is on the couch, her feet propped up on the coffee table. She's shaking a bottle of nail polish, the little ball inside it making that noise that always annoys him.

"I thought you were working today," he says.

"Touché," she says. Her smile is sly and antagonizing.

"Didn't you storm out this morning to go be a *bar-is-ta*?" he says. He's picking a fight. He sees it happening and feels no desire to stop it. She starts painting her nails, as if they are more important than this fight that's about to occur.

"I had the day off. I just stormed out because you were being a dick. I went to Walgreens to buy nail polish for this pedicure you are now witnessing."

Josh's mom never really liked Jess. "She's tart," she said about her once. Josh never knew what that meant, but it made sense now. Tart like a lemon that makes you squint your eyes and contort your face when you take a small bite.

"Where have *you* been?" she asks, still focused on her toenails.

"Just out."

"Well, that's better than playing World of Nerdcraft or whatever the hell it is."

"Jess, stop being like that."

"Like what?" See, she wants the fight too. It's not just him.

"Passive-aggressive."

She looks up from her toes with that smile again. "Oh, sweetie, I'm not trying to be passive-aggressive. I'm trying to be super clear that I'm pissed at you."

"Okay, well, I think you're being . . . tart," he says.

She giggles in a way that's condescending, in a way that tells him he's a fool. "Tart? What the fuck does that mean?" She keeps giggling.

"This isn't funny, Jess."

"It totally isn't. I'm sorry," she says, turning away to stifle more laughter. "You know what else isn't funny? Your ongoing unemployment."

When they moved in together, they opened a joint checking account. It all sounded so romantic at the time, being a team, taking on the realities of adult life together. Josh had never been a team with someone before, unless you counted his mom, which he didn't because that seemed weird. In hindsight, it was a dumb idea. They barely knew each other. Now they will go their separate ways and, when they meet someone new and have the obligatory talk about past relationships, they will describe the failure of theirs by saying, "We were just so young."

"You really think I'm a loser, don't you?" he says.

She shrugs. "I'm open to argument."

He knows how it looks to her. It looks like they moved in together and he became a deadbeat. But could she at least give him the benefit of the doubt? Could she care enough to consider that it might be more complicated than him being a stereotypical loser? Could she ask him if something else is going on, if he's okay, like, mentally?

"I don't think I have it in me to argue with you," he says, suddenly exhausted.

"See what I mean? You're lazy."

That's it.

"Jess, we're done."

She blows on her drying nail polish.

"Okay, go play your nerd game then."

"No, I mean, we're done for good. We're over."

She looks up at him with surprise that quickly morphs into smug satisfaction.

"Um, okay, are you serious?"

He nods.

She shakes her head in disbelief. "You are seriously crazier than I thought."

She stands from the couch, her toes raised off the ground and spread as far apart from each other as they will go. She attempts to walk past him with an air of superiority, but it doesn't quite translate because she's on the balls of her feet, looking idiotic.

"You can have the apartment," he says, his voice projecting at the blank space on the couch where she had been sitting.

"Well, I'd assume so. You can't afford it," she says from the bedroom.

He hears her on the phone with someone, probably Stacy, repeating, "Un-fucking-believable" before launching into an exaggerated, dramatic summary of what's just transpired. He probably shouldn't have done this so hastily. He should have crafted a better exit plan. He looks around the apartment. Most of the furniture and electronics and appliances they bought together on Craigslist or at garage sales. He isn't particularly attached to any of it. She can have it. All he needs is his computers, his clothes, and his electronic toothbrush—listed in order of importance.

When he goes into the bedroom, she's furiously packing a bag, throwing in clothes with no apparent rhyme or reason.

"I'm going to Stacy's tonight."

"You don't need to do that. I'll be out of here in a half hour."

She looks at him like he is certifiably insane.

"Don't we need to, like, divvy things up?"

"You can have it."

"*It?*"

"All of it," he says.

She furrows her brows and says, "Um, are you okay?"

Finally, the question she should have asked weeks ago. Then again, if she had, if she'd pried into his melancholy, would he have told her the truth? Probably not. Even now, knowing that he could make her feel really guilty by saying, "No, I'm not okay. I hit and killed a little girl a month ago," he can't tell her—not because he wants to protect her, not because he thinks she'll say the wrong thing, but because he still can't manage to state the reality out loud. He hasn't told a soul, and as the weeks tick by, he starts to wonder if he ever will.

"I'm fine," he says.

"Okay, well, I tried," she says.

She throws her bag over one shoulder with dramatic flair and marches out of the apartment, with a predictable door slam as the exclamation mark to their breakup. She'll go and tell Stacy all about it. Josh will be villainized. He probably deserves that, but for reasons different from hers.

It really does take him only a half hour to collect the things he needs. He makes three trips back and forth between his car and the apartment and that's it, he's done. He takes one last look around, grabs a few things from the pantry. *We need cheddar cheeeeeese. Love you, cheesy bear.* That's what it says on the whiteboard magneted to the side of the fridge, a month-old note from Jess. They did love each other, as much as two naïve kids could. He just isn't naïve anymore. That's the problem.

He's not sure where to go. He sits in his car, scrolling through contacts in his phone. He's always been a bit of a loner. His closest friends are online. He could call his mom, ask to stay with her. He'd be a burden though. She has her crappy apartment in Anaheim that's barely big enough for her and her cat. Maybe he'll just sleep in his car until he saves up enough money to get his own place again. It won't take long. He just needs a few big jobs. He can do his work in coffee shops and then just park the car somewhere inconspicuous at night. Like, today, he noticed an empty lot for sale near where the Foresters live. An empty lot means nobody to complain about a hobo parked in front of their house. He'll start there. And maybe, just maybe, he'll work up the nerve to talk to Nate and Annie.

SEVEN

NATE wakes up Monday morning to find that Annie is not in bed next to him. She's always in bed next to him. Or, at least, she's always been in bed next to him since the accident. She used to wake up early, before six most mornings, so she could do the dishes from the night before and make breakfast before Penelope woke up. They had a very traditional domestic existence, their duties split according to 1950s gender roles. It surprised both of them. They had always thought they were so progressive. Before Penelope, he did most of the cooking and cleaning because Annie's career was busier. They considered having Nate be a stay-at-home dad or work only part-time once the baby came along. Annie said she wanted to pump milk and bottle it in the afternoon so Nate could be the one to wake up at night and tend to Penelope. To keep up with her job at the firm, Annie would need her rest. But when Penelope arrived, the best laid plans became obsolete. Annie wanted to breastfeed, and she wanted to be home as much as she could. So they rearranged their life to accommodate her surprisingly fierce maternal instincts.

Nate changes into his running shorts and T-shirt and wanders down the hallway, shoes in hand. "Annie?" he calls. Lucy follows behind him, her need-to-be-clipped nails tapping on the slate floor.

"Hi," Annie says. She's sitting on the couch, laptop open. He worries about what has her attention. A couple weeks after the accident, she was glued to the internet, following the story of an orca whale carrying her dead baby calf through the waters of the Pacific Northwest. "They say the mother may die because she's not eating," Annie had said. The mother didn't die, though. She let go of the carcass, after eleven days, and went on swimming. This was presented as a happy ending, but it seemed to make Annie even sadder. It was like she wanted the mother whale to die, to lend credibility to her own despair. The fact that the mother whale went on meant Nate had won in the silent argument they were having.

"You're up early." It's just before seven.

"I couldn't sleep. I can never sleep. My mom's probably right—I should see a doctor."

It's obvious her mind has been up for hours. Is this progress from her complete lethargy, or is this something worse? He rubs the sleep from his eyes.

"Yeah, that's probably a good idea."

It would be a relief if she saw someone. It would mean her mother might not call him every fucking day.

He peeks over her shoulder. She's looking at a website for a medical center in Fullerton.

"Fullerton? Isn't your doctor in Laguna Niguel?"

Dr. Grace, that's her doctor. There was a time when Nate didn't know that. He longs for that time of ignorance, simplicity. Once they started trying to have a baby, he became a real husband, suddenly privy to all kinds of information, like the length of Annie's menstrual cycles (twenty-six to thirty days). *Dr. Grace says that's really good, regular.*

"I want to see someone new," she says.

He doesn't ask why because she probably has a convoluted reason that will only frustrate him. And, honestly, she's taking initiative with something, expressing the will to live, so who cares what the reason is?

"Okay, whatever you think is best."

"They open at eight. I'm going to see if I can get in today."

He has several meetings today, including a big one with a rich real estate mogul who wants a dedicated property manager for his six multiunit properties in San Clemente.

"Uh, okay," he says. "I've got that big meeting today with that mogul and—"

She stops him. "I hate that word. *Mogul*," she says. "I can drive myself."

Being that she hasn't left the house, save for one alleged walk, he's not sure about this.

"Are you sure you—"

She slams her laptop shut and expels an angry breath. "Some days you are so impatient for me to get back to normal, whatever the hell that means. And then when I try, you act like I'm incapable."

That about sums it up, he thinks.

"I'm sorry," he says. "You're right."

In their marriage, this has always been the way to deflate her.

"You going for a run?" she says, softened again.

"Yep."

He sits next to her on the couch to lace up his shoes. Their thighs touch, and he takes note of the fact that this is the most physical contact they'll probably have today. He's waiting for Pete the grief counselor to bring up their sex life, or lack thereof. They used to be a two-or-three-times-a-week couple. He understands that Annie isn't in the mood. He just wishes she'd

understand that he has—there must be a better way to say this—
needs. He's not proud of that, but it's a fact. Another fact: he's
taken to jerking off in the shower a few mornings a week, like a
girlfriendless teenager.

"Oh, I forgot to tell you the other day. One of the palm tree
fronds is going to fall on my car," she says.

"Okay, I'll get it."

They have a reaching tool specifically for this purpose.
The trees have dropped their fronds and pods on their cars on
multiple occasions. After the first time, they went to the trouble
of having the scratches buffed out. Then they stopped caring.

He gets the reaching tool from the garage and stuffs Lucy's
leash into his pocket. He has no intention of using it, but doesn't
want to piss off Annie.

"I'll be back in an hour," he says.

She doesn't look up, just nods distractedly.

He always feels better outside in the morning air, just him
and Lucy. After this weekend's digging and treadmill episodes,
he's thinking maybe he'll sign up for a marathon. It's for the good
of everyone if he gets his energy out somehow. And there are all
those endorphins that are supposed to be good for you. Even
grief counselor Pete would approve.

"You think you could run twenty-six miles?" he says to Lucy.
She just wags her tail. "I might have to leave you at home for that
one." She still wags her tail. That's what's great about dogs—
the consistency of emotion, the stalwart joy of being alive. It
probably has something to do with their tiny brains, but who
cares? Ignorance is bliss, as they say.

He examines the palm trees alongside the driveway. No
about-to-fall fronds that he can see. He goes to the sidewalk
and looks from another angle. No, nothing. Maybe it fell in the

neighbor's yard? He looks over there. Nothing. He shakes his head and wonders if Annie is losing it a little, or more than a little.

He walks down the block with Lucy, scrolling through his phone to find the book he downloaded, that stupid *On Grief and Grieving* book. It disappeared from his nightstand. Annie must have taken it, stashed it somewhere, resigned herself to the fact that he had no interest in reading it. He wants to prove her wrong. He'll listen to it on his runs, then incorporate it into dinner conversations. They used to talk about their days and Penelope over dinner. Now they will talk about grief and grieving. They can have their own therapy sessions. It sounds awful but necessary. Like a prostate exam.

He stops at the end of the block to adjust his earbuds and stretch out his hamstrings. Lucy whines at the car parked next to them. He glances over and sees what she sees—someone sleeping in the front seat. It's a young guy, maybe twenty or so, though it's hard to tell exactly. He's wearing a hooded sweatshirt. Can't see his face. His hands are jammed into his armpits. He must be freezing.

Nate was this kid once, sleeping in a car. His mom's hatchback. They lived in Oregon—his mom still lives there—and it was winter, probably thirty degrees. He was fourteen, a freshman in high school. His father had just dropped dead of a heart attack at the age of fifty-one. There were no warning signs. He went to work one morning and didn't come home. The day after the funeral, Nate asked his sixteen-year-old neighbor for weed. Nate knew he had some, had smelled it wafting from his window many times. The kid must have felt sorry for Nate because he refused to take any money, just gave him a little plastic baggie and sent him on his way. Nate smoked it in his room, not interested in hiding his disobedience. He knew he'd have to assume the role of "man on the house"; this was his brief rebellious phase before that. His mom, face puffy from crying, eyes squinty, yelled, "Get out! I can't handle this right now." So he left. He walked around the neighborhood until sundown and then climbed inside his mom's unlocked car, parked on the street in front of their house. His teeth chattered the entire night. His mom rapped on the window the next morning, told him to get inside. Years later, during one of his biannual Oregon trips to visit his mom, he asked her about the pot incident. "I'm surprised you didn't leave me out in that car for a week."

She said, "Oh, honey, you have no idea how lonely I was."

Nate looks in at the kid in the car, seemingly dead asleep, unmoving. The windows are slightly fogged up, so he's definitely breathing in there.

"I think he's okay," he whispers to Lucy. "We'll check on him when we come back."

Nate starts running at a pace he knows is unsustainably fast. Lucy does her best to keep up. He decides he'll do a few short runs with her during the week and then a long, hard one by himself on the weekend.

Denial and shock help us to cope and make survival possible. Denial helps us to pace our feelings of grief. There is a grace in denial. It is nature's way of letting in only as much as we can handle.

This stupid book.

Maybe he's doing better than Annie with everything because he dealt with death at an early age. *Formative years*, Pete the grief counselor would say. He hasn't mentioned his dad's death to Pete because he knows it would become *a thing*. Pete would want to "dig deeper" and all that shit. Frankly, he could dig until his arms fell off; there isn't anything there. Nate can't even remember if he cried when his dad died. His mom cried. He remembers her tears, the force of them. He remembers thinking she would drown them both.

He wasn't in denial then; he isn't now. He knows Penelope is gone. He *saw* it happen. He can't disbelieve it. He *saw* it. Annie says she still expects to see Penelope playing when she walks by her room. He wants to tell her, *But, Annie, she's not there.* He doesn't, of course. He may not be the most sensitive guy, but he's not an idiot. He wishes he could explain to Annie that they're just different. If he was desperate and thirsty in the desert, he wouldn't be one of those people to imagine an oasis with a lake of water. She would. That's the difference. He's realistic. He takes things as they are.

Anger is strength and it can be an anchor, giving temporary structure to the nothingness of loss. At first grief feels like being lost at sea: no connection to anything. Then you get angry at someone. Suddenly you have a structure—your anger toward them.

That's Annie's problem—she's so angry. She's angry at Nate for damn near everything. She's angry at her mom. She's angry at Beth. She's angry at the neighbors. She's angry at Lucy, for God's sake. Speaking of which, she's angry at God. Nate's never believed in God, much to Annie's parents' chagrin, but that seems to be serving him fine now. He's not really angry at anyone. He's frustrated with Annie and her wallowing. Sometimes, he has nightmares of the accident—he strong-arms the scene out of his consciousness during daytime hours—and he wakes up angry with the guy driving the truck. It's not a rational anger. He hasn't mentioned it to Annie because he doesn't want to add another person to her shit list, though the driver is probably already on it. They just don't talk about him. It would make them nuts to wonder how things could have been different. What if the driver of the truck had hit a red light and just wasn't there when Penelope ran into the street? What if he had stopped for gas? What if he had taken a different route? Of course, that line of thinking could go on indefinitely: What if they hadn't run into their neighbors at the park and taken their eyes off Penelope? What if they had heeded Penelope's impatient wish to go on the swings? What if they hadn't told her, "Just a minute, honey"?

All these *what-ifs*. The book calls that bargaining.

Empty feelings present themselves, and grief enters our lives on a deeper level, deeper than we ever imagined. This depressive stage feels as though it will last forever. It's important to understand that this depression is not a sign of mental illness. It is the appropriate response to a great loss.

Lucy starts to lag behind him, and he slows, begrudgingly. Pete the grief counselor must use this book as a script. Maybe Nate is dealing with some anger—at Pete. Pete and his "depression is okay" mumbo jumbo. Pete doesn't live with Annie. He spends a couple hours a week with her. He doesn't know what she's like. What if this depression of hers *is* a mental illness? Even his mother-in-law agrees with him on this one.

Depression after a loss is too often seen as unnatural: a state to be fixed, something to snap out of.

Isn't it unnatural, though? How long is he supposed to let Annie go on like this? According to that damn "grief exception" thing, depression is "allowed" for a year following a loss before it's considered an *issue*. A year seems too long. Of course, when Pete mentioned "the grief exception," Annie seemed offended by the time limit: "A *year*? That's it?"

It's not like Nate's happy, but he's putting one damn foot in front of the other. He's walking forward. Hell, he's *running* forward. He's going to sign up for a marathon. He has that meeting today, which could bring him more work than he's ever had. Maybe he's an expert griever, already at the acceptance stage of this whole thing. This horrible accident happened. Their family of three is now two again. This is their life now.

Go forth.

Run.

He jogs all the way to Dana Point Harbor, a couple miles past his usual stopping point, pausing only to turn off the book so he can listen to music instead. Lucy is tired but forever loyal. Instead of walking up the giant hill back home, they run it, albeit slowly.

"You think our car sleeper is still there?" he says to Lucy. She pants.

They turn the corner onto their street and see that the car is gone.

ANNIE IS IN the shower when he gets back. It's been a while since he had to wait his turn. She doesn't shower much lately. She's taken a few baths, usually in the middle of the day.

"Did you make an appointment?" he asks her.

"Yeah, they had a cancellation this morning," she says, her voice reverberating off the shower walls. The echo makes her sound stronger.

"That's good," he says, though he still feels uneasy about her driving. She could have a sudden crying fit on the freeway. The tears could obstruct her vision. "Call me to tell me how it goes."

"Okay."

"Oh, and there's no palm frond," he says.

She turns off the water, steps out. Her naked body is thinner than he's ever seen it. She covers it up with sweatshirts most of the time. He can count her ribs stretching across her back—one, two, three, four. *The doctor will say something*, he thinks.

"Really?" she says. "That's weird."

"Maybe you dreamt it," he says.

"You actually think I sleep long enough to dream?"

He steps into the shower, grateful for the water pounding down on him, obscuring anything more she has to say. She can't let him go five minutes without reminding him of her misery.

NATE MEETS WITH the real estate guy at a café on Avenida Del Mar in downtown San Clemente. His name is Marcus Sandoval, which sounds like a name a rich mogul would have. The fact that Marcus contacted him proves that the universe is trying to make things right again. The email came just yesterday, out of the blue:

> Hello, I am a friend of Alfredo Salas. He recommended you
> for property management. My current manager is moving, and
> I need someone to take over my six properties in your area
> ASAP.

Alfredo Salas is the owner of the Laguna Beach house with the "emergency" mudslide. It's a good thing Nate didn't tell the Tommy Bahama tenant to fuck off.

Marcus is wearing a suit, complete with a tie and shiny black shoes. Nate's wearing what Annie calls his "professional clothes"—button-down shirt, blazer, slacks. He feels woefully underdressed.

"Alfredo says he hasn't had a single problem with the property you manage for him," Marcus says. He has an accent—Spanish.

"I like to think I run a tight ship," Nate says.

Tight ship? He has this terrible habit of dragging out all the clichés he knows when trying to impress business people. *Par for the course. Think outside the box. Take it to the next level.* Annie thinks it's hilarious.

The waitress brings Marcus an espresso. Annie always giggles at men drinking out of tiny cups. He can't stop thinking about her.

"Do you think you can handle six properties? I know Alfredo's is just one house. My properties are duplexes and triplexes. Multiple tenants, multiple *problemas*, if you know what I mean."

Nate's mind spins. He will need to hire someone to help him, maybe two people. He's never worked on this scale before. All in all, he has eight properties on his roster right now—six single-family homes, two duplexes. That's ten contracts. Marcus has six properties—three duplexes, three triplexes. That's fifteen contracts. Nate will be increasing his business, including income and hassles, by 150 percent.

Take it to the next level.

"We can definitely handle it," Nate says, already implying with the "we" that he has a team of people under him.

Marcus spins his wedding ring around his finger. Nate picks up on the nervous cue and says, "I assure you, Mr. Sandoval, you are in good hands."

Marcus takes his espresso like a shot of tequila and says, "That is what I like to hear."

What's he going to tell Annie? *So, I know the timing isn't the best, but I'm going to be pretty preoccupied for a while.* Will she be okay if he's not around to look after her? If she's not okay, is it his fault? He doesn't seem to have much of an effect on her, even if he is around. She's in her own little world. He wants her back in his, giggling at grown men drinking out of tiny cups, but she refuses.

Marcus stands from the little, round bistro table, briefcase in hand. He pats the briefcase and says, "I've got all the paperwork in here for the contracts, but let's go look at the properties first."

Nate stands and shakes his hand, making sure his grip is strong and confident. *Fake it till you make it.* That was probably the first cliché he ever learned. He was sitting at the dinner table with his dad, his mom clearing dishes. His dad asked him how school was going, and Nate said he was getting As in everything but speech class. He felt dumb admitting to his dad that public speaking made him nervous. His dad spoke with a booming voice, like an old-time radio personality. He was the top salesman at the local Ford dealership. Big personality, that's what people said. But he leaned over to Nate and said, "We all get nervous. You gotta just put on an act for a while, until it's natural. Fake it till you make it."

Nate remembers this in vivid detail because it was the night before his dad died.

"I can drive us," Marcus says, dangling his car keys.

Nate shakes off the memory and gives Marcus his best confident smile. And just like that, they are off, top down in a BMW convertible.

EIGHT

ANNIE slides a tube of ChapStick across her lips and takes a look at herself in the mirror. She doesn't feel like shit today. She doesn't feel *good*, but she doesn't feel like shit either. It's something to do with that kid coming by to tell her about the palm frond. He restored a little of her faith in humanity. Or something.

She puts on a pair of jeans, which feel tight and constricting compared to her sweatpants. But sliding her thumb between her stomach and her waistband, she notices a gap; she's definitely lost some weight. She pulls a knit sweater over her head, slides her feet into a pair of flats, and heads to the driveway.

Sure enough, the dangling frond isn't there. She walks around the Prius, looking for where it may have fallen, but it's not there. She shrugs it off, assumes the neighbor got it, even if it was on their side of the property line. See, faith in humanity.

She sits in the front seat for a few minutes, punches the address into her on-screen navigation. *I can do this.* She just has to avoid looking in the rearview mirror. Penelope's car seat is still in the back seat. She knows it will make her heart seize all over again to see it empty.

It's weird to be driving again, after a month of not driving. It reminds her of how she felt when she came home from college, after a few months of doing all her commuting on foot or by bus. She grips the steering wheel as tight now as she did then. Thankfully, there's morning traffic to keep everyone well under the speed limit. She stays in the same lane because changing lanes would involve looking over her shoulder at where Penelope isn't.

The medical center is easy to find, a big square building occupying the entirety of a street block. She parks, confirms the suite number on the office directory, and takes the elevator to the fifth floor. The waiting room is stereotypical: magazines fanned out across the coffee table, more magazines in holders mounted to the wall, a couple fake plants, elevator music, a sign-in sheet on a clipboard, a bored-looking receptionist. Annie writes her name on the sheet and checks the "new patient" box. The receptionist asks her for her driver's license and insurance card with the speech cadence of a robot.

"The doctor's running about a half hour late this morning," she says with an I'm-so-sorry face that looks rehearsed and definitely not sorry.

Annie wants to ask how she's already a half hour behind when it's only nine o'clock, but she bites her tongue.

"You can fill out this new patient paperwork while you wait." She says it like it's a privilege.

Oh goody.

The paperwork annoys Annie almost immediately. It asks her to write how many children she has. She skips the question and lazily answers the others before returning the clipboard to the receptionist in a noticeable huff. She grabs a *People* magazine off the table and starts flipping through it. There's a whole page dedicated to pictures of celebrities eating. It makes Annie sad, this page of famous people stuffing their faces. There was a time—not so long ago chronologically, but seemingly eons ago—when Annie could appreciate such petty things, when she had a sense of humor, when she liked seeing that George Clooney enjoys pizza like everyone else.

She stops at a feature spread showing a couple standing in front of what looks to be a giant dollhouse. It's a tiny, Victorian-style A-frame with a purple door. The couple appear to be in their thirties, same as Nate and Annie. The title of the article spans across the page: "Tiny Living, Big Joy." She starts reading.

Joey and Kristen are high school sweethearts, and they look to be just as in love now as you would guess they were as teenagers. Kristen is short, with a pixie haircut and a smile meant for someone with a much larger face. She is looking up adoringly at Joey. He's a big guy—not fat, but thick. The cheerleader and the football quarterback, quintessentially.

After Kristen was diagnosed with stage III breast cancer, they started to reassess their lives and ask themselves how they could maximize their potentially limited time left together. Kristen beat the cancer, but the question remained because "Ultimately, we all have limited time together," Joey says.

They decided they needed to simplify. Too much of their time and energy was spent at jobs they didn't like but remained chained to so they could pay bills for all the things they were supposed to want: a house with a two-car garage and a pool, cars, clothes, the latest gadgets, and various other components of the standard American Dream. Serendipitously, they read an article in the *New York Times* that mentioned Dee Williams, a woman who radically downsized to an eighty-four-square-foot home she built herself and then parked in a friend's backyard. Kristen read the article first and then showed it to Joey, saying only, "Tell me what you think." Joey said, "We should totally do this."

They spent about eight months learning, researching, and securing materials and then a year and a half building their tiny house in the backyard of their regular-sized house. Then they put their regular-sized house up for sale and drove their new home to a plot of land they'd purchased a hundred miles away.

"I feel free now," Kristen says. "We have fewer bills, fewer debts, fewer chores, fewer hassles. In this tiny house, I have more mental space than ever. Life has become very simple, so we can focus on what really matters."

Joey concurs: "Living in a tiny house is not living without—it's living with exactly what you need and only that."

"Ms. Forester?"

Annie looks up to see a small Asian woman in white scrubs standing in the doorway that leads to the exam rooms.

"We're ready for you," the woman says with the same mechanized smile as the receptionist, who is now thoroughly engaged with something on her phone.

Annie puts down the magazine and follows the woman down the hallway.

"So how are you doing today?" she says flatly, in a way that suggests she doesn't care at all how Annie is doing.

"Fine," Annie says.

The Asian woman has her step on a scale and then inputs the number into her iPad—115, about ten pounds less than the last time Annie went through this routine. They don't have a scale at home. It's only at doctor's appointments when she realizes how life circumstances affect her body.

Annie follows her to one of the rooms. The woman shuts the door.

"Take a seat," she says, patting the paper-lined exam table. Annie does. The paper crunches as she shifts around. The woman takes her temperature, which always makes Annie feel like a little kid. She wraps the blood pressure cuff around her upper arm, pumps it a few times. The cuff constricts and then releases. Annie looks at the ceiling.

"Okay, Dr. Ruben will be right in."

Dr. Ruben is a forty-something woman with long, dark hair in tight curls. She probably hated that hair growing up, lamented its inevitable tangles. It's unique though. Nobody has hair like that—not naturally, at least. There was a time, when Annie was a teenager, when perms were popular. They probably will be again. All trends are regurgitated.

"Hi," Dr. Ruben says, extending her long, slender fingers for a handshake. She looks Annie in the eye with a genuine care that compensates for her staff's indifference.

"Hi," Annie says.

Dr. Ruben sits on a rolling stool, takes her iPad out of the big pocket of her doctor's jacket. Everything is online now. Somehow, Annie and Nate are part of a generational shift. They remember doctors with clipboards, everything being on paper. Penelope would have grown up so much differently.

"So," Dr. Ruben says, "what brings you in?"

"Well, I wanted to find a new doctor. I've been experiencing some depression lately, similar to what I had in college."

She can't bring herself to say, "I'm here for medication." She doesn't really want the medication. If she didn't owe her husband and mother some mental stability, she would just continue on in her despair. In a strange way, she relishes the sadness. It's the last thing her daughter will ever give her. Once it's gone, there is nothing.

"Okay, well, let's go through a few of the usual questions, and then we'll talk about the best route to take with that," Dr. Ruben says.

She reiterates some of the questions from the intake form about Annie's medical history. She asks how long she's been experiencing her symptoms. She asks if she's suicidal. Annie says no. She's not suicidal, exactly. She doesn't aspire to kill herself. She feels like she did in college—hoping a meteor will fall from the sky and crush her in her sleep, hoping a car will come out of nowhere and kill her instantly.

"When was your last period?" Dr. Ruben asks.

Annie sorts through the weeks in her head. "I don't know. I can't remember," she says. She wants to tell Dr. Ruben about Penelope, as a way to explain why she doesn't know this basic thing that most women do.

"This month? Last month?" Dr. Ruben persists.

"Maybe last month. I'm not sure."

Dr. Ruben holds her stare. "And you're not on any kind of birth control?"

"No," Annie says. It seems silly now, birth control. She has no desire to even touch Nate. From this point forward, she will always associate love with loss.

"Is there a chance you could be pregnant?"

Annie starts to shake her head, but then stops. *Pregnant?*

Right before Penelope died, they had decided they wanted Penelope to have a sibling. Annie had been an only child. Though it was nice to have the attention and devotion of parents who weren't pulled in multiple directions like other parents, it was lonely. There was no coconspirator, nobody to share games and secrets and stories with. Nate and Annie had asked Penelope if she wanted a sibling, and she had answered, quite definitively, "Yes, a brudder." They asked her the name of this "brudder," and she said, just as definitively, "George." They thought it was hilarious, chalked it up to all those episodes of *Curious George* she was watching. And they started trying. Meaning, one time, maybe two, Nate stayed inside Annie instead of pulling out, which was their usual form of birth control. She couldn't be pregnant though. It had taken almost a year to get pregnant with Penelope.

"No, I don't think so," Annie says. "We haven't had sex in quite a while."

"Okay," Dr. Ruben says. "Are you eating well enough? Your weight is a bit low."

"I don't know. Probably not," Annie says, with a sheepish laugh. "You know how it is."

Dr. Ruben doesn't look like she knows how it is at all.

"Well, I'm going to run blood tests anyway so we'll get a more complete picture of things. I'll send the request in now," she says, punching directives into her tablet. "You can swing by the lab on your way out."

"Okay," Annie says.

"Now, let's talk about the depression."

ANNIE LEAVES THE medical building with a piece of cotton taped to the inside of her arm and a prescription for the same antidepressant that's always come to her rescue. The white knight, her mother called it. She goes directly to the pharmacy, like the compliant patient her loved ones want her to be, and then drives home, without a single glance in the rearview mirror.

Nate is in the driveway, just getting out of his car. She pulls in, gives him a little wave.

"How'd it go?" he asks when she gets out.

She holds up the Walgreens bag, gives it a shake so he can hear the pills inside.

"Success, then?"

She shrugs. "I guess."

He walks to the front door, and she follows on his heels.

"Why don't we park our cars in the garage?" she asks him.

He sticks the key in the front door and stops to look at her before turning it. He's got that look in his eye, the *are-you-nuts?* look.

"Because the garage is full of stuff," he says.

"Well, I know that," she says, which seems to relieve him, "but why do we have all that stuff in there?"

He turns the key, and they go inside.

"Because we don't have anywhere else to put it," he says, extending both arms out to their respective sides, indicating the depth and breadth of their small, but not *tiny*, house.

She sits on the couch, opens her laptop.

"I was reading this article, in the waiting room," she says. "Did you know that only twenty-five percent of people actually park their cars in their garages?"

"It doesn't surprise me," he says. He goes to the fridge, takes out a soda.

"And most people don't wear eighty percent of the clothes in their closets."

He gets that look in his eye again, the look that makes her feel like she must prove her sanity to him.

"It just got me thinking, that's all," she says.

"What was the point of the article?" he says. He sits next to her on the couch. He's humoring her, because he's kind that way.

"Just that we all have so much *stuff*," she says. "There are people who are starting to build their own tiny houses with just the bare necessities. Like, a hundred-square-foot homes."

"Annie, that's a tenth of the size of our house," he says. "That's like a generous closet."

"I know, but people make it work," she says. "The article says the average home in this country is two thousand square feet. That's double our house. In Europe, it's only eight hundred or something."

"Well, then, we have a European mansion." He says this like it's a good thing. He doesn't get it.

"Never mind," she says.

She starts googling tiny houses, clicks through images. They all look so cozy, so nice and tidy and simple. It makes her heart some version of happy to consider having everything important to her in one small space, so contained.

"I had that meeting today," he says.

"Uh huh."

There are all different kinds—some built by people with their own hands, some manufactured by tiny house companies and sold to people who want the lifestyle without the construction.

"It's going to be a lot of properties, a lot of money."

"Uh huh."

Most of them look like the one in the *People* magazine article, with the pitched roof. But there are some box-shaped ones with flat roofs. Most people put the beds in a loft space above the living area, accessible by ladder. It's all so efficient. But not like Annie's first "efficiency" studio apartment that seemed so cold with its plain white walls, a mix between a cheap hotel room and a jail cell. These are homey. The photos make it seem like they are always warm, like cookies are always in their ovens, though some of them probably don't have a heating system or an oven. They have funky-colored walls and adorable reading nooks and clever built-in shelves. Coffee cups hang from hooks next to porthole windows above kitchen sinks. Eating tables fold out of walls and double as work desks, complete with vintage lamps. A few select pictures line walls, each one meaningful, purposeful to the owner. If Annie lived in a house like this, she would have room to hang only a few photos of Penelope. She would have to learn to forget about the thousands of others and be grateful for those few. Maybe it would be like the woman in the article said—freeing.

"Annie?" Nate says.

How long has he been talking? What has he been saying? She has no idea.

"Hmm?" she says, looking up from the computer.

"Have you been listening?" he asks. He's more annoyed than worried, which is progress. She hates his worry. It makes her feel heavier than she already does.

"Sorry," she says.

"Are you going to be okay with me working a lot?"

So this is what he has been talking about. She tries to appear like she's been following along.

"Yeah," she says. "Whatever you need to do."

"You sure?"

She clicks on a link about a tiny house manufacturer in San Diego County, off the 76 freeway, an hour and a half away.

"Yeah," she says again. "It's like you've been saying—we need to move on."

NINE

JOSH tilts his head forward, trying to get his chin to touch his chest. Just a couple nights of sleeping in his car and he already has a nagging pain in his neck. He's at the university library in Irvine, has the fourth floor pretty much to himself. It's a Tuesday, classes are in session, but it's quiet. The only sound is from the little rubber wheels on carts transporting books back to their proper places. He's been hunched over his laptop since the library opened at eight o'clock, finishing up work on the website for his chiropractor client. It's almost noon. His stomach growls.

He keeps checking his phone, thinking Jess will text him. She doesn't though. She's stubborn. He's not even sure if, or why, he wants her to. They're done. It's not so much that he misses her already as it is that he hates that she will always remember him as an asshole. If only it were that simple. He'd gladly accept the fate of being an asshole over the fate of being behind the wheel when a toddler darted into the street in front of him.

He stuffs his laptop in his backpack and heads out. There are about twenty eating establishments within walking distance, but he decides he'll drive south. There's a deli near Nate and Annie's house with the best turkey club he's ever had. And, while he's in the area, he'll swing by and see what they're up to. He's parked on their street the last few nights. He hasn't seen Annie since Saturday though, when she went on her walk and he told her about the palm frond. He worries about her. It's probably strange that he does, stalker-level strange, but he can't help it.

NATE'S CAR ISN'T in the driveway. He seems to be gone a lot lately—working, Josh guesses. Josh looked him up online and found out that he's a property manager. He has a dinky website that looks like it hasn't been tended to in years. Given a few hours and a liter of Mountain Dew, Josh could make it a hundred times better. Now wouldn't that be something? *Hi, I hit your daughter with my car, but I'll spruce up your website for free.*

He parks across the street, sandwich in his lap. Some people eat their lunch while reading a book or listening to music or chatting on the phone with an out-of-state friend; he chooses to eat his lunch while checking in on the parents of a dead three-year-old. Yes, stalker-level strange.

Annie's car is in the driveway, as it usually is. As he bites into the second half of his sandwich, he sees the front door open. He slouches down in his seat. She'll think it's weird if she spots him parked across the street. She'd tell Nate about it later: *You know that kid who came to the door the other day, about the palm frond?* She has a purse swung over her shoulder, sunglasses on. Her car beeps twice as she unlocks it. She's going somewhere. He hasn't seen her leave the house like this. She may have, while he was working at the library or Starbucks, but he hasn't seen it.

As she pulls out of the driveway, he wraps up the remainder of his sandwich and puts it on the passenger's seat. The moment has come when he has to decide how psycho he will be. Should he follow her? She's probably just going to the grocery store or something. What's the point? Maybe that's exactly the point— to see her doing usual errands. It would give him some kind of pleasure to see her engaged in life's dull routines, scanning the shelves for whatever's on her list, sorting through a bin of apples, looking for the unbruised ones.

He trails a few car lengths behind her down the street, holding his breath, waiting for her to look in her rearview mirror and recognize him. She doesn't. They meander through the neighborhood, and then she puts on her turn signal to get on the freeway, going south toward San Diego. He does the same. For a split second, he thinks, *What if she's going to leave all this shit behind and start over in Mexico?* But that's ridiculous. All she has with her is a purse and sunglasses.

She's a careful driver, slow. He wonders if she's always been this way or if what happened made her this way. She sticks to the far right lane. People pass her, giving her sideways glances as they do, probably expecting to see an old person in her seat. He remains a few car lengths behind.

They drive past San Clemente and past the border check that Josh has never understood because it's fifty-something miles north of the actual border. They drive through Camp Pendleton, acres and acres of land dedicated to Marine Corps training. It's a weird juxtaposition—war preparations, with the peace of the ocean in the background. Camp Pendleton ends in Oceanside, San Diego County. Annie puts on her turn signal to get on the 76 freeway going east.

Josh knows this freeway. It goes to Pala, the Indian reservation with the casino. His mom went through a gambling phase when he was in elementary school. She would take him with her to the casino when she couldn't find or afford a babysitter. She'd drop him off at the buffet, always making it sound like it was a special treat: *You can eat whatever you want!* This was exciting for about a half hour. He stuffed his face, mostly with cakes and cookies, and then he was bored. Sometimes he'd wander into the casino, even though she told him specifically not to. It was a strange place, the casino. No windows, unfriendly servers in skimpy outfits, cigarette stench, the barrage of noises: slot machines spinning, games dinging, coins hitting metal, the hollering of winners and losers. He was just a kid, so it was all kind of scary. It seemed like a maze, every row of games looking the same as the next. In hindsight, this was probably on purpose, to encourage people to get lost. Inevitably, he'd find his mom at a blackjack or craps table, with a drink in her hand, usually talking to some guy and giggling in a way she reserved for casino flirtations. If she saw him, she'd get mad and tell him to go wait for her in the buffet area. She'd say it wouldn't be long, but it always felt like forever. On the days she won money, she'd apologize to him profusely on the way home and talk manically about how they would be rich one day and wouldn't have to drive to casinos in the middle of nowhere. On the days she lost money, she wouldn't apologize to him, wouldn't say much of anything at all.

Annie isn't going to Pala though, thank God. Josh couldn't handle seeing her trying to find some version of happiness standing at a slot machine. She drives past Pala, toward Pauma Valley, then puts her turn signal on (though the freeway is empty except for the two of them) and gets off near Lake Henshaw, right before the 79 Junction. What the hell is out here?

What's out here is lots of land. It's how Josh imagines Southern California was before millions of people called it home: prairies of dry yellow grass dotted with green oak trees. He can almost imagine women in bonnets and long cloth skirts carrying buckets of water and men on horseback rounding up cattle. They drive by a small building with a clearly homemade sign out front that says The Hideout Saloon. He has to slow to five miles an hour to keep her from noticing him. She's going only ten miles an hour herself.

He sees her brake lights up ahead and slows to a stop. There's another clearly homemade sign, a slab of knotty wood that says, in marker, Rolling Stone Co-Op. Josh parks at the bend in the road. There's a tree blocking Annie from seeing him. She gets out of her car and walks past the sign, down a dirt road to whatever the Rolling Stone Co-Op is.

He takes out his phone to look it up, but his reception is shitty. Doesn't matter anyway—what are the chances of a place with a homemade sign having a website? He decides to hang back at his car for a while. If he follows her and ends up at the same destination as her, face-to-face with her, there will be no reasonable explanation for his presence. They're an hour-and-a-half drive from the only place she's seen him before. She will be frightened. He couldn't live with himself if he frightened her any more than life already has.

While he waits, he gnaws at one fingernail at a time, moving on to the adjacent one only when he feels a sting and sees blood. He's always been a nail-biter, even when he was a little kid. *You get that from me,* his mom said. At the time, he thought she meant the nail-biting, but he came to realize she was talking about self-destruction in general. He doesn't remember her biting her nails that often, but she went through phases of drinking too much and taking pills that kids use for ADHD and dating losers who ignored her when she said, "Keep your voice down. Josh can hear."

An old, rusty blue Chevy truck pulls out onto the road by the Rolling Stone Co-Op sign. A guy is driving. Is that Annie in the passenger's seat? They drive down the road, out of sight. Josh wonders if he should follow, if she's being abducted or something.

But no, she came here on her own free will. He's thinking crazy. He'll just wait.

He leans against the headrest, closes his eyes. He could so easily fall asleep right now. Not surprisingly, he hasn't gotten good sleep in his car the past few nights. It's not just that he's uncomfortable, his body contorted and crammed into the seat; he's been having dreams, or nightmares, of the day it happened. All the details of that day are coming back, against his will. It's like parking near Annie and Nate's house at night has created emotional osmosis, like his subconscious is more in tune with their pain. They probably replay the scene every hour of the day. There's no resolution to the dreams. The sirens blare louder and louder until they become the sound of his phone's alarm, set to wake him up before people start leaving their houses and calling the police about the bum parked on their street.

About an hour later, the truck reappears, coming up the road toward Josh's car. It turns off by the Rolling Stone Co-Op sign. It's definitely Annie in the passenger's seat. Where did they go? Ten minutes later, Annie reappears. She gets in her car and sits there for a while. Then she starts the car, makes a U-turn, and drives back down the road from where they came. Josh slouches in his seat as she passes. When she's out of view, he pulls forward and parks next to the Rolling Stone Co-Op sign. Sure enough, there's a dirt path about as wide as a truck leading from the road, through some shrubbery. There is something back there, behind the trees. He gets out of the car and follows the dirt path until it opens to a small clearing. There, in the clearing, is a little shack of a house. It looks like an elaborate playhouse for a child, transported from a rich person's backyard and dropped here accidentally. What's weird is that it's on a trailer, with wheels, like it's primed and ready to leave its spot at any moment.

There's movement in the house's front window. Before Josh can think up a reason for why he's here, a man appears and says, "Howdy."

He's a hippie, mountain-man type, in his late twenties or early thirties, with a scruffy, unkempt beard, long Jesus-like hair, holey jeans, an overly worn T-shirt, hiking boots, and the kind of eyes that smile.

"Uh, hi," Josh says, trying to appear like he belongs here, though he's still not sure what "here" is. Maybe it's some kind of spiritual center, though all he sees is the one shack, and that doesn't appear big enough to fit more than three people at any given time.

The guy approaches Josh with a walk that's more of a saunter, slow and easy, like he has all the time in the world.

"I'm James Harper," he says, extending his hand. Josh shakes it, noticing callouses built up on his palm.

"Uh, Mike," he says. A fake name seems wise. Maybe this James Harper runs some kind of cult. He wouldn't blame Annie for seeking out a cult. People do desperate things, like sleep in their cars parked outside strangers' houses and follow them to mysterious locations.

James is one of those people who really looks you in the eye, who doesn't shy away from that kind of contact. Josh is not one of these people. He glances over James's shoulder and looks around awkwardly.

"What can I do you for, Mike?" James says, overly polite, from another era.

"I'm not sure."

"You interested in tiny houses?"

Tiny houses? What the hell? Does he mean like the shack he came out of?

"I might be," Josh says. This is as close to the truth as he can get.

James looks at his wrist. Where a watch would be, there is a yarn bracelet. What did they call those when Josh was a kid? Friendship bracelets? James seems like the type to have adult friends who make these for each other.

"Hey, I owe a buddy of mine some cash. Going to meet him at the saloon. You're welcome to tag along," James says. He must see the apprehension on Josh's face, because he adds, "Otherwise, you'll have to wait here a while for me to get back."

"Oh, okay, I guess I can come along," Josh says. He doesn't have anything better to do. It would be nice to pass some time out here, get back to Orange County after sunset. The hours in the late afternoon are the weird ones, when his "work day" is done and he has nowhere to go but his car.

The rusty old Chevy belongs to James. They get in. When he starts the ignition, the truck roars like it's being disrupted from a nap.

"So how did you hear about us?" James asks.

"A friend," Josh says. "But I don't really know much. She just said to come here and check it out."

James laughs. "Sometimes the best things in life start with vague propositions."

He talks like a fortune cookie.

"She said you would tell me what I need to know," he says, continuing on this story line because it seems to be believable.

"Wow, I'm flattered. I've never been the source of what someone needs to know," he says. He gets this suddenly ponderous look on his face. "At least, I don't think I have."

They pull up in front of the saloon, which looks like someone's kind-of-dilapidated house from the outside. James leads the way, opens up an old screen door that's missing the screen part, and goes inside. There's a bar, some stools, and some card tables with plastic folding chairs next to them. Nobody is there. A ceiling fan turns languidly overhead. Flies buzz about.

"Yo, Kyle," James shouts.

A few moments later, another hippie mountain man appears, shorter and stockier than James. They give each other a loose hug and slap on the back. James reaches into his pocket and hands Kyle a stack of cash.

"That was fast," Kyle says.

"I told you it would be. We're selling like crazy. That solar panel just broke in between payouts, that's all."

"Nice, man," Kyle says.

James pulls up a seat on one of the barstools and motions with a nod for Josh to do the same.

"This is my buddy Mike," James says to Kyle.

Kyle is already behind the bar, opening the mini fridge. He pulls out three beers and pops off their caps.

"Nice to meet ya, Mike," Kyle says.

These guys are way too friendly. It's weird.

"Friend of his says I can tell him everything he needs to know," James says. They have a good laugh about that.

"You must not need to know much," Kyle says. More hearty laughter.

Kyle says he has to go out to the garage. He's in the middle of bottling his latest homemade brew. They agree they'll have one together later in the week. When Kyle is gone, James turns his attention back to Josh.

"So, you want me to sell you on a tiny house or what? Your friend must think it would be a good choice for you, huh?"

Josh just nods. He's still not sure what the hell this guy is talking about.

"Well, I'll tell you my story. We'll start there," he says.

James grew up in a fairly typical, upper-middle-class community in San Diego. He went through all the usual motions—graduated high school, college, grad school even. He worked at a successful investment firm, making six figures when he was still in his twenties. He bought a nice condo in La Jolla, a nice car. That mystical *something* was missing though.

"I started to wonder what's important in life. I started to separate needs from wants in my mind. I felt like I was just buying into—literally *buying* into—consumerism, man," he says. "I started to look at alternative lifestyles. Thought about moving out of the country or something. Thought about holing up in an RV and driving around the country. Then I found out about the tiny house movement, and it just, you know, *clicked*."

The tiny house movement? There's a *movement*?

"It's not just about living in a tiny house. It's a lifestyle, man," he says. "You start to realize that life is for living, not having. You start to want to simplify, break it down to its bare essentials. You see that all these things you considered to be mandatory parts of life were just, like, suggestions. And most of the suggestions are based on this social belief that more is better. I gotta tell you, living in a tiny house for a few years now, less is more. It's fucking so much more."

Josh wonders if James is stoned or if he's just like this naturally. He seems like the type who would shun drugs, saying they distract from the beauty of pure life, or some shit like that.

"I don't have a mortgage. I get all my electricity from one solar panel for, like, twenty bucks a month. I don't have to go to a stupid job in a suit anymore. I can actually do something I love.

That's how I started Rolling Stone."

"Which is . . ."

He laughs. "Your friend, she didn't tell you anything, did she?" He laughs more. Josh just shakes his head.

"Rolling Stone is a tiny house community, man. I got the land for cheap. We've got five houses on it. People rent them, live in them. We all share common expenses. Collectively, we make money building houses for other people. The movement is getting so much bigger. We can't keep up with the orders. People even come from out of state. We build their houses, and they come back some months later and drive off into the fucking sunset."

Josh drains the rest of his beer and then sets the empty bottle on the counter.

"So that shack—you live in there?" Josh says.

"Shack!" James startles at the word, laughs absurdly loud. "Shack!" he says again, like he has that blurting-out disease. What's it called? Tourette's, that's what it is.

"Sorry," Josh says.

"No, man, it's hilarious. Yes, I live in that shack. Dude, it's so much more than a shack."

Josh nods, trying to understand. "Like, how big are the houses, then?"

"Well, that's the thing. Until people catch on and there are some changes to the fucking building codes, there are all these minimum size requirements for houses. That's why we put the tiny houses on wheels, so they're not technically houses. And if they're on wheels, they gotta be short enough to slide under freeway overpasses and skinny enough to fit in a single traffic lane. That means no wider than eight-and-a-half feet, no taller than thirteen-and-a-half feet. All the houses in Rolling Stone are less than two hundred square feet. The biggest one we've built for someone else is about three hundred forty."

Even Josh's mom's crappy apartment is five hundred square feet.

"Where do you put all your stuff?" Josh asks.

James turns to him, like they're sharing an epiphany, puts his hand on Josh's forearm and says, "There is no *stuff*. Just necessities." He leans in close, and Josh tries to hold his intense stare but has to look away. He'll never be as eerily calm as this guy.

"You want to come see 'em? The houses?" James says.

There's obviously no other acceptable answer besides "Sure."

ABOUT A HUNDRED yards past the Rolling Stone Co-Op sign, they turn off onto an unmarked dirt road. This must be where Annie went with James earlier. They take that road maybe a half mile. Suddenly, in the middle of nowhere, there's a campground area, but instead of tents, there are five tiny houses. Josh's grandpa's second wife—the first one, Josh's grandma, died when Josh was only four—collected cuckoo clocks. These houses look like giant, mobile versions of those. They are all structurally alike, but they are each painted different bright, flamboyant colors—purples and yellows and reds.

The houses form a semicircle, separated from each other by a hundred feet or so. There are barbecues and firepits and planters with vegetables or herbs or whatever. A bank of solar panels is stationed next to a big oak, doing its job, collecting sunlight.

"Hey, James," a woman says. She's sitting on a chair on the tiny front porch of her tiny house. It all looks way too idyllic. Maybe it *is* a cult.

"Oh hey, Dawn." He waves. Josh waves too because it seems rude not to.

"How long do people stay?" Josh asks.

"Leases are a year. Renters pay two hundred bucks a month, mostly to cover basic expenses for the community."

"And they build houses?" Josh asks.

"Sure do. We encourage them to build their own home while they're here, then mosey along after their year's up," he says. "I'll show you."

They drive past the tiny house community or campground or whatever and come to what James says is the construction area where the renters build tiny houses—their own, for when they leave, or for people who commission the Rolling Stone Co-Op to build them. There is one mostly done tiny house. It doesn't look like the others, with their pitched roofs. It's more like a bungalow—four sides with a flat roof.

"That's for a guy up in Montana," James says. "He's coming down to get it next week."

There are three other homes in various stages of construction and a trailer with nothing on it yet.

"How much do people pay for them?" Josh asks. It's fascinating, really.

"Depends on the style. That bungalow is twenty-two grand."

Josh doesn't know if this is a little or a lot for what is essentially a shack.

"I put half of what we make in a communal account, for expenses that come up. Divvy up the rest of the proceeds among everyone who helped build. Everything's in cash. Keep the institutions and the government out of it," he says. "Seems to be working so far. No complaints. Though with the increased interest, we might have to grow the community so that more than five people can stay here and help build. Or we could just hire construction workers to help us fill our orders. I haven't decided yet. I like that the community is small, intimate."

He's a dreamer, this guy.

"Are all the houses rented now?"

James turns around, and they head back out to the main road. They both wave at Dawn on their way.

"Yeah, they're all rented. People come and go, come and go. Like a rolling stone, right?"

Josh gets the reference. He had a Bob Dylan phase, like any teenager who fancies himself different from everyone else.

"There was a lady who came right before you showed up. She put her name on the waiting list. We have a waiting list—isn't that a trip?"

It isn't what Josh would qualify as "a trip," but he nods.

"If you're interested, we can put you on our list."

They pull up in front of James's house—which Josh still insists is a shack—and get out.

"That's okay. I'm gonna think about it," Josh says. "Do you have a brochure or something I can take with me?"

James laughs. "No, man, nothing like that."

He could offer to create a website for them, but that would likely also get a laugh.

"You got your phone on you though? I'll give you my number."

Josh takes out his phone, halfheartedly punches in James's number, giving him the name "Tiny House Weirdo" in his contacts list.

"Cool, thanks," Josh says, "and thanks for your time and everything."

"Sure, sure," James says. They shake hands, and Josh wanders back toward the road.

"You know, it can take time to really embrace this," James calls after him, arms out like he's giving "this," the tiny house world that he occupies, a hug. "You can start by getting rid of things at home. You'd be surprised how little you need to be happy."

"Right," Josh says. "Thanks."

If only this guy knew Josh's home was now a car.

If only this guy knew that Josh was unlikely to ever be happy.

NATE usually dreads the appointments with grief counselor Pete. He's looking forward to this one though. Maybe "looking forward to" isn't the right way to put it . . . He's anxious for it.

"You okay?" Annie asks him as they sit in the waiting room. It's only when she stares at his leg that he realizes it's bouncing up and down.

"Yeah," he says, stopping it.

He's not really okay though. Well, *he's* okay; Annie isn't. When she was in bed all day, mute save for the crying every couple hours, he thought that was the worst of it.

But this new phase of grief, or whatever the hell you want to call it, is worse. He woke up yesterday to her rummaging through the hall closet, pulling out all of their bath towels. "Do you realize we have ten different white towels?" she said before he had the chance to ask what she was doing. "Ten!" she said. The intensity of her dismay worried him. And it worried him more when she threw out eight of the towels, saying, "There is just you and me. Two towels is plenty."

It wasn't just the hall closet and the towels either. She opened every cabinet in the kitchen, pulling out all the dishes and pots and pans. She surveyed the inventory, a pad of paper in her hand. "We got so much stuff for our wedding that we never use," she said, with a disbelieving shake of the head. "We have three cutting boards!" She started putting things in boxes labeled Goodwill. She moved with the force of a hurricane to the living room, riffling through books on the shelves, throwing them in the boxes. In the bedroom, she sorted through clothes in the closet; the sound of the metal hangers flying across the wood bar was like nails on a chalkboard to Nate's ears. No room, except Penelope's, was safe.

Her mother had called her while she was in the garage, going through boxes they hadn't touched since they'd moved in years ago. He heard Annie on the phone with her: "No, Mom, I'm just cleaning up. It's good for me to stay busy." Then: "Mom, I'm fine."

Predictably, her mother called Nate later that day, saying she was concerned. "They say people start going through possessions, giving things away, when they're going to, you know . . ." Neither of them dared to complete that thought.

"MY FAVORITE COUPLE," Pete says, coming out of his office with a smile on his face. Nate assumes he says this to all his couples, as a little esteem boost to get the session off on the right foot.

They follow him into his office and take their usual seats: Nate on the couch against the wall, Pete at his desk, Annie in the upholstered chair. Their therapy triangle. They've been seeing him twice a week, per his prescription. The day after the funeral, Annie's mother had given them a list of therapists covered by their shitty insurance. Pete's was the first name on the list. Nate made the initial appointment because Annie couldn't. "If I see a grief counselor, that means it's all real," she'd said. She was like that at first, deep in denial. The day of the accident, she refused to take off her shoes and get in bed, saying, "If the day ends and I go to sleep, that means this all happened."

Nate had never been to a therapist before. Annie had, wore her experience like a badge of honor. "Therapy isn't going to help with this," she'd said. "I've been to therapy. A lot. It can't handle this." And maybe that was true. But Nate felt it was his duty to at least try, to go through the expected motions. Besides, Annie's mother would be on his case about it if he didn't.

It hasn't been as bad as he thought it would be. Pete is easy enough to talk to, a "guy's guy," Annie says. He's in his midfifties, though his hair has already gone stark white. He wears jeans. When first introducing himself, he said his background was in post-traumatic stress disorder. He used to counsel soldiers coming back from Iraq. "Talk about grief," he'd said. Then, as if to lighten up the mood, he added, "I see you live in Capo Beach. I love it there. I surf down at Doheny at least once a week."

After the first session, Annie said she didn't trust him yet. She was bothered by the fact that he had a dying succulent on his desk. "It's so easy to keep a succulent alive," she'd said. "So easy."

"So," Pete says, his chair creaking as he leans back in it. He interlaces his fingers and rests his hands on his belt buckle. He's one of those guys who wears a belt with jeans. "How are things?"

He flips through his notepad, searching for his pages from the previous session. Sometimes Nate wants to reach over and grab the paper, see what Pete has scribbled about them.

"I haven't been as isolated," Annie says.

Over the last couple weeks, they've spent a lot of time talking about her isolation, about how it's normal, about how it will pass, about how it annoys her that Nate asks if she wants to go see a movie. *Isolation is a darkness to experience, but not a place in which to live.* That's what the stupid book says. Nate listened to it again on his run this morning.

Annie tells Pete about how she went out for a walk, though she doesn't mention that Nate is the one who suggested it. She speaks of this walk like it was climbing Mount freaking Everest. She mentions the kid who came by about the palm frond and says something like, "Maybe the world has some good left," which makes Nate want to roll his eyes. He doesn't, of course. She talks about her doctor's appointment, the medication now in her possession. She says she feels more energetic, that she's been on a cleaning spree. That's what she calls it—a cleaning spree.

Nate can't help but interject. "It's more than just that. She's throwing things away."

"*Donating* them," Annie corrects, as if this difference is important.

Pete furiously jots all this down.

"Why are you cleaning?" Pete asks, using her original term for the madness.

"Because," she says.

That was Penelope's most recent favorite word. She used it all the time. The morning of the day of the accident, Annie asked her, "Penny, why did you draw on the wall?" and she answered, "Because." Her other favorite word: "Nothing." The day before the accident, Nate picked her up from preschool and said, "Tell me what you did at school today," and she said, "Nuffing." He and Annie laughed that night about how she was already a defiant teenager.

"I read this article in *People* magazine," Annie continues, seemingly coming to her senses and realizing that "because" is not a valid adult response. "Have you heard of the tiny house movement?"

Pete shakes his head. Nate sits back on the couch, rests his head against the wall. He knows Annie is about to reveal her craziness. For once, Pete will agree with him that something is wrong with her. For once, grieving will not be a good enough reason for her behavior.

"Well, there was this article in *People* magazine about it. And then I looked it up online. Lots of people are doing it," she says.

"It?" Pete asks, pen primed and ready, hovering over a clean page of his notepad.

"People give up their homes to live in tiny houses. Like, a hundred square feet, sometimes less than that. It's all about simplifying, stripping down to bare essentials, focusing on what really matters."

She's repeating something she read, that much is obvious. Pete writes this down and then looks up.

"Do you want this? A tiny house?"

Nate tries to make eye contact with him, so he can say with a raised eyebrow, *This is weird, right?* Pete won't look at him though, as if he knows that doing so will rush him to a judgment he should reserve. Instead, he stares at Annie, who looks down at her lap. "No, not necessarily," she says, shyly and unconvincingly. "I just think there's freedom in getting rid of the clutter. I support the philosophy."

Again, Nate almost rolls his eyes. It's that word—*philosophy*—that gets to him.

"With the donating, how much stuff are we talking about?" Pete asks.

"Almost everything we have," Nate says, again unable to stop himself.

Annie executes the eye roll he's been politely resisting.

"That's an exaggeration," she says. She stares daggers at Nate, and it suddenly feels like they are in couples counseling instead of grief therapy.

"Okay, she left us two bath towels, two sets of silverware, two bowls, two plates. So not *everything*," Nate says. He knows he's being a dick, but he can't seem to find it in himself to care.

"What about furniture?" Pete asks.

Annie laughs. "Of course I haven't gotten rid of furniture," she says. *Right*, Nate thinks, *as if that would be crazy and the rest of this isn't.*

"What about Penelope's things?" Pete asks.

Annie looks down at her lap again. She shakes her head slowly and solemnly. She will not even put words to this—Penny's things—yet.

Pete sits forward in his chair, hands on his knees.

"What's happening isn't unusual," he says. Nate closes his eyes so he can roll them under the darkness of his lids. This is Pete's common refrain: *It's not unusual.* Apparently nothing in the "grief process" is unusual. Every insane action is fair game.

"To go through Penelope's things would be to face the fact that she's gone," Pete says. "It makes sense that you're not ready for that."

Annie nods. It angers Nate that she's getting this validation, this approval.

"It seems that you are trying to control the rest of your life, your environment, in preparation for tackling feelings related to Penelope," he says.

Annie nods more.

"It's a form of staying busy, what you're doing," he says.

"That's what I told my mom," Annie says. "I mean, it's better than doing drugs or something, right?"

Pete doesn't confirm or deny this. "Lots of people stay busy because the emptiness would be too much. They distract themselves."

"Nate's signing up for a marathon. And he just signed this big property management deal," Annie says.

So this is what it's come to—tattling with the end goal of proving to the mental health professional which one of them is more fucked up.

"Annie, that is irrelevant. You're not working, so I'm taking on more work. It's simple math," Nate says. "We have bills to pay."

Pete extends his arms out to the sides, one palm facing Nate, one facing Annie, like a referee.

"Guys, let's focus on what matters here. What matters is surviving this grief," he says.

Nate and Annie sigh simultaneously. If there's one thing they can agree on, it's that "surviving this grief" is sigh-worthy.

"Whether it's running a marathon or cleaning or working, we all do things to avoid dealing with the grief. Just know that it won't go away. It can fester."

"I feel like the cleaning is helping me," Annie says.

Cleaning. Nate makes a fist, digs his fingernails into the center of his palm.

"And that's good. We can just be mindful of it and talk about it in here," he says.

There is a moment of silence as he writes more notes.

"Now," he says, looking up, establishing a change of subject, "what memories did you guys bring this time?"

Every session, they are each asked to share a memory of Penelope. It's supposed to put them in direct contact with the pain of losing her. In other words, it's a way to pick at the wound before a scab can even begin to form. In other words, Nate fucking hates it.

The only way out is through. That's what the stupid book says.

"A few days before, we were at the park and she pointed at a bird. She loved to point at birds and dogs, any animal really," Annie says. "I asked her if she wanted to be a bird one day, and she said, 'No, Mama, because I'd miss you.'"

Annie starts crying before she even finishes the sentence. Nate swallows hard.

"Sometimes," she says, struggling with the words, "I think of her as a bird now."

Pete reaches over, touches her arm. He hands her the box of tissues that is always at the ready on his desk, next to the dying succulent. She takes one.

It's Nate's turn now. The both look at him expectantly. God, he hates this.

One of Nate's favorite memories is of Penelope giving what they called "dinner hugs" every night when they sat at the table to eat. More often than not, she gave out only one, as if she had a limited supply, and it was usually to Nate. Secretly, he loved this, relished in feeling like the chosen parent. Another favorite was going into her room in the mornings and watching her sleep. When she woke up, he always asked to see her "granny thumb," all pink and wrinkled from sucking it through the night, looking decades older than the rest of her. When she learned to talk, he didn't even have to ask; she would show it to him and say, "Granny thumb!" The day before the accident, she was slow to wake up. He cuddled her in bed, enjoying the silence. The first words out of her mouth were "peanut butter." Maybe she'd been dreaming of it. He wished she'd had the language to tell him about it, about all her dreams.

Nate hasn't shared these memories though. And he doesn't plan to today. Pete, bless his grief counselor heart, was a stranger a month ago. Why does he get the privilege of such details? He doesn't. Period. So Nate always shares some inane fact, which probably makes him look like an asshole, but he doesn't care.

"Nate?" Pete says, too gently.

"She liked to put ketchup on everything," he says. "Especially pizza."

THE DRIVE HOME is mostly silent, as it usually is after these things. When they're stopped at a light, he looks over at Annie in the passenger's seat, her arms wrapped around her middle like she's giving herself a hug. She's staring out the window. In their first year or two of knowing each other, she loved the "What are you thinking?" conversations, always asking him, always disbelieving and annoyed when he said, "Nothing." Part of him wants to ask what she's thinking now, but a bigger part of him doesn't want to know.

They pull into their driveway, and Annie gets out of the car. He watches her walk to the house. Lucy greets her at the door with unadulterated excitement and joy, her mood as constant as Annie's is volatile. Is it that Annie wants to move? Is that what this tiny house thing is about? It would make some sense. This house was for their family, and there is no family now. This is the house where they welcomed their daughter into their lives and then watched her leave. It seems implausible that Annie will be able to make new happy memories here.

What about the old happy memories though? Nate isn't the sentimental type, never has been, but he can't help but feel attached to these walls, to the things that have happened within them: the birthdays and Christmases and Saturday morning pancake breakfasts. Grief counselor Pete would say something lame like, "You can take the memories with you wherever you go. They're always with you, just like Penelope." Nate isn't sure though. Penelope isn't with him. He doesn't feel her.

When Annie was seven or eight months pregnant, she woke up one weekend morning and declared, "I need an omelet." Knowing they didn't have the makings of an omelet in their fridge, he offered to go pick up breakfast at Turk's in the harbor. They loved Turk's, used to go there every weekend before Penelope came along. It's the diviest of dive bars, catering to fishermen who need greasy food before heading out on the water and those who need stiff drinks when they get back. Nate used to joke that all of the waitresses looked as if they'd spent at least one night on railroad tracks and instigated or broken up a dozen fights. That's why they stopped going after Penelope came; it wasn't exactly kid-friendly.

"I don't know," Annie said, in response to his offer to go fetch an omelet. She scrunched her nose. "Eggs don't travel well."

That, right there, is why Nate doesn't want to move. Memories might be like eggs. If they leave their house, they might leave the memories with it. But hell, if Annie wants to move, he will. Not to a damn tiny house, but he will move. For her. It's crystal clear that he will have to be the strong one. Her needs trump his. She's the one losing it. She's the one falling apart.

ELEVEN

ANNIE sits up against the bed's headboard, laptop on her thighs. She stares at the cursor blinking on the email login page. She's up again at 3:30 a.m. Sleep eludes her, like clockwork, at this hour. She used to blame Lucy for waking her. The dog's been itching a lot at night; they've probably let too many weeks go by since her last flea treatment. But it's not always Lucy's fault. It's just 3:30 a.m., a witching hour.

One of the first things Nate did when they brought Penelope home from the hospital was set up an email account for her. "She'll thank us one day for reserving it now. Trust me," he said. Penelope.Forester@gmail.com. The fact that it was untaken had filled Annie with pride. Their daughter was truly unique. "Twenty years from now, she'd have to settle for Penelope.Forester.78 or something," Nate said, pleased with himself. It was like he was trying to make himself useful. He admitted to feeling like he was just in the way in those early days. The baby wanted Annie—or Annie's boobs, more specifically.

Even though Annie made fun of it in the beginning, she came around to using the email address. She started sending Penelope messages, telling her how much she loved her, sharing memories with her that she knew her forming brain would never save on its own. That's strange, isn't it, how nobody remembers anything from their first few years? It's like the brain has so much to take in, so much to process, that things are discarded on a daily basis. Annie catches herself thinking, "Thank God Penelope won't really remember the accident," before realizing, all over again, that Penelope is dead.

Annie logs in to the account. The last message she sent Penelope was a couple months ago. It's a short one: "When you start dating, please remember that every boy should treat you like a queen, even on the days you don't feel like one. If they don't, you can't blame me if I kill them." She assumed her daughter would share her sense of humor.

She remembers what motivated that particular message. She'd been with Penelope at the outdoor mall, pushing her in her stroller. It was midday, prime time for "stroller derby," when Annie was surrounded by moms just like her and still felt out of place. She was intimidated by other mothers, in their premium yoga pants, looking like they had it all together. Annie was there to return a sweater her mom had bought for her. She couldn't remember the last time she'd gone to a mall with any kind of enjoyable purpose. They stopped in the food court because Penelope wanted a snack. At the table next to them, a teenage boy was in the process of breaking up with a teenage girl. She was sobbing. She had on way too much mascara, and it was starting to run down her cheeks. Annie's heart broke with the thought that Penelope would probably feel like that one day. All women do.

She clicks the button to compose a new message, starts typing:

Penny, I wish you were still here. It feels stupid writing that. Duh. Of course I wish you were still here. I feel so lost. What was life like before you? I can't even remember. And even if I could, I don't think this current life could be that. It's not that simple. This email account was supposed to be to store messages for you to read later, like in your teenage years, when your hatred of me would reach an inevitable and irrational fever pitch. Now what is it? A place for me to pretend like we are pen pals? Can you read in heaven? I like to think anything is possible there.

"What are you doing?" Nate asks. He's staring at her, wide-eyed, from his side of the bed. How long has he been watching her?

"Did I wake you?" she says, angling the laptop closed.

"No," he says, probably lying.

He turns flat on his back, stares up at the ceiling. Something is different with the two of them lately. That chasm between them is wider. It's probably Annie's fault. She went to the Rolling Stone Co-Op, and now she can't stop fantasizing about this new life in a tiny house. What's worse is that her fantasies don't include him. She sees herself there alone. Nate wouldn't want to be there anyway. He thinks it's crazy, the whole thing. So she hasn't mentioned it, not since their therapy session last week when he seemed hell-bent on proving to Pete that she had lost it.

"Well, I guess I'll go for a run," Nate says, as if he has no choice in the matter, as if that's the only option when you wake up before dawn.

He swings his feet out of bed and directly into his running shoes, always on the floor next to his nightstand, ready for him.

"I have a busy day today. I'm doing walk-throughs of some properties, meeting with some tenants," he says, lacing up.

What if she blurted out, "I don't care"? What if she just said it?

"What are you up to today?" He persists in asking even though she never gives him an answer that suffices. And they call her the crazy one.

"Cleaning," she says. She needs to finish tackling the garage.

"The spree continues?" He gives her an amused smile, a smile that pities her.

There was this time when Penelope pulled out a pair of hiking boots from the very back of Nate's side of the closet. She put them on and said she was going on a trip with Lucy. They gave her one of those same smiles, and she got mad and said, "Put your teeth away!" What if Annie had the gall to order Nate to do the same? He has such stupid, fucking perfect teeth. His mother got him braces when he was a kid. He's probably never thanked her. *Asshole.*

"Yes, Nate," she says, knowing they use each other's names like this only when they're arguing, "it continues."

SHE LIKES HIS morning runs. They give her an hour or two to herself, an hour or two away from his judgment, an hour or two to relax her shoulders away from her ears. She starts sorting through her drawers of clothes, imagining she's packing to up and leave, to go live in the tiny house village. That's what James, the Rolling Stone Co-Op guy, said he thought of it as—a village, a little city unto itself.

Really, all she will need is a couple pairs of old, ratty jeans (she'll be helping build houses, after all), a few T-shirts, a jacket, pajamas, a few pairs of socks, sandals, sneakers, underwear, bras. She goes through the bathroom cabinet, cursing at herself for all the stupid lotions and potions she's bought over the years. In the tiny house village, she'll just need a toothbrush and paste, deodorant, shampoo, conditioner, soap—that's it. Maybe she'll become a hippie with leg and armpit hair. Or maybe she'll bring a razor. A razor doesn't take up that much space.

She goes to the kitchen, pulls out a bowl, a coffee mug, one set of silverware, a dinner plate, a salad plate, a medium-sized pot, a medium-sized pan, a spatula. Before they had Penelope, she and Nate went on camping trips. It was easy to get by with very little. Just a simple bowl of pasta felt like a delicacy at the end of the day, sitting around the fire. This new life will be like that. Simple.

The sentimental things are harder than the practical ones. The shelves of the bookcase in their living room are jammed with so many framed pictures. There are ones of her and Nate before they got married, at their wedding, after they got married. There are pictures of Penelope as a newborn, as a one-year-old, as a two-year-old, as the three-year-old she will always remain in Annie's mind. That's another of the many injustices—being denied seeing her daughter grow. It's not just about missing out on school performances and sports events and graduations and weddings and grandbabies; it's about missing out on seeing her physical growth. Would she have looked more like Nate or Annie? There was no consensus in her three years on earth. Some people said, "She looks just like Nate," and others said, "She's your mini-me, Annie."

She surveys the framed photos. In her tiny house, she will have room for just a few. She could probably cram in more, but that's not the point of a tiny house. Like James said, it's a lifestyle. It's about stripping away. She decides on one photo of her and Nate, taken just a few months after they met, out in Joshua Tree. They were drunk on tequila when they snapped the picture. She can almost hear Willie Nelson playing at their campsite. There was so much ahead of them then. It's hard to imagine that ever being the case again. They seem like two people who will perpetually have so much behind them.

Choosing a photo of Penelope is not so easy. She chooses the frame she likes best, a natural wood one, with a picture of Penny at the beach. It's her profile. She's looking out at the ocean. A blur of black—Lucy, running—is in the background. Penelope looks like she's having deep thoughts, though the thoughts of a three-year-old can be only so deep. Annie then goes about systematically removing all the other Penelope photos from their frames. She will insert them behind the one chosen picture. She can rotate them out on a regular basis. It's genius, really. There are boxes of photos in the garage, but it seems like if the lids are on those, she shouldn't go disturbing them. It would only make things harder.

Just as she exhales a big, telling breath, the phone rings, startling her. It's six o'clock. Who would be calling this early? She doesn't recognize the number, a 760 area code. She answers anyway. Morning calls are usually emergencies, after all.

"Allie?"

Her initial thought is that it's a wrong number. But then she remembers that Allie is the fake name she used when visiting the Rolling Stone Co-Op. There wasn't really a reason to use a fake name, but it was enticing to be someone else—specifically, a woman who hadn't lost a child.

"Yes?"

"Sorry to call so early," he says. It's that James guy, the one who showed her around. She recognizes his voice. "I'm just so excited to tell you we have a tiny house available today."

"Today," she parrots back to him.

"Yes, and you're first on the list. We had someone leave a bit unexpectedly, so we're trying to fill the spot as soon as possible." This stressed-out version of James still sounds pretty relaxed.

"Wow, um, okay," she says. "Wow."

Standing there holding the chosen framed picture of Penelope, she wonders if this is God, the one she's come to doubt, finally telling her what to do. What are the chances that James would call right as she's packing for her hypothetical departure? But that's the thing—it's hypothetical. She didn't expect him to call so soon. Now that he has, she has to decide if the tiny house fantasy will remain just that—a fantasy—or if it will become her life, her reality.

"Can I get back to you in a little bit?" she asks. "I'm just . . . I'm in the middle of something."

"Oh, sure, sure," he says. "Today, preferably."

Right as she says, "Of course," Nate walks in, sweaty from his run. Lucy goes straight to her dish, laps up water.

"Who was that?" Nate asks, still breathless, hands on his hips.

"Telemarketer."

In that instant, with that lie, she knows that she will go. She can tell by Nate's face that he would have run all day if he could, just to avoid her. They need to be apart. She needs to simplify things for herself, break life down into little pieces and then put them back together again. She won't tell him; she'll just up and go. But she'll leave a note or something so he won't worry—tell him she needs space, as cliché as that is. She's sure he'll breathe a sigh of relief. That will be his first reaction, before he goes into the obligatory concerned husband mode.

Nate goes to the shower, and she calls James.

"That was fast," he says.

"I'll take it," she says. "I'll be there today."

"Awesome," he says with an excitement in his voice that eases her doubts. "We'll be ready for you."

"Great," she says, but she thinks, *Holy shit.* She retrieves a suitcase from the guest room closet. The last time she used it was on their honeymoon. They went to Maui. They fit all their stuff, Nate's and hers, in the one suitcase. Clothes necessary for Hawaii are lightweight. They spent half the trip in bathing suits, the other half naked in their hotel room.

The pipes squeak as Nate turns off the shower. She shoves the suitcase back into the closet. There's something exciting about this secret, something invigorating. She goes to the bedroom, sits on their bed, watches him get dressed.

"You'll be gone most of the day?" she asks. He looks at her suspiciously. She hasn't been showing much interest in how he spends his days lately.

"Yeah, you need something?" he asks, buttoning one of his nicer pairs of pants, pulling a belt through the loopholes.

"No."

When they were in Maui, they thought about going to a psychic in Lahaina. They were half drunk when they saw the neon lights in the window promising fortune-telling. They decided against it. What if they had gone? What if the psychic had predicted that they would lose a child? What if the psychic had told them that they would become tense and uncomfortable with each other? They probably would have dismissed her with a laugh. When they were in Maui, there were no plans to even have a child, so they wouldn't have bothered imagining the way that losing one destroys the most loving of people.

"I can pick up something for dinner," he says. "It might be late though."

"Don't worry about it."

She follows him to the kitchen, where he grabs his work binder off the island, along with his keys.

"Okay, then, have a good day," he says.

If he knew this would be the last time he'd see her for a while—maybe ever, who knows?—what would he say? She feels bad for him, for the way he'll berate himself for not even making eye contact with her in their last moment together. Her eyes start to well up.

"Nate," she says.

He looks up now.

"I love you," she says.

Instead of saying "I love you too," he says, "Oh geez, Annie, why are you crying?"

She wipes her eyes with the sleeve of her shirt. "Sorry," she says. "I'm fine." Ultimately, that's what he wants to hear. He goes to her, puts one arm around her shoulders. The other arm is encumbered by his binder.

"You going to be okay today?" he says, his voice slightly condescending, like he's talking to a grade schooler who scraped her knee at recess. "This is why I asked if you were alright with me taking on more work. I can't have you crying all day."

"I'm fine," she says again.

He's probably not satisfied with this response, not fully, but he allows it to be enough. He's running late now, after all.

"See you later," he says as he opens the front door.

Saying "okay" would add one more lie to her list, so she doesn't say anything at all.

IT TAKES ONLY an hour to pack the suitcase. It's heavy when all is said and done, but she's succeeded in packing up the essentials of her life in one bag. She carries it outside, to her car. She has to balance it on her thigh, use the force of her leg to heave it into the back of the car. Lucy watches everything. She is the only witness to this. She lingers at the car even when Annie heads back to the house.

"Lucy, come on," Annie yells at her. Lucy doesn't budge. It's the suitcase. Lucy knows what a suitcase means.

"Lucy, damn it, come on," she yells louder. It feels good to yell.

Finally, the dog listens, wanders back, seemingly accepting that she's not going to wherever Annie is going.

Back in the house, Annie does a once-over. She walks through every room, except Penelope's, taking stock, making sure she hasn't forgotten anything that she can't live without. That's a big requirement—*can't live without*. Most things can be lived without. God seems to think she can live without her daughter. If that's the case, it seems unconscionable to bring an extra pair of jeans.

Then there's the matter of the note. She riffles through the junk drawer, finds a pen and a pad of paper, one of those cheap promotional ones that real estate agents pass out. There are doodles on the first page, probably the result of her boredom while waiting on a customer service call long since forgotten. She rips off that page, throws it away, starts writing. Lucy watches her intently, knowing the junk drawer is where they keep her treats. She sits at Annie's feet waiting, begging. Annie caves and gives her a biscuit.

"Okay, take care of Nate," she says to Lucy, though this is a ridiculous thing to say to an animal.

It's weird to walk out of the house, to lock the door behind her, not knowing when she'll be back . . . if she'll be back.

Opening the hatchback, she verifies that the suitcase is there. She has this OCD-like anxiety sometimes. She used to check the time set on her alarm clock at least three times before bed when she was nervous about something going on at work the next day. Those were the days, when happenings at work were the biggest concern.

What if she never returns? What if she builds a tiny house and drives it somewhere far away? What if her interaction with Nate is reduced to divorce papers sent through the mail? She gets in her car despite, or maybe because of, all these unanswered questions.

The key is in the ignition when her phone rings, another number she doesn't recognize, an Orange County number. Normally, she would let calls like this go to voice mail, but something compels her to answer.

"Hello?" she says.

"Is this Annie Forester?" the woman asks.

"Yes."

"This is Dr. Ruben."

"Oh, hello," Annie says.

"I am embarrassed to say this, but we've had your blood test results for a few days now and I didn't realize nobody had called you yet. We're going through some staff changes at the office and, well, anyway, I'm calling you now."

"Oh, okay," Annie says.

She had assumed the tests were normal because she hadn't heard otherwise. Maybe she's anemic. She was anemic for months after Penelope was born. Anemia would explain her recent fatigue.

"So, everything looks fine," Dr. Ruben says, "but you are, in fact, pregnant."

Annie shakes her head no, forgetting that Dr. Ruben can't see her through the phone.

"Annie? You there?"

"Yes," she says, still shaking her head. "This has to be a mistake."

"Blood testing for pregnancy is absolutely accurate."

There was just that one time, maybe two, when Nate didn't pull out, on their just-started mission to give Penelope a sibling. The past implies she's not exactly a Fertile Myrtle. When Annie was first trying to get pregnant, her mother used that phrase: *Be patient, honey. It won't take long. I have a feeling you're a Fertile Myrtle.* When she didn't get pregnant, those words taunted her. She was so angry with her mother for getting her hopes up she refused to speak to her about the whole endeavor.

Point being: what are the chances she got pregnant *right away* this time?

If Penelope was still alive, she and Nate would laugh about it, call it dumb luck. But Penelope isn't alive, and now it just seems . . . dumb. *Pregnant*? What business does she have being pregnant?

"I don't *feel* pregnant," she says, her voice sounding high-pitched and strange.

"You're probably less than eight weeks along. Some women don't know they're pregnant that early, unless they take a test."

"Right, right," Annie says. She flicks at the keys, dangling from the ignition, with her index finger.

"I have referrals for an ob-gyn," she says, "if you want."

"That's okay," Annie says. Then she adds, "I guess it's good I came to see you."

"Well, you would have figured it out sooner or later," Dr. Ruben says with a good-natured laugh.

Annie thinks of that TV show about women who didn't know they were pregnant. One day, they think they just have diarrhea or something and out comes a kid in the toilet. Absurd, truly.

"Oh, have you started taking the antidepressant?"

"Not yet," Annie says. She hadn't been able to bring herself to do it, to begin this process of leaving behind the sadness, leaving behind Penny.

"Okay, good. It's not proven safe for pregnancy, so just see how you do without it. You may feel fine. Pregnancy hormones work wonders."

She sounds so excited for Annie, for her hormones.

"Right," Annie says.

"Call my office if you need anything, okay?"

Annie grunts in agreement and ends the call.

She pats her still-flat stomach. Does this change anything? Or does this just give reason to why James called today, at six o'clock in the morning, before doctor's offices open to make their first calls of the day? She looks over her shoulder, past Penelope's empty car seat to the suitcase in the back. She's come this far; there seems to be no choice but to keep going.

TWELVE

JOSH eyes the bottle of NyQuil in the cup holder, wondering if it's time for another dose. Living in a car, on its own, isn't so bad, but living in a car while sick with the flu is another thing entirely. At least it seems like his fever has broken. He still has chills, but that may be because it's so freaking cold outside. He burned through a quarter tank of gas by letting the car run with the heater on last night.

As he's pouring another dose of NyQuil into the little plastic cup, he hears yelling. It's Annie, yelling at the dog to get back in the house. She seems angry, frantic. He watches as the dog—named Lucy, apparently—trots back to the front door, and then Josh throws back the NyQuil like a shot of booze. He winces, same as he would with tequila.

About ten minutes later, Annie comes outside again. No dog this time. She opens up the hatchback of her car. There's a suitcase in there, obviously filled. She pats it with her hand and then shuts the hatch. Then she gets into the driver's seat and sits there for a little while. Is she leaving? For where? The tiny house place?

She pulls out of the driveway and disappears down the street. He thinks about following her, but the NyQuil is going to make him woozy real soon. He decides to wait until Nate comes home later, probably after seven o'clock, which has been the norm as of late. He'll see how Nate reacts, if he reacts at all. Maybe there's a reasonable explanation, like she went to her parents' house. There was something worrisome in her face though, something anxious.

⌂

NATE COMES HOME closer to eight o'clock, well after sundown. Josh can barely keep his eyes open, he's so exhausted. He blows his nose into a shirt he's using as a handkerchief. His grandfather always used handkerchiefs. Josh couldn't understand why, with all the germs trapped in that cloth square.

He watches Nate go inside the house. Lucy greets him at the door, as usual. Five minutes later, he comes back outside with a piece of paper in his hand, Lucy trailing behind him. He is actually scratching his head, just like a caricature of a person who's perplexed. Nate looks at the driveway, as if confirming that Annie's car is, in fact, gone. He takes his phone out of his pocket, dials someone. He starts pacing the sidewalk, back and forth, back and forth. Whoever he calls doesn't pick up. He mouths "fuck" and places another call.

Josh rolls down his window so he can hear. He has to strain, but he can make out some of the conversation from where he's sitting.

"I don't know. There's this note, and she's gone," he says to the person on the phone.

"Obviously, I tried calling her," he says. He's clearly irritated.

There are lots of "yeah"s and "okay"s. He ends with, "That's a good plan. Okay, see you soon."

Nate looks up and down the street and catches Josh's eye. *Crap*.

"Hey," he calls.

Josh freezes. Nate sees him, is calling to him. Josh scrambles to find his sunglasses in the center console, puts them on quickly, and pulls the hood of his sweatshirt over his head, hoping it will cast a shadow over his face.

"Hey," Nate says again. He's approaching the car.

Josh sits up straighter in his seat, covers the NyQuil and food wrappers and clothes with a jacket so it's not obvious he lives in his car. And then, there's Nate, at his window. Josh's heart pounds as he waits for Nate to recognize him.

"Did you happen to see someone leave my house? A woman, brown hair?" Nate asks.

There is no recognition. Nate doesn't know who Josh is. The sunglasses and the hooded sweatshirt have done their job.

"Uh, no, sorry," Josh says. "I just got in my car. Haven't been out here more than a few minutes."

He puts the key in the ignition as proof that he's just a normal guy, on his way to somewhere more interesting.

"Right, yeah," Nate says. The paper in his hand crinkles in the breeze.

"Everything okay?" Josh says. It's touchy; he has to be careful not to pry too much. A normal kid his age wouldn't be interested in Nate's plight. A normal kid his age would go on his way without asking questions. If he shows too much concern, he'll seem suspicious.

"I don't know," Nate says, still looking up and down the street. "Anyway, thanks."

Josh watches him walk back across the street. He goes into the house, but leaves the front door open. Lucy lies on the doormat.

Considering how flustered Nate seems, that paper in his hand is probably a note from Annie. Saying what? That she's left him? Maybe she is at the tiny house place. Josh scrolls through the contacts in his phone. He saved that guy's number, didn't he? James was his name, right? There's no phone number for James though. He does a quick search through his list. There it is: Tiny House Weirdo. He laughs to himself and then calls James.

"Rolling Stone Co-Op" is how James answers the phone.

"Hi, James? This is, uh, Mike. I came to see you a few days ago."

"Hmm," James says, obviously racking his brain. He doesn't seem like the type to have a good memory, to get attached to any specific moments. They all move freely, like river water over rocks or some shit.

"I went with you to the saloon or whatever, asked you some questions."

"Oh, right!" he says. Josh can almost picture the characteristic light bulb flashing on over his head.

"Let me guess," James says. "You've thought about it, and you want on the waiting list?"

"Uh, well—"

"That's awesome, man, awesome."

Josh can hear him turning pages of a notebook or something, primed and ready to write down his name on the list.

"Do you have any available right now?" Josh asks.

"Actually had one open up last night. Guy decided to get back together with his girlfriend, so he peaced out."

"Oh, so that one's free?"

"Nah, already got someone for it. She came out today."

She. It must be Annie.

"And if you'd have put your name on the waiting list the day you came, you'd be right after her," he says. "But nope, now you got someone else in front of you."

"That's okay," Josh says. He figures he'll play along with this notion of wanting to live there, in the tiny house community. James wouldn't have any reason to talk to him otherwise. This way he can call on a regular basis, ask a few questions, check in on Annie in a roundabout way. Maybe he can even make another trip out there, with the pretense of needing to acquaint himself with a few more things in preparation for his tiny house life.

"I'm not really in a hurry," Josh says.

"That's good. Hard to say when the next one will come available. Everyone's on a one-year lease, but some people just take off before the lease is up. Like this guy last night. If nobody breaks a lease, the next person will leave in"—Josh hears him flipping through more papers—"April."

"Okay, sounds good," Josh says.

He gives James a fake full name—Mike Clinton—and his phone number. Now he is officially on the list. He can always back out, if and when James calls saying there's a tiny house with his name on it.

"Would it be possible to, you know, talk to some of the current residents, see how they like it?" Josh asks.

"Sure, man. Most of them love to talk about it."

"Cool. I'll probably want to do that."

"Right on," James says. "Listen, man, I gotta go check on the new tenant. See you when I see you?"

"And not before that."

James laughs and hangs up without a formal goodbye.

It's obvious Nate doesn't know where Annie is. Does he even know about the Rolling Stone Co-Op? Is it Josh's duty to tell him? It's really none of his business. He shouldn't even be sitting here, in this car, across the street from their house. It's creepy. How would he possibly explain why he knows Annie's whereabouts?

Well, I killed your kid, so I've been watching you to make sure you're okay. I saw Annie leave the house last week and followed her all the way to San Diego County, to this tiny house community. Yeah, it would sound ludicrous. And besides, maybe Annie needs this. Maybe he shouldn't get in the way of what she wants. If it becomes an issue, if Nate starts really losing it, then maybe he'll come up with a way to tell him. Or he'll leave a note in the mailbox. Or something. Annie will probably be back in a week or two. James said so himself—some people don't stick around.

A car pulls into the driveway, into Annie's spot, right as Josh is getting ready to find a new place to park for the night. After all, if Nate comes outside again, he'll think it strange that Josh is still parked there. Josh doesn't need to be pegged as a suspicious person right now.

Josh lingers, his foot on the brake, watching as two people —a man and a woman—get out of the car in Annie's spot. They must be Annie's parents. They're older, and they look very concerned. The woman, in particular, looks like she's about to freaking faint. They rush through the front door. Even from the street, Josh can hear them talking. They are using their "in case of emergency" voices. He can't make out what they're saying, but it's all very panicky.

What if they call the police? Will Josh be an accessory to something if he doesn't tell them what he knows? But an accessory to what—a woman leaving her husband? That's all it is now, after all, a grown woman leaving her husband. By all appearances, she left a note. She didn't disappear without saying something. This isn't, like, an abduction. They're just worried because they don't know where she is.

Or maybe they think she's going to kill herself. Fuck, *is* she going to kill herself? Josh thinks about her opening the hatchback, patting the suitcase with her hand. There would be no reason for the suitcase if she was going to kill herself. Unless, maybe, the suitcase is packed with rocks and she's going to tie it to her ankle and throw herself off the San Clemente Pier. That's the NyQuil talking. Josh is thinking crazy. He's watched too many of those crime dramas. Jess loved those fucking crime dramas.

The thing is that Nate and the in-laws don't know she left with a suitcase. They don't know that she looked like a woman with a plan, a woman with a destination in mind. Only Josh knows this. It might comfort them to know what he knows.

It would help if he could see the note. Maybe Annie didn't clarify enough. Maybe she just said "Farewell," and that's why they're freaking out. That would be bitchy of her, thoughtless, selfish. Annie doesn't seem like the bitchy type. Maybe she said she was going somewhere for a while, but they think that's a lie and she's really going to kill herself. People do commit suicide after tragedies. And losing a kid is a pretty big fucking tragedy. But the suitcase . . . the way she patted it with her hand. Josh is sure she's not killing herself. He's sure. She's going to live in a tiny house. That's all. A tiny, simple, away-from-it-all house.

THIRTEEN

NATE stands at the kitchen island, watching his mother-in-law read the note for a third time. She recites it aloud, over-enunciating, as if it's written in a language other than English.

> Nate,
>
> I know this seems weird, but I just need to get away for a while. I don't want you to worry. I'm okay. Consider it a retreat of sorts. I don't want to be found, so please don't come looking. My phone will be off. I'm getting some money from the ATM, so I won't be using my credit cards. I hope you're not angry with me. This is good for us, promise. I love you and just want us both to be happy again, if that's possible.
>
> Love,
>
> A

She sets the note on the counter and looks up at Nate.

"I think we need to call the police right now," she says, with an authority that dares him to challenge her.

He wishes they weren't here. They're making it worse—or, rather, Sheryl is. Steve is just hovering like he usually does, shoulders slumped as if to accentuate his uselessness.

Sheryl thinks Annie's going to "end it all," that's how she keeps phrasing it.

Steve keeps saying, "Now, Sheryl, we don't know that."

Nate would like to think that as unfamiliar as his wife has been to him since Penelope died, he knows her well enough to say that she's not going to "end it all." She just wouldn't. The note says she's okay, that he shouldn't worry. He has to believe she's being truthful.

"We can call them if you want, but she hasn't even been gone a day," Nate says. "For all we know, she just left an hour ago."

Sheryl eyes him like he's a suspect, like he's one of those husbands who kill their wives.

"What harm does it do to call the police? I mean, if she is in danger, the sooner they know, the better."

He can't disagree with her, though he thinks her premise—that Annie is in danger—is flimsy. If he fights her, he looks like he doesn't care. He knows, though, from watching too much TV, that the police won't be able to do much. Annie is a grown woman who clearly articulated that she does not want to be found. A woman going on a trip, or whatever, is hardly worth investigating.

"Have you talked to the neighbors?" Steve asks. This interjection of his, rare in its occurrence, suggests that maybe he's on Nate's side and agrees calling the police is a bit rash.

"Not yet," Nate says. "I came home, read the note, called you. Oh, well, I asked this kid across the street if he saw her, and he said no."

"Why don't we start there, Sheryl?" Steve says to his wife, whose arms are now crossed defiantly against her chest. "If the neighbors can't offer any insight, we'll call the police." He gives Nate a conciliatory nod and adds, "Just to file a report."

Sheryl huffs. If something is wrong, if something does happen to Annie, Steve and Nate will be to blame. That much is clear.

"Okay, then," she says, stomping toward the door, "let's go."

They march from one house to the next like a group of off-season Christmas carolers. Sheryl takes the lead, introducing herself and extending her hand like it's a business meeting. She asks if they've talked to Annie recently. Most of them look perplexed, not registering the name. Nate and Annie have always been polite with their neighbors but never overly friendly. A few of them glance past Sheryl and see Nate there. They recognize him, know him as "the guy whose kid got hit by the car." Then they seem concerned, ask if everything is okay. Sheryl does not have the patience to explain. If they don't have information for her, she moves right along.

Half an hour later, they have gone up one side of the street and down the other with no leads. Sheryl gives Steve an exasperated *I told you so* look and then takes out her phone, making a show of dialing 9-1-1. She tells the operator that she wants to report a missing person. Nate can't deal with her drama. He leaves her out on the driveway, goes back in the house with Lucy, and reads the note again.

I don't want you to worry. I'm okay.

When Sheryl comes back inside, she says they connected her to the local police department—probably because an adult woman leaving a note to say she will be gone for a while is not a valid emergency—and they are sending out a couple officers to take a report. She seems very proud of herself.

Nate grabs a beer from the fridge. Sheryl gives him a look that asks how he can possibly enjoy *alcohol* at a time like this. Steve gives him a look that asks if he can have one too. Nate opens the fridge, throws a can at Steve. Immediately, Steve looks to Sheryl, like a child in need of instruction. She just rolls her eyes. He cracks the can open anyway. Nate has never before liked his father-in-law so much.

It takes an hour for the cops to come. They don't come with sirens blaring. They just park along the curb out front and stroll up to the house. One of the guys is really young, baby-faced, fresh out of the academy. The other is older, in his fifties, clearly the mentor. They probably took this call as a leisurely practice run, a learning opportunity for the young'un.

"I'm Officer Martinez, and this is Officer Banks," the older one says.

Nate's never had police officers in his house before. He stares at their holstered guns, their shiny black shoes. Even though he thinks Annie's fine, or wants to think that, the presence of these guys makes him uneasy, makes him think something more serious is at hand. They each take out small, spiral-bound notepads. Sheryl motions for them to sit, but they insist on standing. They must think this won't take long.

"So how long has she been gone?" the older one, Martinez, asks. He's already making notes on his pad, not looking up.

"We don't really know," Nate says. "She was here this morning, when I left for the day. She seemed fine then, nothing out of the ordinary."

Nate goes through the details of the morning in his head. She was already awake, on her laptop in bed, when he woke up. Her laptop—is it still here? He'll have to check, after they leave. He went for a run. She was on the phone when he came back—with whom? She said it was a telemarketer, but it was still early in the morning, so maybe it was someone else. Was she having an affair? At first, it seems like a totally logical possibility, but then he remembers that she's been holed up in the house for most of the last several weeks. She's barely had energy to shower, let alone have sex with some other guy. He wishes it was that, secretly. That would be so mundane and trivial.

He remembers the way she said "I love you" before he headed out for the day, the way her eyes welled up. Was she crying because she knew she was leaving him? That must have been it. He had been preoccupied and impatient. He regrets it now.

"So it's been less than twenty-four hours," the younger cop says, stating the obvious.

"Yes," Nate says. He wishes he could pull them aside, tell them that he knows this is ridiculous and premature. Martinez seems like the type that would commiserate with him about the annoyances of mothers-in-law.

"And there's a note?" Martinez says.

Sheryl takes it from the counter and hands it over, treating it with the kind of care given to an ancient scroll found in an Egyptian cave.

The cops read it together, their eyes scanning the words quickly. Then they hand it back.

"Your wife," Martinez says, glancing down at his paper, "Annie? Not to be rude, but she's over the age of eighteen, correct?"

Nate can't help but laugh, just a little. "It would be illegal if she wasn't," he says. Nobody is smiling though. They all have straight faces. He clears his throat. "She's thirty-five."

"Well, based on this note, we can't really do anything at this time," Martinez says.

"What if we think she may harm herself?" Sheryl says. Playing her trump card, that's what she's doing.

Banks, the younger cop, raises an eyebrow and says, "Is there something that would make you think that?"

"She has a *history*," Sheryl says.

Both of the cops' bodies are angled toward her now, away from Nate.

"She tried to kill herself when she was in college," Sheryl says.

"And her daughter just passed away," Steve chimes in.

"Our daughter," Nate says with a possessiveness to his tone that probably makes him seem like an asshole.

The cops' eyes ping-pong from one person to the other.

"She hasn't said anything about harming herself," Nate says.

"She's been giving away a lot of her possessions," Sheryl says. "That's a common sign."

"She's been giving them away to simplify her life," Nate says. It's strange to be suddenly in the position of defending his wife's recent madness. Really, though, he thinks Sheryl is wrong. He thinks Annie is, as the note says, okay.

Denial and shock help us to cope and make survival possible.

That stupid book.

Martinez sighs. "Look, I feel for you guys, but it doesn't appear that there is anything to investigate at this time."

He takes two business cards out of his pocket—cops have business cards?—and hands one to Sheryl and one to Nate.

"Call us if there is any more information, okay? We'll keep a report on file," Martinez says.

"Might be she needed some time away," Banks says. Martinez shoots him a look of caution. Cops probably aren't supposed to speculate on people's lives. Only shrinks can do that.

"Thank you, anyway," Steve says. Sheryl can't bring herself to thank them. She is silently fuming, convinced she knows all and the rest of them are inept idiots.

Muffled voices come booming out of the younger cop's

walkie-talkie. He apologizes too much, turns down a dial, and they continue their exit.

"Well," Sheryl says after they're gone.

Nate waits for more, but that's all he gets: *Well*.

"Let's just regroup in the morning," Nate says. *Regroup*— another one of his overused business terms. "I'm not sure what else there is to do."

Steve nods in agreement, but Sheryl isn't having it.

"Did she drop any hints about this? You must remember *something*."

Nate is a failure in her eyes, a sad excuse for a husband. And maybe there's some truth to her perception. Maybe a good husband *would* remember something.

It feels as if it were somehow your fault. You were there. You saw it all happening. In your perfect hindsight so many things stand out that could have been done differently.

That stupid, stupid book.

"Is there a friend she would go to stay with?" Steve asks. He's ready to go home, but he's humoring his wife.

"You know Annie," Nate says. "She didn't have a ton of close friends. There's Beth, but she hasn't talked to Beth much since Penelope—"

"Have you tried to call Beth anyway?" Sheryl interrupts. Sheryl retired from teaching kindergarten a couple years back, but she still uses her talking-to-a-five-year-old voice.

"Not yet," Nate says. "I'll text her."

He scrolls through his phone, brings up the last conversation he had with Beth, more than two weeks ago. She had texted him to ask how Annie was doing, said Annie wouldn't return her calls. He just wrote back, "Don't take it personally. She's still having a hard time."

Beth responded with, "Ok, well, let me know if I can do anything." He didn't write back.

He types: *Hey, been a while, I know. Have you heard from Annie?*

Less than a minute later, Beth responds: *No. Why? Everything ok?*

Yeah. She said she had to get away for a while. Any idea where she would go?

Jesus, no. Beth goes on, sharing a barrage of worries that Nate simply can't deal with right now.

"Beth hasn't heard from her," he tells Sheryl and Steve, clicking off his phone.

Sheryl expels a theatrical sigh, bows her head, shakes it side to side. "I'm just at a loss," she says.

Steve manages to convince her that they should go home, sleep on it. It's close to midnight. They're all tired. He escorts her out, his big, fat arm around her shoulders. It's one of the only times Nate has seen them touch.

Nate goes to the bedroom, looks for Annie's laptop. It's not on her nightstand, where it usually is. He looks in the nightstand drawers and then in all the clothes drawers, for good measure. Nothing. He looks for more proof that she's just on a trip, or retreat, or whatever. Her toothbrush is missing. This is a good sign. He goes to the guest room closet, where they keep their big suitcase. That's gone too. Back in the living room, he notices some pictures have been taken out of their frames. Pictures of Penny, he thinks, though he can't recall exactly. And there's a picture of him and Annie missing, the one of them in Joshua Tree. The only reason he knows this for sure is because it's always been his favorite.

That confirms it—she's okay. But wherever she is, she must be planning to be there for a while. She took pictures, after all.

He checks the bank transactions on his phone. Sure enough, she withdrew two thousand dollars in cash at the branch in San Clemente, right at 9:00 a.m., when it opened for the day. Maybe she came back to the house after, or left for her mystery destination straight from there. Two thousand dollars can't get her that far. Airfare would eat up a sizable chunk of the two grand, so she must be somewhere within driving distance. Even if she chooses the cheapest, dirtiest motel, the two grand will run out in a few weeks. And Annie isn't the type to choose the cheapest, dirtiest motel. She shrieks at the sight of cockroaches.

Lucy looks at Nate, watches the wheels turn in his brain, seemingly waiting for assurance.

"She'll be back before we know it," he tells her, and himself. "She will."

FOURTEEN

ANNIE lies awake, staring at the wood-beamed ceiling of her tiny house. *Her* tiny house. She lives here now. The bed—a queen-size mattress on the floor— is just a couple feet from the ceiling, in a loft space that Annie thought would be cozy but now seems a little claustrophobic. If she has a nightmare that causes her to jolt up in bed, a not uncommon occurrence since Penelope died, she will hit her head on the ceiling. And that's not the only danger. If she has to pee in the middle of the night, which she did at least once a night as a nonpregnant person and is sure to do more often now, she has to climb down a ladder.

How could she be pregnant? She touches her belly again. With Penelope, there were signs, symptoms. Her forehead broke out in vicious acne, something that caused Beth to predict early on that she was having a girl; "Girls make you ugly," she'd said. Her breasts swelled seemingly overnight so that she started overfilling her B-cup bras. During sex, Nate touched them more, her breasts. She teased him, asked if he was imagining having an illicit affair with someone better-endowed than his wife. Certain smells—coffee, a cigar someone gave Nate at that wedding they went to, a Sharpie marker—made her gag. And the peeing. She had to go ten, fifteen times a day.

Maybe there *have* been signs, symptoms. Maybe she's been too distracted to notice. There were some passing waves of nausea, now that she thinks about it. She attributed them to stress, depression. Any mother would want to throw up when thinking about her child dying, right? She'd even mentioned it to Nate, last week or the week before. "I feel so sick about it some days," she told him.

His eyes said, "Still?"

She feels sorry already for this new baby, for ignoring its attempts to make itself known. *It.* She can't dare say he or she. She can't dare acknowledge the human life in progress. She can't dare love again. It's like that book says: *To love is ultimately to lose what we have had the privilege of loving.*

Her house is the farthest one from the road, at the end of the semicircle of tiny houses. It's one of the plainer styles, one of the first ones built, according to James. It's a simple A-frame, with a little porch and a bright-red front door that seems friendlier and more welcoming of guests than she will ever be. There's a window next to the door that James refers to as "giant." It's maybe two feet square.

The inside is quaint and tidy. With a straight face, James calls the entry area the "great room." It's about six feet by six feet. Nate wouldn't be able to lie down on the floor without his head and shoes hitting the opposing walls. Beyond the great room, there's a small galley kitchen—James correctly calls it a kitchenette— adjacent to a bathroom that's barely big enough for an adult to stand in. "It's like a phone booth," she said to James with a little laugh. He looked perplexed for a second. Was he too young to know what a phone booth was? Surely he'd seen pictures.

The loft with the bed is above the kitchen and bathroom, accessible only by climbing up six rungs. It's bigger than the "great room." There are two skylights over the head of the bed that make it feel even bigger. James said, "If you need to get out in an emergency, like a kitchen fire or something, you'd go out through these windows." Somehow, Annie doubts she would get out at all in the event of a kitchen fire. In this small of a space, she'd pass out from smoke inhalation before she knew what was happening.

Being in the loft reminds her of the long summer weekends she spent at her grandparents' house in Arizona. That's where her mother was born, Arizona. She was one of three kids and the only one to leave the state. Even as a kid, Annie could tell her mom and dad didn't like to go back to visit. It was an obligation. Grandma Bea and Grandpa Joe had a designated kids' room in their house, complete with two sets of bunk beds for Annie and her cousins. Her cousins lived nearby, but they slept at their grandparents' house only if their parents went on a trip without them. When Annie visited, her cousins slept in their own beds at their own homes, and she was alone with the two bunks. She always took the top bunk next to the window. The leaves of a giant elm tree pressed up against the window, making it easy for her to imagine she was in a tree house. There was something thrilling and secretive about it, being way up there.

She blows a breath on the window over her head, draws a heart in the fogged-up circle. Penelope used to think this was magic. She was just beginning to understand that her first name started with a P. A few weeks before the accident, on a rainy day, Annie blew a hot breath on the window in her bedroom and helped Penny write P with her finger. Penny clapped her hands with a pride that made Annie excited for all her future achievements. There would be so many, she had been sure.

For now, Annie's giant suitcase is sitting in the great room. James gave her the key, told her to make herself at home, but she's not ready to unpack yet. Maybe this is a stupid idea.

Maybe she should just go home. She could tell Nate about the pregnancy. Would he be happy about it? Was she happy about it? No. Was it crazy to admit that? She was shocked. She was terrified. *Happy* did not seem like a word that would apply to her ever again.

She falls asleep at some point, because the next thing she knows she's waking up from a dream. In the dream, Nate tells her it was a mistake—the truck didn't hit Penny. It was another child who got hit. The two of them do their best not to jump up and down, reveling in the tragedy of this other child. There is a knock at the door, probably a police officer returning Penny to them. She had gotten lost in the madness at the park, but she's home now. The knocking gets louder. Annie goes to answer the door, and that's when she wakes up. She barely misses hitting her head on the ceiling. Her heart races. Which nightmares are worse—the ones when she relives Penny running into the street, or the ones when she thinks it was all a misunderstanding?

The knocking is at her front door. Of her tiny house. She gets her bearings, momentarily alarmed at where she is. What time is it? She doesn't have a single time-telling device near her. She's turned her phone off, tucked it away in the outer pocket of her suitcase, determined not to turn it on. Nate or her parents might pick up her GPS signal if she does. Her mother has probably already contacted the authorities. Nate, if she knows him at all, is trying to respect her note; her mother, if she knows her at all, isn't.

The light outside the window is bright. It must be late morning. There is another trio of knocks.

"Just a minute," Annie calls, her voice muffled by phlegm caught in her throat. It's as if she's been sleeping for years.

When she opens the red door, she's greeted by a woman holding a basket of spinach bundles.

"Oh my God, did I wake you?" the woman says, looking genuinely horrified at the notion.

"It's okay. I have no idea why I slept so long."

Annie squints in the light, taking in this stranger. She's fifty-something, wearing a big gardening hat, a long gray braid sneaking out from under it and resting on her shoulder.

"I can come back later," the woman says.

"No, that's okay." And then, because there doesn't seem to be any other appropriate thing to say, "Come in."

She's tall, this woman. Tall and—what's the politically correct term?—big-boned. The tiny house vibrates as she walks.

"I'm Dawn," she says, sticking out the hand that isn't holding the basket of spinach.

Her grip is firm, announcing a desire for a friendship that Annie isn't seeking. She hadn't thought this part through, the "community" part of the tiny house community. She had envisioned herself holed up in a small container of a house, packed in tight, with no room for all the questions about why life is unfair.

"Allie," she says. She'll have to persist in using the fake name. That's what James knows her as. She can't go back now. Maybe it's for the best. Maybe it will be a relief not to be Annie.

Dawn looks around and sits on the tiny window seat next to the front door.

"It took me two weeks to unpack," she says, jutting her chin toward the suitcase.

Annie goes to the suitcase, sits on it. She'll need to get a small couch or something for the space, after she unpacks of course.

"Really?"

"Oh yeah. It took me two weeks to convince myself that I wasn't crazy for moving here."

"But you did eventually convince yourself?"

She lets out a hearty laugh that's totally unaware of its own volume. "That's a good point. Maybe I just became okay with being crazy."

"They say insanity is a matter of perspective," Annie says, thinking of all the times Nate told her, with his concerned eyes, that she had lost it.

"Do they say that? I never know who 'they' are."

"Nobody does," Annie says.

"Well, speaking of crazy, our spinach production is out of control this winter," she says, handing over the basket. "I manage the community garden."

There's that word again. *Community.* Annie does everything in her power not to wince.

"I have a black thumb, so not sure I'll be much help with that," Annie says. This is what she will do—back away slowly from any social obligation.

"Black thumb. Ha," Dawn says, again with the laugh. "Everything you touch dies?"

Annie swallows hard.

"Oh, don't feel bad. My husband was the same way," Dawn says with a quick wave of her hand, as if she's swatting away Annie's guilt like it's an annoying fruit fly. "So what brought you here?" Dawn asks.

Black thumb.

"Just wanted a life change," Annie says. It's a dumb answer. Dawn nods though, seemingly understanding not to press further.

"I came after my husband died," she says. She's doing that thing of sharing in hopes of reciprocity. Annie's initial regard for Dawn starts to morph into annoyance.

"Oh," is all Annie says.

"ALS. I watched him deteriorate over two years. That's how fast it was, two years," she says with a snap of her fingers. "He biked a hundred miles a week, so when he said he was having weird pains in his legs, I didn't think anything of it. That's where it started, his legs."

Some people are like this, needing to talk through their grief, rehash it. Annie was like that with Nate. She wanted to talk with him about it, even if they went in circles for hours on end. She wanted to take comfort in him because they had this one unbelievable thing in common: they were the parents of Penny. He wanted nothing to do with those conversations though, was stubbornly committed to the cause of moving on. She bothered him, just as Dawn is bothering her. There is no fault in the matter; it just is.

"I'm so sorry. That must have been hard," Annie says, using the very words she hated to hear from all the condolence-offerers who bombarded her.

"It was, but it brought me here," Dawn says, with a toothy smile. She's a "lights up a room" type. It's no wonder she's the unofficial welcome committee.

"How long have you been here?" Annie asks. As much as she would like to be, she's not immune to the social pressure to make conversation. She hears Nate: "Annie, you have to at least *try*."

"Six months," she says. "John died, and I moved three weeks later. I just had to, ya know?"

Annie does know.

"Lots of people come here after a loss." She eyes Annie, looking for some glimpse of her tragedy. "It's something about realizing what matters in life, wanting to simplify."

"Makes sense," Annie says.

"You'll meet everyone later today, probably. We usually gather around sunset, have a glass or three of wine."

Since Dawn's been here in her house, there's been this familiar feeling—the Notre Dame feeling, that's what Annie's always called it. It's this sense of being lonely in the midst of people trying to make you anything but. The girls in her dorm tried so hard to get her out of her funk. They did. They invited her to parties. They offered her wine coolers. She was hell-bent on isolation though.

"Okay, sounds good," Annie lies.

Dawn takes her cue, stands.

"If you need anything at all, you just let me know. I'm like the mother hen here. Raised three kids and miss it, so sorry in advance," she says with her laugh.

"Thank you," Annie says, "for stopping by." She walks behind her toward the door, shooing her outside like she would Lucy.

Then she stops. There is something Dawn could help her with.

"Actually, do you know of a doctor nearby?" Annie says.

Dawn pivots on her heels, looks at Annie. She probably thinks Annie has cancer, that she's here to live her last days in a tiny house. Maybe that's not so bad. Maybe people will leave her alone then. Nobody likes to be around dying people.

"Like, a general practitioner type or what?" Dawn asks. She's prying as much as she's trying to be helpful.

"Yeah, sure." She can start there. The general practitioner will refer her to an ob-gyn.

"There's Dr. Franklin. Old as dirt. Works out of his house about forty minutes away. We usually go to him for little things," she says. "Is it a little thing, hon?"

Right now, the baby is about the size of a lentil. That's what the baby book said when she was six weeks pregnant with Penelope.

She remembers because she made lentils for dinner that night and then couldn't eat them. Nate laughed so hard that he had to stop and catch his breath.

"Yes, a little thing," she says.

"I'd be happy to drive you, show you the way."

I'm sure you would, Annie thinks.

"That's okay. Maybe just write down the directions. No rush. It's not any kind of emergency."

"Right, of course," Dawn says. They don't trust each other, not yet. "Do you have a notepad?"

Annie goes to her suitcase and takes out a pad of paper, the same pad of paper she used to write the note to Nate. Looking closely, she can see the indentations of the pen. She hands it to Dawn, along with a pen, and Dawn writes down the directions.

"Here you go," she says, handing it back. "Easy as pie."

"Thanks," Annie says.

"And we'll see you tonight then?"

It's clear that Annie's presence is required, that she has no choice in the matter. Dawn gave her directions to the doctor; she must make an attempt to fit in. Tit for tat. *Annie, you have to at least try.*

"Sure," she says. "See you tonight."

FIFTEEN

JOSH knows he has a problem when he's pissed off about having to go see his mom for her birthday. He doesn't want to abandon his post outside the Forester house. It's not like there's anything much going on, but he's sure that with his luck, something big will happen if he leaves.

In the last couple days, since Annie left, Nate has been leaving the house early and coming back late, seemingly going to work as usual. There's been no sign of Annie. Josh is sure she's living at the co-op. He'll call today, under the guise of looking to ask the newbie some questions in preparation for his eventual move. He has to talk to her, to make sure she's okay. Then he'll be able to rest. See, he has a problem. He's like an addict: *One more hit and I'll be fine.*

He's supposed to be at his mom's house in an hour. Does he have time to call the co-op now? He'd be better able to enjoy, or at least tolerate, the evening with his mom if he could just hear Annie's voice. It'll take about forty minutes to get to his mom's house. And he has to pick up her favorite takeout (Luigi's) and a Baskin-Robbins ice cream cake on the way. His mom loves those fucking cakes. This is their tradition every year. They eat and drink whatever liquor is his mom's latest favorite and catch up on life, each pretending that they are happy as hell so as not to disappoint the other. He'll be back at his post in four or five hours.

He texts his mom: *Might be a little late. Wrapping up a job. See ya soon.*

He knows that's a soft spot for her, his career. She's so fucking proud of him. It kills him a little sometimes. It's like she has nothing to live for but his success.

Predictably, she texts back, *No problem, Joshie.*

He scrolls through his phone contacts for James's number. It rings a few times. Josh is about to hang up when James answers.

"Rolling Stone Co-Op," he says.

"James!" Josh says with too much enthusiasm. "It's Mike." It takes him a second to remember his fake last name. "Mike Clinton."

The silence that follows confirms that James has yet to register Mike Clinton as someone of any importance.

"I called the other day. I'm on the waiting list for a house there."

"Oh right. Sorry, dude. What's up?"

"I was just wondering . . . I know you said someone new moved in, and I'd love to talk to her about her experience so far," he says. "You did say it's a 'her,' right? I think you said that." His heart races as he remembers their conversation. He's pretty sure James told him it was a woman. He's pretty sure he doesn't sound like a creep, yet.

"Oh, yeah, Allie?"

Allie? Who the hell is Allie?

"Um, I guess," Josh says, suddenly disappointed and confused. Maybe it's a freak coincidence that a woman moved into the co-op on the exact day Annie left. Maybe it isn't Annie. But it must be, right? Maybe James misremembered her name?

"She's just getting settled. Not even sure she's unpacked her suitcase yet," James says.

The suitcase. Josh clings to that as proof that Annie didn't kill herself. She just went somewhere. She must be Allie. Of course she wouldn't use her real name, just like he isn't using his. Josh is about 60 percent convinced of this story line, 40 percent still unsure.

"Okay, well, it would be good to talk to someone who is brand new about the transition and whatnot."

Transition and whatnot? He sounds like such a tool.

"Cool, man. I get it. Allie doesn't have a phone, so she'll have to use mine. I'll talk to her, see if she's into it."

"That would be awesome."

"Alright, will call you back later then, hopefully with Allie."

Josh wants to ask what "later" means. In James's head, it could be an hour or a week. He refrains, for fear of sounding like a crazy person who is way too uptight to live in a tiny house village.

HE ENDS UP getting to his mom's apartment in Anaheim right on time. He always feels a little sick to his stomach coming back to his old neighborhood. There's Disneyland and all its affiliated restaurants and attractions, and then there are the poor neighborhoods tourists never see. It's depressing, the dichotomy. His mom doesn't see it that way though. She tells people she lives minutes away from the happiest place on earth.

His mom has this old "wipe your paws" doormat, dirtier and more scuffed up than the last time he visited, which was months ago . . . with Jess. They'd brought Luigi's that time too, and Jess made a show of explaining to his mom how evil it was to eat veal parmesan. "It's a *baby cow*," she announced, as if his mom didn't know this fact and would immediately put down her fork now that she did. She just shrugged though and went on eating. Jess didn't really have a right to judge. It wasn't like she was a vegetarian or anything. She just had a thing about the baby animals.

"Joshie," his mom says when she opens the door. She's already had a drink, probably a beer or two. She tends to start with beer and then progress to the harder stuff. She wraps her arms around him, pulls him close to her chest. It's weird how that hug is at once comforting and uncomfortable.

"Hey, Mom," he says, walking past her into the apartment. She's attempted to clean it up, that much is obvious. It still smells bad though, like cigarette smoke and fabricated flower scent. He sets the food on the kitchen table and puts the cake in the fridge. His mom is already rummaging in her liquor cabinet, pulling out bottles. She mixes them each a drink in cocktail glasses that she says are for special occasions, but Josh assumes are for every night.

"So, honey," she says, opening the Luigi's containers in search of her veal parmesan, "how's life? I haven't talked to you in ages."

Josh sets his phone on the table next to him, his eyes glued to it.

"Good, fine," he says. His mom would probably keel over if she knew he was living in his car. Or she would insist he live with her, and then he would keel over.

"You seem distracted," she says, taking a long pull on her drink. The ice cubes rattle.

"Sorry," he says, lifting his eyes from his phone after confirming the ringer is turned on. He forces a smile. "You still working at that restaurant?" he asks her.

Last he heard, she was waitressing at one of the tourist restaurants by Disneyland, wearing some kind of lame outfit and buttering up people on vacation.

"Sure am. Tips are good. Can't complain," she says. She always says that—*can't complain*. And she always ends up complaining.

"That's good."

"It would be nice if my asshole manager gave me more of the prime weekend shifts though," she says.

Can't complain.

"It's probably a seniority thing, Ma."

"A what?"

He doesn't bother, changes the subject. "How's Marty?"

Marty is her cat. They got him when Josh was ten. They went to the pound to get a kitten, and Josh overheard some guy saying they were putting down this orange tabby the next day. Josh insisted on taking that one home, even though he was "old" (five years they said). If they were right, he's on his way to his twentieth birthday and doesn't seem any the worse for wear.

"He caught a bird the other day, out on the balcony."

Josh taps through his phone to double-check that he hasn't missed a call.

"Is this about a girl?" his mom says, nodding toward the phone.

"This? No. Just work, sorry," he says, meeting her eyes.

"Are you still dating that Jessica?"

"No, we broke up."

His mom hated Jess, but she still sticks out her bottom lip in a pitiful pout and says, "Oh, Joshie, I'm so sorry."

"It was for the best."

"Well, yes, probably, but that doesn't always mean it's easy."

His mom would know. She'd dated every variety of loser and been in tears every time things ended.

"You're not on drugs, are you?" she says.

"What?" Josh says, alarmed. "No. Why would you say that?"

"You're all fidgety."

"I just have a lot on my mind."

His mom stares at him, as if trying to determine whether or not he's telling the truth. Then, apparently satisfied with whatever she sees or doesn't see in his face, she resumes eating.

"I'm glad work is keeping you busy," she says.

"Yeah."

They eat in silence, save for the sound of ice cubes rattling in their glasses and forks hitting plates. The silence is broken by Josh's phone blaring. It's James calling.

"Ma, I'm sorry, I gotta take this," he says, already standing from his seat and going to her bedroom for privacy. There's no time for her to protest.

Her bedroom is musty from a recently taken shower. Clothes are strewn about. There are a couple beer bottles on the nightstand, next to a weird statue of Jesus. Josh's mom always said she was sure God didn't exist. Josh sits on the edge of her bed, immediately aware that she needs a new mattress. Maybe he'll buy her one, when he gets back to his normal work routine and makes some more money.

"Hello?" he says.

"Mike, this is James. I've got Allie here with me. She's our newest addition."

He hears James tell Allie to say hello, and a small, female voice mutters, "Hi."

"Thanks for calling back."

"Sure thing. I'm gonna turn the phone over to Allie," James says. There's a shuffle in the background, and then Annie—or Allie or whoever—comes on the line.

"Hello," she says.

He can't tell from just that greeting if it's her.

"Sorry to bother you like this," Josh says. There is something in the way she said hello that tells him she is, in fact, bothered. She doesn't want to be on the phone with him.

She sighs. "No problem." An obvious lie.

"It's just that I—I'm not sure about this tiny house thing. I wanted to talk to someone who just moved there."

She doesn't say anything. She just exhales a breath—a sign of frustration? Annoyance? He needs her to speak in complete sentences to see if he recognizes the voice. Maybe it's silly to think he'll be able to. He's talked to her face-to-face only once, about the palm frond threatening to fall on her car.

"When did you move in?" he asks.

"A couple days ago," she says. That tracks with when he saw her pull out of her driveway with that suitcase in her car.

"Do you like it?"

"So far, yes. Getting adjusted."

He's about 90 percent sure it's her, Annie. It's something about the edge in her voice. There's this apprehension, like she has things she doesn't want to talk about.

He has to just go for broke. "Is it hard to leave everyone behind?" he asks.

"It is hard," she says, somewhat defensively, "but sometimes you have to."

It's her. This is the same voice that snapped, "Lucy, shut the hell up" when he showed up at her door. He thinks of a way to confirm it's her for sure.

"My dog, Lucy, will have to stay with my mom," he says.

"That's funny," she says. "I had a dog named Lucy too."

It's definitely her. Definitely. He cringes at the past tense, at her insinuation that Lucy is no longer her dog. Maybe she doesn't plan on going back.

"It seems freeing," he says, "to start over, be someone new."

"Be someone new," she says. "Right."

From Annie to Allie. It makes sense now.

"Are you happier there?" he dares to ask.

She gives a little mocking laugh. "It's only been two days."

"Right."

There's more silence.

"Look, I'm sorry, can we talk some other time?" she says.

If she's intent on ending the conversation, this isn't the worst way it could happen. There's hope in "some other time."

"Yeah, definitely, of course," Josh says. "You don't mind if I call again, like if I have questions?"

She sighs, probably considering whether or not she wants a rapport with this strange guy on the phone.

"Sure," she says. "Though there are other people who have been here longer than me. There's this woman Dawn—"

"I wanted to talk to a new person. I figure I can live vicariously through you, see what it's like to leave it all behind."

"Okay," she says, noticeably defeated.

"I won't be annoying, promise."

"It's fine. I just don't know if I'm the greatest source of information for you."

"You seem perfectly adequate."

Perfectly adequate? What a dope.

She hands the phone back to James, who says, "Look at me, making connections."

Josh thanks him and ends the call. He stays sitting on the edge of his mom's bed until his heart stops pounding.

HIS MOM HAS moved to the couch, entertaining herself with a fresh drink.

"Sorry about that," he says.

"No problem, sweetie. You gotta do what you gotta do."

"Everything's better now," he says.

Annie is alive and well. Josh feels guilty being the only person on the planet to know this besides Annie herself. Should he find a way to tell Nate?

"Glad to hear it," she says.

He goes to the fridge, pulls out the cake, and sticks a candle in it. When he comes out singing "Happy birthday," his mom looks at him like everything is right in the world. And maybe it is.

SIXTEEN

NATE takes down a box labeled "photos" from a shelf in the garage. It's Sheryl's fault that he has to do this. She said, "We should put up flyers with Annie's picture, in case anyone knows something or saw something suspicious." *Like what?* Nate wanted to ask but didn't, in favor of gritting his teeth, knowing Sheryl could probably see his jaw muscles flex in frustration.

So he has to find a good picture of Annie—one that's flattering, because she would want that, and one that accurately depicts her features. Usually Annie is the one behind the camera, so he's prepared for this to take a little time.

The albums at the top of the box are the most recent ones. Last year, Annie announced that she wasn't going to print photos anymore. They had so many, filling up album after album. Maybe this simplification thing of hers started when Penelope was still alive. Maybe it's not a sign that she's gone nuts.

With the exception of a few photos printed for frames, the last hard copy photos they have are from when Penelope was two. There's a photo of her on the toilet, smiling big and proud. They started her young with the potty training. After a few times taking her to the bathroom, she started going completely on her own. They didn't even know she was in there until she came walking out with her pants down. It took a while for her to figure out pulling up her underwear. When she mastered it, Annie said,

"She already doesn't need us." Her eyes were watery when she said it, and Nate made fun of her a little.

There's a picture of Penny at the petting zoo, touching a baby goat. Penny's face wears a look of complete awe. That's why people like kids—they're so impressed by everything that adults have learned to ignore completely.

Nate closes the album and sets it on the ground. He does the same with the next one, trying to get to the pre-Penelope pictures so as not to torture himself. Maybe memories aren't all that great. Maybe they're kind of awful. Taunting. Haunting. Maybe they should sell the house, start anew. He'll suggest it to Annie if she comes back. When she comes back. *When.*

He opens the third album from the bottom of the box. It's safe. No Penelope photos. These photos are from before they were married. There are lots of pictures of just Annie in this album, lots of pictures of just Nate too, probably because in that falling-in-love phase you're so absorbed and enamored with each other that you pass the camera back and forth and snap away, intent on capturing each other's amazingness. There are lots of selfies too, before selfies were a thing, when the person with the longest arms (Nate) just held the camera out in front and hoped that faces ended up in the resulting photo. Annie printed even the mistake ones, the ones that cut them off at the noses.

The photo he decides to use for the flyer is from when they went to the Huntington Gardens in Pasadena. It's five years old, but Annie looks exactly the same, a fact he didn't know to appreciate until now, in this moment, with these photo albums. She's sitting on a bench, looking straight at the camera, though obviously not quite ready for her picture to be taken. She's not smiling big enough to show her teeth. Her lips are slightly upturned, in a Mona Lisa–type grin. She looks content, but not happy, which seems appropriate for a missing-person flyer. Though, really, who the fuck knows how to choose a photo for a missing-person flyer?

He slides the photo out of its slot and takes it to the computer to scan it. He's not sure what to write on the flyer. He starts with "Missing Person" and then deletes it. That's what Sheryl would write. Dramatic Sheryl. Instead, he writes, "Have you seen me? Looking for information on the whereabouts of Annie Forester," along with his name and phone number. Short and simple, not too alarmist. He can't bring himself to add "Last seen" because that's what goes on posters for people who turn up dead.

He prints off fifty flyers. He'll start with that. Nobody will call, except maybe ambulance-chaser types looking for gossip. Sheryl will be pleased though. She will check the "put up flyers" box on the list he imagines she has, titled something ridiculous like "Bring Annie Home!"

"Come on, Lucy. You wanna go for a run?"

He may as well put up the flyers while on a run. He's trying to get in as many miles as he can. His marathon is at the end of next month. He's been running in the morning and then again at night. Lucy looks leaner. He's lost six pounds already.

He goes out fast—too fast. Because he's angry. Pissed off, actually. He doesn't have time for this, for these flyers. Annie is fine. She has to be. She will come back. She'll probably see the flyers and be appalled that they went to such lengths. *I don't want to be found, so please don't come looking.* That's what she wrote. And here he is, disrespecting her wishes.

What he needs to focus on right now is work. Because work has become a clusterfuck. He can't tell Sheryl and Steve that though. They don't even know he took on all the Marcus Sandoval properties. Sheryl would say something like, "Why would you do that when Annie needs you?" She would imply that's why Annie left. Maybe she would be right.

It was probably stupid, taking on all this work. He can't keep up. Well, he could keep up if all the properties were quiet, but nearly all of them have some kind of problem. This is why Nate doesn't believe in God; if there was a God, he would cut Nate a fucking break at a time like this.

The pool pump is broken at the Via Contente house. The Calle Tranquilo house is not so *tranquilo*; the tenants have missed rent for the second month in a row and are dodging phone calls, meaning the dreaded eviction process is probably imminent. Thankfully, those houses aren't Marcus Sandoval's properties. He's the one to impress or, at the very least, not upset. His Avenida Oso duplex has a water heater leak that is affecting both units. Nate hasn't had a chance to even inspect the damage. Anything involving water can be a major problem. He has to get over there. Today, ideally—after this run/flyer fiasco. There's a homeowners' association complaint for the Sandoval duplex on Calle Miramar, something about how they suspect the roots of the ficus tree in the backyard are pushing against the fence, so the tree needs to be removed. Fucking ficus trees. The roots are always a problem. They should be illegal. There was a noise complaint against the duplex on Avenida Corona too. He needs to call the tenants, just to make sure everything's kosher. They probably just had a party, which Marcus Sandoval doesn't need to know about. Last on the list: A family is moving into the Via Barcelona triplex tomorrow, or is it Sunday? He needs to contact them about doing a final walk-through of the property.

He needs a drink. That's what he needs.

He needs to get one of those accounting software programs, because he has only a vague notion of all the money changing hands. Someone could owe him thousands of dollars, and right now, in this moment, he would have no idea.

He needs to hire someone to help him. He should put up an ad on Craigslist or in the paper. Do people still read the paper? If his website wasn't a piece of shit, he could put up an ad there.

He needs to update his website.

Lucy starts resisting as he runs. He's going too fast for her, sprinting to compensate for the stops he's making to put up the flyers. He slows. He's about halfway through his stack of flyers. He must look like an idiot, running with a dog leash and flyers in one hand, a stapler and tape in the other. His phone beeps, one of his calendar alerts. Fuck, is there a meeting he forgot about?

No, not a meeting—an appointment with grief counselor Pete. Those appointments are for Nate and Annie, together. With Annie gone, it's like Pete is gone too. Except that he's not, and he requires advance notice for cancellations. "If you don't call twenty-four hours before, I'll have to charge you. I'm sorry, it's just policy." That's what he said at their first appointment. It was the only time during that appointment that he didn't, couldn't, make eye contact with them.

"Fuck," he says out loud. Lucy tilts her head to one side. She's heard this word a lot recently.

The rest of the flyers will have to wait.

"WHERE'S ANNIE?" PETE says, looking over Nate's shoulder as he walks into the room. Pete sounds just as uneasy about Annie not being there as Nate feels.

"That is an excellent question," Nate says, sitting on the couch. He's still wearing his running clothes, sweat cold on his skin.

Pete closes the door and sits in his chair, looking more concerned than Nate has ever seen him. Pete is an easygoing, there-is-no-problem-too-big guy.

"She left," Nate says.

"Left?"

Nate tells him the story, recites the note. He knows it verbatim by now.

When he is done, Pete leans forward and says, "And she's been gone how long?"

"This is day four."

"Day four," Pete echoes. "And you haven't heard from her at all?"

"Nope."

He's annoyed with Pete's tone. It's the same tone Annie's mother has been using, the doomsday tone. Why can't these people just take the note for what it is? *I don't want you to worry. I'm okay.* The words replay in his head like a commercial jingle that won't leave you alone.

She'll be back in a week, two weeks, tops.

"How are you doing with it all?"

Oh, Jesus. This is what Pete asked in their first session, when Annie told him through tears about Penelope dying. Nate, not knowing how to respond, had answered, "It's been hard," because that seemed like the right thing to say. Pete gave him a squinty-eyed, compassionate stare, begging Nate to join his wife in crying.

"I'm doing fine because I trust Annie. I trust the note she left."

Pete nods and jots down something on his infamous pad of paper.

"What are you writing?" Nate dares to ask. It's kind of freeing without Annie here. Most of the time, in these Pete sessions, he's just trying not to upset or embarrass her. Without her here, his inhibitions are gone.

"Excuse me?" Pete says, glancing up, pen paused.

"I'm just wondering what you're writing," Nate says. "Does the fact that I'm not freaking out irrationally about my wife being gone mean I'm insane or something?"

"Do *you* think it means you're insane?"

Nate's face is getting hot. He's really tried to like Pete, for Annie's sake. Without her here, maybe he doesn't need to try anymore.

"Of course I don't think I'm insane," he says. "I think I'm saner about this than anyone else."

"Tell me more about that," Pete says. He's ever calm, like Teflon to Nate's obvious agitation. That must be a requirement to be a therapist, Teflon coating.

"I'm keeping a level head. Someone has to," he says. "We can't all freak the fuck out."

"Why not?" Pete says with a sincerity that makes Nate laugh.

You laugh when you're nervous, did you know that? Annie said that to him once. He'd laughed in response to her.

"Look, I'm just trying to be logical. I don't know why that's a bad thing," he says. He resents having to defend himself to Pete, but can't help going on. "I pride myself on keeping it together. Sorry to disappoint you."

"Disappoint me?"

"It's pretty fucking obvious you want me to lose it. You and Annie both. Somehow that's a breakthrough, if I fucking lose it."

He sounds angrier than he intends. If there's a poor soul in the waiting room, he probably thinks Nate is, in fact, losing it right about now.

"You seem angry, Nate."

No shit, Sherlock.

"This therapy thing, it's just not for me."

He starts to stand. He expects Pete to stand too, but he just sits there in his chair.

"I think it would be a good idea if you stayed," he says.

"Why's that?"

"So we can talk through this anger. You're upset, clearly."

"With all due respect," Nate starts, knowing people use this phrase only when they are about to say something disrespectful, "talking about it with you is making it worse."

"You didn't have to come today. You must have come for a reason."

Nate takes the folded check out of his shorts. It's damp. He sets it on the little table next to the couch.

"I would have had to pay you if I canceled. It's the principle of the thing," he says. "Consider this my more-than-twenty-four-hour notice of cancellation for all future appointments."

Pete sighs audibly.

"Oh, and I suppose you want me to share a Penelope memory before I go? That's your thing, right?"

Pete starts to say something, but then his mouth looks paralyzed, lips slightly parted, no words coming out. It gives Nate pleasure to stump him.

"One time, our dog took her favorite stuffed animal—this unicorn thing—and chewed off its horn. She said to the dog, with all this conviction in her little face, 'You asshole.'"

And with that, he leaves, closing the door behind him. It's probably the most dramatic exit Nate has ever made in his life. And it feels good. This must be how Annie felt when she made her own dramatic exit—resolved, vindicated, purposeful. Pete is probably writing something in his notes about how Nate is "projecting" onto him. Isn't that one of the favorite therapy terms? Everything has a reason in therapy. That's the problem with it. In life, so many things don't have reasons.

You asshole.

Nate and Annie had laughed about that hysterically. Not in front of Penny, of course; they didn't want to encourage her. "She learned it from you," Annie said. "You're to blame on this one."

Today still has the chance to be good, productive. He'll visit his properties, starting with Avenida Oso with the water heater leak. He knows himself well enough to know he'll feel better when he checks some things off his list. He'll tell Annie's mother he put up a hundred flyers. What's she going to do, count them? Maybe at the end of the day, with a glass of whiskey—which he never drinks, but seems appropriate—he'll put up an ad on Craigslist, find someone to help him with the properties. By the time Annie comes back, life will be back in order. He'll have all his accounting sorted out. His marathon is in San Diego. They can make a weekend of it. He'll find a good Italian restaurant down there. Annie loves Italian.

She'll be back in a week, two weeks, tops.

She has to be.

SEVENTEEN

ANNIE has become part of the tiny house community, in spite of herself. They've all welcomed her with impossible-to-reject open arms. There are five residents in total, not including James, who stays in his house up the road but hangs out with them during the day—chatting, working on the houses, drinking beer.

Matt is about James's age, early thirties. He's tall and thin with long, sinewy muscles and sunken cheeks. He used to be a rock climber until he saw his friend fall and die, a story told with little emotion. *Maybe that's how all men are*, Annie thinks— *emotionless*. Matt lives in the bright-yellow house. He's been in the community for a few months, says he plans to stay the full year, learn about building, then take his own house and go "off the grid." His whole goal in life is to live simply and cheaply so he can travel the world. His eyes get big when he talks about it.

Ken is in his late fifties, though with his leathery, wrinkled skin, he looks like he's seventy. He tells a sob story fit for a country song. His wife left him, he lost his job, and he had to foreclose on his house. He worked in construction and happened to see an ad James posted online, looking for people with building experience to "live and work peacefully in a unique community." He said, "Why the hell not?" and moved to the co-op ten months ago. He has only a couple months left here, technically, but James says he might let him stay longer because he's such a help with the building. The two of them, James and Ken, do most of the construction, as far as Annie can tell. All Annie has done so far is help paint a soon-to-be-sold bungalow, stack wood, and organize the nail inventory (so many different sizes!). James gave her a book to study with standard construction plans in it.

Lia is petite, skinny. Her hair is always in a bun, like a ballerina. She's just twenty-three, a fact relayed by Dawn. Lia's quiet and seemingly uninterested in sharing her story. It's a relief to Annie. She's not the only one who prefers a little privacy.

Dawn said, "Don't worry. Lia's just shy. She'll warm up."

Annie wanted to say, "It's perfectly fine if she doesn't." She wanted to say, "Leave the poor girl be."

The days feel like summer camp. They do most of the construction work in the morning. Besides the soon-to-be-sold bungalow, there are three other houses in progress. One is for a client, an Alaskan, according to James. One is for Ken. It's a cabin style, with knotted pine side paneling. It's almost done, just needs some finishing touches. And one is for Dawn. Hers is framed out, a phrase Annie has learned means all the wood beams are up. Matt's house is just a trailer right now. All the houses start with a trailer base. James scours the internet for used ones because they're so expensive new. He says the online scouring occupies 50 percent of his day. There is no house-in-progress for Lia yet. She's still deciding if she wants one. Annie will have to decide that for herself at some point too. She hasn't thought that far ahead, can't commit to her own tiny house, to a permanent life without Nate.

They work until noon, then take a lunch break. They work after that, but with less gusto. By three o'clock, most of them retreat to their individual tiny houses. Read. Nap. Whatever. The wine-and-sunset community happy hour is a nightly occurrence. It's not so bad. Even Lia goes. There's an understanding that attendance is part of being a member of the community. You pay very little rent, you help build houses, and you chat with people at sunset.

"You survived a week," a soft voice says.

Annie's sitting at the campfire. She turns around. Lia is there, holding her wine glass with both hands, as if she doesn't have the strength in just one.

"One week," Annie says.

Lia remains standing a few feet away. Annie finds herself patting the chair next to her. She senses Lia requires invitation.

"I hated my first couple days here," Lia confesses, sitting next to Annie.

"Me too," Annie admits.

"I didn't think it would be so . . ."

"Social?"

"Yes, exactly."

Kindred spirits. Peas in a pod. Annie told Nate once, "You're the U to my Q." He looked at her strangely and she explained: "Q is nothing without U. Q needs U to make words. Otherwise, it's just alone, useless."

Lia sets her glass on the ground, leans closer to the fire to warm her hands. Her knee bumps Annie's.

"How long have you been here?" Annie asks.

"Five and a half months. I showed up a couple weeks after Dawn. I probably would have left right away if Dawn hadn't convinced me to stay."

"She's a little . . ."

"Pushy?"

"Yes."

"She means well," Lia says. "She reminds me of the lady who ran my Girl Scout troop when I was little."

It seems like Lia was little just yesterday.

"Den mom," Annie says.

"Exactly."

They are quiet.

"Have you decorated your house yet?" Lia asks.

"I haven't even unpacked my suitcase."

Lia nods like this makes sense to her. "There's a thrift store out in Santa Ysabel," she says. "I'll go with you if you want. That's where I got my couch."

"I'd like that, actually," Annie says, meaning it.

"Tomorrow afternoon?"

Tomorrow is when Annie is going to see Dr. Franklin. Tomorrow may be a very strange day.

"How about this weekend?" Annie says.

"Deal."

🏠

DR. FRANKLIN'S OFFICE is in Julian, a historic gold rush mountain town stuck in a simpler time. In fall, people flock there to pick apples. It's famous for apple pie. Annie had planned on taking Penny in September. Annie kept a list in her phone of fun things to do with Penny: the flower fields in Carlsbad, the Griffith Observatory, whale watching. It's still in her phone, probably always will be.

The main drag has a bookstore, a soda fountain, a pie shop, a coffee house, and a cute bed-and-breakfast. Penny would have loved it. Nate too, probably. It could have been a nice family weekend. Thankfully, it's mostly desolate today. That all-too-familiar anger would come back if Annie was faced with just one annoyingly happy family.

The doctor's office seems like it hasn't been updated since 1960. Olive-green shag carpeting in the waiting room and all. There is no receptionist; this isn't that type of operation. A bell rang when Annie opened the door. That's enough to alert Dr. Franklin, seemingly the only person on the premises, to the arrival of his possibly only appointment of the day.

He's old . . . very old. The age spots on his hands are dark, wide circles. He wears bifocals and looks like a kind-but-mad scientist.

"You must be Allie," he says.

She must be.

"And you must be Dr. Franklin."

"Come on back."

She follows him, slowly, so slowly, down the hallway to his one exam room. She hops up on the table, shifts around on the paper lining. He sits in a chair facing the table, a clipboard in his lap, and starts asking her questions about her medical history, making notes on the paper in front of him. This is how medicine should be—personal, intimate, no computers.

"So, then, what brings you here?"

"I just moved into the tiny house community out by Pauma Valley. One of the people there recommended you."

"Must be Dawn," he says, a smile spreading across his face. He still has all his teeth, which Annie takes as a good sign.

"Yes, Dawn."

"She's a good egg," he says.

Annie likes him, this Dr. Franklin who refers to people as eggs.

"I just found out I was pregnant, right before I moved in."

He has very little reaction. He scribbles something on his paper and then says, "Any idea how far along you are?"

"Six, seven, eight weeks—somewhere around there."

With Penelope, she knew so many more specifics. She took copious notes in her day planner. She still has a paper day planner, refuses to go digital. When they were trying, she recorded the dates of her periods, her estimated ovulation, when they had sex. She found out she was pregnant on a Friday, exactly twenty-eight days after her last period. She marked that as "four weeks pregnant." Nate didn't understand how she was already four weeks pregnant. She had to explain that they count back to the date of your last period as the starting point. They consider the whole time since that period—the release of the egg, the union with the sperm, the implantation in the uterus—part of the pregnancy. He didn't get it. His eyes glazed over. It didn't matter. She was so excited that she proceeded to label every Friday after that: five weeks, six weeks, seven weeks, all the way to forty weeks. She worried she might jinx it, labeling in advance, so she wrote in pencil.

"Well, I can do an ultrasound to see," he says.

"You can?"

She sounds more surprised than she intends. It just seems preposterous, this old man operating any kind of technology.

"Sure can," he says.

"Okay, well, sure, can we do that?"

He leaves so she can get undressed. When he returns, he has an ultrasound machine on wheels with him. As he's setting it up, he says most women in the area deliver at the hospital in Murrieta. He can refer her to a doctor there, but he's happy to do her ultrasounds and any necessary blood tests "along the way." When Annie was pregnant with Penelope, she would have laughed at this man. She needed the very best care. Now though, she's aware that even the very best care can't prevent all misfortunes. And she likes Dr. Franklin.

"That sounds fine, for now. I don't really have a plan in mind yet," she says, with a nervous laugh. She sounds like a clueless teenager at a free clinic. She shifts around uncomfortably, the paper gown crinkling.

"This early on, we do internal ultrasounds," Dr. Franklin says. "Feels kind of like a Pap smear, just some pressure."

Annie doesn't tell him that she already knows this. She requested an early ultrasound with Penelope because she was so paranoid.

It looks like a dildo. That's what Nate whispered when the doctor revealed the probe at that first early ultrasound. Annie slapped his arm. The technician pretended not to hear.

Dr. Franklin puts a condom over the probe. Nate snorted like a teenage boy telling a fart joke when this happened before. "Better safe than sorry," he'd said.

It's weird that Nate isn't here.

"I used to be an ob-gyn, if that makes you feel better," Dr. Franklin says, once the probe is inside, moving around, searching for her baby.

"Oh, really?" Annie says. It does make her feel better.

"Switched to family practice 'bout fifteen years ago. I'm too old to get up in the middle of the night and run down to the hospital."

She watches him watch the little screen, looks for signs of concern on his face. He shows none.

"Ah, there we have it," he says, pointing his shaky, arthritic index finger at what looks like a small white jelly bean.

"That's it?" Annie says.

"Sure is," he says. "You see that flutter?"

It looks like it could just be a blip in the screen, but Annie sees it.

"Heartbeat," he says.

It's so, so weird that Nate isn't here.

It's so weird that she *is* here, looking at this grainy image, implying to this old man that she is ready to bring a baby into the dark, terrible world. Dr. Franklin doesn't ask about her husband (or boyfriend or sperm donor or whomever), the man half responsible for the on-screen flutter. How very PC of him. He might think she got knocked up during a one-night stand. He might think this is an "oops" pregnancy. When she was trying to get pregnant the first time, the very idea of an accidental pregnancy seemed so unbelievable, so flippant. She didn't have the personality for that. She wasn't the whimsical type. She didn't get caught up in moments. Her life was very planned. . . or it used to be. Now, here she is, with a pregnancy that was planned at the time it began but feels so accidental now.

Can babies hear thoughts? Absorb them? She hopes not.

"Measuring about eight weeks now. Which puts you due in"—he consults a wall calendar behind him—"early September."

September. Nate's birthday is in August. Hers is in October. Penelope's is in November. This baby falls right in line. Fits right in.

September. What's the astrological sign then? She knew all this with Penelope. Penelope, a Scorpio. She'd researched it. A water sign. Intense personality. She'd told Nate, "This does not bode well for her teenage years."

"Well, everything looks fine right now," Dr. Franklin says.

He's wise to say it this way. *Right now.* Whatever is to happen next month, or in three years, is a mystery.

"When should I come back?"

"A month," he says, "unless you want to come sooner than that for peace of mind."

Annie gives Dr. Franklin a knowing smile, a smile that says she has lived and seen things that even he hasn't seen.

"Peace of mind?" she says. "There's no such thing."

AFTER PENELOPE'S FIRST ultrasound, Nate and Annie went to dinner and talked excitedly about their future baby. They didn't know at that point if they were having a boy or a girl. Annie always had a feeling it would be a girl. She feels like this one will be a boy. She can't help but remember Penny saying she wanted "a brudder." It seems like, with everything that's happened, Penny should at least get what she wanted. A part of Annie still wants to believe the world is fair, that there is rhyme or reason. A part of her needs to believe that.

She gets back to the tiny house community in the late afternoon. The construction area is quiet; everyone is done working for the day. She feels guilty for missing some of the day, for going to her appointment. They probably talked behind her back: *She just got here and she's already missing work? Lotta nerve, that one.* James assured her it was fine, but still. What will happen when her pregnant belly grows, when they realize that she will be of little help to the community when it comes to building houses? *One thing at a time*, she tells herself. That mantra has never worked though. She's always a thousand steps ahead.

"Hi, there," a voice calls.

It's only when Annie looks up that she realizes she's been walking with her chin glued to her chest. It's Lia, sitting out on her small deck, a book in her lap.

"Hello," Annie says with a wave.

"I was just going in to make some tea, if you want to join," Lia says.

Annie gets the feeling that Lia doesn't extend invitations often. She extends this one in almost a whisper, as if she doesn't want anyone else to hear because they might wonder why she never asked them in for tea.

"Sure," Annie says.

Annie has been inside everyone's tiny house except Lia's. The others mandated tours—*this is my humble abode*, both Dawn and Ken said with a sweep of their arms. All the houses are structurally alike inside, but the personal touches make them seem so different. Matt's house is bare, much like Annie's. He has a beanbag chair in lieu of a couch. He uses an upside-down wooden crate as a coffee table. He has a few books, no pictures in plain sight. Dawn's house has character. That's how Nate would describe it in one of his property listings: *overflowing with character*. She has lace curtains on the windows, a couch covered in a magenta paisley sheet, colorful dish towels and throw pillows. Even the most mundane objects have personality—a bright-green teakettle, a bowling-ball-and-pin salt and pepper shaker set, a table lamp in the shape of a blossoming flower. She has lots of pictures of family, lots of dishware. Every inch of space in her home is used. Ken's house is similarly lived-in, but in different ways. He has shelves of tools, too many coffee mugs, piles of books—thrillers, mostly, as far as Annie could tell. He's messy. When Annie visited, dirty dishes were stacked in and around the sink, random articles of clothing were strewn about. Annie wondered if this was Ken's rebellion against the wife who left him, the wife who made him pick up after himself for however many years.

"Come on in," Lia says, opening the front door.

It smells like vanilla. Annie spots the source, a candle burning on the kitchen counter. Lia's house is clean, fairly sparse. An antique-looking, flower-patterned green couch is the star of the space.

"From the thrift store?"

"Yep," she says. "It's not very comfortable, but I love it anyway."

There's a framed poster on the wall next to the couch, a Robert Frost quote. *In three words I can sum up everything I've learned about life: it goes on.*

This is supposed to be comforting, this quote. But Annie sees it as completely overwhelming. *It goes on.*

"I love that quote," Lia says, catching her looking at the poster.

You must not know what it's like to wish it would just end, Annie thinks. And just like that, Lia joins the list of people who cannot be fully trusted.

Lia's shelves are dotted with a few personal items: a succulent in a clay pot, a stuffed teddy bear with worn "fur" and a missing nose, and a framed photo of two older people. Her parents, Annie guesses. It feels like a home. Annie wonders if her tiny house will ever feel that way, if any house without Penelope will ever feel that way.

Lia goes to the kitchen, fills two mugs with water and puts them in the microwave that occupies most of her counter space.

"Did you have a nice day?" Lia asks, oh so sweetly, as the microwave whirs.

Annie has the intense urge to tell someone. Nate is the person she thinks of, but she can't call him. Not now, not yet. Maybe she should tell Lia. Maybe she just needs to not be the only person who knows.

"I'm pregnant," she blurts.

Lia's eyes go big, as if she's never known a pregnant person before, as if she's never heard of this phenomenon called pregnancy.

"Oh," she says. "Wow."

The microwave beeps, and Lia takes out the mugs. She dunks a tea bag in each of them.

"I had my first ultrasound today," Annie says.

It does feel better, to say it out loud, to speak of it as something that is actually happening, not just something existing in her own mind.

"Did it go okay?"

"Yeah, fine, so far," Annie says.

Lia goes to the couch, and Annie follows.

"I'm scared," Annie says.

Lia blows cooling breaths on her tea. "Why?" she asks, brows furrowed.

Annie looks down at her tea, at the water becoming brown.

"My three-year-old. She died. Right before Christmas."

It feels good to say this out loud too.

Lia reaches over, puts a hand on Annie's thigh. Her fingers are warm from holding the mug of tea.

"That's why I came here, I guess," Annie says. "I haven't told anyone though."

Lia squeezes Annie's hand, not in the gentle, grandmotherly way, but hard, tight. Her grasp says she understands, though Annie doesn't think she possibly could.

"You don't have to talk about it," she says. "Unless you want to, I mean."

Then: "I know how it is."

Then: "I lost a child too."

EIGHTEEN

JOSH needs to tell Nate what he knows. He has to. It's been an entire week since Annie left, and there are signs up now. *Signs.* They're all over the freaking neighborhood. Nate must have put them there, or Annie's parents. Probably Nate. The signs say, "Have you seen me?" with this picture of Annie sort of half-smiling. It's not the best picture of her. There are so many on Facebook that are better.

Josh felt better after talking to Annie. She's alive and seemingly well, a relief. But he's the only one who knows this; that's the problem. Nate doesn't look good. Strung out, that's how he looks. Josh sees him go for runs, sometimes twice a day, in the very early morning (the motion detection light on their driveway usually wakes Josh up) and again in the late evening (sometimes after Josh has closed his eyes for the day). Nate's always got his head down, staring at the ground. He's in his own world. Josh has been parked in the same spot on the street for a few days now, and Nate doesn't even seem to notice.

So, yeah, he has to tell him. He has information about this man's wife. It's selfish to possess it. Sharing it, that's the right thing to do.

But how? Of course, he can't just walk up to Nate's front door and say, "Hi, I'm Josh. I happen to know your wife is safe and sound in a tiny house community in eastern San Diego County."

Nate would have questions, obviously. Josh couldn't give him answers.

He could just leave a note, but that seems weird and creepy. Nate would probably turn it over to the police or something. They might check for fingerprints. Josh is in the system because of that time he was busted for pot when he was seventeen. He was a minor though. Do juvenile records disappear after you're no longer a juvenile? He should know this. He doesn't though. He could write the note wearing gloves, to prevent fingerprints, but no . . .

Calling Nate is the best bet. Josh can find a pay phone, assuming there is one still in existence within a ten mile radius, and disguise his voice a little. He'll say he has an anonymous tip. Nate's number is printed on the missing-person flyer; it's not even like Josh would have to go digging around the internet to find it. Maybe Nate wouldn't believe him. He's probably getting lots of calls from weirdos because of the signs. But hell, chances are he'll at least check it out, go visit the tiny house place or whatever. Josh would, if it was his wife who was missing. *His wife*. It's strange to think about, a wild hypothetical if there ever was one.

Turns out there's an app that identifies locations of pay phones, showing them as little blue dots on maps. It treats them like they are endangered animals, approaching extinction. There's no way anyone using this app is not a criminal of some kind. If they use the app, that means they have a phone. They just need to make an untraceable call for some reason. Definitely suspicious.

The nearest pay phone is just five minutes away from Nate and Annie's house, in Dana Point, in front of a donut shop. Josh parks and then goes in to buy a donut. He doesn't really want a donut, but he feels like it will look less weird if he buys something. Otherwise, he's just a guy who pulled up to a donut shop to use a pay phone.

"That one," he says, pointing at a glazed donut with rainbow sprinkles.

IT'S BEEN TEN, fifteen years since he ate a donut. On certain occasions, when his mom was in one of her good moods, she'd buy a dozen donuts on Saturday mornings. She liked the ones with the goo in the middle; he preferred the classic ones, the rainbow-sprinkled kind being his favorite. It was like she saw those donuts as her parental good deed of the day. Most weekends, he was on his own while she was "out," doing things that were unclear to him until he got older and realized what drugs were. Cocaine, that was her drug of choice—though it seemed she would do anything available. She got clean a few years back, but her liver will probably give out soon because of all the replacement booze.

He sits at one of the orange plastic tables inside the donut shop. The youngish Mexican guy behind the counter looks at him funny, probably because nobody ever sits inside; they take their dozen and run. Someone has carved "chinga tu madre" into the tabletop. Josh knows, thanks to his public schooling, that this means "fuck your mother." Josh laughs to himself. *I was actually just thinking about your mother*, he imagines telling the punk who etched the offensive words. He wouldn't punch the guy. Five years ago, he would have punched the guy. He likes to think he's more mature now. Now he would just say, "How about you go fuck yourself instead?" Yes, mature.

He throws his napkin in the trash can and gives the guy behind the counter a "goodbye and thanks" nod of the head.

When he steps outside, he pretends like he's just seen the pay phone and remembered he has to make a call. He acts out the scene dramatically, like an old-timey actor in the silent movies Jess used to make him watch. She liked to think she was cultured. And then she'd turn on the *Kardashians* show and blow her cover.

He has Nate's number scribbled down on a little piece of paper. He picks up the phone, then puts it back on the hook, thinking he should at least practice his voice first. He clears his throat, says "hello" as deeply as he can. Even after puberty, his voice remained on the squeakier side. He'll never sound manly. He'll never be able to pick up a girl in a bar based on voice alone.

He clears his throat again, repeats "hello" until he feels comfortable. He sounds ridiculous, but whatever, it'll get the job done.

He picks up the phone and puts in the required coins, fished out of his car's cup holder. The only time he even uses coins is when he gets fast food. He has this thing about giving exact change. OCD, Jess used to say.

It rings. It's midday Thursday; Nate is probably working. He's never home during the day, it seems. One ring, two ring. If there's no answer, should Josh leave a message? That seems riskier, to have his voice on this recording that could be saved and shared with the police. He's paranoid, probably. But still, he'll just hang up and call back later. He'll have to buy another donut.

As he's about to give up, as the fourth ring begins, there's suddenly an answer: "Hello?"

It's just one word, but it's the harshest greeting Josh has ever received over the phone. Nate sounds rushed, stressed, irritated.

"Um, hi," Josh says, forgetting to use the fake voice, forgetting everything he was going to say.

"Yes?"

Josh is silent, not sure what to say in response to the edginess of Nate's tone. What's wrong with the guy? Well, Josh knows what's wrong, overall—with his wife missing and all—but Nate seriously sounds like he's going to jump through the phone and strangle this person who is wasting his time. Josh being that person.

"Sorry," Josh mutters.

"Hello? Look, I'm really busy. Are you calling about the job opening or what?"

Job opening?

Before Josh has a chance to think, he says, "Um, yeah."

And before Josh can backtrack or explain or inquire or *something*, Nate says, "Okay, can you meet at Turk's in the harbor in an hour?"

Josh has no idea what Turk's is—or "the harbor," for that matter. And he has no clue what the job opening is. But he says, "Okay."

Nate hangs up before Josh can confirm the place. He takes a pen out of his back pocket and scribbles "Turk's" on the piece of paper, under Nate's phone number.

What the fuck is he doing? He doesn't have to go, of course. But shit, Nate might jump off a bridge if he's a no-show, if he proves to be one more annoyance in his day. Straw that broke the camel's back or whatever. Maybe it's meant to be that they meet face-to-face. Josh can just tell him, in person, that he's sorry about Penelope. Finally. He can tell him that he was coming to their house to deliver his condolences when he saw Annie leave with a suitcase. He'll say he followed her; it will sound weird, but whatever. Nate will just be happy to know where his wife is. Maybe Josh will even come out looking like some kind of hero. Maybe Nate will clap him on the back and say, "Thank you, man."

Or maybe he'll punch him square in the jaw. And maybe that's okay. Maybe Josh deserves it.

He looks up Turk's on his phone. It's just a short drive away, in the Dana Point Harbor area. As he drives there, he feels like he's going to barf up his donut, make a rainbow-colored mess all over the car. He takes deep breaths, wills the nausea away.

There are only a few people in Turk's, mostly middle-aged men with big bellies hanging over their belt buckles. They're each sipping whiskey and chasing it with Bud Light. The waitresses are also middle-aged, with big bags and smudged mascara under their eyes. It smells like a bar, that musty alcohol stench. Josh knows it well, grew up with it. Most people would be turned off by places like this, but to Josh it's nostalgic. The fact that Nate picked this place to meet about a job opening makes Josh like him that much more.

Josh sits at the bar, orders a Coke. It doesn't seem appropriate to be drinking beer when Nate shows up. *Hi, I'm the guy who hit your daughter, and here I am enjoying a Coors.* No, not appropriate. Josh rubs his palms on his jeans. They're sweaty. They're always sweaty when he's nervous. If he has to shake Nate's hand, it'll be embarrassing. But no, Nate won't shake his hand. Why would he shake his hand? *Oh, I know you. You're the guy who hit my daughter. Nice to meet you.*

He pulls down the sleeves of his hooded sweatshirt (fuck, he's wearing a hooded sweatshirt!) to cover up his tattoos. Turk's is the type of place where tattoos are standard, but Josh doesn't want to look like "that kind of guy" to Nate. It will just incite him more. Like when you're driving and some guy cuts you off and you pull ahead and realize he's morbidly obese and you latch onto that and think, *You fucking fatass.* He doesn't want Nate to think, *You tattooed asshole.* No, the guy responsible for killing his child should look as respectable as possible. A churchgoing type. He wishes he wasn't wearing this stupid sweatshirt.

"You want another one?" the bartender asks. She's fifty-something, wearing cutoff jean shorts even though it's cold outside, big gold earrings dangling from her ears.

"Sure," Josh says.

He's two sips in when Nate arrives, twenty minutes early, probably hoping to compose himself with a drink before meeting Josh. Instinctively, Josh cowers, slouching on his bar stool, turning his face to the side so Nate won't see him. It works; he doesn't see him. And Nate must take a seat in the booth behind Josh, because Josh doesn't see him come around to the other side of the bar. This is awkward. Now Josh is going to have to approach him. He hadn't anticipated this.

Maybe he should just sit here until the appointed job interview time. Yes, that's what he'll do. He finishes his Coke. He pretends to use his phone while trying to see Nate in the reflection on the screen. He's there, at a booth, by himself, sipping a beer. Sierra Nevada, it looks like. A good choice. He's looking down at his phone, his brows furrowed in concentration. He won't notice if Josh leaves and then comes back in, as if he's just arrived. Yes, that's a good plan. Josh leaves a ten dollar bill on the counter, which is way too much for two Cokes. He'll probably forever be a good tipper, always trying to prove he's a good person.

He lingers outside, watching the boats in the marina, a couple sea lions sunning themselves on the wood docks. When fifteen minutes have passed, he goes back inside, trying to stand up straight. An upstanding citizen, literally. Nate looks up when he walks in. This is it—the reckoning.

Except that there is no look of recognition on Nate's face.

Josh holds his eye contact, asking Nate with his stare, *You know who I am, right?* No response, though. Just a blank look, with a forced smile of the professional variety.

"You must be who I talked to on the phone," Nate says, holding out his hand.

Lo and behold, they do, in fact, shake hands.

"Um, yeah," Josh says.

"I didn't even get your name," Nate says with a polite, aw-shucks laugh.

"Mike," Josh spits out. Because Nate must know the guy who killed his daughter was named Josh. He must. It's included in the police reports. And even if Nate doesn't think this is *the* Josh standing in front of him, he must hate all Joshes.

"Mike, I'm Nate," he says. "Have a seat."

Josh sits across the table from him, still waiting for that telltale light bulb to go off in Nate's head. Nothing, though. He knows Nate saw him on that day, the day it happened. Josh had gotten out of his truck and gone straight to the girl. Before he had a chance to kneel down, to see if she was okay, Nate came seemingly out of nowhere and said, "Move," and shoved him out of the way. Josh watched the rest of the scene from the sidewalk. He doesn't remember seeing Annie take her eyes off Penelope, but he remembers Nate looking up at him once, his eyes communicating nothing but disbelief and alarm; it was too soon for condemnation. The ambulance hadn't arrived yet. They didn't even know for sure if the girl was gone.

Is it possible Nate's blocked out the whole thing?

"Sorry if I was short with you on the phone. It's been a hell of a day," Nate says.

"I know how those go."

"Can I get you anything? Beer?" Nate asks.

Wouldn't that be something—the father of the girl Josh killed buying him a beer.

"No, thanks. I'm good."

"So," Nate says, setting aside his phone and leaning back in his seat, giving Josh his full attention. "Do you have experience with property management?"

What is the right answer to this question? Josh has already lied once. The truth seems only fair.

"Not really," he says.

It's not like he wants a job with Nate anyway. Shit, that would be crazy. He came here to apologize for what he did, to tell Nate about Annie. All of that seems so surreal now.

"That's okay, honestly. I didn't have experience before I got into this either," he says. He's being kind . . . too kind. "You're young. What are you, eighteen?"

Baby face, his mom calls him.

"Twenty-two, actually."

"That's still young," Nate says. "I really just need someone to help me with workload. An apprentice, if you will."

He's desperate, that much is clear. It's like he's trying to talk Josh into the position, instead of Josh talking him into hiring him.

"What kind of stuff do you need?" Josh asks.

"Well, I've got all these properties to oversee. I need to manage the tenants, be on top of money coming in and out, deal with any problems that come up. I need a system. I haven't had time to figure out the system. Life's been busy and . . ."

It's strange to hear Nate reduce his wife's disappearance to "life's been busy."

"I'm good with systems," Josh says. "I do computer programming and stuff."

What is he doing? It's like he wants the job. Maybe he does. To help Nate. Nate seems so fucking desperate.

"Really? Man, my website needs work," Nate says.

Yes, it does.

"I can set up a program for you, like a dynamic spreadsheet to keep track of each property."

"That would be awesome," Nate says. "Because, right now, all this shit is up in my head, and I'm kind of losing it."

Yes, you are.

"Okay, well yeah, sure, I think I could help you," Josh says.

"It's part-time. The ad on Craigslist said that. I'm guessing you saw the ad there."

Josh just nods.

"I figure fifteen bucks an hour. Is that fair?"

Nothing in life is fair, dude.

"That's great," Josh says.

Nate claps his hands together once.

"Well, that's done," he says. "I'm not sure I should tell you this, but you're the first person I interviewed."

He is truly desperate.

"Oh, really?"

"I've just gotta get some help, ASAP, ya know?" he says. He tips his beer into his mouth, sets it down, empty. "Can you start tomorrow?"

Josh shrugs. "Sure, that's fine."

"Okay. How about we meet at my house in the morning? I don't have an actual office. I'm usually at my properties throughout the day. But we can meet at the house, and then I'll take you around, show you each property, give you a rundown. You can take notes and start working on this program of yours."

"Sounds good," Josh says.

"You have your phone on you?"

A silly question in this day and age. Everyone always has their phone on them. Always.

Josh takes it out.

"Lemme give you my address," Nate says.

Josh nods and punches in the numbers, pretending they are not at all familiar to him.

NINETEEN

NATE is fine until the sun goes down. Then he feels strange. That's the only word for it—strange. It's weird without Annie in the house at night. Even in those terrible first few weeks after Penelope died, when Annie was just a ghost of her former self, floating around aimlessly, she was still *there*. He was so irritated with her grief, and now he wants nothing more than to have it back, to have her back.

It's been eight days now, since she left. He tries calling her at random times during the day, on the off chance her phone is on. It never is. Sheryl and Steve check in daily to see if Nate has heard anything. He wants to tell them, "Don't you think I would fucking call you if I heard something?" They come by the house every other day, snooping around as if Nate's got Annie stuffed in a closet somewhere. He keeps telling them to give it another week. She has to be back after a couple weeks. She only has enough money for a couple weeks.

Predictably, there have been no leads with the flyers. He's gotten calls, but no leads. Most of the calls are from curious neighbors who say some version of, "So, she just *disappeared*?" They don't sound particularly concerned. They sound interested, in-fucking-trigued, likely wondering if the crew from *60 Minutes* is going to show up and interview them. They would act aghast on camera, say things like, "This is just such a peaceful neighborhood, and she seemed like such a sweet person.

I can't believe this happened." Nate knew the flyers were a bad idea.

At least he has Lucy. Through everything, she continues to wag her tail and smile. Annie might have insisted dogs don't actually smile, but he chooses to believe otherwise. He talks to Lucy more than ever now. Just yesterday, when the new assistant kid came over, he said, "Lucy, this is Mike." And Mike looked at him like he was certifiably insane, then he gave Lucy a tentative wave.

He seems like a good kid, Mike. Has absolutely no experience with property management, but he's smart. Nate took him around to all the properties yesterday. Mike brought a notebook, brand new by the looks of it. He took notes on every property, all twenty-five of them. *Fuck, twenty-five?* Nate was out of his mind to think he could handle this. It's too much. But Mike was already spouting off ideas about this computer program he's going to create to help keep everything organized.

For now, most of the major issues have been handled. The pool pump at Via Contente is taken care of. The eviction is under way at Calle Tranquilo. What a fucking headache, evictions. The water heater leak at Avenida Oso is fixed, with minimal damage to the lower unit, thank God. The ficus tree at Calle Miramar has been yanked out of the ground. They've gotta put something in its place—a nice, trouble-free shrub of some kind. That can wait. The noise complaint at Avenida Corona turned out to be no big deal; just an enthusiastic party celebrating the tenant's thirtieth birthday. And the new tenants at Via Barcelona seem happy as can be. Nate sent them a welcome basket with jams and cookies and coffee and some other shit, and they took the time to thank him, which most tenants don't. He read that "thank you" email three times. It made him feel good, like he was doing something right. For once. Nate's talked to Marcus Sandoval twice. He seems pleased. He has absolutely no idea that Nate is losing his mind, which is the goal.

"Lucy, you ready?"

He wants to get a run in before Mike comes over. He told the kid he can set up shop at the dining table. Mike said he usually works at Starbucks or the college library. "Lots of roommates at my place," he'd said. "Hard to concentrate." Nate remembers those days. In the year between graduating college and meeting Stephanie, he lived with five guys in a house in Huntington Beach. Whoever would rent a house to five twenty-somethings is an idiot. Nate would never take on managing a property like that. In the first week, the police were called—twice. They weren't even having a party. They were just drinking and playing darts in the backyard. Five guys, bonded by beer and competitive activity, can make a hell of a lot of noise.

He's at the front door, Lucy at his side, ready to set out on a short run (a five-miler), punching information into the running app on his phone, when a call comes in. "Mom" flashes on the screen.

"Fuck," he says.

Lucy looks at him like, *What now?*

He hasn't talked to his mom much. She doesn't know Annie is gone. She would freak out. His mom had been devastated about Penelope. Nate couldn't handle it. He'd never heard sobbing like hers before. Bellowing, almost. He doesn't remember her crying like that when his father died. Maybe she did, and he's blocked it out. It would be worthy of blocking out; it was that bad. Even Annie seemed unnerved by it, skeptical of how anyone besides her could feel so much pain.

His mom was in town for the funeral and then flew back to Oregon. She called every day until Nate stopped answering. He felt bad, hitting that red button on his phone, declining her calls. But come on, he couldn't take care of all these falling-apart women in his life. How could he be expected to comfort them, to hold all their sadness? He should have told Pete the grief counselor, before stomping out, that the reason he doesn't cry is there's no fucking room left for his tears. They evaporate, preemptively.

He'll make this quick. Get it over with. It's been a couple weeks since he's talked to her. He owes her his voice.

"Hi, Mom," he says, sitting on the wicker love seat next to the front door, its red cushions faded by the sun. When they bought the house, they had visions of sitting out here, drinking wine, chatting with passing neighbors. In reality, the love seat is used only as a place to put things while unlocking the front door.

"You're alive," she says.

"Of course I am," he says. "Just been busy."

That's always the excuse. *So busy.* Isn't that what parents want for their adult children—a full life?

"How's Annie?" she says. As if she knows. Mothers always know.

"She's fine."

"Fine?" Her voice sounds doubtful. Of course Annie can't be "fine." Penelope is gone, and that reply is unacceptable forevermore.

"I mean, she's okay, considering," he says, annoyed with having to amend his response. What's so wrong with being "fine"? Even if you're not fine, what's wrong with saying you are?

Fake it till you make it.

"And you?"

"I'm good, Mom," he says. "Busy."

"Back at work?"

"Yes. I've actually got twenty-five properties on my roster now. Just hired an assistant," he says, hoping this will impress her, elicit some of that pride every son wants his mother to have.

"An assistant? Wow," she says. "Are you sure you aren't taking on too much?"

He tilts his head from one shoulder to the other, stretching his neck. She's not proud; she's concerned. Why is everyone so fucking concerned?

"Mom, it's good for me. It's good for us. It's good to get back in the swing of things. The money is good."

Good, good, good.

She expels something between a laugh and a sigh.

"You're so much like your dad," she says.

It's a bad thing, the way she says it.

"Too strong for your own good," she says.

Too strong? There is no such thing, is there?

"Mom, really, I'm fine," he says.

"Are you? Are you *really*?"

What is with the prevalence of this question? Do people expect him to think about it and change his mind? *On second thought, I'm not fine at all. I'm terrible. Thank you for helping me realize that.*

"Mom, you need to stop worrying. I—we are getting on with life as best we can," he says.

"I just don't want you to bottle it all up. That's what your dad did. I'm sure his heart attack was caused by stress. I'm sure of it."

"I'm not going to have a heart attack." Well, he might, if this conversation continues.

"And you'll talk about things, if you need to?" she says.

Holy fuck, did grief counselor Pete put her up to this?

"Mom, are you watching too much *Oprah* again?"

Sometimes after a death, people turn to religion. When Nate's father died, his mother turned to Oprah.

"She's not even on the air anymore," she says, with a don't-be-ridiculous tone. Somehow, in these types of conversations, he always ends up being the ridiculous one.

"Mom, I have to go. I'm going for a run."

"You're running again?" she says, high-pitched.

"Yep." Maybe this will get her off his back. Who can criticize good, old-fashioned exercise? Everyone's heard of endorphins. "Signed up for a marathon next month."

"A *marathon*? That's a big deal, Nathan."

The "Nathan" tells him she's seriously concerned now.

"Mom, Jesus, I'm trying to be healthy."

"Okay," she says with a defeated groan, "just don't exhaust yourself."

"Uh huh," he grunts.

They exchange their "goodbye"s and "talk soon"s, and he heads out with Lucy. He planned on it being an easy run but decides a faster pace is good, necessary even. His mother doesn't understand all the benefits there are to exhausting yourself. It's only when he's completely spent that his mind goes quiet.

WHEN HE TURNS the corner back onto his street, five miles done, Mike is lingering on the driveway, hands jammed into the pockets of his slightly slouched jeans. Apparently, that's still a trend, the slouched jeans. "Isn't that uncomfortable, walking around with your butt crack exposed?" Annie said once. "Kids these days make me feel old and grumpy."

Nate looks at his watch. The kid is ten minutes early, probably thinking that looks good to an employer. To Nate, it's annoying. He's all sweaty. He would have liked to take a shower in peace, to refuel with some peanut butter on toast, before having to be Boss Nate.

"Hey there, Mike," Nate calls as he approaches the driveway.

Mike doesn't respond so Nate calls out again, louder. Mike turns around, waves.

"I guess I'm a little early," he says with a shrug.

"No problem," Nate lies. He looks around, notices there are no cars parked out front. "You find the house okay? You could have parked in the driveway."

He doesn't want to explain why there's currently an extra space.

"Oh, yeah, thanks," Mike says. He seems nervous. "I, uh... my grandma lives in this neighborhood, actually. Parked at her house and walked over."

A twenty-two-year-old kid visiting his grandma? Mike is either an unusually kind soul, or a liar. Nate doesn't have time to figure out which. He just says, "Okay, then."

Nate jogs to the front door, opens it, lets them inside. Lucy goes straight to her water bowl.

"You run a lot?" Mike says, hands still in his pockets.

"Lately, yeah," Nate says. "Training for a marathon."

He goes to the fridge, takes out a water bottle. He offers one to Mike, but Mike shakes his head, mutters, "No, thanks."

"I'm going to jump into the shower. Make yourself at home. I figure the dining table will be a good place for you to work."

Mike looks at the table, as if assessing its merits. "Okay," he says.

After Nate showers, he comes out to find Mike staring at the pictures on the bookcase shelves, the ones Annie left behind, that is. It unnerves Nate, watching this kid analyze his family that isn't.

"Oh," Mike says, startled. "I was just—I didn't know you were married."

He says this like the fact that Nate is married is some kind of modern marvel.

"Yes. Annie. That's my wife."

Nate waits for the next question: *Where is she?*

"She's out of town," he says, before the question comes. "On business."

It occurs to him that Mike may have seen the signs with Annie's face on them. He holds his breath, waiting for Mike to say something, but Mike just nods, steps away from the bookcase, and sits at the dining table where his laptop is open and ready.

"When did you get married?" Mike asks, typing away, his back to Nate.

It's a weird question for a kid to ask, isn't it? Nate thinks back to when he was twenty-two. He'd just started dating Stephanie. By the end of their relationship, he knew much more about giving a shit about people other than himself, but at the beginning— when he was Mike's age—he was so immature. Maybe Mike's trying to be polite, make conversation. Nate wants to tell him that's really not necessary.

"Uh, let's see, 2008," he says.

This summer will be their seventh wedding anniversary. When Annie comes back, he'll say, "You must have had a hell of a seven-year itch, huh?" She'll laugh. Wouldn't that be something, to hear her *laugh*?

"Long time," Mike says. Then he goes quiet and continues typing away.

Nate starts scrolling through his phone, prioritizing his emails for the day. Nothing too urgent, yet.

"Any kids?" Mike says, still typing.

"Huh?" Nate says.

"You have kids?"

So weird, these questions.

"Uh, no," Nate says. Suddenly, it's like a walnut has lodged itself in his throat. He has to swallow three times for it to go away. "No kids."

Thankfully, the questions cease—the personal ones, at least. The next several are about the program Mike's creating: *What kinds of information do you want to track for each property? Do you want alerts emailed to you when rents come through? Do you have any print records, like of repairs done, that you want digitized?* He has kind of a genius air about him, this kid. He's the type who probably skipped out of classes for the simple fact that they bored him.

"Once I get this working for you, you'll be set," he says. He seems so excited by this project. It's baffling. Nate's never had that kind of intellectual passion for anything. "I wish I had your simple mind," Annie said to him once. She didn't mean it as an insult.

"You're pretty damn smart, aren't you?" Nate says.

Mike shrugs.

"Why the hell are you looking for jobs on Craigslist?" he asks him. "Shouldn't you be working for NASA or something?"

For the first time in two hours, Mike stops typing. It's like this question finally stumps him.

"Uh, I don't know," he says. "It's good for me to stay busy."

"I know what you mean."

"And I'm saving up for my own house." He says this with a hint of surprise, like he's just decided right now, in this moment, to save up for his own place.

"That's great, man," Nate says. "When I was twenty-two, I was saving up for beer."

Nate laughs at this memory of his younger self, but Mike just sits there, fingers still, hovering over the keyboard.

"I'm thinking of getting a tiny house," he says, his hands gripping the arm of the chair as he twists around to look at Nate. The intensity of his stare makes Nate take a step back. It's like he's daring Nate to ask about this venture, fishing for either a fight or approval.

"A tiny house?" Nate says. Like what Annie was yammering on about? Are they so popular that hipster kids want them too?

"I can buy the whole thing for, like, twenty-five grand."

"Yeah," Nate says. He looks to a picture of Annie on the bookshelf, one of her at the beach. "My wife was talking about that."

"She wants one?" Mike says, seemingly not surprised that Nate's wife would be interested in such a thing.

"She was talking about it," Nate says.

Mike turns back around, but he doesn't resume typing.

"There's a builder, down in eastern San Diego County. You should check it out," Mike says.

"Maybe we will."

Maybe when Annie comes back, if she's still interested in that, he'll humor her. At this point, he'd do more than humor her. He'd sell everything and live in a fucking tiny house forever if it would make her some version of happy.

"Do you want the name of the place?" Mike says.

Ever helpful, Mike.

"That's okay," Nate says.

Mike's shoulders slump, like this really disappoints him. Apparently, he's as passionate about tiny houses as he is about computer programming.

"You know what? Sure. Give me the name," Nate says.

Mike practically jumps out of his seat.

"Awesome," he says. "You really should go."

He tears a piece of paper out of his notebook, scribbles on it, and hands it to Nate. He has horrible handwriting, quintessential chicken scratch. Nate remembers an article saying that most geniuses do. Their brains run impatiently ahead of their hands. They can't get the thoughts down quickly enough.

Mike's note is legible, though barely: *Rolling Stone Co-Op.*

ANNIE hasn't been able to stop thinking about Lia. It's not just the shock of her story, the sadness of it, but this unsettling realization that Annie isn't the only one on the planet suffering. It should comfort Annie, make her feel less alone. Instead, it makes her a combination of embarrassed and angry. Her pain is not unique. She was so convinced it was. When it's that profound, it feels personal. It feels like the universe has it out for you, specifically.

Lia told her story with alarming efficiency, over just one cup of tea.

"My boyfriend, Caleb, and I got pregnant a couple years ago. I was just twenty-one. It wasn't planned, just sort of happened."

So Lia was a flippant, non-planning fly-by-the-seat-of-your-pants-er. Annie caught herself thinking, *If it wasn't planned, then the loss can't be so bad.* She immediately chastised herself for that thought. Here she was, mad at Nate for implying she should "get over it," and she was thinking the same thing about Lia.

"We kind of talked ourselves into being cool, young parents, ya know?" Lia went on. "Hipster parents, that's what Caleb said." Lia laughed to herself at the memory. The laugh alarmed Annie. People with this kind of pain shouldn't be able to *laugh*. It's absurd!

"I was at this bookstore, in one of the fiction aisles, the *M* to *P* aisle. I was looking for this new book by a guy named Brandon Nickel. It's weird I'll always remember that."

She laughed again after that, a pensive little *giggle*. Annie felt heat rise within her. If Nate heard Lia's story and heard her giggles, he would turn to Annie and say, "See, you can get better." She doesn't want to get better. Getting better, moving on, laughing again means she's accepted Penelope's gone. She can't accept it. She won't. Why doesn't anyone understand that?

"I started having this painful cramping. I went to the bathroom, and I was bleeding."

Just a miscarriage, Annie thought to herself. *It's not like you had three years with your child before she was taken.* It's a terrible thing to think, but Annie couldn't help it. She's bitterly possessive of her sadness, convinced it's worse than Lia's, worse than anyone else's. The Worst. It's hers. It's the last thing Penelope gave her, and she will cling to it fiercely. It makes her think of when Lucy took Penelope's stuffed animals, collected them in her dog bed, and Penelope marched over, took them back, and said, angrily, her little lips pursed, "Mine!"

"They had to induce labor. It's not like I could miscarry at home, ya know? I was seven months in. It was, like, a baby. Not an embryo or whatever."

This is when Annie started feeling especially guilty for all her bitchy thoughts. *Seven months in?* She can't imagine that, giving birth to a dead baby. A new thought crept into her mind: *At least I got to know mine.* That's unnerving—thinking of herself as the lucky one.

"I pushed and pushed, and the doctor pulled him out by his two tiny arms. I could feel them dislocating inside me. I screamed, but the baby was silent."

Lia started crying right then, so soon after those giggles. Why does grief have to be so confusing, so nonsensical? Instinctively, Annie reached out, squeezed her hand. Annie's eyes started to well up. A tear escaped, rolled down her cheek. *Mama, water's coming out of your eyes.* Penny said that once, the day Annie found out her grandmother had passed away. She'd died at the age of ninety-five, in her sleep, months after declaring she was ready to go—and, yet, Annie had still sobbed. How in the world did God think she could handle her three-year-old being hit by a truck?

"They cleaned him and swaddled him and asked if I wanted to hold him. Caleb said he didn't think that was a good idea, but I had to, ya know? How could I not? How could I let the nurse take him away as if he was nothing? I had to hold him, look at him, this person who never quite was. I had to confirm his short existence, tell him, 'Yes, you were here. I saw you. I loved you.' I had to, ya know?"

Annie did know. She did. She'd told Nate, a couple weeks ago, "You can't possibly understand. Nobody can." But maybe that's wrong. Maybe some people can understand. Maybe she is just one of many. Maybe her loss is dreadfully common. She doesn't want to believe this. Somehow, it makes Penelope seem less special.

"Caleb left the room. I held him, our son, for two hours. I named him—Ethan. I couldn't let him go. I just stared at his perfectly clasped fingers, his tiny arms pulled close in to his chest. He had the tiniest frown on his little face. He looked peaceful. I know everyone says that, but he really did."

Penelope looked peaceful too. Even in the middle of the street. Internal injuries, they said later at the hospital. On the outside, she was perfect. "She's just sleeping, she's just sleeping," Annie repeated over and over again after the doctor said she was gone. Nate took Annie by the shoulders, tried to get her to look into his eyes, to see the truth. She couldn't.

"They moved me into a small room to recover. I put my maternity clothes back on. That's when I lost it, putting on those stupid pants with the elastic waistband. They gave us a little card with Ethan's footprints on it. They handed it to Caleb, but he just passed it right to me, couldn't look at it," she said. "I still have the card."

She got up from the couch and went to a small wooden box on her bookshelf. She retrieved the little card from inside and brought it over to Annie. The feet were so small . . . so, so small. Nate wouldn't have been able to look either.

"My milk came in a few days later. I told Caleb it was like my breasts were crying for Ethan. He hated when I called him by his name. Ethan. He couldn't handle thinking of the baby as, like, a real person."

"It's hard for men," Annie found herself saying, her only verbal contribution thus far.

"Yeah," Lia said, a solemn confirmation. "We couldn't survive it, Caleb and me. We tried for a year. We just couldn't."

"Nate and I . . ." Annie began, realizing she hadn't mentioned to anyone in the tiny house community that she even had a husband, let alone that his name is Nate. "We were having a hard time. That's why I left."

Lia nodded, like she understood completely. What a bizarre thing, to be understood completely.

They just sat there, in silence, for what felt like an hour but was probably only a few minutes. Finally, Annie asked the question weighing on her mind.

"Does it upset you that I'm pregnant?"

Lia was still looking at the card with the tiny footprints. She turned it over and over again in her palm. Annie got the feeling this was some type of self-soothing ritual, like how her grandmother used to run her fingers over her rosary beads.

"No," Lia said, looking up. "It doesn't."

Annie waited for her to change her mind, to add, *Well, maybe a little*. She didn't though.

"Really? I hate other mothers," Annie said. When she told this to Nate, he'd said things like, "Come on, Annie, that's not really fair." He'd *winced*.

"Oh, I went through that," Lia said, like it was a phase three decades ago.

"I think you must be a better person than me," Annie said, trying her hand at adding a pensive giggle. It felt odd coming out of her mouth.

"No," Lia said. "I've just had more time."

THEY'RE GOING TO the thrift store to get Annie a couch. That's the mission. Lia shows up at Annie's house right on time, wearing a long, flowing white skirt. She seems like one of those ethereal, always-at-peace people. Annie continues to fluctuate between being annoyed with this and envious of it. Plain and simple, she just doesn't know how it's possible. Maybe that's why she's entertaining the idea of a friendship with Lia; so she can find out.

"I'm almost ready," Annie says, looking around for her purse. You would think it would be impossible to misplace anything in a house this small.

She finds her purse up in the loft, not remembering she'd left it there. It's a force of habit, having her purse by the bed. She keeps her phone in it, and she's used to scrolling through Facebook during insomniac hours. True masochism, really, seeing all those photos of people and their happy, alive children. Nate told her to stop, but she couldn't. It made her feel bad, yes, but that's how she was supposed to feel. "You're picking the scab," he'd said. She knew it was just a phrase—*picking the scab*—but she was appalled that he could think she was already scabbed over. Did he not see the gaping gash in the center of her chest?

Since she's been here, she's turned on her phone twice—mindlessly, accidentally—before remembering that she has cut ties with her old world. Not just the Facebook friends, but Nate, her parents. If she thinks too hard about it, she can't take a deep breath.

Lia offers to drive because she knows where the thrift store is. One Person's Trash it's called. Clever.

Their drive is pleasantly silent until—"Does he know? About the baby?" Lia's voice is cautious, soft and soothing, like the yoga teacher in the prenatal classes Annie took before Penelope was born. Lia's obviously been wondering this, waiting for the right moment to ask the question.

Now is as good a time as any. Annie's always preferred having uncomfortable conversations in the car, when you don't have to look someone in the eye. When she moved in with Nate and realized he wasn't exactly great with finances, she waited until they took a road trip to Santa Barbara to say, "So, I was reviewing the credit card charges . . ." It was their first real fight, ending, per usual, with Nate apologizing. He was always good to her that way, always willing to admit fault when there probably wasn't any. They just had different ways of doing things, of living, of feeling. Why was it so hard for a couple to accept such a simple truth?

"He doesn't know," Annie says. Then, as if to make this fact less horrifying, she added, "I didn't even know. I was literally in the driveway, leaving to come here, when the doctor called me. I had no idea. We had just begun trying for another baby before Penelope died."

Lia holds the steering wheel with both hands at six o'clock. Annie used to do this when she was a teenager. She thought it made her look cool, relaxed. Her mother hated it: "Ten and two, Annie. Ten and two."

"Do you think he'd be excited?" Lia asks, voice still soft.

Annie hasn't even thought about this. He would *say* he was excited, she knows that. Because that's the right thing to say. Whenever she asked him how his day was, for example, he'd say, "Good," even if it wasn't. "You don't want to hear about a bad day," he'd tell her when she asked how it was possible that every day was good. Nate is dutifully committed to life's designated talk tracks, the greatest hits. *Oh, sweetie, that's great news.* That's what he'd say. She can even imagine him saying something about the circle of life. In truth, he would probably be terrified to know she's pregnant. Or he should be. They're not ready for this. It's too soon, too fast. How can they be parents together when they can barely talk to each other?

"I don't know," she says. "I don't even know if I'm excited."

"It's a lot to take in," Lia says. "So soon after and all."

Annie flips down the sun visor and looks at herself in the mirror. She doesn't have a mirror in her tiny house, just a small compact one in her purse. She hasn't been wearing makeup, hasn't paid much attention at all to her appearance. Her lips are chapped. It's been dry out. She turns her head slightly to confirm the dark shadows under her eyes are real, not tricks of light.

"I look like I have two black eyes," she says, marveling. She flips up the sun visor.

"Can't sleep, right? Wide awake at three in the morning?" Lia says. She doesn't even wait for Annie to confirm. "I went to see a psychic after what happened. I was desperate, I guess. I wanted to know what happened to Ethan. She said early morning is when the ceiling is the thinnest, when we have the greatest access to the heavens. That's when nuns wake to pray. It's the most common time people die."

"Hmm," Annie says.

"Who knows if that's all bullshit," Lia says, reading Annie's mind, "but I was waking up at three for months."

"What did she say happened to him?" Annie asks. It's silly to ask. As if a psychic knows anything.

"She said he's my angel now."

That's what they all say, Annie thinks. "He's always with you," they say. "He's watching over you," they say. Idiots.

"She said she could see him, that he was at peace."

Would she tell you if he wasn't?

The bitchy thoughts continue. Annie picks at her cuticles, a nervous habit.

"You and Caleb, do you still talk?" she asks.

"We did, for a while. I mean, how do you just stop communicating with someone who's been through that with you?"

You run away, Annie thinks. *You leave.*

"But now? You're not in touch?"

"We text each other on holidays, birthdays, that kind of thing. He has a girlfriend now, which is weird."

"That is weird," Annie says. She can't imagine Nate with someone else. Or she doesn't want to imagine that. Who would he choose? What type of woman? Someone less complicated, that's for sure. Someone who was a cheerleader in high school, someone with a perpetual ponytail, someone who likes to swim in the ocean, someone whose glass is always half full, someone who says "fudge" instead of "fuck," someone who laughs at corny jokes, someone who joins clubs—book clubs and jogging clubs and cooking clubs.

"It's for the best. I don't think he wants to remember me, and I don't want to remember him. We both remind each other of Ethan."

Is this what will happen to her and Nate? She can't imagine it, occasional text messages the only remnant of what had been. But, somehow, she can't imagine going back to before either, watching their TV shows, eating pasta, having sex.

"I can't even look at Nate sometimes," Annie says. "I see Penelope in him, in certain expressions, like when he furrows his eyebrows. He's been furrowing his eyebrows a lot."

Lia gives a little shrug, eyes still fixed on the road in front of them.

"Maybe, one day, you'll be grateful for that," Lia says. "Maybe, one day, you'll love when he furrows his eyebrows because you'll get that flash of her."

Annie can't imagine feeling anything but complete agony, but she says, "Maybe."

She hates the insinuation, common among condolences-givers, that time heals all. It's so helpless, waiting for hours and days and weeks and months and years to pass, hoping enough distance from the present moment will blunt the sadness. She'd told Nate she wanted to be in a coma, to wake up months later, to skip the grieving. He'd said, as if taking her proposal seriously, "I don't think it works that way."

The parking lot in front of the thrift store is mostly empty. There is one car, a red Camry that looks to be about twenty years old. The passenger's side mirror is off, dangling by a cord. The store sign is missing a couple letters, so it reads, On Person's rash. Under the sign is a huge cardboard box filled to the brim with clothes. A couple T-shirts are on the ground, as if discarded, deemed unacceptable for the bin. Lia paws through the clothes, holds up a purple knit cardigan, assessing it. For undisclosed reasons, she puts it back, and then they go inside.

"Mornin'," a woman at the front counter says. She's clipping her nails, doesn't bother to look up. She's probably the owner of the Camry with the dangling mirror.

There are racks and racks of clothes, shoes in piles against the walls, and a few rows of household items. It's like one massive indoor yard sale.

"Furniture's over here," Lia says, leading them beyond a wall that Annie thought marked the end of the store but is really just a divider.

It's all in the back corner: chairs (so, so many chairs), couches, tables of varying heights and purposes (dining, patio, bedside, poker).

"Oh, this is perfect," Lia says, going straight toward a periwinkle-blue velveteen couch with just one long cushion. It's outlined in wood trim and has wooden claw feet.

"It's the right size," she says, sitting on it. It's big enough for two people to sit comfortably, much like Lia's couch. She finds the price tag, taped to the back of the couch.

"Only fifty bucks," she says.

Annie can't find anything wrong with it, specifically, but it's still wrong. She can't even bring herself to sit on the thing. Lia pats the cushion next to her—the miraculously unstained cushion—and Annie just shakes her head.

"I don't know," she says. Her heart is racing, like she's a panicky bride-to-be standing in a dress shop, feet not just cold but frozen.

Lia stands, not questioning Annie's rejection. She spins on her heels, points to another couch, a plaid one.

"That one's a good size too," she says.

Annie's heart is still racing though. She can't do this, the couch. It makes her tiny house more real, more permanent. She can't. Her face feels suddenly hot, a rush of heat overtaking her. She closes her eyes, but that makes her feel dizzy, like she's had too much wine. She opens them again. Lia is looking at her, mild concern mixed with bafflement, a look Annie would give Penny when she threw a temper tantrum, kind of like *Are you done yet?*

"You don't have to get anything today," Lia says.

She walks past Annie, back toward the household items, the smell of lavender in her wake. When Annie turns around, she's perusing the clocks. There are about a dozen of them, stacked on top of each other. Lia picks up a small wooden one, inspects it.

"I'm sorry," Annie says.

"You don't have to apologize," Lia says, nonchalantly, like Annie's small panic attack in the middle of a shitty thrift store is no big deal.

She holds up the clock to Annie. "What do you think?"

"I like it."

"Okay then," Lia says. She marches toward the cash register. The woman is still clipping her nails. Lia pays for the clock with two dollar bills, and they leave.

"Here," she says, when they are outside. She hands the clock to Annie. "For you."

"You don't have to do that."

"Well, you're not ready for a couch, so you can start with a clock."

She leads the way back to the car, Annie holding the clock dumbly in her hand like it's a fragile little pet bird.

"Thanks," Annie says. She supposes she can put the clock on the shelf in her tiny house and see how it feels. She can always get rid of it, if need be. Getting rid of a couch is much harder.

Start small. That's what Nate said when he told her to get out of the house, go for a walk.

"I freaked out in there, I guess," Annie says, once they are back in the car and they can speak again without looking at each other.

"It's okay," Lia says.

Why couldn't Nate just say those two words? *It's okay.*

"They had perfectly fine couches," Annie says, still feeling the need to explain herself. She blames Nate for that need to explain. He always looked at her with such longing for rational thought. "It's not just about the couch."

Lia takes her eyes off the road to look at Annie, emits one of her little laughs, and says, "You don't think I know that?"

TWENTY-ONE

JOSH is alone in Nate and Annie's house. Nate had to leave in a hurry. He got a call about the water heater at the Avenida Oso duplex leaking again. And then, not five minutes later, Marcus—who Nate refers to as the Big Kahuna—called to say he'd driven by the Via Salvador triplex and was "not pleased." Those were his words. Nate had answered the call on speaker. "I thought I told you to hire a gardener. The lawn is dying."

Nate mouthed "Fuck," but out loud, to Marcus, he said, "I'm on it, Mr. Sandoval."

"What's that arcade game?" Nate asked Josh on his way out the door. "The one where you hit one thing and another pops up?"

"Whac-A-Mole?" Josh said. The only reason he knows that is because his mom's favorite bar was next door to an arcade. He spent hundreds of hours there.

"Yes. That's what my life feels like right now," Nate said. "Whac-A-Fucking-Mole."

"Is there anything I can do to help?" Josh asked.

Nate motioned toward the laptop sitting in front of Josh and said, "You are helping. This program you're working on is going to be clutch. I'm just in over my head."

Josh is almost done with the computer program, then he'll get started on redoing Nate's website. Once those projects are done, Nate will realize he doesn't have much need for Josh. Or Mike, rather. The name thing is confusing as hell. Josh has been working at Nate's house for five days straight and, on three separate occasions, Josh didn't respond when Nate said, "Hey, Mike." Nate probably thinks he's a fucking weirdo.

Somehow, before the projects are finished and Josh is effectively out of Nate's life, Josh has to think of a way to let Nate know where Annie is. Tomorrow will be two weeks since she left, and anyone can see Nate is stressed. He might say it's about work, but Josh knows better.

Josh keeps waiting for Nate to confide in him, say, "My wife is missing." But Nate is clearly uninterested in sharing his life's grievances. He continues to say his wife's out of town on business. The other night, Josh stayed kind of late and Nate offered him a beer. With that dose of liquid courage, Josh dared to ask Nate if his wife traveled "like this" a lot. Nate said, straight-faced, "Not a lot, no. This is a long trip." Josh hasn't even asked what she does for work because he doesn't want to watch Nate squirm in search of a lie.

It was stupid to mention Rolling Stone Co-Op to Nate. It seemed like a decent idea at the time. But Nate didn't take the bait. If he'd just admit that his wife is missing, Josh could say, "Didn't you say she was into tiny houses?" He could lead Nate to the truth. But no. Josh has tried to force the issue. That night with the beers, he asked Nate, "Did you think any more about checking out that tiny house place?"

Nate looked at him strangely, like he had no idea what he was talking about. "Oh, no," he said finally, "not yet."

Josh clings to the "yet," hoping Nate will have a middle-of-the-night epiphany. Annie had expressed interest in tiny houses. Why can't Nate see that she might be pursuing that interest?

It seems so obvious to Josh. Nate might think Josh is a fucking weirdo, but sometimes Josh thinks Nate is a fucking moron.

In any case, Josh's ruined any chance of sending an anonymous note in the mail: *Your wife is at Rolling Stone Co-Op.* Now that he's mentioned the name of the place to Nate, the anonymity is blown. Nate would confront him, say, "How do you know where she is?" The whole awful truth would come out, and Nate would hate him forever. Josh hates himself enough for what happened; he can't handle Nate's hate too. And Annie—he can't be responsible for causing her more pain.

Of course, he could just finish up his projects for Nate, disappear, and then send the note. That's always an option, though it would mean he could never see Nate again. He likes the idea of seeing Nate again. Annie too. Keeping tabs on them will keep him sane, he thinks.

Quite the pickle. His mom always says that.

IT'S WEIRD BEING alone in the house. He continues to work for a little while after Nate leaves and then gets up and looks out the window, peering through the shutters to make sure Nate's car isn't in the driveway. He doesn't want to get caught snooping again. When Nate saw Josh staring at the family photos on the bookshelf that first day he came over, Nate got that "you're a fucking weirdo" look in his eyes. In that moment, Josh almost blurted out, "I'm the guy who hit your daughter." Like confessional Tourette's or something. He just couldn't handle the "you're a fucking weirdo" look in Nate's eyes. He felt the need to explain.

He didn't explain, of course. It's not just that he doesn't want Nate to hate him. It's that, more and more, he wonders if confessing his identity and delivering some heartfelt apology is selfish. Maybe Nate wouldn't even want that from the guy who hit his daughter. If he did want that, or if he wanted to punch the guy in the face, wouldn't he have come after Josh? Tracked him down? Maybe Nate doesn't want to even know the guy. Maybe he would consider it a burden to put a face to that guy. Maybe he just wants to pretend the truck was driverless and go about his life.

After all, he continues to say his wife is out of town on business.

Josh wanders down the hallway, previously unchartered territory. Whenever he comes over to work, he walks straight through the front door and sits at the dining table, which is part of the kitchen and overlooks the family room—one of those open floor plans that were all the rage on the home renovation shows Jess watched. He's gone into the hallway only to use the bathroom. He's never stepped into the bedrooms. There's an unspoken understanding that those are off-limits, too personal.

Now that Nate is gone, though—whacking moles at the rental properties—Josh can't help but venture beyond the bathroom. There are three bedroom doors, all half-closed. It's not like he's looking for something, specifically. He's just curious.

He pushes the first door open. It's Penelope's room. He stands in the doorway, his hands gripping the frame. He leans in, looks around, hesitant to plant a foot into the space that used to be hers. It's like he thinks it's another dimension, that room, and if he steps into it, he might not be able to return.

The bed isn't made. The pink polka-dot comforter lies askew. They seem to be preserving the room, leaving it exactly how it was the day she died. There's a book next to her pillow—*Love You Forever*. Did Nate or Annie read that book to her the night before the accident? It would seem so appropriate. It makes Josh think of Rachel Gomez in high school. She flipped her Jeep Cherokee on the freeway and died instantly. The night before, she'd baked cookies in the shape of angels. Everyone said it meant that, on some level, she knew her fate. It meant there was a bigger plan that all of those left behind had to accept. Josh couldn't accept it though. To him, it was better to assume there was no plan, that it was an unlucky accident the day after she happened to bake angel cookies, than to think there was a plan that included a young girl dying.

A bunch of other books line shelves on the walls, one cover stacked over another. There's a toy kitchen set, complete with toy pots and plastic food. It appears Penelope was in the middle of making fake spaghetti. A giant wooden *P*, painted pink, is on the wall above the kitchen set. Next to it, a framed print reads, "Sweet Child of Mine." Like the Guns N' Roses song.

No wonder Annie left, he thinks. It's less shocking that she went to the tiny house community than it is that Nate continues to live here, walking by this room every day. How can he stand it?

Josh dares to take a step inside. He sits on the bed, wondering if he's somehow disturbing the scene. What if he leaves an indentation in the comforter that Nate notices? What if Nate knows every little thing about this perfectly preserved room?

Her closet door is open, revealing shelves stuffed with clothes and shoes. A tiny jean jacket is on the floor, next to the pink polka-dot hamper—matching the bed comforter. A stuffed dog and a plastic baby doll sit against the dresser, facing each other, as if in conversation. It's these little details—how can Nate stand it?

Josh lies down on the bed, looks up at the ceiling, thinks about how Penelope must have done the same every night before falling asleep. He flips open the *Love You Forever* book, thumbs through it. The same little passage repeats throughout:

> *I'll love you forever,*
> *I'll like you for always,*
> *As long as I'm living*
> *my baby you'll be.*

It's a weird thing for a children's book to mention: *As long as I'm living*. It seems like kids shouldn't have to consider that there is something besides "living."

Josh hears Nate's car pull into the driveway. He hops off the bed, doing his best to arrange the book and comforter exactly as he found them. By the time Nate is opening the front door, he's back at the dining table, staring at the computer screen, a look of contemplation put upon his face.

Nate makes a beeline straight for the fridge, takes out a beer, cracks it open, and chugs it with impressive ease.

"How'd it go?" Josh asks, though everything about Nate suggests it didn't go well.

"Fucking water heater is leaking again," he says. "I didn't even get over to the Salvador place because I've got a fucking flood on my hands. My HVAC guy is heading over. I figure I'll go by Salvador and then head back over there to make sure the repairs are done right this time."

"Do you want me to go by Salvador?" Josh asks. He should make himself useful, so Nate will want to keep him around even after the website work is done.

Nate crushes the can in his palm like he's at a frat party and tosses it into the trash.

"If you could, that would be awesome," Nate says.

"Well, I'm your assistant, so I can do whatever you want."

Nate relaxes his shoulders away from his ears, as if an actual load has been lifted.

"Okay, yeah, go by there if you can. You remember where it is, right? See how bad the landscaping looks. Then if you can research some gardeners, that would be great. My usual guy says he can't do it."

"No problem," Josh says, already googling gardeners, perusing their online reviews, their pricing. "I'll have options to you in a couple hours."

Nate nods along to this plan while scrolling through his phone. His eyes shift from side to side rapidly. He mutters, "always something" to himself.

"Nate," Josh says. He has to at least try to ask.

Nate doesn't look up, but says, "Yep?"

"You okay?"

Please, just tell me, Josh thinks. *Let me help you.*

Now Nate looks up. "Fine," he says. "Why?"

Because you seem like you're losing it, that's why.

"You just seem stressed," Josh says, already aware that these efforts to get Nate to talk are in vain.

"I *am* stressed," Nate says, agitated. "Look, I gotta go, but let's talk about the gardener situation in a couple hours. I'll call you."

And just like that, he's out the door, gone again.

JOSH PARKS HIS car several blocks away because he worries Nate will recognize his Civic as the one that's often parked on his street. He's even invented a grandmother, whom he claims to visit before going to Nate's house to work. The lies just keep coming.

The long walk to his car is as annoying as it is necessary. Today, because of Nate's sense of urgency, Josh jogs the last block, wondering how in the world Nate runs for miles.

He drives by the Via Salvador triplex, and it does, in fact, look like shit. The small lawn out front is completely dead, just a patch of yellow straw, and all the rose bushes that line the front of the house are dried up. A passerby would assume deadbeats lived here. Josh takes a few pictures and texts them to Nate.

Shit, Nate texts back.

Looking up gardeners now, Josh texts.

Back at the house, he compiles a list. It takes him just a half hour to find five well-rated gardening services for Nate to evaluate. He's even called to verify their pricing and availability and then input all this information into his computer program for future reference. He can't wait to tell Nate, to be responsible for easing his mind. He's not back from the water heater emergency yet.

Josh wanders down the hallway again, peeks into the second bedroom. An office, it looks like, with a desk, chair, and futon. It's a mess, file folders everywhere—probably Nate's attempts at organizing himself. The third bedroom is Nate and Annie's. At first glance, there's no sign of her. But then Josh opens the closet and sees all her clothes hanging there alongside Nate's. That must be weird for Nate, to paw through her shirts and dresses while getting ready every day. The bathroom is littered with products only women use—face creams and lotions and potions and whatever. Only one toothbrush, though. If Nate's at all observant, he must realize she went somewhere purposefully. She's not *gone* gone.

Josh hears the front door open and bolts out of the bedroom as fast as he can. Thankfully, Nate's looking down, fiddling with his keys, when Josh emerges in the hallway. To Nate, it probably looks like Josh just came out of the bathroom.

"Water heater okay?" Josh says.

"I sure hope so." Nate collapses onto the couch, lets his head fall against the back cushion. He closes his eyes. His chest rises and falls rapidly, like he's hyperventilating or something.

"You okay?" Josh asks.

Nate opens his eyes but doesn't look at Josh. He stares straight ahead, at the television mounted on the wall in front of him.

"I'm fine," he says.

Josh doesn't buy it for a second. Annie has to come home, and soon, or else Nate is going to have a mental breakdown and Josh is going to witness the whole thing.

"Mike?" Nate says, finally looking at Josh.

Maybe this is it, the moment Nate admits his wife has disappeared: *The truth is my wife isn't on a business trip. She's missing. I need help.*

"Yeah?" Josh says eagerly.

We can find her! That's what he'll say. *Let's make a list of everything we know. Didn't you say she was interested in tiny houses?* Within twenty-four hours, they'll be on their way to Rolling Stone Co-Op and Nate will be thanking Josh profusely for making his life whole again.

"You gotta do me a favor," Nate says.

"Yeah?"

"Please stop asking me if I'm okay."

TWENTY-TWO

NATE has marked this day in his mental calendar with a big X. Today is two weeks since Annie left. Today is the day she's supposed to be back. Mike is here, sitting at the dining table like usual, and Nate keeps expecting Annie to walk through the front door. He imagines she wouldn't be dramatic about it. She wouldn't throw open the door and yell, "I'm back!" No, she'd walk in like it was any other day and just say, "Hey." And then they would talk about everything, whatever she wanted to talk about. Nate would say how much he missed her. He would apologize, though he wouldn't be able to pinpoint his exact wrongdoings if she asked. He just knows that he must have fucked up if she left for two weeks.

Or more.

If she doesn't come back today, it will be more than two weeks. If she doesn't come back today, part of him thinks she never will.

"I'm going to set up the website so you can update it on your own when I'm done," Mike says. He rambles about the "platform" he's using, listing its attributes, touting its benefits. Nate isn't listening. It's like he's underwater, aware of the conversation going on above the surface but unable to decipher it.

"Sounds good," Nate says, hoping that's the correct response. It must be, because Mike nods and resumes doing whatever he's doing.

Nate's phone buzzes with another email from Marcus. Ever since the landscaping snafu at the Salvador property, Marcus has insisted on daily check-ins, which make Nate feel like a child in need of tending. So he let the lawn and rose bushes die—it's not the end of the world. It's not like the roof caved in. *Knock on wood*, he thinks as he taps his knuckles on the butcher block counter. Mike looks up. He's like an anxious dog, this kid, aware of every little sound.

Just then, Nate hears footsteps approaching the front door. It's too early for the mailman or UPS guy, and he's not expecting any packages anyway.

Maybe it's Annie.

Right on time.

Maybe she guessed that two weeks was Nate's deadline.

Maybe they know each other better than he thinks.

He stands still, as if his feet are glued to the stone tile. He doesn't want to go to the door. If it's her, he wants to let her come in on her own. She won't want him bombarding her with a hug and questions.

If it's not her . . . Well, it has to be her.

There's a trio of knocks. Annie wouldn't knock. This is her house. Unless she doesn't think of it as her house anymore.

Nate remains standing on his little square, as if it's his life raft in a tumultuous sea. Mike turns around in his chair, eyebrows raised like *You gonna get that?*

Reluctantly, Nate goes to the door. He turns the knob slowly, as if he's in a horror movie and the much-feared supernatural monster is on the other side of the door.

"Nate. So you *are* alive."

It's Beth. He must have about forty unanswered text messages and ten voice mails from her sitting in his phone. She looks pissed off. She has a right to be. The last she heard from him, he said Annie left and he didn't know where she went. She probably resorted to calling Annie's parents for information. They, unlike him, are probably more than willing to talk about everything ad nauseam. At least, that's what he told himself to make himself feel better.

"I'm sorry," he says immediately.

She walks past him into the house like it's her own home. At one point, in what feels like a very distant past, it was like her own home. She used to come over all the time. She and Annie had what they called their "date nights," named in jesting reference to all the women on Facebook who posted pictures of their special outings with their husbands, like *Look at us, we are so in love.* Annie never liked other women, Beth being the one exception. Sometimes Beth would come over, and they would just sit in the backyard and drink wine. Sometimes they would go out somewhere, leaving Nate and Beth's husband, Todd, to watch the kids. Nate became friends with Todd by necessity. They have very little in common. Todd is some kind of investment guy and spends all his free time golfing. He's nice enough, though. And Nate knew it made Annie happy that they could all get along harmoniously. Before Penelope died, they'd been talking about doing a vacation together—Yosemite, maybe, or Lake Arrowhead if Yosemite seemed too ambitious. Then Penelope died, and it was like Beth and Todd and their kids did too.

"What the hell, Nate?" Beth says. Her arms are crossed against her chest, and she's got that look in her eye, the same look she had when she pulled Nate aside a month into his relationship with Annie and gave him her version of the you-better-not-hurt-my-friend speech. If he remembers right, her exact words were "You better be as great as you fucking seem."

Maybe I'm not as great as I fucking seem.

"I've been meaning to get back to you, I just—"

"It would take all of five seconds," she says, arms still crossed. "And I've tried to come by here, like, six times, and you're never home. What the hell?"

She keeps walking into the kitchen. Lucy greets her. She takes a moment to forget her fury and nuzzle Lucy's face. When she finishes with that, she turns around, sees Mike, and startles.

"Jesus!" she says.

"Hi," Mike says. He gives an awkward wave.

The last thing Nate wants is for Mike to hear about the drama of his wife being missing. He hasn't been able to talk to Annie's best friend about it; he sure as hell doesn't want to open up to this twenty-two-year-old.

"Can we talk outside?" Nate says to Beth in a whisper, nodding toward the front porch. He shifts his eyes in Mike's direction, shakes his head lightly, hoping Beth understands this means they shouldn't discuss things in front of him.

She gives Nate a weird look and rolls her eyes. "Yeah, whatever," she says.

She marches back outside with Nate following behind. He shuts the door and checks to make sure the front window is shut.

"Who's the kid?" she says. When she sits on the wicker love seat, a cloud of dust fills the air. "Nice," she mutters.

"He's working on a website for me."

"A website? Really?" she says. Her whole appearance changes suddenly. She looks sympathetic, concerned. "Are you offering a reward and all that?"

A reward? What is she talking about? Then Nate understands: she thinks the website is for Annie, to alert the public to her disappearance and collect leads or something. Should Nate be creating a "Find Annie" website? He shakes off this idea. *Trust her note*, he thinks. *Trust her note.*

"No, it's just a website for my work," he says. He knows this will baffle her, but he isn't quite prepared for the shrill, you-can't-be-fucking-serious laugh that comes out of her mouth.

"*Work?*" she says—or spits, rather. "How are you even thinking about *work?*"

It's easier than thinking about Annie.

"I'm trying to just go on with things. I'm assuming she'll be back. The note says she'll be back."

Beth looks skeptical.

"This note," she says. "Can I see it?"

"Sure," he says. "But I can just recite it for you too. I've read it a thousand times."

"Okay," she says, "go."

He does. Certain lines echo in his mind after he's done.

I just need to get away for a while.

I don't want you to worry.

I'm okay.

I don't want to be found.

Please don't come looking.

This is good for us.

Beth nods, taking it in. Finally, she says, "I want to see it." As if she doesn't believe him. As if she wants to confirm the handwriting is Annie's. As if she thinks Nate is a suspect in the disappearance.

"Fine," Nate says. He goes back inside, to the kitchen junk drawer where the note is still stashed.

"Everything okay?" Mike asks.

Fucking fabulous.

"Yeah," Nate says. He slams the drawer shut and goes back outside.

He hands the note to Beth, watches her scan it. When she's done, she places it next to her on the seat and sighs heavily.

"It's just so weird," she says, the bitchy tone completely gone.

"I know."

She looks beyond Nate, at the palm tree behind him. "Steve and Sheryl want the police involved," she says.

He knew she must have talked to them. He's been trying to avoid them, though they still "pop in." Sheryl is working on getting a GPS trace of Annie's phone. It's hard to get approval to do that, apparently. Annie would have to be a minor, or there would have to be obvious foul play. Besides, Nate keeps telling Sheryl that Annie's phone is off. The note says so. Sheryl seems to think Nate is maliciously discouraging her whenever he speaks the truth.

"They're not going to get involved. She's a grown woman who left a note saying she's going away for a while," he says.

Beth nods. "I know, but Sheryl will keep trying anyway. You know how she is." She looks straight at him, bites her lip. "They keep saying you must know where she is."

"I don't."

She ignores his denial, talks right over him: "And I see why they think that. I mean, you're working like normal. You don't seem that freaked out. It's like you *know* she's okay."

"I don't *know* that," he says. "I *assume* that. I have to assume that."

She smiles a little. "Annie always said you were annoyingly optimistic."

He doesn't like this way of talking, as if Annie is gone forever.

"This one time, she said you asked her, 'What's the worst that could happen?' I don't even remember what it was about.

But she said she was appalled you even asked her that, like you had no understanding of her ability to think up the most horrible catastrophes."

He's not sure if this little antidote is meant to compliment him or make him look like an idiot.

"We balance each other out," he says, sticking to the present tense, committed to the idea that Annie is not gone forever.

"Yeah . . ." Beth says. She looks back at the palm tree again.

"She never said anything to you? About leaving?" Nate says.

If Annie were to tell anyone, it would be Beth. She confided in Beth more than she did in Nate. She always said she hated when women referred to their husbands as their "best friends." She said, "Husbands are husbands. Best friends are best friends. They are good for different things." Nate's always assumed Beth knows things about Annie that he doesn't, and he's been fine with that, until now. Now he has to wonder if he's been gypped, if he's been denied access to some important part of his wife, a part of her that would want to up and leave.

Beth shakes her head, though.

"We weren't really talking much, you know, since Penelope died," she says.

She picks up the note, scans it again. Nate knows how this goes. You read and read and read, hoping to find some clue you missed the previous time.

"Yeah, she wasn't talking much to me, either," Nate says.

They are bonded, sadly, by this fact, by Annie's isolation.

"Where the hell would she go?" Beth says, looking straight at Nate again.

"I have no idea. And I thought for sure she'd be back by now."

Beth puts down the note again.

"Do you think she would . . . ?"

Nate knows what she means, and he absolutely doesn't think that. Can't think that.

"No," he says with confidence. "I don't."

But then a moment passes, and he can't help but ask, "Do you?"

She takes a deep breath, as if she's considering the possibility for the first time, though she's probably thought about it again and again.

"I don't know," she says. "You know about what happened in college, right?" She asks this tentatively, like she's not absolutely sure if Annie's told him about this part of her past. Does Beth really think Annie wouldn't tell him that? Did Annie insinuate to her best friend that she'd kept secrets from Nate?

"Yeah," he says. "Of course I know about that."

They both nod together, solemnly.

"I just don't think she would," she says. "Or not like this, if that makes sense."

"It does."

When Annie tried to kill herself in college, it was with Advil of all things. There was no elaborate scheme. She left a note that said she couldn't do it anymore. She apologized to her parents. These are all facts, known by Nate and Beth and Steve and Sheryl. It doesn't make sense that Annie would go away somewhere to kill herself and leave a note saying she was fine.

"Her toothbrush is gone," he says. "And our big suitcase. And some photos."

Beth looks at him, mouth agape. "You're seriously just telling me this now?" she says. "That's very important information. Do Steve and Sheryl know that? They didn't mention it to me."

He can't remember if they were aware of the missing items.

"You should probably make sure you tell them," she says.

"It's a good thing, then, right?" he says.

"Absolutely."

"You think it means she's okay?"

"Well, she wouldn't give a shit about her teeth if she was going to kill herself."

The way she says this, with such definitiveness, relieves him. He exhales a breath that feels like it's been trapped in his chest since Annie left.

"Maybe she wanted to take a trip before, you know, doing the deed," Nate says. A small voice of doubt has been whispering this possibility in the very back of his mind.

Beth shrugs. "She still wouldn't care about her teeth, would she?"

He doesn't like the question—*Would she?* She's slightly doubtful too.

"I don't know, but I don't think she would write a note full of lies," he says.

"I agree," she says, with an emphatic nod.

She stands, apparently ready to go, satisfied with the visit.

"I wish you would have told me all this sooner. I've barely slept," she says.

"I'm sorry."

She gives him a hug, long and tight. "I know," she says. "I forgive you."

"I'll call you if I hear anything," he says.

"I'll call you even if nothing has changed," she says, "and you better fucking pick up."

Nate goes back inside and finds Mike standing next to the couch, looking guilty. Was he listening?

"I, uh, think I'm at a good stopping place with the website," Mike says.

He's trying to make it seem like he just got up to stretch his legs and come notify Nate of his progress. But the expression on his face says he was listening at the door like a gossip-hungry high school girl.

"Okay, then," Nate says. It comes out harsh. Nate can't help it. He isn't sure why he cares so much if this kid knows about Annie being gone. He does though. It's his personal business. He doesn't want Mike's, or anyone's, pity. He doesn't want advice or consolation. What would a twenty-two-year-old know about anything anyway?

"I'll probably work at home tomorrow," the kid says.

At least he's observant, aware of Nate's irritation. At least he's not saying something like *I couldn't help but overhear, and I'm so sorry.* If one more person tells Nate they're "so sorry," he will lose it in the way everyone expects him to.

"Sounds good," Nate says.

Mike goes to the dining table, closes his laptop, and shoves it in his bag.

"It's looking really good, the website," Mike says, slinging the bag over his shoulder. He gives Nate a smile that also reads like an apology.

"Cool," Nate says.

Mike says, "Okay, see ya," and leaves.

Nate opens the kitchen junk drawer and puts the note back inside, but not before reading it one more time.

This is good for us, promise. I love you and just want us both to be happy again, if that's possible.

He slams the drawer shut.

Of course it's possible, he thinks.

This is the first time he's let himself be angry at Annie. He reopens the drawer for the sole purpose of getting to slam it again.

Just come home and see.

TWENTY-THREE

ANNIE appreciated morning sickness when she was pregnant with Penelope. Beth thought she was crazy, described the waves of nausea throughout the day ("It's not just the fucking morning," she'd said) as complete hell. Annie just liked that there was an obvious symptom to remind her that the baby was in there, growing.

Now though, she agrees with Beth's past assessment: she was crazy to "enjoy" morning sickness. Maybe this time around is worse. It must be. With Penelope, she remembers the queasiness went away if she ate a small snack. That doesn't seem to be the case now. Now, if she thinks about it too much, she throws up. She's vomited three times in as many days. She never vomited with Penelope.

"You sure there's just one baby in there?" Lia says.

Lia has been coming over every day since the nausea hit. She makes tea and cooks macaroni and cheese for Annie (the from-the-box kind, because that's all that sounds appealing). Annie lies in bed, and Lia sits next to her because Annie still doesn't have a couch or anywhere else to sit. Annie hasn't been able to work on the houses much. Lia is her liaison, telling everyone that she has a bad flu. They've agreed, Lia and Annie, that nobody needs to know about the pregnancy yet.

"Unless that old doctor is blind, which is a valid possibility considering his age," Annie says, "there's just one." She looks down at her belly. Anyone else would say it's still flat, but Annie knows her body. She can see just the slightest bump. With Penelope, her pregnancy wasn't obvious to anyone but her until the fifth month. Even Nate claimed he couldn't see much of a difference until that fifth month. It's funny how simultaneously aware and unaware men are of women's bodies.

"Maybe it's a boy this time," Lia says. "They say the sex of the baby affects the body differently."

"Maybe," Annie says.

She keeps remembering how Penelope said she wanted a "brudder" named after Curious George. Annie doesn't let herself fantasize much about this baby-to-be—she still can't quite believe the baby's real—but when she does, she imagines him or her as Georgie. Boy or girl, the name will be Georgie.

"Did you get sick when you were pregnant with Ethan?" she asks Lia.

Annie's never sure how much she should ask about Ethan. She wants so badly to know why he died. *Why, why, why.* She's so hung up on the why. Lia never talks about that. She may have given up long ago on ever knowing the answer to that one-word question.

"Is it weird that I don't even remember?" Lia says.

It would be hypocritical of Annie to call anyone weird.

"It's like I've blocked out all of it," Lia says.

"Protective amnesia," Annie says. "I don't remember Penelope's accident. I mean, I know it *happened*, but I can't recall any details."

Lia probably has questions about Penelope, about the accident, but she spares Annie the asking of them. They have an unspoken agreement in regards to each other's tragedies.

"I should probably get back out there," Lia says, looking out the window above the bed.

The Alaskan client is picking up his house tomorrow. Today is the day they stick a gigantic bow on the front door and put a welcome plant on the porch.

"Have you thought any more about what James said?" Annie asks.

James said it's time to start building a new house, and it's Lia's turn, if she's interested in designing hers. That is, after all, what most people do when they come to the Rolling Stone Co-Op.

"I don't want to do it," Lia says. "I'm afraid to tell him. I'm afraid he'll think it's stupid that I even came here."

"James doesn't seem like the judgmental type," Annie says.

"Like . . . how can I possibly know if that's the future I want—me, alone, in a tiny house? Maybe I want to have a boyfriend again, a husband. Maybe I want a family one day."

Such brave daydreams, Annie thinks, for someone who knows what it's like to lose it all.

"What about you?" Lia says.

"Me?" Annie says, her voice coming out timid, meek. She doesn't know about her. She feels more convinced than ever that she knows nothing at all.

"You don't know if you're going back to Nate, do you?" Lia says.

Annie shakes her head. "Not yet."

Lia gives a small smile, a smile that says, *That's okay. Everything in time.* Then she crawls off the bed and climbs down the ladder.

"If you feel better, come on out," she says before she leaves.

TODAY MARKS FIFTEEN days since Annie left. Fifteen days. She's thought about Nate during every single one of those fifteen days. In the time they've been in each other's lives—this summer will be eight years since they met—they've never gone this long without talking. A few months after they got married, Nate went on a weeklong backpacking trip in the Sierras with his cousin. He didn't have cell reception. That was the longest they ever spent apart, and Annie hated every minute of it. She tried to be enthusiastic on his behalf, said things like, "You're going to have so much fun" and "Take so many pictures" before he left. But she hated being away from him. She told Beth, "I think I'm coming down with something," because all of her limbs seemed heavy, and she just wanted to sleep. The embarrassing reality was that she was going through withdrawal from him. There was no other explanation for it. See, in those days, not an hour went by without some kind of communication with Nate. They texted like crazy-in-love teenagers, bombarding each other with impulsive "I can't stop thinking of you"s in the middle of boring, ordinary days. And they had this thing about texting each other bizarre facts. Annie still remembers some of the best ones:

Maine is the closest US state to Africa.

Anne Frank was born in the same year as Barbara Walters.

Hippo milk is pink.

Armadillos nearly always give birth to identical quadruplets.

Honey never spoils.

Turtles can breathe out of their butts.

They hadn't played that little game in years, since before Penelope was born. But they still talked all the time. It was weird to go a few hours without a call or text. Until Penelope died. Then it was like they completely forgot how to be with each other. Then it became mostly silent.

"It's weird—I'm not depressed here," she told Lia last night. "It's always been part of me, the depression. Sometimes it goes

dormant, like a volcano, but I always fear it will erupt again."
Then she admitted something that's been on the border between
the back and front of her mind: "Sometimes, when I'm really
desperate, I think God took Penelope because he knew she'd
inherit my depression. He was sparing her."

"I don't think there's any reason God took her from you,"
Lia said.

"That's almost worse. If there's no reason, then that just
means life's a crapshoot."

Lia nodded but didn't say anything, letting Annie come to
the conclusion herself that this was probably the case.

"It's good you're not depressed, though," Lia said. "Right?"

"It's just weird."

Maybe it's the pregnancy hormones working their magic, but
she tends to think it's not just that. It's something to do with
being away, with not having to walk by Penelope's room every
day, with not having to feel Nate's impatience and judgment and
frustration, with not having to see herself as a burden, with not
having the pressure to "move on."

"It makes sense," Lia said. "Here, you have space from
everything that happened."

How ironic, to find so much space in a hundred-square-foot
house.

The sad truth is that she doubts she can have this peace
back at home, with Nate. She misses him because she's used
to him being there, but she's still angry at him. She thinks of
the way he looked at her in those weeks after Penelope died,
like he didn't understand her at all, like he couldn't stand
who she'd become. She resents him for refusing to share her
sadness. Did he not love Penelope that much? Had she really
married someone so cold? She keeps wondering if maybe they

were compatible when life was light and easy, but not now. Fair-weather spouses, or something. There are couples who can survive trauma and tragedy, and there are those who, well, can't. She keeps wondering about the vows "till death do us part." They don't specify whose death. For Nate and Annie, it could very well be *till our child's death do us part*.

So no, she doesn't know yet if she'll go home.

What she does know is that she won't leave him wondering. He's probably worried, unless he doesn't have capacity for that emotion either. Her parents are definitely worried, though. She hopes they're taking comfort in the note. She was in a hurry when she wrote it, but she tried to make it clear that she's okay. She tried to make it clear that they need to let her do this. She will call when she has a resolution. She will.

THE CURRENT WAVE of nausea crashes and then retreats. The reprieve is instant. She changes into a pair of jeans and a sweatshirt, drags a brush through her hair. She must look like shit. It's nice, really, that she doesn't have a full-length mirror here to confirm. Her sneakers are sitting next to the front door, a pair of socks stuffed into one of the shoes. She puts them on and goes outside, taking a moment to let her eyes adjust to the brightness.

They're all in the construction area—Lia, Matt, Ken, Dawn, and James. Ken sees her first, shouts, "Well, look what the cat dragged in." They all turn and wave as she approaches.

"You feeling better?" Dawn asks. She scans Annie up and down. It's obvious from the glimmer of suspicion in her eyes that she knows, somehow, that Annie's pregnant.

"I am," Annie says.

"I wonder if it's something you ate," James says. Men, so oblivious to things women know intuitively.

"Maybe," Annie says. If the morning sickness comes back tomorrow, there's not going to be an easy way to explain why she's incapacitated yet again. She just hopes the worst is over. If it's not, everyone will know what Dawn seems to have already figured out.

"You're just in time for the bow," Lia says.

The bow is big and red. It's just like the one Nate stuck on the Prius when he bought it for Annie—a birthday present. There are those Lexus commercials around Christmastime featuring people surprising their significant others with bow-adorned cars. Annie thought they were absurd, those commercials. She couldn't fathom making such a big, nonrefundable purchase for someone without their official participation and agreement. She wasn't the type for that kind of radical surprise. But then Nate went and bought her a Prius based on a few occasions when she'd mentioned how much they could save on gas "and help the environment too," she'd said, "because we're supposed to care about that." Sure, she needed a new car; her Honda had surpassed 200,000 miles. But it was still a shock to see the Prius in the driveway.

"You like it?" Nate asked.

There was no suitable answer besides "I love it." But, in reality, she always wished he'd gotten the dark interior. She hated the tan. It's things like this, the surprise Prius, that make Annie wonder if she and Nate are more different than she ever realized.

"You want to do the honors?" Ken says, holding out the red bow to Annie.

She raises her hands like people do in front of cops to show they're not holding a weapon.

"You guys have worked much harder on this house than I have," she says.

"Let's make it a group effort," Dawn says. That's Dawn—all about group efforts. Matt rolls his eyes, but with a smile so it comes across as good-natured.

The six of them approach the house with the bow. Dawn says, "One, two, three," and they all press the bow onto the door.

"Ta-da," Dawn says.

"What time's he coming to pick it up?" Matt asks.

"Sometime tomorrow," James says. "He's driving down with his wife. From Alaska! Talked to him yesterday, and he was in San Francisco."

With his wife, Annie thinks. She can't imagine living in a tiny house with someone else. There's just not enough space. Then again, the Alaskan's house is larger than the others; it's almost three hundred square feet. Still, though. Nate and Annie couldn't tolerate each other in a thousand square feet. Frankly, they probably couldn't tolerate each other in a hundred thousand square feet.

"I always assumed living in a tiny house was a solo thing," Annie says.

"It will be for me," Ken says. "Otherwise, there would be a high risk of homicide."

Everyone but Annie laughs. Yes, Nate would kill her if they lived in a tiny house. Well, not *kill* her. She's being dramatic. He would leave her, though, which would be so much worse.

"I don't even know if I should get a dog," Matt says.

"Small dog would be fine," Dawn says. "I bet you could even live in a tiny house with a child." She gives Annie the quickest of little winks.

"Who said anything about a *kid*?" Matt says. Matt speaks of having children the way Annie used to before she had a completely unexpected change of heart. He sees them as a drain on time and resources—his own and the earth's. Annie doesn't dare tell him he'll change his mind. She hated every person who told her that. She still can't help but wonder if God took Penelope from her because she used to think like Matt.

"I wasn't talking about you, specifically," Dawn says to Matt. "We all know your thoughts on procreation."

"My kids would have loved a tiny house," Ken says. He hasn't mentioned his children since Annie's been here. They must be grown, living on their own, in different states, probably.

"Kids should be playing outside most of the time anyway," Dawn adds.

Annie used to agree with this idea of kids playing outside. Now she wishes she had kept Penelope indoors, always. If she had, Penelope would still be alive. She fears for the baby growing inside her. She wonders how she'll ever be able to let go of his hand.

"Enough about kids," Matt says.

"Amen," James says, which is the closest he gets to expressing an opinion on the matter.

Everyone gets silent, waiting for someone to step up and change the subject.

James assumes the responsibility. "So, Lia here says she's not going to build a house for herself," he says. "Which means you're next in line, Allie."

Allie. It still throws her off.

"I'll have to think about it," Annie says.

"I think Allie's got a man in her life," Dawn says, with another wink.

Dawn seems to be the only one interested in this potential gossip. The men have started a side conversation about what work they're going to do on Matt's house today. It's no longer just a trailer, Matt's house. They've started building the wood skeleton. He wants a cabin-style house, like Ken's. Slowly, they wander over to his work site about a hundred feet away.

"Or she *had* a man in her life," Dawn says.

Instinctively, Annie touches her ring finger. She took off her wedding band on the drive to Rolling Stone Co-Op, put it in the center console of the Prius like it was spare change. It's weird not to wear it. Sometimes she looks down and panics, thinking she's lost it. It always takes a moment to get her bearings. It's like when you wake up in a hotel room and don't know where you are or why you're there.

"Who cares?" Lia says. "It's her business."

"I'm just curious," Dawn says with a playful smile that means no harm. She saunters off and joins the guys at Matt's house.

"She is so annoying sometimes," Lia says.

"Yeah."

"What's wrong?" Lia says. She knows Annie so well already. It's both heartening and unnerving.

"I was just thinking there's no way Nate and I could live in a tiny house together," she says. "We would last a day, maybe."

"That bad, huh?"

"The way he looked at me . . ." she says. "It's, like, this person you thought would love you through anything saying with his eyes that he doesn't know you at all. Doesn't *want* to know this version of you."

"He was scared," Lia says. "Grief is terrifying."

"Well, I was scared too," Annie says. It comes out angrier than intended. She *is* angry, though. Why couldn't Nate just hold her? Why couldn't he just sit with her instead of running—literally, running—away? At their wedding, the officiant said something like, "When things get hard, talk to each other the way you talk to

Lucy." All the guests laughed. Annie laughed. She never thought it was advice they would actually need to take seriously. If Lucy stepped on a fucking thorn, Nate would use this *poor baby* voice with her for the rest of the day and give her extra treats. He coddled that stupid dog. Why couldn't he just coddle Annie?

"Men are programmed to fix things," Lia says. "They get upset when they can't."

Beth had said something similar about her husband, Todd: "He won't just *listen* to me. He always has to offer fucking solutions." Annie can't even remember when she said this, specifically, because she said some version of this on a regular basis. Annie remembers thinking to herself that Todd was such a stereotype. She humored Beth, but secretly Annie was a smug bitch, relishing the fact that she got the better husband. She'd had no idea she had married a stereotype too.

"It's like he couldn't *stand* being around me," Annie says. "He was dead set on moving on, and I was like this quintessential ball and chain holding him back."

Lia opens her mouth, starts to say something, then stops, as if thinking better of it.

"What?" Annie says.

"You were afraid he'd move on without you? Leave you behind?"

Yes, something like that.

"So you left him first," Lia says.

It sounds so simple, the way she sums it up. Annie sounds like a coward, the way she sums it up.

"You left Caleb," Annie says, immediately hating her childish tone.

"Caleb left me," Lia says.

Caleb left her?

"I'm sorry," Annie says. "I didn't know."

"I gave him no choice, really," Lia says. "I stopped eating after I lost Ethan. It started with not wanting to look pregnant anymore, ya know? I couldn't stand seeing myself in the mirror, seeing evidence of a mother and not having a baby to show for it. I lost thirty pounds quickly. And then I kept going. It became this obsession. I'd spend all my time counting calories so I didn't have to think of anything else. Caleb said he couldn't watch me kill myself."

"So he left you?" Annie says, incredulous.

Lia sighs. "Technically, yes, he left me. But I guess I was leaving him with each pound I lost."

By the looks of it, Lia still isn't eating like she should. She's so thin. It makes Annie feel better in a weird, twisted way to know that Lia is a work in progress just like she is. *Nobody grieves perfectly.* Grief counselor Pete had said that.

Lia goes up to the porch of the Alaskan's house. The welcome plant next to his door is a succulent, green and spiky with a flower about to blossom. Lia adjusts the pot to her liking, then looks up.

"I hope the Alaskan isn't taking this tiny house back to Alaska. This succulent will never make it up there."

"I think James said they're taking it to Arizona," Annie says.

"So maybe the succulent was intentional." She gives the flower-to-be a little tap, like her index finger is a magic wand that will make it grow, and then she hops down the porch steps.

"I was wondering," Annie says. Lia raises her eyebrows expectantly. "Can we go back to the thrift store this weekend?"

"Sure," Lia says.

"I think I'm ready for that couch."

TWENTY-FOUR

JOSH is in Starbucks, in a corner he's deemed "his corner." He told Nate he'd work at home today—but, of course, he doesn't have a home. He's still sleeping in his car. He parks it a few miles away from Nate's house to avoid any possibility of Nate seeing him while out for one of his morning runs. How would Josh possibly explain that? *Uh, I was too tired to drive home, so I just decided to sleep here.* That would be taking his "fucking weirdo" persona a bit too far. The thing is, he doesn't have money for a place yet. Working for Nate isn't nearly as profitable as working for his usual clients. He should be doing bigger jobs if he wants to get on with his life. He can't though, until all this is resolved.

And it's far from resolved.

A lady came over to the house yesterday to talk to Nate. Josh had to press his ear against the front door to listen in. Nate practically opened the door on him, caught him standing awkwardly next to the couch looking dumb and guilty. That's one reason Josh is at Starbucks today. Nate seemed pissed Josh was eavesdropping. Best to give him some space.

The other reason Josh is at Starbucks is because he needs to be away from Nate so he can call Annie. He has to find out what she's up to, when (or if) she's coming home. Nate and the lady were talking about the possibility of Annie killing herself. Apparently she tried once before, in college. So, yeah, Josh has to make sure she's okay. Somehow, if she's not okay, it will be his fault.

He pushes his laptop across the table once he's at a good stopping point on the website work. The good thing about Starbucks is you can make phone calls and nobody thinks anything of it. There's a constant hum—the click-clacking of keyboards, the whir of the latte foam maker, the elevator music. It's never quiet. Yet, somehow, it's still possible to feel very lonely. Nobody smiles or makes eye contact. Everyone there thinks it's their own personal office; all the other patrons are enemies encroaching upon their space. Someone was in Josh's corner the other day, and he found himself rolling his eyes dramatically at the inconvenience.

When Josh talked to Annie the first time, she'd said it was fine if he called again. He's restrained himself in the interest of being respectful and not creepy. It's been fifteen days, though. That's a while. Nate is slowly going crazy. Annie may be going crazy. He needs to call her—or James, rather. It would be so much easier if she was using her own damn phone.

Josh scrolls through his contacts, finds "Tiny House Weirdo." It still gives him a laugh. He can't bring himself to change the name to "James." The phone rings five times before a robotic voice comes on and says the voice-mail box is full. Of course it is. Mountain man James probably can't be bothered to check his voice mail. Josh decides he'll do some more work and try again in an hour.

An hour later, still no answer. James answered his previous calls. What if something happened there? What if something happened *to Annie*?

Be rational, he tells himself. *She's probably fine.*

He decides that if the next person who walks into Starbucks

is a man, then something bad has happened at Rolling Stone Co-Op. He sits up straight, on alert in his chair, waiting for the next coffeehouse patron. He's always played games like this. *If the microwave beeps before I get to it, then I'll live to be one hundred. If I check the time and it's after one o'clock, then I'm going to get a big job soon.* Jess used to say he was so superstitious. That's not it, really. It's more that he likes to think he can predict the future. He likes having that sense of control. Logically, he knows it's dumb, but he still plays the little games.

The next person who walks in is a middle-aged man, phone pressed to his ear, stress all over his face. He's angry at whoever he's talking to. When Josh listens hard, he can hear him saying, "This is unacceptable." It's a bad sign, this angry man walking into Starbucks.

Josh tries James's number again. Nothing.

It occurs to him that he can just drive out there. It's not that far. He could just see for himself if she's there. He knows what her car looks like.

It's a risk. If Annie sees him, she'll probably recognize him from when he told her about the palm frond. He can wear a hat and his glasses that he never uses since Jess convinced him to get contacts. He'll have to cover up his tattoos; he knows she saw those. Still, it's a risk.

He googles "Rolling Stone Co-Op," thinking if something did happen, there would be a news story about it. Nothing though. There are very few mentions of the place at all. The ones he finds are on pages about tiny houses—Rolling Stone is listed briefly as a manufacturer. It's incredible, really, how this community has managed to stay off the grid.

Yes, he'll go. A quick drive-by, just to check, to make sure she's there and okay. He'll try calling James on the drive out there. Maybe James will pick up and prove that all this fretting is absurd. Josh packs up his stuff and leaves, telling himself that if one of the baristas says "goodbye" or "have a good day," then Annie is fine.

The baristas don't even look up.

THE DRIVE OUT is fast. It's the middle of the day, no traffic. He tries James three more times. No luck. He really does think something is wrong now. He has a bad feeling. Granted, he's had lots of "bad feelings" in his life that haven't materialized into anything significant. It's like he's falsely psychic. The day he hit Penelope, he didn't have any "bad feelings." Go figure.

He drives past the Rolling Stone Co-Op sign to the turnoff in the road that leads to the community. His heart hammers in his chest. Is this a stupid idea? Probably. If Annie sees him and recognizes him, what will he say? *What a strange coincidence!* She won't believe that. What are the chances that he appears on her doorstep one day about a fucking palm frond and then shows up at a random tiny house community where she's now living? It's suspect. She'll be freaked out. He supposes that's all she'll be though—freaked out. That first time he saw her, she didn't appear to know he had anything to do with the accident. So she'll just think it's odd. She'll come to the same conclusion as her husband: *what a weirdo.* Josh can live with that. He is a weirdo. Clearly.

The semicircle of five tiny houses comes into view. He sees people milling about the construction area, their faces indistinguishable at this distance. He does a quick scan for Annie's car but doesn't see it. He doesn't see any cars though. They must park them in a separate area. He slows, not wanting to get too close. What should he do now? He tentatively inches closer to see if she's among the people in the construction area.

Suddenly, out of nowhere, there's a knock on his driver's side window. He flinches. His heartbeat's in his ears now, pounding. It's James, with a big dopey smile on his face.

"Dude!" James says.

Josh rolls down his window.

"Hey," Josh says. His mind is racing. He has to come up with a story for what he's doing here, fast.

"Coming for another visit?" James says. James is wearing overalls and work gloves. That's why he didn't pick up the phone; he was working. *Duh*.

"Yep," Josh says. The less he says, the better. Let James fill in the details for himself.

"We're all working over there if you want to come say hello," James says.

Oh, that's okay. I just want to stalk from a distance. Really, what the hell is he supposed to say?

"Uh, sure," he says. He's always prematurely agreeable, before he thinks things through. That's how he ended up working for Nate. That's how he's ended up in most circumstances of his life. It was just a few weeks after meeting Jess when she said, "We should play house," and he said, "Okay."

James waves him forward like an air traffic controller. As he gets closer, he sees Annie. It's definitely her. He considers putting the car in reverse, peeling out, dust flying up behind him. His palm hovers over the gearshift.

"What was your name again?" James asks him, approaching the driver's side window again. Josh puts the car in park, reluctantly.

"Mike," he says. It's not even hard to remember to say this.

That's what Nate calls him. He may as well just change his name for good.

"Right, right—you came to the saloon with me," James says, memory sufficiently jogged.

"Yep."

"You're on the waiting list?"

"I think so."

"Someone's ahead of you, if I remember right. Might be six months or so."

Josh grunts his understanding. He's not really interested in moving here, but if he says that, then there's no reason for him to be here right now.

"Well, come on," James says. "They don't bite."

Josh follows on his heels. He adjusts the hat on his head, a cheap Angels baseball hat with the Pechanga Casino logo on the back of it. He found it crumpled up under his car seat, a giveaway from a game he went to with Jess. Josh doesn't give a shit about baseball, or any sport for that matter, but Jess's friends had free tickets and she wanted to go. At least the hat is coming in handy. He adjusts his glasses and wonders if this is enough of a disguise.

"Guys, this is Mike. He's considering joining our little community in a few months," James says to the group.

There are five of them: a youngish guy, a middle-aged guy, a middle-aged woman, a pretty girl about his age, and Annie. They all look up. He can feel Annie's eyes on him. He stares at his feet, like a socially inept idiot.

"Hiya, Mike," the middle-aged woman says. She sticks out her hand, and Josh shakes it. "I'm Dawn. This is Matt, Ken, Lia, and Allie."

Allie. He's got to remember to call her Allie.

They all mutter their hellos. The youngish guy, Matt apparently, says, "What's up?"

"Nice to meet you," Josh says, glancing up quickly.

"We just finished a house for a client from Alaska," James says, swinging his arm out to the side to showcase the little house in front of them, with a big red bow stuck on the front door.

"Cool," Josh says.

"And now we're working on Matt's house," James says, pointing to an in-progress minicabin.

"Cool," Josh says again.

"You're the guy I talked to on the phone?"

It's Annie. Addressing him. *Shit.*

He looks up, dares to meet her eyes. She's squinting, either because of the sun behind him or because she's trying to decipher why he looks familiar.

"Oh, right, you talked to Allie a little while back," James says, overly excited about this remembered connection.

"Uh, yeah," Josh says.

"Why don't you guys chat then?" James says. "We're due for a break anyway."

Josh and Annie look at each other, sizing each other up. She doesn't seem to recognize him . . . yet.

"Okay," Annie says, uncertainty in her voice. They seem equally uncomfortable with James's proposal that they chat.

Everyone but Annie and the younger girl go back to work, probably picking up on the fact that Josh isn't interested in chatting.

"You're the guy with the dog named Lucy," Annie says, pointing a playfully accusing finger at Josh.

Right, that's what I told her. Pretty soon, there will be too many lies to keep track of. Pretty soon, he'll fuck up everything.

"Yeah," he says.

She looks at him hard. She's going to say something. She knows.

"You look so familiar . . . I can't place it," she says.

She looks at the other girl like she might know, like she might say, "Yeah, he looks like the guy from blah blah blah," but she just shrugs.

"I'm Lia, if you didn't catch it," the girl says, extending her hand.

It's the softest hand Josh has ever held. He can't help but hold it a little longer than is appropriate. What is this pretty girl doing here, in this tiny house community, building houses that will put callouses on her palms?

"Nice to meet you," Josh says. Maybe he'll just talk to this girl, to avoid any more eye contact with Annie.

"So, you want to move here?" Lia says.

She sits on a stack of wood. Annie does the same. He stands before them feeling like a jackass at an interview.

"Maybe," he says, tugging at the bill of his cap, pulling it lower over his face. He can't help but think that Annie's silence means the wheels are busily turning in her head. Something is bound to click. *Palm frond.* Or worse: *accident.*

"You might be even younger than me," Lia says.

"Twenty-two," Josh says.

"I'm twenty-three," she says.

Annie is still quiet.

"Usually, when young people come here, it's because something big happened to them," Lia says.

"Yeah," he says, nodding in agreement. "Something big."

"Gosh, I just can't place it," Annie blurts. She's shaking her head in disbelief at her own inability to remember. Josh stares at his feet. He's got to get out of here—fast.

"He kind of looks like the lead singer of the Contradictions," Lia says.

Now they are both analyzing him, or trying to; he keeps staring at the ground. They probably can't see, but he's smiling at this comparison to the lead singer of the Contradictions. Jess used to say that guy was "so hot."

"As if I have any idea who the Contradictions are," Annie says.

She and Lia share a laugh. They're friends; that much is clear. Annie has made a friend. At first, this relieves Josh. But then it concerns him. If she was planning on coming home, would she bother making friends?

"You guys going to stay here long?" he says, trying to sound very nonchalant.

It's no use though. They both shrug.

"We'll see," Annie says vaguely.

Then she turns the focus right back to him: "Where are you from?" she asks. "I know I've seen you somewhere."

Maybe her brain doesn't want her to remember, for self-protection or whatever. Even if she just recalls the palm frond incident, she'll have to think about why this twenty-two-year-old kid would be stalking her. She must know the driver of the truck that killed Penelope was his age. Some part of her must know that.

"San Diego," Josh says. Another lie. He's got to leave before more tumble out of his mouth. He takes his phone out of his pocket, looks at it with mock concern.

"Sorry to cut this short, but I've gotta get home," he says, pretending like he's responding to some kind of emergency. Isn't this what girls do when they want to ditch out on blind dates?

He starts walking backward toward his car. They stand, but

don't follow him.

"Tell James I said goodbye," he says.

"If you have any questions, feel free to call," Lia says, using her hand as a visor against the sun.

Annie says something to Lia that Josh can't hear. "Lia has a phone," Annie calls out to Josh. "You should get her number."

Lia looks embarrassed, horrified. They giggle like the girls who used to make Josh nervous in high school.

"Allie doesn't have a phone, or isn't using it, or whatever," Lia says, approaching Josh, finger combing strands of hair that have escaped the bun on top of her head.

Is she flirting with him? Josh can be pretty clueless, but he thinks she is.

"Oh, okay, what's your number?"

She dictates it to him, and he types it into his phone under the name "Tiny House Pretty Girl." Then he changes his mind and types "Lia."

NATE turns the corner onto his street at the end of his fourteen-mile run and sees a police car parked in front of the house. Usually, he can't muster up enough motivation to run this last little stretch, but now he sprints.

The cops are at the front door, midknock. All Nate can think is that they've found Annie. They're coming to tell him they've discovered her body. He lingers at the end of the driveway, unsure if he's ready for this news.

The cops turn around, apparently giving up on someone answering the door. Nate recognizes them as the same guys who came to the house when Sheryl wanted to report Annie missing. Officer Martinez was the older guy's name. He can't remember the younger guy's.

"Mr. Forester?" the younger cop says. They're on their way back to their car when they see him.

"Yes," Nate says. He wipes the sweat from his forehead with the back of his equally sweaty hand.

He can't move. He just stands there, waiting, bracing himself. *We're sorry to have to tell you this . . .*

"Officer Banks," the younger one says. That's right—Banks. "And this is Officer Martinez."

"I remember," he says. He can't bring himself to ask: *Is everything okay?*

"Do you have a few minutes?" Martinez says.

Their faces betray nothing. They're stoic, solemn, calm. There's probably some rule book about this type of thing. Rule number one: keep it professional.

"Uh, sure," Nate says.

"Do you mind if we talk inside?" Martinez says.

They don't want to tell him out here, on the driveway. They don't want to cause a scene. Rule number two: deliver the news in the recipient's house, where they are most comfortable.

Nate opens the front door—he never locks it when he goes running—and they follow him inside. They take off their hats when they enter the house. Did they do this when they came the first time, or is this a display of respect to accompany their condolences?

Lucy starts sniffing them, conducting her usual full inspection. Nate calls her off, and she jumps up on the couch, uninterested. Nate goes to the sink, wets a paper towel, and covers his sweaty face with it. Can they just tell him now, while he's hiding under this paper towel? They are silent, though. He takes off the paper towel to find them standing there at the island, looking impatient.

"Is it bad?" Nate says.

When Nate and Annie first started dating, she'd had to get her wisdom teeth removed. She needed a ride home from the hospital because of the anesthetic, but she wouldn't ask him outright. He offered, confirming for both of them that they weren't just casually seeing each other. When he came into the recovery room, she was out of it, still doped up. Her first words: "Is it bad?" In any other circumstance, he would laugh at that memory, but he can't now.

"We just want to ask some questions about your wife," Banks says.

"Questions?" Nate says.

So are they just following up? Is that what's happening?

"Yes, about her disappearance," Martinez says. They are looking at him like he's an idiot.

"I thought you were coming to say you found her," he says. His voice is shaky.

"Oh, no," Martinez says.

"You haven't found her," Nate says. He needs them to say these words, to confirm that she is not a body floating in a river somewhere.

"We haven't found her," Banks says.

He grabs onto the edge of the island, bows his head until it hits the butcher block countertop, sighs.

"You're relieved?" Martinez says.

"Yeah," Nate says.

"Don't you *want* us to find her?" Banks says. There's accusation in his voice. Nate realizes how this looks to them.

"Oh, yes, I mean, of course," he says, too quickly. "I just thought you were going to say you found her, you know . . ."

"Her *body*?" Martinez says.

Nate forces a laugh that comes out strange and psychotic.

"I've watched too much TV," he says. "I was thinking the worst."

The cops look at each other, doubt all over their faces.

"Sorry, then why are you here?" Nate asks. "I haven't received any new information or anything."

"We're just looking into things a bit more," Martinez says.

"Okay," Nate says, not sure what this means.

Both of them whip out their little spiral notebooks and click the ends of their identical, government-issued pens.

"Do you want to sit?" Nate says, motioning toward the dining table. They don't even turn to assess the seat offerings, though. They both say, in unison, "No, thank you." There is no friendliness about them. None. If Nate's not mistaken, he's the bad guy.

"So, walk us through the days before she disappeared and the day of," Martinez says, pen primed.

"The days before?" Nate says. "I mean, she was doing better, I thought."

"Better than what?" Banks says.

They're going to make him say it again: *Our daughter died.* Didn't he already tell them this?

"Our little girl died, right before Christmas," Nate says.

They write this down as if it's news to them, though he's sure it's not.

"She'd been depressed," Nate says, "understandably."

He hasn't really said that before—that Annie's depression was understandable. When she was here, home, he was so impatient with it.

"Did she talk of suicide?" When Martinez asks this question, he doesn't make eye contact with Nate. He just stares at his stupid little notebook.

"No," Nate says.

She'd said things like, "I don't know how to go on" and "I'm too sensitive for this world" and "I hate being alive." He'd dismissed these statements as dramatic. Was that a mistake? Was she warning him of her intentions?

"I mean, not explicitly," Nate adds.

"What does that mean?" Banks says. This guy, Banks, seems convinced that Nate is withholding important information. He reminds Nate of Annie's mother.

"It just means she was depressed. Maybe there were signs of this that I missed. I don't know," Nate says.

"Signs?" Banks presses.

"Dude, I don't know. I'm just saying maybe I wasn't as attentive as I should have been or something," Nate says. "You all seem to think I must know where she is and the fact that I don't certainly makes me ineligible for Husband of the Year."

"Whoa, now, no reason to get upset," Martinez says with the same *just calm down* tone Nate uses with Annie, the one that pisses her off every time.

"I'm not upset," Nate says. He's defensive, though, so it sounds like he is, in fact, upset. He finally understands how Annie felt when he told her to calm down or—her favorite—*relax*. He finally knows why she'd yell at him. "Stop acting like you think I'm irrational." Or, "Stop implying that you're so sane and I'm nuts."

"Okay, okay," Banks says, like he's talking someone off the fucking ledge of a high-rise.

"You said maybe you weren't as attentive as you should have been," Martinez says.

Is Nate supposed to have a lawyer here, to make sure his words aren't recorded and used against him like this? Probably. But if he asks for one, that seems like an admission of guilt. What do they think he's done, exactly? *Killed* her? Is that what they think?

"We were grieving in different ways, that's all," Nate says, recalling all the therapy sessions with Pete. *It's very common for spouses to mourn differently.* That's what he'd said.

"Would you say there was any marital discord?" Banks asks. Martinez gives him a quick, scolding look. Perhaps Banks shot his wad too soon. They'd probably discussed this in the car: *Don't go for broke until he's weak.*

"*Discord?*" Nate says.

"Conflict," Martinez says.

"I know what it means," Nate says. He tries, but fails, to repress the defensive tone.

"Were you getting along?" Banks adds, as if Nate needs him to dumb down the question even more. Nate's starting to really hate these two.

"We were getting along as well as two people can when they've lost a child," Nate says. There's the defensiveness again.

"And you say you saw her the morning she disappeared?" Martinez says.

"Yes," Nate says. *I already told you cocksuckers this.*

"How did she seem?"

She was crying.

She'd said, "I love you."

Martinez and Banks shouldn't get to know these details.

"She seemed fine," Nate says. "There certainly wasn't any indication she was going to *leave*."

"What time did you return that night and find she was gone?" Banks asks.

"I don't know exactly. Around eight o' clock, I think. It was dark outside."

"You didn't call the police, though," Martinez says.

"She left a note," Nate says. "We've *discussed* the note. You've *read* the note."

They nod but don't say anything.

"Can anyone confirm your whereabouts during that day?" Martinez says. It's a big question, full of implications and accusations, but Martinez's face remains emotionless.

"My *whereabouts*?" Nate says. He's shocked they're even asking. What the fuck do they think he did?

"Where you were," Banks says.

"I know what it fucking means." That damn defensiveness.

Nate is sure multiple people can confirm his whereabouts, but he doesn't know who those people are, specifically. He had just gotten all the Sandoval properties on his roster. He visited many of them that day, introduced himself to tenants, chitchatted with neighbors. It's a blur, though. It's not like he knew at the time that it would be crucial to remember the details, the hourly play-by-play, of that day. All he knows is that he was exhausted when he came home, and then he read the note and everything before the note became part of another life, meaningless.

"I was visiting the new properties on my roster," Nate says. "I'm sure I can find people to attest to that fact."

Attest to that fact. He sounds so formal, like he's testifying in court. Are these asshole cops going to see to it that he testifies in court?

"Your business became very busy after your wife disappeared," Martinez says.

How do they know this?

"I signed on to a bunch of properties right before she left," Nate says.

They nod like this means something, like it's relevant in some way.

"I don't see what that has to do with anything," Nate says.

Martinez clears his throat. "People might think it's odd that you're able to just go on working while your wife is missing."

This sounds like what Beth said. *They keep saying you must know where she is*—they being Steve and Sheryl.

"Did my mother-in-law put you up to this?" Nate says.

The way Banks looks up, like someone just fired a shot that grazed right past his eyebrows, answers the question.

"We're just doing our due diligence," Martinez says.

Fucking Sheryl.

"She's crazy, you know," Nate says, "Annie's mother."

Instead of expressing confusion over Nate's mention of Annie's mother, Martinez says, "This doesn't have anything to do with her," which just confirms that it has everything to do with her.

Sheryl actually thinks Nate did something to Annie? She's probably concocted some strange story in her head. Nate can see the newspaper headline now: Man Goes Insane After Daughter's Death, Kills Wife.

"You guys have read the note," Nate says. He always comes back to the note. *Trust the note, trust the note.*

"We can't confirm your wife actually wrote the note, Mr. Forester," Banks says.

So now they're calling him Mr. Forester. And now they're implying he forged the note.

"Jesus, you guys can't be serious."

"We're just doing our due diligence," Martinez says.

"Yeah, you said that already," Nate says.

"Is there any other information you want to tell us?" Banks asks.

In the movies, this is where the guy breaks down in a surprise confession.

"She took a suitcase with her. And her toothbrush. I can show you where they were," Nate says. He knows this is a futile effort though. They can't confirm there was ever a suitcase or a toothbrush. They can't confirm that Nate didn't throw them in the Pacific Ocean.

"She said her phone would be off, but maybe you can get a trace off it," he says. He sounds desperate now, which is not how a suspect should sound.

"We'll be looking into that," Martinez says.

"You want my DNA?" Nate says, sticking out his tongue as if they're ready with cotton swabs in their pockets.

"Not at this time, Mr. Forester," Martinez says. "But we'll be in touch."

I'm sure you will.

They put their notebooks back in their pockets simultaneously. Nate walks them to the door—not to be polite, but to make sure they fucking leave.

As the police cruiser pulls away, he mutters to himself, "I can't fucking believe this."

Then his phone rings.

Marcus Sandoval.

Shit. He was supposed to meet him at the Calle Miramar duplex at four thirty to discuss some possible renovations that Nate will need to supervise. It's ten till five.

"Marcus, I'm just looking for a parking spot," he says.

"There are plenty, so I should expect to see you shortly."

Fuck.

Nate runs to the bedroom, changes out of his running clothes and into slacks and a cashmere sweater that Sheryl bought for him one Christmas—his most impressive article of clothing, by far. He puts on too much deodorant and then is out the door, in his car, on the way to Marcus.

This—all of this—is Sheryl's fault.

He dials her number in the midst of mild hyperventilating. She answers on the first ring because, even if she thinks Nate is an insane murderer, she also needs him for information regarding her daughter.

"Is there any news?" she says, before any proper greeting.

"Big news," Nate says, relishing in this cruel opportunity to get her hopes up.

"What is it?" she says. There is such eagerness in her voice. It makes Nate feel like a dick.

"The cops think I'm a murderer," he says. "That's the news."

Her disappointment comes out as a long sigh.

"You wouldn't happen to know why they would think that, do you?" he says.

"Nate, you and I both know they weren't going to give any attention to this case."

He hates the way she says "this case," as if it's an official criminal investigation. Annie just needed to get away. That's all. Why can't anyone accept that she's fine? *She has to be fine.*

"So, what, you told them I was involved?"

"I didn't say that, not exactly," she says. But whenever anyone says "not exactly," they mean "pretty much exactly."

"You've got to be kidding me."

"This will get them to pay attention, maybe track her phone," Sheryl says.

She's implying they can be in on this together, for Annie's sake. But that might be a front. He can't trust this woman at all. She might really think Nate is an insane murderer. Of course she wouldn't admit that to him for fear that he would kill her, which is an appealing idea at this point.

"Fuck you, Sheryl."

He hangs up.

He wishes so badly that he could call Annie, tell her about this. She would be appalled. Eventually, they would laugh about it— *Remember when my mom told the police you might have killed me?*

He calls Beth.

"Nate," she says. "Hi." There's an edge to her voice, like she's nervous about why Nate's calling.

"I haven't heard anything about Annie," he says so she can relax a little. "But I just had the cops interrogate me. Sheryl told them I might be involved."

"You've gotta be shittin' me."

"They're probably listening to this phone call," he says. That might not be true. That might only happen in the movies, but he doesn't know for sure.

"She's really lost it."

"You don't think I'm involved, right?" Nate says. He needs someone, anyone, on his side.

"No," she says. "I mean, I did, kind of. It's always the husband or whatever, right? But, no, not now."

It really is always the husband. Annie loves all those real-life crime shows—*Dateline, 20/20, 48 Hours, Cold Justice*—and it's always the fucking husband. Five minutes into most episodes, Annie would say, "Whelp, we know how this one's going to end."

"I can't believe this," Nate says.

"It's not like they're going to find anything," Beth says. "Right?"

Just that one word, that question—"Right?"—makes Nate feel absolutely alone. That one word reveals that Beth isn't quite sure.

"I gotta go," Nate says.

"Okay. Well, call me if they arrest you," Beth says, with a tense laugh.

"Yeah," he says. "Right."

He hangs up as the Calle Miramar duplex comes into view. Marcus was right—there are plenty of parking spots. The sun is setting, but he can make out Marcus standing on the sidewalk in front of the property, hands on his hips. Even at dusk, with his face not fully visible, it's obvious he's pissed.

"I'm so sorry I'm late," Nate says, turning off his phone because he knows how much Marcus will hate it if Nate's distracted by an incoming call or text.

"I don't care if you're sorry," Marcus says. "And your sweater is inside out."

TWENTY-SIX

ANNIE finally has a couch. It's an ugly thing, blue-and-yellow plaid. It's hard to believe a couch like this was ever in style. It seems like it was made for a garage rec room and, ultimately, a garage sale. It's comfortable, though. When she sits, the cushions sink down just enough, as if it's been lovingly used over many years. She imagines it was owned by an elderly man who passed away. She's rescued it from a trash dumpster destiny. When Lia asked her, with a look of true bewilderment on her face, "Why this one?" Annie had answered, "I feel sorry for it, I guess."

Lia's coming over for dinner. Annie realized she's never actually seen the girl eat. She's only seen her drink tea—and a few sips of wine at the evening happy hours. Maybe it's maternal instinct, exacerbated by the pregnancy, but Annie feels the need to make sure Lia's not starving herself.

"Did I tell you I'm a vegetarian?" Lia says when Annie opens the front door to find her standing there on the doormat holding two paper grocery bags. She insisted on doing the cooking.

"No, but that's fine by me," Annie says.

"I was planning to make bean burgers," Lia says, walking past Annie and setting the grocery bags on the kitchen counter. "I hope that's okay."

"Sure," Annie says, though she's never considered those two words together—bean and burger.

"I became a vegetarian after what happened with Ethan," Lia says. "It's like I was suddenly too sensitive about things that didn't used to bother me, like eating animals."

She forces a nervous laugh that prompts Annie to ask, "Are you okay?"

Lia holds a red onion in her hand like it's a baseball she's about to throw across the room.

"Caleb just texted," she says. "I guess he's getting married."

She sets the onion on the counter and continues unpacking the rest of the food. There are so many vegetables for what Lia has described as a "bean burger."

"Wow," Annie says, not knowing what else to say.

Lia busies herself lining up the vegetables in an order that makes sense only to her. Then she empties a can of beans into a colander and runs water over them.

"I thought I would be fine with it, ya know? I mean, I knew they were dating. It's just—it's weird."

"Of course," Annie says.

Annie tries again to imagine Nate with his next wife, the not-a-care-in-the-world, glass-half-full former cheerleader with the perpetual ponytail. She hates this woman who does not even exist yet.

"They'll probably have a baby soon," Lia says. She's got a knife in her hand now, aiming it at a carrot.

Annie hasn't even thought about this possible future yet—Nate having a baby with the perpetual ponytail woman. Somehow, Annie's sure tragedy would never befall them. They would be the quintessential happy family, and Annie would be left to resent them from afar. And what of this new baby in her belly? She would have to send little Georgie to visit Nate every other weekend, or whatever's usual when it comes to child custody arrangements. Georgie would probably like the perpetual pony-tail woman better than Annie, would request her as a mother. *She's more fun, Mom*—that would be the common refrain.

"I can't imagine," Annie says, though she just has.

"I guess it's that it all happened so fast for him," Lia says. "We split up a year ago, he meets her a month later, they move in together, and—*bam!*—they're getting married."

Nate would probably move on quickly too. He's been in a rush to get over this grief thing since day one. He's been fixated, annoyingly so, on being "normal" again.

Lia adds the carrots and some spices to the beans and starts mashing everything together.

"You'll get your happy ending too," Annie says. And, while she doesn't believe this for herself, she does believe this for Lia. Because Lia wants it, clearly. Annie doesn't know what she wants.

"Yeah, I know," Lia says unconvincingly.

She creates four patties out of the mysterious mixture and places them in a pan. Annie feels like she should hug Lia, or at least give her a comforting pat on the shoulder. She's never been that type though. She used to worry it would make her a bad mother, but she was different with Penelope; she couldn't keep her hands off Penny.

"I have to pee for the hundredth time today," Annie says, walking past Lia to the bathroom.

Did she have to pee this often when she was pregnant with Penny? She can't remember. Or she remembers it in the third trimester, but not the early months. In so many ways, this pregnancy feels novel, like she's never had a child before. She hates that she's forgotten so much from the first time. She hates how inadequate her memory is. It's all she's got to keep some of Penny alive, and it clearly sucks.

In the tiny bathroom, she struggles to turn around and sit on the toilet.

"How am I going to fit in this thing when I'm nine months pregnant?" she says.

"That's a good question," Lia says. Annie can hear the patties sizzling in the pan. "You think you'll be here when you're nine months pregnant?"

"That's another good question."

Sometimes she can't imagine life without Nate. Or, rather, she can't imagine Nate having a life without her. But sometimes she can see herself here, in this life, long-term. She can see herself living without Nate—not because she wants to, necessarily, but because she has to, because she has come to associate him with too much pain. She can even see herself raising a baby on her own, with the help of Lia. Aunt Lia, the baby would call her. Or maybe Aunt Li-Li, since kids seem to like syllabic repetition. Annie has to remind herself that Lia wants another kind of life, though—a husband, a family, a do-over of her own.

"Allie, do you want cheese on your burger?" Lia asks.

Allie. It's so strange that she can envision Lia as an aunt to her baby, but Lia doesn't even know her real name. Should she tell her? When?

"Sure, yeah," she says.

When Annie comes out of the bathroom, Lia is placing slices of cheddar on their patties. Annie resumes her seat on the couch. There simply isn't room for two people in the kitchen. And, for all intents and purposes, the couch is basically in the kitchen.

"That guy hasn't even called me yet," Lia says.

"What guy?"

"The one who visited the other day—Mike."

The guy who looked so familiar. Annie couldn't place him, still can't. Annie had no idea Lia was waiting on this guy to call her. Maybe she wasn't until she found out about Caleb getting married.

"I know, it's stupid to think he'd call," Lia says.

"Maybe he still will," Annie says. She suddenly feels very old. She remembers her mom attempting to comfort her with similar words in high school when Annie lamented that her crush-of-the-moment didn't even know she was alive. Annie had simultaneously dreaded and looked forward to Penelope's romantic woes, knowing they would be angst-ridden but would bond them as mother and daughter.

"I guess I thought there was a little spark with him, ya know?"

Annie doesn't know though. She used to know. She felt it when she met Nate. He will be the last. Even if she meets someone new, she'll never again be a giddy, instant-spark sort of person. She's too mistrusting of life now. From here on out, any happy moments will be tempered by a voice in her head whispering, *It won't last.*

"So, you think you're ready to date again?" Annie asks.

"I don't know. I want to be ready."

That, right there, is the difference between the two of them.

THEY EAT ON the couch because there's really no other place to eat. The burgers are good, better than Annie expected. Annie watches Lia eat hers, peering up discreetly so as not to make Lia feel self-conscious. Lia takes bites gingerly, each mouthful seemingly calculated, part of some tally in her mind. She eventually finishes her food. It just takes her a while.

"Sometimes I wonder if Caleb and I could have made it work," Lia says, balancing her plate on her thighs, her legs crossed in a yoga pose.

"Maybe," Annie says. "But you're probably just thinking that now because you're upset he's getting married. You said you guys tried for a year to make it work. You tried."

"We thought we tried. We said we tried. That's what you're supposed to say. We didn't *really* try though. It got uncomfortable, being with each other, and we gave up."

"Sometimes it's hard to know the breaking point." Annie was convinced she and Nate had been at theirs, but now she's not so sure. Something in her, the same something that got her through depression and law school and a year of failing to make a baby, can't stomach the idea of just giving up.

"I miss him a lot," Lia says, her eyes welling up. "I hate that he told me he's getting married over a *text message*."

Annie has no idea what to say, so she says nothing. She feels the urge to say things like "It will be okay!" and "Everything happens for a reason!" She refrains, shuddering at the thought that she's just as guilty as Nate and everyone else of being programmed to deliver canned emotional support.

"God, I'm being ridiculous," Lia says. She stands abruptly and takes her plate to the sink.

"You're not."

Lia starts doing the dishes, despite Annie's insistence that she leave them. When she's done, she says, "Do you mind if I head home?"

They had planned to watch a movie on Lia's laptop, up in the loft, like teenage girls at a sleepover.

"Not at all," Annie says. "But I'm here if you want to talk."

"Thanks," she says. "I'll be fine in the morning, I'm sure."

Annie walks her to the door, opens it. The night air is crisp and cold. Lia wraps her arms around herself.

"Just promise me something," Lia says, looking Annie in the eyes with an intensity that makes her think, *Oh God, what?*

"If there's any chance of making things work with Nate," she says, "don't blow it."

She turns quickly, not giving Annie a chance to respond.

ANNIE CLIMBS THE ladder up to her loft. It's just after eight o'clock. She's not tired but figures she'll lie in bed until she is. She likes looking out the window at the stars. She was never a stargazer before, never took the time. Nate was always into that kind of stuff—red moons and solar eclipses and passing comets. He's like a little boy that way, fascinated by everything.

She does miss him. It's not that she doesn't think there's a chance they can work it out. She just doesn't know for sure. Shouldn't she know for sure? How can a marriage survive without that confidence? Without it, what do the vows even mean? *In sickness and in health, till death do us part . . . I suppose, if it's convenient for both parties.*

She's been gone almost three weeks now. She wonders what Nate is thinking. She wants to talk to him, she does. Her instinct is to talk to him. She just doesn't want to be disappointed. Some part of her can imagine him scolding her, saying, "Annie, what were you thinking?" If he said that, or something like it, they would be done, stake-in-the-ground done. She needs him to understand, or at least try to understand, why she's doing this.

She reaches into her purse, takes out her phone. She stares at the black screen, considering, and then pushes the power button until the screen flashes awake with light. It takes a long time to come to life completely.

A plethora of text message notifications populate the screen—forty-two notifications, to be exact. They're from Nate and her mother and Beth. She's not sure if she should read them or not, if they will convince her to stay or come home. She starts with Beth, on the assumption she'll tug fewer heartstrings than Nate or her parents.

Where are you?

That's the first one. They get progressively more desperate.

Everyone is looking for you.

Just tell me where you are. I'll come there. I don't even have to tell anyone. Are you OK? Can you please just tell me you're OK?

She deletes the rest of Beth's messages without reading them.

Maybe she's a selfish bitch for coming here, for worrying everyone. This possibility sends a rush of heat and shame through her body. It's the same rush you get when you realize you've done something horrific, like walked out of the bathroom and into a meeting with toilet paper trailing from your skirt.

Nate is listed in her phone with his full name—Nate Forester. That's how she originally entered his name, when she first met him, and she never updated it to say just "Nate" or "Hubby" or some other nauseating nickname. Beth has Todd in her phone as "Better Half." Annie teased her about that for months, took to calling Todd "Better Half" to his face: *Hey, Better Half, Beth says you got a promotion at work. Congrats!*

What will she say to Nate?

It's me.

Will he cry? Yell? Hang up?

She taps his name. Her heart pounds so hard that each beat reverberates in her eardrums. She waits for the ringing, holding her breath. There is no ringing though. It goes straight to his voice mail.

Hi, you've reached Nate Forester. Please leave a message, and I'll return your call just as soon as I can.

Hearing his voice, the way he adds "just" to "as soon as I can" for an extra-friendly touch, makes her heart pound harder.

She hangs up, doesn't leave a message.

Why is his phone off? His phone is never off. Shouldn't he have it on, in case she calls? There she goes again, being a selfish bitch, expecting that he's just sitting upright and still on the far right cushion of their couch—his cushion; hers is the left, and Lucy's is the middle—waiting for her to figure things out. Maybe this is a sign that she isn't supposed to call him. Not yet. She holds down the power button on her phone until the screen goes dark again. And then she lies there, staring at the dark sky, sleep eluding her, until morning.

TWENTY-SEVEN

JOSH is on the phone with his mom, on the way to Nate's house to present him with the final website. It looks good, professional. Nate will be pleased, impressed even.

"I haven't heard from you in a while," Josh's mom says.

"I know, I know. I've got a lot going on," he tells her. "How about I come by tonight? I'll get takeout from Luigi's."

"Veal parmesan for me, please," she says. "I'll pick up some wine."

Pick up. As if she doesn't have a stash of bottles within arm's reach, Josh thinks.

He turns onto Nate's street and sees a police car parked in front of Nate's house.

"Ma, I gotta go," he says.

There's just the one car. Not many, which is good; many would imply an emergency. Still, he parks hurriedly across the street and jogs to the front door, just as Nate and two officers are coming outside. Nate looks agitated. All Josh can think is that something happened to Annie. He should have told Nate she was at Rolling Stone Co-Op. He should have told him a long time ago. She really did kill herself, and it's all his fault. Josh feels dizzy with this potential reality, like he might pass out.

"Hey," Josh says to nobody in particular, to the three of them as a group.

The officers give small chin-juts of acknowledgment. Nate doesn't even look at him. Josh doesn't know whether to leave or go inside or what.

"I, uh, have the finished website to show you," he tells Nate, holding up his computer bag as evidence.

"Just wait inside, okay?" Nate says.

He's definitely agitated. Not sad-agitated though—angry-agitated. Maybe Annie is okay. Maybe this isn't about her. Josh goes inside, sets his bag on one of the dining table chairs, and peers between the slats of the plantation shutters at the cops and Nate talking on the driveway. The cops look stern. Nate looks flustered. He is making excessive arm gestures.

After a few minutes, the cops walk toward their car and Nate comes back toward the house. Josh sits at the dining table and opens his laptop, pretending to be working.

"Jesus fucking Christ," Nate says when he walks in, slamming the door behind him.

Nate has requested that Josh not ask if he's okay, but Josh can't help himself. "Everything okay?" he says tentatively, unsure if Nate's wrath will soon be directed at him.

"No," Nate says. He starts pacing from the front door all the way down the hallway and back again, running his fingers through his hair.

Again, Josh can't help himself. "Did something happen or—"

"Nothing *happened*," Nate says. "The cops *think* something happened. That's the problem."

They think something happened? What? Is it about Annie? That must be it. *Shit*. This is getting bad. And complicated. Bad and complicated.

"They think you did something or . . . ?" Josh starts typing nonsense into his programming application. He wants it to look like whatever's happening is of no consequence to him. He's just a curious kid, that's all.

"Yeah," Nate says. "They're fucking harassing me."

Josh dares to ask, "What do they think you did?"

Nate stops pacing and looks at Josh like he's a complete idiot, like *What? Did you think we're friends?*

"I don't want to talk about it," Nate says. *With you,* his tone implies.

"Okay," Josh says. It's got to be about Annie. Do they think he offed her or something? How could they think that?

"Actually, dude, I'm sorry, but I'm not going to be needing your database or your website or whatever," Nate says. He resumes pacing.

"Oh, uh, okay," Josh says. He starts to close his laptop.

"Marcus fired me."

"Man, that sucks," Josh says.

"It does suck. It's one of the many things sucking right now."

Josh wants to spit out, *I know where she is.* But he swallows back the admission, unsure if Nate would punch him or hug him. Maybe he can call the police, leave an anonymous tip or something. That's a thing, right? Anonymous tips?

"You can get other contracts, right?" Josh says.

Nate mumbles something Josh can't make out.

"It doesn't matter," Nate says. "None of it fucking matters."

Josh watches Nate stop at the end of the hallway and bang his head on the door to the water heater closet—once, twice, three times, solid thuds.

Josh has to call Annie. That's what he has to do. He has to tell her to come home. That's the only thing that will fix this. The police have to see she's okay. Nate needs to see she's okay.

"Can I do anything to help?" Josh says, feeling almost as helpless as he did after he hit Penelope, when he was standing there in the middle of the street, next to his criminal vehicle, arms hanging dumbly at his sides, people swarming, ambulance lights flashing, someone—Nate, maybe—yelling, "Move, move, move!"

"No, Mike," Nate says, with an insane-looking half-smile on his face, a half-smile that calls Josh a moron. "There's nothing you can do to help."

Nate walks back into the kitchen, stops at the island, hands on his hips. He points an index finger at Josh and says, "Actually, there is something you can do."

Josh looks at him, his eyes wide and eager.

"Sure, anything."

"Leave," Nate says. "Leave me the fuck alone."

Josh feels his face flush. He knows this feeling, the punching-bag feeling. When he was in high school, during his sophomore and junior years, his mom was having one of her harder times. She was involved with some asshole who was making her drug habit worse than it had ever been. Then she lost her job (because she showed up high) on the same day that her boyfriend decided to take up with a younger, prettier addict, and his mom lost it. On Josh. Because he was there. Because he was just a dumb kid who didn't have any "real" problems. She yelled at him as if he were her boss and her boyfriend in one person. She shoved him hard enough that he stumbled back into the wall separating the kitchen from the den. Josh was so shaken up about the whole thing that he talked to one of the school psychs about it. Tanya was her name. She had dreadlocks that looked dirty. She'd told him, "Your mom's lashing out at you because she knows you'll eventually forgive her."

It's not the worst thing to be pegged as forgiving.

"Okay," Josh tells Nate. "I'm leaving. But call me if you need anything."

JOSH SITS IN his car for a good five minutes, taking deep breaths. He's got to call Annie. There's no choice now. Things have gotten out of hand. He's let them get out of hand. Somehow, on his quest to make everything better, he's made it drastically worse.

Shit. He always forgets that Annie doesn't have a phone, or it's not on or whatever. He can call James. Or that girl, Lia. She gave him her number. If that's not fate, what is?

His fingers hover over the screen, above her name in his contacts list, shaking the way they do if he drinks two Mountain Dews on an empty stomach. He taps her name, and it starts ringing.

"Hello?" she says, her tone prematurely annoyed, in anticipation of a telemarketer.

"Lia?" Josh says.

"Yeah?"

"It's, uh, Mike," he says. "I came by the other—"

"I know who you are," she says, her voice instantly brighter, chipper even.

"Sorry to bug you."

"Why would you think you're bugging me?" she says. "I gave you my number, remember?"

She laughs in that giggly way girls do. It's clear he's not calling for the reasons she's expecting. He feels bad, really bad.

"Right," he says. "Well, how are you?" He may as well humor her, a little bit. If circumstances were different, he would probably be interested in her. She's pretty. But he can't flirt on a good day, and today is most definitely not a good day.

"I'm great. Was just heading out to work on Matt's house," she says.

"I won't keep you."

She giggles again. "You're not keeping me."

Cut to the chase, stop beating around the bush, rip off the Band-Aid.

"I'm actually calling about Annie."

"Annie?" she says, perplexed.

Shit.

"I mean Allie."

"Allie?" Lia says, now suspicious and concerned and no longer giggling. "What about Allie?"

"I, uh, know her husband," he says.

"Nate?"

It's a good thing that Lia knows his name, isn't it? That must mean Annie talks about him, misses him even.

"Right, yeah. I work with him, or for him, or whatever."

"And you know she's here?" Lia says. She sounds guarded, cautious in the way women are taught to be. Jess once said, "Every guy's a psycho stalker until proven otherwise."

"It's a long story," Josh says.

"I've got time."

"Look, you've got to just tell her to come home."

"Why do I have to tell her anything?"

"Nate is going crazy. Things are bad here."

"He doesn't know she's here?" Lia says.

"I didn't tell him. I thought she wouldn't want him to know. I thought I was doing the right thing . . ."

She's quiet, maybe busy considering the possibility that Josh might not be an asshole after all.

"What do you mean things are bad there?" she asks.

"He's going to lose it," he says. "The police are involved. I don't know why, exactly, but I think they're investigating him for her disappearance or something."

"Holy shit," Lia says.

"My thoughts exactly." Then he says, "If she doesn't come home, or at least call Nate and tell him what's going on, I've got to call the police."

Lia exhales a long, drawn-out sigh.

"I'll talk to her," she says.

"Thank you," he says. "I know you're friends. She'll listen to you."

She sighs again. "I kind of think she should go home anyway," she says, her voice slightly lower, as if she fears Annie will hear her. "It's terrible what happened, but I think they can make it work."

"My thoughts exactly."

TWENTY-EIGHT

NATE

NATE paces up and down the hallway for what must be the hundredth time. He didn't have to be such a fucking asshole to Mike. The kid didn't deserve that. But, really, he asks too many questions. He doesn't pick up on "leave me alone" cues. At all. Fucking kid.

And fucking cops. And fucking Sheryl. He should call her and tell her the latest developments in the case of Nate Forrester, Wife-Killer.

"Nate," she says in lieu of "Hello."

"Guess who just paid me another visit?" Nate says.

She doesn't have to guess though. She knows.

"Nate, if you didn't do anything, they won't find anything. What's the big deal?"

If? If!

"Sheryl, I didn't do anything. There is no *if*."

"Fine, then, what's the big deal?" she says. "They're giving the case more attention. They'll help find Annie."

"And make me out to be guilty in the process."

"They're probably just trying to intimidate you," she says.

"They're doing a fucking good job."

During this latest visit, they asked him again where he was the day she left. It's like they're trying to catch him in a lie. They also asked him to put together a list of people who could verify his alibi. Nate can't stand that word—*alibi*. Only criminals need those. Nate asked them, "Should I get a lawyer or what?"

The officer said, "I don't know, do you need one, Nate?"

"I'm sorry if I've made things worse," Sheryl says. But, the way she says it, she's not sorry at all. She's pleased with herself. She thinks this plan of hers is genius. Nate's sanity, Nate's entire life, is of no consequence.

"You'll pay for this when Annie comes back and never speaks to you again," he says. He hangs up, hoping to leave her with that new worry. All this time, Sheryl's feared Annie not coming back. She hasn't stopped to consider what will happen if she does—*when* she does.

Lucy paws at Nate's leg, which she never does. She may be the last mammal on earth who believes in him, who is on his side.

"You want to go for a run?" he says to her.

He just did a fourteen-miler this morning. But Lucy hasn't gotten out today, and it might feel good to get a few more miles in. At the very least, it should exhaust him enough to make him stop pacing and thinking about all this newly introduced bullshit.

Lucy's ears perk when he says "run." She knows what this means.

"Okay," he says. "Let's go."

IT'S OBVIOUS WITHIN the first quarter mile that his legs have nothing more to give. The long run earlier took it out of him. Or the cops took it out of him. He has to think about each step, each breath. His heart pounds. Does his heart always pound like this? He becomes hyperaware of each beat, starts wondering if it's normal. Everyone's heard the stories of runners who drop dead midworkout. Their friends and family members say, "But he was so healthy!"

Nate thinks about his father. Was his heart pounding excessively in the days before it gave out completely? Were there signs? If there were, Nate didn't know. Maybe his father had high cholesterol and high blood pressure and high everything, but Nate was just a blissfully ignorant teenager, believing in immortality the way kindergartners believe in Santa Claus.

Come to think of it, Nate has no idea what his own cholesterol and blood pressure are. He hasn't been to the doctor since before Penelope was born. Back then, he went at Annie's insistence. He'd become one of the many men who need to be cajoled by their wives to be healthy and good people. She'd said, "You don't get annual physicals?" with such exasperation, you'd have thought he'd told her he didn't wash his hands after taking a crap, as a rule. She knew his father died young. She'd said, "Don't you want to make sure everything is okay?"

He'd thought, *Not really*, but said, "I guess." So he went, to make her feel better. He didn't realize how nervous he was about the whole thing until the doctor's office called with his blood results and he had to sit down because his hands got clammy and he felt slightly sick to his stomach. The results were all normal. When the report came in the mail, he stuck it to the fridge like parents do with their kids' report cards.

Annie said, "See? It wasn't that bad," but Nate still dreaded the next time she'd remind him to go. Then Penelope was born, and she forgot all about Nate's annual physicals.

Given recent stresses, Nate wouldn't be surprised if his heart wanted to give up. *I can't handle this, dude.* That's what he imagines his heart saying, if it could speak. He slows to a jog. Lucy licks his palm. He's right in front of the park. *The park.*

Where *it* happened. He usually meanders through neighborhood streets to avoid it, but somehow, here he is. *At the park.* Lucy looks at him like, *What are we doing here?*

That day, if Lucy hadn't been there, Penelope still would be. Nate has thought about this fact over and over again.

Nate and Annie were chatting with the old hippies who live up the street from the park. Greg and . . . the wife's name always escapes Nate. Greg always wears a baseball hat, a straggly ponytail sticking out the back. The wife, she likes to knit. She knit caps for Penelope and Annie; Penelope's was pink, Annie's blue. It felt very old-fashioned, very Midwestern, to have neighbors who knit things for you. Annie was actually wearing her cap on their family walk when they ran into Greg and his wife. They took family walks at least three or four times a week—Nate, Annie, Penelope, Lucy. Lucy was part of the family. She always stuck near Nate. Nate never used the leash. It's not like that particular day was any different. What's different is that something caught Lucy's eye as they were all standing there on the grass. A cat or a squirrel, maybe. She darted out toward the street. And Penelope followed her, calling, "Lucy! Lucy!" and giggling. The adults all yelled, "Penny!" in unison and ran. But it was like they were running through quicksand. That damn truck was coming down the street, at just the wrong time. Nate could see what was about to happen. He could see it so clearly.

Lucy licks his palm again. He shoves her face away. Annie thinks what happened is Lucy's fault. Some part of her knows it's really his fault though. That's why she left. She always warned him about the leash. He didn't listen. And now Penelope's gone— and so is Annie.

He still can't catch his breath. Something is wrong. His chest tightens. What do people say a heart attack is like? An elephant standing on your chest? Is that what this is? He kneels down. Lucy licks his face. He pushes her away. Something is wrong. Is he dying? Is this it? His pulse races. Everything in front of him goes blurry. When he closes his eyes, he sees zeros and ones flying around in the darkness. What does that mean—zeros and ones?

He fumbles around for his phone, stuffed into the pocket of his shorts. He brings it on his runs, in case Annie calls. He never thought he'd need it for some kind of medical emergency.

It takes multiple attempts to unlock his phone because his hands are so sweaty that the touch screen isn't registering what numbers he's hitting. This just makes him panic more. Finally, access granted, he considers dialing 9-1-1, but then he decides against it. He doesn't want two fire trucks and an ambulance arriving while the whole neighborhood looks on. If he's truly dying, he wants it to be with little fanfare. He finds his way to his recent calls screen and scans the names. Sheryl. Marcus. Beth. Mike. Mike will do. He's probably not that far away. He just left the house a little while ago. Nate makes a promise to himself, a before-you-see-the-white-light promise: if he doesn't inherit his father's fate and drop dead, he'll be sure to apologize to Mike for being such a fucking asshole.

TWENTY-NINE

ANNIE is lying on the exam table in Dr. Franklin's office. She had a dream last night that she lost the baby. It was so realistic, the dream. They say you don't see color in dreams, just like they say you can't do math in dreams because the math-doing part of your brain is off when you sleep. Annie's counted things in dreams, though. She's done basic addition in dreams. And she definitely dreams in color. In last night's dream, she was in her tiny house bathroom and there was blood in her underwear—red and threatening.

She woke up with a start, sweating. She put her hand on her belly, hoping for some kind of confirmation that it had just been a dream, that everything was okay. It's too soon for baby kicks, though. She closed her eyes, thinking maybe if she concentrated hard enough, she could figure out what was going on inside of her. It's so strange that a pregnant woman has absolutely no idea what's happening to the human she's harboring. There's so much blind faith. Too much, maybe. She pulled the waistband of her sweatpants away from her body and peeked into her underwear. There was no red. But still . . . *it must mean something.*

"It doesn't mean anything," Lia told her the next morning when Annie showed up at her front door, still wearing her pajamas.

Annie couldn't get a thought out of her head though: *It would serve me right to lose the baby.* It suddenly seemed idiotic to leave

Nate, to come here, on this bullshit mission to find some version of peace. Of course she would lose the baby. Why would God allow her to be a mother again? *Stupid. Stupid. Stupid.*

"Maybe I'm not ready to have this baby," Annie dared to say to Lia. Maybe she said it because she knew Lia would dismiss her theory.

"So that means you'll lose it?" Lia said.

Yes, Annie thought, but she just shrugged.

"If readiness was required for motherhood, there would be very few children on the planet," Lia said. She turned away from Annie and went back to preparing her morning tea. End of discussion.

Annie walked in and sat on Lia's couch. "I just feel like something is wrong," she pressed.

"You think something should be wrong. You think you left Nate and now you deserve a punishment."

Yes, Annie thought.

"Life isn't that simple," Lia said. She joined Annie on the couch. "You're one of those 'everything happens for a reason' people, aren't you?"

Give it to God, Annie's mother used to say. *He has a reason for everything.*

"I guess so."

"You know, I came up with all sorts of reasons for why I lost Ethan," Lia said. "Because I smoked pot before I knew I was pregnant, because I didn't visit my grandpa on his deathbed, because I never finished college, because I'm an atheist."

There were many times when Annie wondered if God took Penny because Nate was an atheist. Or maybe God was punishing Annie for marrying a person who called religion "a crutch, at best."

"What if I hadn't eaten spicy Thai food for lunch?" Lia went on. "That's what I ate the day I lost Ethan. I fixated on that lunch for *months*."

Grief counselor Pete said this was a stage of grief—all the *what-ifs*, all the pleas to go back and do something differently. Bargaining, he called it. "See, it's a *thing*!" That's what Annie had said to Nate, in the hopes that he would realize her feelings were valid, real, even normal.

"The thing is, I lost Ethan, and there will never be a reason good enough for that," Lia said. "Life is just random."

How is Annie supposed to accept such a thing? How is she supposed to accept that there's nothing she can do to ensure a certain life or, at the very least, ward off bad things? How is she supposed to get out of bed every day with this reality?

"At some point, the meaninglessness of everything will be liberating," Lia said. "Until then, call the freaking doctor. I know you want to."

And she did.

And now she's lying on his exam table, thinking about how maybe Lia's right. Yes, Annie left Nate. Yes, she may not be ready to be a mother again. But maybe these facts have nothing to do with the fate of her baby.

"Everything looks just fine," Dr. Franklin says, his eyes on the ultrasound screen instead of on her face.

There's the heartbeat, that steady beat of a drum underwater. She wishes she could lie here all day, listening to it. She wishes there was a way to listen to it at home, connect earphones that would transmit the sound throughout the day.

"Well, now I feel silly for freaking out," Annie says, sitting up, the paper gown crinkling.

"Most first-time mothers freak out," he says.

Her heart drops. She never told him about Penelope. In Annie's future, there will be so many people like Dr. Franklin who won't know about Penelope, and Annie will secretly and irrationally resent them for denying her existence.

"Any guesses on the sex?" he says with a smile. He must humor all the first-time mothers this way; it's unlikely he cares about the sex. Annie humors him with her own smile and says, "I'm pretty sure it's a boy."

ON THE DRIVE back to the tiny house community, Annie wants to call Nate. So badly. Maybe she should. Maybe it's time to go home. She'll ask Lia what she thinks, though part of her already knows what Lia will say.

Everyone's working on Matt's house when she gets back.

"I'll join you guys in a second," she calls to them. "Just gotta change clothes."

Then she realizes Lia isn't with them.

"Where's Lia?" she asks.

They all shrug.

Dawn is the only one to respond verbally. "I think she's feeling a little under the weather."

Annie wanders toward her house and, from a distance, she can see Lia waiting at her front door, sitting on the ground with her knees pulled up to her chest. She stands when Annie approaches.

"What are you doing?" Annie says.

"Waiting for you."

"Dawn said you're sick?"

Lia shakes her head. "No, I'm not. I just didn't feel like working."

Annie opens her front door, and they both go inside.

"Everything okay with the baby?" Lia asks.

"Yes," Annie says sheepishly. "You were right."

"I like when I'm right," Lia says with a little grin.

"Is everything okay with you?"

Lia sits on the couch, pulls her knees up to her chest again. Is it Caleb? Is that what this melancholy pensiveness is about?

"Yeah, I'm fine," Lia says. She starts picking at her cuticles. "It's just—something strange happened while you were at the doctor."

"What?"

"That boy called me."

It takes Annie a second to remember what boy she's referring to. The one who came to visit the other day. The one who looked familiar. Mike.

"That's a good thing, right?" Annie says.

"He said something odd," she says, looking Annie in the eye for the first time since coming inside.

"Odd?"

"Is your name Annie?"

At just the utterance of her name, Annie's ears start ringing. Instinctively, she puts her palms over them in an attempt to mute the ringing. She remembers this happening the day of Penny's accident. She remembers sitting in the back of the police car with Nate, following the ambulance to the hospital—they wouldn't let her ride with Penny—and saying to Nate, "What is that noise?" He looked at her, the first of many *are-you-nuts?* looks after the accident, and said, "What noise?"

"What?" is all Annie can say. She can't very well deny the fact of her name. Somehow, Lia knows. But how?

"That boy," Lia says, "he knows your husband somehow."

"Nate?"

This seems all too strange. This boy. Nate. Lia. All connected. Worlds colliding, as they say.

"Yeah, he works for him or something."

Nate doesn't have anyone working for him. This can't be right.

"I don't understand," Annie says.

"I don't really either."

"So, Nate knows I'm here?"

How could he know? And if he knows, he's just fine with letting her be out here alone? She imagines him telling people she's at a retreat. She imagines him playing down the distress that sent Annie here in the first place. She imagines him smiling and laughing, thinking his poor, troubled wife just needed some time away. This all pisses her off.

"He doesn't know," Lia says.

Now Annie is really confused.

"Mike didn't tell him."

Who the hell is this boy? And how does he know she's here? Annie knew he looked familiar, she knew it. But, still, she can't place him. She can't figure it out.

"I really don't understand," Annie says.

"He says things are bad at home," Lia says. "He says Nate's losing it."

Nate? Losing it? Annie can't picture it. She's never even seen him cry. She asked him once, well before Penelope died, well before Penelope was even born, "When's the last time you cried?"

He'd twisted up his face in a look of angst, struggling to remember, and said, "Sixth grade, I think. Got hit by a pitch in Little League and broke my wrist."

"Losing it how?"

"I don't know exactly. That's just what he said."

It excites Annie in a probably sick-and-twisted way. But the excitement quickly turns to worry. It would take a lot for Nate to lose it. And, being that such a state is unprecedented, she's not sure what this will mean for him.

"There's something else," Lia says, with an unnerving carefulness to her voice. "He says the police are involved. I guess they think Nate had something to do with your disappearance."

My disappearance, Annie thinks. Is that what they're calling this? A *disappearance*? She left a note. Didn't he get the note? What if he didn't get the note? Her ears start ringing again. Suddenly, she knows she has to leave. Suddenly, she has that feeling like when you're in a dream, naked in the middle of a mall, thinking, *Fuck, what am I doing here?*

"Oh my God," Annie says. "I never meant—"

"I know," Lia says. "You just need to call him. If you want to stay here, fine. But he needs to know you're okay. Mike is going to call the police and tell them where you are if you don't talk to Nate."

The police! It's absurd they're involved. Absurd.

She climbs up to the loft and fishes her phone from the bottom of her purse. She turns it on, finds Nate's name at the top of her "Favorites" list. She taps his name and starts going over in her head what she'll say when he answers:

It's me.

I messed up.

I'm so, so, so sorry.

I want to come home.

It starts ringing. Once. Twice.

"Pick up, pick up, pick up," she says.

He doesn't though. She thinks back to the other day, how his phone was completely off. This is unlike him. What does it mean—*losing it*? What has she done?

Clutching the phone in her hand, she climbs down the ladder.

"No answer?" Lia says. Annie shakes her head. She needs to see Nate. It's clear now. She's too flustered to drive, though. Her ears are still ringing.

As if reading her mind, Lia says, "Come on, let me take you home."

THIRTY

JOSH

JOSH paces the lobby of the ER, wondering what he'll do if Nate dies. He would have to call Annie—or Lia—and break the news. He would be associated with yet another tragedy in their sad lives.

He was on his way to his mom's house when he got a call from Nate. He thought that was weird since Nate had made it pretty clear their working relationship was done, and it's not like they had any other kind of relationship. Josh assumed it was about his final pay or something.

"Mike?" Nate said. He sounded out of breath.

"Nate? You okay?" He didn't sound okay.

"Yeah. I mean, no. I don't know."

"Where are you?"

"I'm near the park off Camino Capistrano. You know the park?"

The park. Of course Josh knew *the park*—where he and Penelope were in the wrong place at the wrong time, united for all time by that mutual wrongness.

"Uh, yeah. What's going on?"

"I think I'm having a heart attack."

"Holy fuck, are you serious? Did you call 9-1-1?"

"No, no, I don't want that. Can you just come get me?"

Josh didn't know what to say besides, "Yeah, yeah, of course."

He made a sharp U-turn, tires squealing and all, and headed back toward Nate's neighborhood.

"Just stay on the phone with me, okay?" Josh said.

Nate grunted something that sounded like agreeance.

Josh drove five miles per hour through the neighborhood leading to the park. His mind couldn't help but flash back to that day. He gripped the steering wheel tighter, bracing himself for dogs and small children darting out of nowhere into the middle of the street. He remembered, suddenly, what song was playing that day—a Lumineers song. *I belong with you, you belong with me, you're my sweetheart.* That one. The song was a couple years old but still part of an iTunes playlist on heavy rotation in Josh's car. He liked the Lumineers. He'd taken Jess to one of their concerts. That's what he used to think about when he heard the song— Jess, the concert. Now he will only be able to think about that day.

Nate was crouched down on a patch of grass next to the bus stop sign. An older man and woman were standing next to him, looking concerned. They were wearing matching bright-white sneakers and had two tiny terrier-type dogs on leashes. Lucy walked in circles around Nate. Josh parked and pushed his car door open, leaving the engine running.

"I'm here," Josh said, putting his hand on Nate's back. His shirt was drenched with sweat. Nate didn't seem able to even look up. He was staring at the ground, chin against his chest.

"You know him?" the man said.

"Yes," Josh said.

"We're worried it's a heart attack," the man said.

The woman said, "We were going to call 9-1-1, but—"

"No," Nate said. That one word seemed to require a great amount of effort.

"Can you breathe?" Josh asked.

"Not . . . really."

"I'm going to take him to the ER," Josh said.

The man and woman seemed relieved by this.

"We can take the dog home," the woman said, looking at Lucy's tag on her collar.

Nate nodded at this and Josh said, "That would be great."

"Nate, can you stand?" Josh asked.

"One . . . minute," Nate said.

Nate put both hands on the ground. That's when his phone fell out of his pocket. Josh picked it up.

"You don't even have to stand," Josh said. "My car's right here. You can crawl."

And that's what he did. He managed to look up for a few seconds, enough time to spot the car, his target location. Then he crawled slowly. It seemed to take an hour, but it was probably just a few minutes. Josh saw the man and woman and their terriers at the end of the next block, talking to another couple, pointing.

Josh googled the nearest ER and drove as fast as he could. He had a brief morbid thought of Nate dying in his car, and, well, that just couldn't happen. The drive to the hospital was short. Josh had his eyes on Nate more than the road. Nate was curled in the back seat, his knees pulled to his chest, eyes closed. Josh must have asked him if he was okay thirty times. Nate just grunted. He was awake, at least. Josh thought he remembered that it was important to keep people conscious in times like this.

He pulled into a handicapped spot right in front of the ER because it was closest to the door. He ran inside, like people do on medical drama TV shows. The woman in scrubs behind the reception desk did not look at all alarmed as he approached. She probably saw this type of urgency all the time.

"My friend," Josh said, not knowing what else to call Nate, "I think he's having a heart attack or something."

"Where is he?" the woman said. Her name tag read Anisha.

"In my car, in the back seat," Josh said. "He can't walk."

"Okay, we'll send someone out."

She picked up a phone. Within seconds, two guys and a gurney appeared. Josh showed them to his car and they hoisted Nate onto the gurney with a casual "one-two-three," and then he was gone, wheeled back to a treatment room. Josh was left standing there, not knowing what the fuck to do.

He moved his car to a regular spot and then went inside to the waiting room, where he is now, pacing.

His phone vibrates. His mom.

"Are you still coming over?" she asks.

"Shit, Mom, sorry, something came up."

"Is everything okay?"

"Yeah. No. I don't know. I'll call you later."

He hangs up and puts the phone back in his pocket, only to feel it vibrate again a few seconds later. He curses under his breath, annoyed with his mother, and then realizes it isn't his phone vibrating; it's Nate's.

The name "Annie Banannie" flashes on the screen. *Annie! Annie's calling!* The desperate phone call to Lia must have worked. Josh doesn't know what to do. He contemplates answering the call, but what would he say? He decides he'll tell Nate later, when he's stable. *If* he's stable.

Josh goes to the nurses station, asks if there's any news.

"And you are . . . family?" the nurse says. She nods, encouraging Josh to lie.

"Uh, yeah," Josh says.

The young woman smiles and says, "He's going to be okay.

Just a panic attack. We see them in the ER all the time. We'll let you know when you can go back."

She seems to enjoy giving Josh this news, as if she doesn't get the opportunity very often to put worries to rest. He feels light-headed with relief.

Josh resumes pacing, walking the length of the waiting room area at least a hundred times. He's no longer that worried about Nate; he's just anxious to tell him about Annie calling.

Finally, a nurse—a different one from the good-news-giver—comes toward him and says, "You can see him now."

He follows her down a long hallway, curtains pulled tightly shut. He can't see anything, but he can hear people crying and moaning, and that's almost worse. His imagination goes wild with the possible atrocities—horrific car accident injuries, missing limbs. It occurs to him: Penelope was here.

Nate is at the very end of the hallway. The nurse pulls back the curtain, and he is lying there on a bed, hooked up to an IV. A slim Asian man is standing next to the bed. He must be the doctor, though he looks too young to be a real doctor.

"Hey, Mike," Nate says. He sounds woozy, out of it, like the drunk guy who ends up sitting in the bathtub, philosophizing about life, after everyone's left the party.

"You feelin' okay?" Josh says.

"No heart attack," Nate says, a sleepy grin on his face.

"EKG and bloodwork came back normal," the doctor says.

"They said I had a panic attack," Nate says. He seems to find this amusing. "Too much stress." He seems to find this even more amusing.

The doctor probably assumes Nate is just another asshole working too many hours at a bullshit corporate job. He has no idea.

"He's on Valium right now," the doctor says. "Should be ready to go after we get these fluids in him."

The doctor leaves, and Josh goes to the side of Nate's bed.

"You got a phone call," Josh says, presenting Nate with his phone like it's a delicate gift worth millions of dollars.

"I did?" Nate says with a sleepy grin.

"Yes," Josh says. He forces the phone into Nate's palm because Nate doesn't seem to understand that he should take it. Suddenly, Nate grabs Josh's right wrist and stares at the tattoos traveling up his arms. He fixates on one in particular—a line of zeros and ones wrapping around his upper forearm like a bracelet.

Jess had asked Josh about the tattoo the first night they met. "What does it mean?"

"It's binary code," he told her.

"What?" she asked.

"It's a computer programming thing," he said.

"I've always liked geeks," she told him.

Nate traces the bracelet of zeros and ones with his left index finger, his forehead creased into a look of deep concern.

"Hey," Nate says, finally, "I know you."

"Of course you know me," Josh says nervously.

"No," Nate says, still gripping Josh's arm. "You were *there*."

THIRTY-ONE

NATE ran over to Penelope, thinking, *She's fine, she's fine, she's fine.* The truck wasn't going that fast. Later, he would say that to the doctors repeatedly, and the response would be, "But she's a very small child, Mr. Forester."

Someone was already with her when he got to her. A man. A boy, rather, when Nate got a better look. Nate saw the truck stopped, the driver's side door open. Then he realized this boy with his daughter was the driver of the truck. He was crouched down, his arms—the right one tattooed from wrist to shoulder—reaching toward Penelope, but not touching her.

"Move!" he shouted at him, his voice sounding nothing like his own. The kid scrambled to his feet, and Nate pressed his mouth to Penelope's, cursing himself for never properly learning CPR. You're supposed to do that when you're a parent—one of many ways Nate failed his family.

Annie wouldn't come near them. She was standing on the sidewalk, calling to him, "Is she okay? Nate! Is she okay?" He just yelled, "Yeah, I think so. Stay there."

She wasn't okay, though. And Nate knew right away. In retrospect, maybe it's good that it was instant. Maybe it's good that Penelope didn't have to suffer, that they didn't have to hear her cry in the middle of that street.

"The truck must have hit her just so," the doctor said. "She was as tall as the hood." Meaning it struck her in the head, meaning if the truck had been a normal car, they would be dealing with some broken bones and nothing more.

Nate has always hated trucks. Annie has too. Annie never liked the gas guzzling. Nate just didn't see the point of a truck for 90 percent of the assholes who own them. If you run a cattle ranch and are transporting livestock feed on a daily basis, fine. If you manage a construction company, fine. But if you're just using the truck to help douchebag friends move twice a year, you have a small dick. That was always Nate's thinking.

And now he just thinks trucks are deadly weapons. He thinks their drivers are potential killers.

But Mike?

Mike doesn't even own a truck. Just today, when he came to Nate's rescue, he was driving a Honda Civic. Nate doesn't remember the name of the driver who hit Penelope, has blocked out that particular detail, but he's sure it wasn't Mike. He would remember if it was Mike because that's his cousin's name. Maybe Mike is the driver's twin. Maybe they are so committed to their twinness that they share the same tattoos.

Or maybe his name isn't really Mike.

"You were there?" Nate says again, this time as a question. He releases Mike's arm, and Mike draws it close to him, like he's afraid Nate will grab it again.

"Where?" Mike says, but his eyes tell Nate that he knows exactly where. He looks scared, deer-in-the-headlights scared.

"The accident," Nate says. "It was you. Driving."

Mike takes two steps back. He is wincing, in expectation of an attack, though Nate is in no condition to do any attacking.

Nate wants to scream at him. He wants to get up from this hospital bed and strangle him. He wants his anger, the unleashing of it, to take away the pain of losing Penelope and, possibly,

Annie. Even with the Valium, his heart pounds, hammering in his chest the way it did before he called Mike and told him he was having a heart attack. He takes a deep breath. That's what the doctor told him to do "the next time this happens," as if he is going to be a person who has panic attacks from now on, as if that is who he is now.

He closes his eyes. And maybe because the drugs calm him enough to feel something besides rage, he starts to cry.

He can't remember the last time he cried. Never as an adult, he knows that much.

"I'm sorry," Mike says, his voice small and seemingly far away. "I don't know what to say."

Nate keeps his eyes closed until they are so filled with tears that he is forced to open them, to allow the liquid to escape. Mike is near the doorway, his figure blurry.

"You knew who I was all along?" Nate says.

"I should have said something," Mike says. His voice cracks, like he might cry too. "I just didn't know—"

It's starting to make sense now. He was looking for them—for Nate and Annie. To apologize. To make amends. "It's okay," Nate says. He doesn't really believe these words, but knows he needs to learn to believe them.

"Annie called," Mike says, nodding toward the phone.

Annie? Nate flips over the phone in his hand, sees for himself that there's a missed call from her. He taps her name, and it starts ringing.

Mike hesitates at the threshold between the treatment room and the hallway. "I guess I should go, unless you need—"

"Mike. Wait," Nate says.

"Yeah?" Mike says, his tone apprehensive, scared.

"Can you give me a ride home?"

Mike sniffles—he is crying—but then smiles with one side of his mouth.

"Sure," he says. "And, just so you know, my name's Josh."

ANNIE directs Lia to make a left at the next street—the street Nate and Annie and Penelope called home.

"I didn't know you lived so close to the beach," Lia says. They're at the top of the hill, before the stop sign, when there's a brief but beautiful glimpse of the Pacific. Annie never thought she'd live near the beach. On the way home from work, she used to pause on this hill and think about how lucky she was.

Her phone rings loudly. She'd turned up the volume as high as it would go, on the off chance she couldn't hear it, even though it's sitting right in her lap.

Lia flinches. "You're going to give me a heart attack," she says. "Is it him?"

It is him. Nate. Finally.

"Nate?" Annie says the second she picks up.

"Annie?" he says. He sounds unsure, disbelieving it's her.

"It's me," she confirms.

And then she hears what sounds like . . . weeping.

"I'm so fucking happy to hear your voice," he says.

"Are you okay?" Annie asks.

Lia drives down their street slowly. Annie points at the house, indicates where Lia should park. They stop.

"I'm okay now," Nate says. He's definitely crying.

"I'm home, Nate," she says. "I just got home."

She opens the car door and runs toward the house. The front door is unlocked. She goes inside, and Lucy greets her immediately, tail wagging. Annie kisses her nose. She missed Lucy, as much as she has told herself to hate Lucy forever.

"I didn't know you had a doggy," Lia says, coming in behind Annie, stroking Lucy's coat.

"I'm not there," Nate says.

He's not, Annie realizes.

"Where are you?"

"I'll tell you later. I'll be home as soon as I can. Don't go anywhere."

THIRTY-THREE

JOSH waits in the lobby until Nate is approved to leave the hospital. He didn't expect Nate to ask him for a ride home. He expected Nate to flip out on him and tell him to fuck off. He wonders if that's coming when the Valium wears off.

"Annie's home," Nate says when they get into Josh's car.

"She is?"

Shit. It's great she's home but . . . *Shit*.

How's Josh going to handle this? Annie will recognize him as the guy who came to the tiny house community. And if Nate realizes that Josh knew where Annie was and didn't say anything, then he will flip out. For sure.

"She wasn't on a business trip," Nate says.

"I know," Josh says tentatively.

Nate looks at him, but Josh keeps his eyes on the road. "You saw the signs, didn't you?"

Josh swallows hard.

"I did," Josh says.

Nate sighs. "I didn't want to get into it. She's been missing since—"

"I know," Josh says.

Nate stops talking. Josh feels his eyes on him again, waiting for Josh to explain.

"I was parked outside your house the morning she left. I was going to knock on your door, and I saw her leaving with a suitcase," he says. This isn't the complete truth; it's pieces of the complete truth, crumbs.

"You saw her leave? Why didn't you—"

That's not all, Josh thinks. *You have no idea.*

"I followed her," Josh says.

"What?" Nate says. "Followed her where?"

"To this tiny house community."

"She went to a tiny house community?"

"I tried to tell you. I gave you the name of the place. Rolling Stone Co-Op. Remember? I was hoping you would go see for yourself."

I tried. I tried.

"Why didn't you just come out and tell me?"

He can still feel Nate's gaze on him, boring into his temple. Josh can't bear to look at him.

"I was scared, I guess," he says. "I thought she would be mad. I thought you would be mad. I didn't want to hurt either of you."

"I don't get it," Nate says. "What was your plan with all this?"

He doesn't know anymore. The initial plan was to make sure Nate and Annie were okay. Maybe the secret plan was to find a way to forgive himself.

"I'm sorry," Josh says. "I should have just left you alone."

Did he make everything worse? Annie would have left regardless. Still, ultimately, he had something to do with her coming home. He'd called Lia.

"It doesn't matter," Nate says impatiently, finally taking his eyes off Josh and looking out the window. Here is the anger Josh expected. Here is the anger he knows he deserves. "Just get me home."

Thankfully, home is only a few minutes away. Annie's Prius is in the driveway. Nate opens the passenger's side door before Josh has even put the car in park. He doesn't close the door, can't be bothered. He runs toward the house, and Josh wonders if he should just drive away, leave them all to wonder what happened to the guy who wasn't named Mike.

Before he can decide, though, Lia is out front, looking at him as he sits there in the driver's seat, her head tilted to one side, eyebrows furrowed. She does a beckoning wave, indicating he should come inside. He doesn't move. She comes toward the car.

"What are you doing?" she says, peering in through the still-open passenger's side door.

"I thought they might want privacy."

"I'm here," she says. "And I don't have any way of leaving. I don't want to be alone, feeling awkward."

Josh—ever the pushover, always easily coerced by pretty females—turns off the ignition and goes inside with Lia. He feels better with her here. He feels like Nate and Annie won't lose their shit with her here.

Nate and Annie are hugging and crying. Josh and Lia linger by the door. It's Annie who looks up to acknowledge the two of them there.

"Mike," Annie says.

"Actually, his name is Josh," Nate says.

Here it goes: Nate's going to rat him out. Annie's going to cry. And Josh is going to regret coming inside.

"Josh?" Annie says.

"He said his name was Mike because he was trying to be secretive on his little spy mission," Nate says.

And that's all he says on the matter. He must know it will only cause Annie pain to know the complete truth. Complete truths are overrated.

"I don't care what his name is. I'm just glad he let me know I needed to come home," Annie says.

"He did?" Nate says.

Annie looks confused, like she assumed Nate would have known this.

"Yeah," Annie says. "I mean, he called Lia, and Lia told me."

"Lia?" Nate says.

Lia smiles shyly and waves at Nate.

Annie continues: "I wanted to come home anyway. I just don't know if I would have gotten here as fast."

Nate gives Josh a small nod that says things between them are all good now. Then he goes back to hugging Annie.

"You guys probably want to catch up," Lia says. "Mike or Josh or whatever his name is can drive me back to Rolling Stone." She looks at Josh expectantly and says, "Right?"

There is nothing to say besides, "Right."

THIRTY-FOUR

NATE and **ANNIE** sit on the couch, his hands holding hers. He takes her face in his palms, kisses her, and says, "We can move into a tiny house. Tomorrow. If that's what you want."

Annie's eyes start welling up. There's no way he wants to live in a tiny house. He is saying this for her. He is trying so hard, for her.

"Or Beth can draw up plans so we can build our own tiny house. I thought about this in the ER, and I'm in."

"The ER?"

"It was nothing," he tells her. Because he doesn't want her to worry. Because he doesn't want her to blame herself for the panic that attacked him.

"Nothing? What happened?" she presses.

He remembers now that Annie wants him to be someone who talks about things, who doesn't pretend everything's okay when it's not.

"I had a panic attack."

Her heart sinks. She lets her head fall into her hands and shakes it back and forth. "This is my fault," she says.

"I knew you would think that. And you're wrong. We both know I've never learned how to deal with stress. I'll get better."

"I'm the reason for the stress."

"Penelope dying is the reason for the stress, Annie."

They sit in silent reverence of this fact.

"I don't think I want to live in a tiny house," Annie says finally.

"You don't?" He wants to understand her, what she needs. He hasn't spent enough time trying to do that.

"I think I just needed to get away."

There was something comforting about living tiny, being confined to a small space. Maybe she thought her mind would purge some of its heavy-weighted feelings if there simply wasn't room for them. But, turns out, no matter how tiny the house, the feelings remain.

"I understand," Nate says, which is all Annie ever wished he would say.

"I think I want to move though," she says. "Fresh start."

Since she's stepped foot in the house, she's felt sad at the notion that Penelope's room is still there. She can't walk by that room every day of her life. Even if they turn it into a guest room or an office or some other room that will hardly be used, she will always know what it used to be.

"We can do whatever you want. We can move," he says. "I just want you to be happy."

"You should be happy too."

"You're home," he says. "I'm happy."

She squeezes his hands and says, "What would you think about having another baby?"

He wouldn't think she would want that. He assumes that would be too hard for her. But he's learned from all this that he doesn't always know his wife's mind.

"I want what you want," he says. "Is having another baby what you want?"

She starts crying, and Nate isn't sure why.

"We don't have to," he says. "Honestly, whatever you want."

She looks up at him, with tear-filled eyes, and says, "I don't know what I want—but I'm pregnant."

He pulls her toward his chest, wraps his arms around her, kisses the top of her head. She sobs, not because she's sad, but because she finally feels safe.

"Oh, sweetie," is all he says.

"It happened right before Penelope died. I didn't know until I left. Due in September," she mumbles.

"That's a good month," he says. "And Penelope did say she wanted a brother."

This—the fact that Nate remembers—makes Annie believe for the first time since Penelope died, that she and Nate will be one of the lucky ones who make it.

"We have to call the police," she tells him.

"Yes," he says. "And then your mother."

THIRTY-FIVE

JOSH wishes he was better with making conversation. He never has been. He's always been socially awkward. That's why he became a computer programmer. Or maybe he became socially awkward because of his early love of computers. Classic chicken or the egg scenario.

"I think they'll be okay," Lia says, after several minutes of uncomfortable silence in his car. Josh keeps wondering if he should just turn up the music.

"Yeah," Josh says. "I hope so."

"They missed each other," she says.

"I think so."

"Do you think people can survive tragedy?" she asks.

He remembers that she has no idea of his role in Penelope's death.

"I have to think that," he says.

"Me too."

They are silent again. Then Lia leans forward and turns up the volume. It relieves him to spend the drive listening to his playlist, though he can't help but worry she hates his taste in music. This self-consciousness, it's the first sign of a crush.

It's well after midnight when they get to the turnoff for Rolling Stone Co-Op.

"I was going to give you directions, but then I remembered you know the way," Lia says. It's the first thing she's said since turning up the music.

"Yeah, I know the way."

"So you never had any intentions of living here?"

He shrugs. "Not really."

At night, the community is almost completely dark, except for tiny porch lights on each of the houses. He parks the car and waits for Lia to get out.

"It's a cool way to live," she says. "You should consider it."

It's not a horrible idea. Josh still doesn't have a place of his own. He still doesn't have much direction. Tiny houses are cheap; he's learned that much. As long as there's an internet connection, he can get his work done. And, Lia's here. Lia's pretty and nice and seemingly interested in him, for some inexplicable reason.

"Maybe," he says, the idea starting to gain traction in his mind. "Maybe I will."

"At the very least," she says, "you should call me to have coffee so we can discuss it further."

She leans over the center console and kisses his cheek. It sends a jolt through his entire body. She opens the car door and gets out. Then she leans back through the open window and says, with a sly smile, "So, coffee next week?"

He gives her his own smile and says, "At the very least."

"THAT WAS MY house," Annie says to Nate, pointing at the tiny house with the red door, a house that someone else now calls home.

"It's . . . tiny," Nate says.

He's always been curious about the tiny house community his wife called home for those few weeks, but today marks their first visit there. Josh and Lia had come to visit them at their new home a couple times—once for dinner when Annie was pregnant, and then after George was born. When Josh asked Lia to marry him, Nate and Annie were the first people they called. "We want to get married at Rolling Stone," Josh had said. It made sense. They'd spent a year living together there, after all. The wedding would mark the culmination of that year. They'd built a tiny house together and were planning to drive it to Washington.

"What's in Washington?" Annie had asked Josh.

Lia shouted from the background, "Lots of trees—and the future."

There are four rows of white chairs positioned in front of an arch decorated with pink roses. Annie bounces George on her knee. He's a happy baby, the type of baby who seems wise beyond his years, the type of baby who doesn't fuss because he seems to understand that a little discomfort is both inevitable and temporary.

"Do you recognize anyone?" Nate asks Annie.

She looks around and shakes her head. "Just James."

They'd said hello to James when they first arrived. He was serving as usher, wearing a button-down white shirt with a much-too-large red bow tie. When he saw Annie, his eyes just about bugged out of his head. "Allie!" he'd said. They didn't correct him.

The white chairs fill with people. When everyone is seated, a violinist in the back starts playing, and Josh walks down the aisle with his mother. He gives Nate and Annie a nod. There are no bridesmaids or groomsmen. The next person down the aisle is Lia, her mother on one arm and father on the other. She wears a crown of flowers and a giddy smile. During the past year, her face has become fuller, her cheeks rounder. It relieves Annie in the way Annie's parents must have felt relieved when Annie survived her own tumultuous young adulthood.

The officiant is one of the other tiny housers, a young man about Josh's age wearing a bolo tie and black cowboy boots. He tells everyone to be seated and begins his musings on love. Annie takes Nate's hand, like she always does at weddings. She's never considered herself much of a sap, but weddings get to her. There's so much hope at a wedding, so much faith in the ability of love to conquer all. And, well, maybe it can conquer all. Maybe Nate and Annie are proof.

They still see grief counselor Pete, even though they are doing well. Preventative measures, they say. Nate and Annie have cried together during these newborn days with George, unable to stop comparing him to baby Penny: *Remember the faces she used to make when we unswaddled her first thing in the morning? Remember how she giggled?* There are still boxes to be unpacked in their new house, many of them with Penny's things. The new house is just ten minutes from their old house, but it feels a world away. It's east of the freeway, what locals refer to as "the non-beach side." They are up in the hills, their backyard butting up to a horse trail. When they get up before dawn with George, they see packs of coyotes roaming beyond the fence, silhouetted against the rising sun.

Annie's mother still insists on asking, "Are you happy?" Neither Annie nor Nate know how to answer that question. Penelope is gone. They will never be what they once were. They will never *not* be sad. But they are not only sad.

Josh takes both of Lia's hands in his as he says his vows: "Lia, you've shown me more than I ever thought possible. We've lived in this tiny house together for a year and, yet, life has never felt bigger."

Annie squeezes Nate's hand. He looks at her, winks. They feel like veterans of vows like these, in on a secret about just how big life really is, how messy and scary and redeeming and joyful. George squirms, and Nate lifts him off Annie's lap and places him in his own. They already talk to George about his sister. They want him to know her. It will take him years to understand why she is gone; maybe he will never understand. Nate and Annie don't.

Penelope used to associate all things that are leaving or gone with "going home." She would point at planes flying overhead and proclaim, "Home." When the Easter eggs were all gone, she proclaimed they had "gone home." Perhaps this is how they will explain Penny's absence to George. They will tell him there is a home from which we all come, far more spectacular than any earthbound house. That is where Penny is. She has gone home.

ACKNOWLEDGMENTS

FIRST AND FOREMOST, thank you to Turner Publishing. Todd Bottorff, you have built something so great. Stephanie Beard, you are one of a kind (or two of a kind? I'm convinced you have a clone because there's no way one human could do what you do).

It seems every author says, "this book would not be what it is without . . ." and I have no interest in being unique: This book would not be what it is without the editorial expertise of Heather Howell and Kathy Haake. And the cover would not be what it is without Madeline Cothren. Kathleen Timberlake and Katie Kurtzman, thank you for doing all the marketing stuff I'm not good at. (Heather/Kathy, is it okay that I just ended that sentence with a preposition?)

Carey Burch, thank you for loving this story so much, for understanding that my books are my babies, and for treating them as such.

Brenna Eckerson, thank you being such a cheerleader. Meeting you reinforces my belief in fate.

Mom and dad, thank you for supporting my writing all these years. I take it for granted that you've always believed in me. Mom, our two-person book club is my favorite.

To all my reader and writer friends, you are my people. Thank you for existing and loving words as much as I do. Without you, I'd feel way weirder in this world.

Chris, you are the most loyal, dedicated, committed person I've ever met. Thank you for all you do every day to make our life as amazing as it is. We are two strange peas in a cozy pod . . . watching "Dateline."

And, last, Mya. It will be several years before you read anything I write (unless I write a children's book . . . hmm), but I'm leaving this note for you anyway. Your dad and I went through so much grief before you came along. That grief inspired this book. And you inspired its happy ending. You've proven all the clichés true—you are the light of my life, you are the best part of every single day. I love you so much, my girl.